THE FIVE ELEMENTS

BY
STEPHEN SALAM

ASTRELLION BOOKS

Copyright © 2022 Stephen Salam

All rights reserved.

ISBN: 9798835085620

First Edition, August 2022

Published by Astrellion Books

Cover design by Stephen Salam

Cover illustrations by Martyn Pick
www.martynpick.com

The characters and events portrayed in this book are fictitious. Any similarity to real persons, living or dead, is coincidental and not intended by the author.

No part of this book may be reproduced, or stored in a retrieval system, or transmitted in any form or by any means, electronic, mechanical, photocopying, recording, or otherwise, without express written permission of the publisher.

DEDICATION

This book is dedicated to my great friend and partner in crime, Robert Hartshorne. Without him this novel would not have been written.

It is also dedicated to the wonderful Jackie Withey, whose backing and encouragement kept me going through the long years of development.

I would also like to thank my family; Susan, Alex, and Lara for allowing me the time, space and support needed to get this book written and published.

CONTENTS

Preface

1	Danger in the Dungeon	1
2	A Boy In Trouble	20
3	Making Contact With The Past	35
4	Back to reality	39
5	The Next Dragon	43
6	The Empire of Darkness	51
7	A Vision Comes True	56
8	The Return Of Cyax	64
9	Back To Bad Habits	70
10	A New Team Member	78
11	An Away Mission	85
12	The Wand Of Xylos	96
13	Escape	109
14	Out Of The Shadows	116
15	The Library Of The Astraxi	120
16	How To Train Your Dragon Warrior!	134
17	The Cup Of Souls	145
18	The Calm Before The Storm	155
19	A Warrior Turns	166
20	Conflict Begins	172
21	Retreat	182
22	Treachery	188
23	Lost In The Forest	194
24	What Next?	204

25	Pinned Down	216
26	The Celestial Plane	229
27	Back On Mission	241
28	The Fortress of Thanatos	250
29	Evacuation	255
30	Regrouping	269
31	The Consequences Of Failure	272
32	The Lost Ship	279
33	Shifting Sands	293
34	The Eve Of War	306
35	Return To Astrellion	310
36	The DragonStone	318
37	Desperate Times	328
38	The Return Of The Fallen	334
39	A Farewell To Comrades	351
40	Picking Up The Pieces	355

PREFACE

The Five Elements is the first in a series of books about the mythical land of Astrellion and its group of legendary heroes, known as The Astraxi, who are fulfilling an ancient oath to protect the land.

The untimely death of a brave warrior draws teenage misfit Nico into the Astraxi, and the re-emergence of their immortal foe Cyax, triggers a race to find and control the Five Weapons of Elemental Power, whose combined magic would make him invincible.

With Four Undead Kings, a ruthless Warrior Princess, and legions of Cyber-demons ranged against him, can Nico learn to harness his Dragon Lore in time to prevent Cyax unleashing a new era of Darkness and suffering upon the world?

I hope that you will enjoy this story of action and adventure, with a little bit of science fiction, sorcery and humour thrown into the mix.

Stephen Salam

CHAPTER 1
Danger In The Dungeon

When asked to locate the land of Astrellion on a world map, people usually point to somewhere in the middle. It is neither in the East, nor is it in the West and you wouldn't say it was particularly in the North or the South either. It sits by the sea, near the mid-point of the large land mass that runs across the northern hemisphere.

There is more to Astrellion than its geography suggests. Trade routes and travellers have always converged there, but it's also a place where other dimensions, unearthly realms, and planes of existence intersect with the Earth. Remarkable people and fabulous creatures arrive at these intersections, bringing all sorts of new ideas and new ways of thinking, as well as all manner of problems.

When Astrellion's capital city of Astrapolis was founded by its first King, Theokeis, he built his palace high up on a hilltop, overlooking the city that was hemmed in by a thick defensive wall.

Over four thousand years later, the modern city of Astrapolis had grown so large as to completely surround the old one, by some considerable distance.

Just inside the old city walls, near the remains of the Great Gate, stood an inconspicuous café. From the outside it appeared nothing special, a single storey stone building with two windows, screened with latticework for privacy.

On top of the café's tiled roof was a kinetic sculpture made from intertwined glass tubes twisted into a double loop, like a figure 8 lying on its side: ∞. A neon glow rippled across the tubes, changing colour in a repeating pattern, but the sculpture's timing mechanism was faulty, sometimes causing the glow to stop or leap randomly between the tubes.

Attached to the sculpture was a battered electronic billboard. Every ten seconds or so, letters would slide along it, one character at a time, spelling out the establishment's name: 'THE PERPETUAL MOTION CAFÉ.'

Behind its creaky old doors, the Perpetual Motion Café concealed a centuries-old secret. It was really the headquarters of a mysterious organisation, known as *'His Royal Majesty's Most Excellent and Ancient Order of The*

Astraxi' known as *The Astraxi* for short. The Astraxi were a group of warriors established four thousand years ago, by King Theokeis, to protect the land of Astrellion from Evil.

Beyond the battered tables etched with graffiti and the slightly shabby booths, stood a very basic serving area topped with a worn-out laminate surface. On any normal day you would find Xin the café's chef, cooking and serving simple, tasty food to anyone who came in. Particularly popular was his special chilli prawn dim sum.

Xin was a tall, wiry, middle-aged man, who looked around fifty or maybe even older. It was hard to tell how old, as his pale skin had very few wrinkles, just a set of deep furrows on his brow and around his eyes. His almond shaped face generally wore a genial smile and perched on top of his shaved head was a chef's hat, which was comically too small for his cranium, and had a habit of slipping off while he was working.

Xin was a great cook, but his most impressive skill was the speed with which he prepared his dishes.

His hands were a blur from which emerged a stream of items that were tossed around in a wok for a short while and blended with sauces, before being tipped hot and steaming into a pile of fresh noodles.

To most people it looked as if some kind of sorcery must be at work. And they were right, because Xin wasn't just a modest cook, he was in fact a very powerful Warrior Mage.

Beyond being a chef, Xin's true purpose for over four thousand years, had been to lead, train and provide guidance to successive generations of Astraxi warriors.

On this particular day however, Xin was not behind the serving counter, the lights were off and the sign on the front door read 'CLOSED.'

Xin had shut up shop early that day to join the Astraxi on a mission to recover an artefact known as the Cup of Souls, which was one of five powerful weapons that had been created in ancient times harnessing the Lore of the Five Elements. It had long been suspected that the Cup of Souls was hidden under the Royal Palace, which was now a World Heritage Centre.

Inside the museum complex, Xin was standing near the visitor centre with the six young people who were the current serving members of the Astraxi: Phaedra, Ciara, Ben, Eleni, Eduardo, and Ash.

They appeared to other visitors as a slightly odd-ball collection of tourists, an unconventional group of people, but nothing special, for it was not the way of the Astraxi to draw too much attention to themselves.

Xin was nervous about this mission to find the Cup of Souls. His young team were well trained but had never faced anything as powerful or as dangerous as this magical artefact.

The elemental weapon of Earth, the Cup of Souls had been missing, presumed lost, for over a thousand years following the Great Battle of Astrellion, when the forces of darkness had invaded and almost destroyed the city of Astrapolis.

Using her enhanced sensitivity to the five forces, Phaedra, the Astraxi's Tiger Warrior, had detected an unusually strong concentration of earth elemental energy in the ruins.

While doing some research in the archives of the Astraxi, Phaedra (also known as Phae to her friends) concluded that the energy she felt would most likely be explained by the presence of the Cup of Souls. She was very excited at the thought of finding the lost artefact and made a very forceful argument to Xin to agree a mission to try and find it, but he wasn't sure it was such a good idea.

After an assessment of the potential dangers of such a mission, and under mounting pressure from Phae, Xin finally agreed that the group of young warriors should explore the secret passages below the palace and retrieve the artefact to prevent it from falling into the hands of Evil once more. Xin reasoned that the risk of the Cup falling into the wrong hands vastly outweighed the risks involved in its retrieval.

'It's been a long time since I was last in here, but from memory I think we can get down to the secret underground chambers via a staircase hidden behind this wall,' said Xin to the assembled group, pointing to a thick stone wall of large blocks covered in yellow and white lichen. The wall formed part of a solid stone plinth several metres high, upon which stood some of the citadel's most impressive remains.

'This staircase was only accessible to the King, his close family, his personal guards, his most trusted officials, and personal servants. It's protected by a spell rendering it invisible to most eyes, and that's why it has never been found by the many archaeologists who have studied the Palace. The spell is powerful enough to fool any modern scientific techniques. I just hope I can remember the words to break it!'

Despite his modesty about whether he could remember the spell after so long, Xin spoke the word '*Yoshara*' confidently and waved his hands at the wall, which shimmered like a mirage before part of it disappeared revealing the entrance to the stairwell.

'Pretty cool! Nice one Xin' said Ben, a young Australian boy with a sunny disposition, and a mane of curly hair, who looked like he might have just stepped of the beach at Bondi. He smiled brightly up at Xin with his broad, square face, deep brown eyes, and slightly snub nose, set neatly into his bronzed complexion. Ben's Astraxi superpowers were drawn from the Celestial Dog, Canis Major, whose image is in the night sky running alongside that of his master, the mighty hunter Orion.

'Yes, it's easy when you know how! The mage who hid the entrance fished that section of wall out of another dimension and put it there to keep out any nosey parkers!' replied Xin and waving his hands he urged the Astraxi towards the stairs.

'Well, come on then, chop-chop! I'll need to close this portal again before the museum staff catch us in the act and ask us to pay the entrance fee. I don't imagine any of you have brought any money, have you?' He smiled at the group, already knowing the answer.

'That's because we're here by royal appointment! We don't need to carry entrance money when the King's chief servant is with us,' teased Ciara in her cheeky Irish lilt.

Ciara, whose powers were drawn from the Celestial Monkey, was a teenage girl, but with enough attitude and natural wit to carry herself easily with much older company. Her complexion of fair skin, flushed with pink at her cheeks, with a delicately freckled nose, pale blue eyes and rounded chin were topped with a shock of wayward auburn hair, all of which were testament to her Irish heritage. Her fast wit and her fiery temper got her into trouble as often as her humour made her friends. She pursed her cupid-bow lips and looked the old man directly in the eye smirking, fit to burst out laughing.

'Such impertinence, I would have had you locked up, or worse for that four thousand years ago!' Xin shook his head and rolled his eyes at Ciara's comment and urged the group forward once more before raising his staff. 'Honestly, it's like herding cats!

'Luxeïs' he called out, and the head of his staff lit up, glowing brightly as if illuminated from inside. Under the torch light, they edged slowly forward down the stairs, through a narrow passage into a dark underground chamber, soon finding themselves surrounded by ancient works of art depicting the history of Astrellion. The beautiful murals, statues, and carvings showed kings long dead, and depictions of the Astraxi in their past glories fighting alongside magical creatures while battling vast armies of demons. But if Astrellion was all powerful and victorious, why had its power faded? Xin knew the entire bloody history, having lived through every minute of it. Maybe he would explain that someday, or maybe he preferred not to talk about it, who could tell.

'Is that you?' enquired Eduardo, who had stopped to admire a very detailed mural with a handsome bald man leading a group of Astraxi into battle against an enormous multi headed beast.

Eduardo was a teenage boy of mixed heritage, from South America and like Ciara a well-established member of the group. His Astraxi power came from the constellation of Serpens, or the Celestial Snake as it is more often known. Eduardo was always stylishly dressed, and today was wearing a long dark leather coat lined with green silk, with a crisp plain white cotton shirt, pale green faux snakeskin trousers and pointy toed ankle boots. His hair was black with a long, green-tinted fringe that fell over one eye and he usually wore an interesting collection of earrings to match a brooch or other adornment he was wearing, often with an inset emerald stone.

'Er, yes, that is me!' replied Xin, slightly embarrassed, yet also very proud of his bold depiction in the mural. 'That was a war we fought in the earliest days against Golteria, shortly after it had been established.'

'Nice armour' remarked Eduardo, 'I bet it's worth plenty now if you've still got it.'

'I donated it to the Central Museum many years ago. You'll see it on display in the main hall of antiquities, that is, of course, if any of you young people ever go to museums these days!' replied Xin, with a knowing grin.

'I am surprised they didn't put you on display in the museum too Xin!' quipped Phae, with a wide smile spreading across her face.

Phaedra had the look of a very lean athlete, with long sleek black hair tied in a ponytail and was dressed casually in high quality sportswear. It was hard to decide just by looking at her face with its strong, symmetrical features, exactly what her heritage was, as she seemed to defy any obvious classification.

But the most striking were her Eurasian eyes, which were the most brilliant shade of amber, and flecked in the same way as the precious stone; eyes which always totally captivated the attention of anyone who was brave enough look into them for any length of time.

'Ha ha, very funny, you'll pay for that later when the washing up needs doing after dinner!' retorted Xin. 'Oh look, here's an interesting scene, one that for once doesn't involve a battle with Cyax and the armies of Golteria.' Xin pointed to a mural depicting himself and two Astraxi facing a giant humanoid creature with the head of a toad and webbed feet that had fought its way past the Royal Guard and was poised to attack the King.

'This is a demonic toad from one of the more exotic planes of existence. The artist has made it look much bigger and more dangerous than it really was. Heaven knows how it got here, I suppose some sorcerer must have added a bit too much incense to his breakfast potion and during the resulting fit of uncontrollable coughing accidentally yanked it through a portal, but it was a most curious beast. Anyway, for some reason it got very agitated and was trying to attack the King. It was almost impossible to stop it. We tried using swords, pikes, arrows, lightning bolts and even a fireball, but it was very resilient. It must have had quite a tough hide!' said Xin, raising an eyebrow as he enjoyed the memory of the moment.

'We didn't really know what to do with it, until a combination of Monkey magic and Snakish charm solved the problem.'

Xin pointed to two figures painted on the wall. 'Jana, who was the Monkey Warrior at the time, used her powers of illusion to disguise Megara the Snake Warrior as a female version of the same demonic toad creature. Then Megara used her irresistible charm to persuade the creature to look inside an iron flask that she had taken from a display cabinet in the throne room. Megara must have been very convincing because the creature seemed mesmerised by her. What the creature didn't know was that the flask was in fact a magical device designed to imprison extra-planar demons. All it took was a small wave of Megara's hand and he was sucked inside and locked in it for ever.' Xin paused for a moment in reflection, 'Hmm. She never did tell me how she knew the flask was magical!'

'What did you do with the flask afterwards?' asked Ash, who was always looking for the fine detail in any story. Ash was the oldest member of the Astraxi, having been the group's Stag Warrior for almost twenty years, since he was a boy and whose power came from the Celestial Stag, a constellation which was well known to the people of ancient Astrellion.

Ash was an enigmatic character, who generally only tended to speak when he thought it necessary to say something. Most of the time he was inconspicuous, even when in a small group, trying not to stand out from the crowd. He tended to wear the same combination of t-shirt, jeans, sneakers, and a dark lightweight cotton jacket without any obvious branding and with lots of pockets to store the things he felt necessary to carry with him, mostly tools and gadgets.

He was as close to a true ethnic Astrellian as you could get, but behind the shy, fidgety exterior lurked a fearsome intellect, constantly analysing the world around him, while shrinking from any emotional engagement.

'Hmm, yes whatever did happen to that flask?' mused Xin. 'I hope nobody found it and opened it, that would have been a most unpleasant surprise!' he laughed softly, and the others joined in. 'Come on, let's stay on task,' he said urging them forward once more.

Passing through another ornate archway, the vaulted roof of the next chamber was decorated with heavenly bodies, asterisms and planets surrounded by a vast, gilded airborne dragon blasting fire across the ceiling at a horde of demons on the wall opposite. Eleni, the Astraxi warrior whose power came from the constellation of Draco the dragon, smiled, and pointed upwards.

'Look upon the glory of Dragon power and despair at your own frail inadequacies, losers!' announced Eleni in tones of comic grandeur spreading her arms out wide as if to reflect the dragon's majestic pose.

Being in her twenties, Eleni was also one of the oldest of the group and had studied archaeology at university, while training to be a member of the Astraxi under Xin's guidance.

Like Phae she had an athletic physique, resulting from her martial arts combat training, along with the natural self-assurance and leadership that all Dragon Warriors have in their personalities. An elaborate dragon tattoo adorned her upper arm just below the shoulder upon which cascaded her long hair.

Since their founding, each of the Astraxi had carried a magical amulet, a different amulet having been created for each one of the Warriors. The amulets allowed the Astraxi to 'power up' their lore and to summon their companion creatures from the celestial plane.

Ciara the Monkey Warrior reached for her amulet and squeezed it, causing the inscribed image of the monkey at its centre to glow, while also enabling her superpowers. She was going to have a little fun at the Dragon's expense!

Using her imagination and her powers of illusion she made the vast dragon in the mural shrink to something worm sized that wriggled and writhed and whined on the ceiling, before disappearing in a small puff of smoke with a pathetic whimpering squeak.

'That's more like it! I give you Eleni, mistress of worms!' she laughed. But Eleni knew the girl was just taunting her overly grandiose gesture and joined in the joke, pushing Ciara's shoulder in mock anger.

'Sshh, calm yourselves!' hissed Xin firmly, 'Don't lose your discipline and stay focused. If I recall correctly, this underground chamber has many other entrances so we may not be alone, who knows what else is down here. Let's just find the Cup of Souls and get out, there's no time for anything else, do you understand? And remember don't touch anything, you never know what you might find down here.' The group stood still for a moment, understanding the seriousness of Xin's warning.

At the far end of the chamber, they passed more ancient objects covered in the thick dust of forgotten centuries.

Arranged on stone shelving was a collection of ancient earthenware pots and vases. Some of them looked very ornate, clearly having been created by master artisans at the peak of their talents, while others were much more rustic in their form. One dusty iron flask looked remarkably similar to the one in the mural they looked at earlier, 'Best leave that where it is for now,' said Xin raising his eyebrows slightly.

'What about that one,' said Ben enthusiastically pointing to an elegant white vase, finely decorated with a scene of wealthy people in fifteenth century robes riding through the countryside against a backdrop of snow-capped mountains. His cheerful personality always had something of a wagging tail about it, making him an endearing and loyal companion, but as the Dog Warrior he had powerful senses that made him a great hunter and an even better fighter.

'From what I recall the Cup of Souls disguises itself as a very humble item, so that it attracts as little attention as possible to prevent it from being stolen,' remarked Xin drily as he peered into the gloom studying the pots while illuminating each one with his glowing staff.

Phae concentrated and focused her senses on earth elemental energy. Slowly and to her eyes only, most of the pots on the shelves faded away into the darkness, except for one unremarkable unglazed, earthenware bowl with loop handles that seemed to have an aura around it. Indented roughly into its surface, were symbols that looked as if they had been made with a crude implement, poked into the surface of the clay with a shard of wood.

'I can sense its energy. I think it's the one on the left of the top shelf, the one with the strange markings?' exclaimed Phae. 'I wonder what those inscriptions mean?'

She was about to step forward to take the bowl from the shelf but was held back by a firm grip on her shoulder from Xin. 'Just wait a minute Phae.' he warned. 'Remember what I said. We don't know what we're dealing with here.'

'The inscription looks a bit like Linear A,' said Eleni. 'An ancient form of writing that's never been deciphered by archaeologists.'

'If only they'd asked me, I could help them with that!' mused Xin. 'But I don't recognise that script. It's like nothing I have ever seen before.'

Without warning, the group were engulfed by a huge cloud of dust thrown into the air by a prolonged blast of icy cold wind, scattering the papyrus scrolls across the floor and blowing grit into their eyes, which they hastily protected with their hands. As they staggered in the confusion and darkness, a terrifying howl pierced the air and the light on Xin's staff faltered, while a look of dread spread across his face.

Out of the flickering shadows of a nearby tunnel appeared two hideous wraith-like figures walking towards them. Dead, watery eyes were set deeply into the faces, which were covered in a very thin paper-like flesh of a greenish-grey hue, embellished with tattoos of ancient mystical symbols.

Locks of hair made from the backbones of snakes hung limply from beneath their helmets, draping over the shoulder plates of their heavy armour, which was engraved and decorated with the heraldic symbols of long dead kingdoms. The apparition in front was carrying a vicious looking sword clearly designed to inflict pain and suffering rather than a quick and merciful death.

The Astraxi's stunned expressions gave way to a deep fear that chilled their bones and paralysed their bodies. Despite their training, they were unprepared for the aura of terror being projected by the undead creatures, a *Bane* spell.

'Taotie and Hundun!' whispered Xin before composing himself and calling out an order, loudly and clearly. 'Star shield! Now!' There was a brief but agonising pause where nothing or no one moved, as the Astraxi were so gripped by the visceral terror of the Bane spell. 'NOW!!' Xin barked with all his energy.

Breaking from their deathly stupor, the Astraxi squeezed the amulets on their wrist bands. A cloud of golden plasma-like points of energy flowed out of each amulet, quickly merging with the others to form a glowing dome shaped translucent barrier, separating them from the ghostly figures. The shield's surface shimmered with energy as constellations were formed in the star light. The shapes of the six magical creatures of tiger, stag, snake, dog, monkey, and dragon flowed across the shield's surface, melting in and out of existence and forming other star patterns.

As the shield was forming, each of the young warriors also went through a physical transformation, in which armour of a style from times long gone by, magically enveloped their bodies.

The style of the armour was broadly similar for each warrior, plates of shining metal and leather, highly decorated with the symbols of Royal Astrellion. Each warrior's armour carried a different decoration on the breastplate and the helmet, to match their associated celestial companion. After the transformation, the six were now instantly recognisable by anyone who had ever encountered them, as the legendary warriors of the Astraxi.

It had been many centuries since Xin had last encountered any of the Four Fiends, the undead remnants of four corrupt ancient sorcerer kings from the lands to the East. Destroyed by their lust for wealth and power, the Four Fiends possessed unnatural magic to extract the souls of their victims, which in turn would increase their own strength. They hunted humans for their life force and revelled in the pain, suffering and misery they inflicted in doing that.

Normally all four would be present, Hundun, Taotie, Taowu and Qiongqi. But today only two of those, Hundun and Taotie were present. Xin was very wary indeed, as facing even only two of these malevolent beings was extremely dangerous and he was well aware of the fact that these young warriors had never been tested in this way, never having had a face-to-face encounter with an enemy even half as powerful as the Fiends. 'Do not let them touch you' he commanded in a very slow and clear voice.

'Astraxi, be strong!' added Eleni the Dragon Warrior. Being noble and proud, as you would expect of a Dragon, Eleni made an inspiring leader. But the Fiends made the most of their moment of surprise and charged the protective star shield, attempting to smash it down.

Next to Eleni stood Phaedra, the Tiger Warrior, whose power was drawn from the Celestial White Tiger. Phae was graceful and intelligent, her family being descended from the rulers of the lands along the ancient trading routes that extended from Astrellion towards the great empires of the East.

But she was also highly impetuous and had a very short temper. Phae was a natural hunter with sharp instincts and an even sharper tongue. Tiger Warriors are dangerous because they often react without thinking, believing that their strength will allow them to win in any situation and this was exactly what happening in Phae's mind at that moment. Despite the ferocity and danger of the attack from the Fiends, Phae had her mind set on taking the Cup of Souls, and in her head, nothing was going to stop her. 'I can get it,' she shouted.

'We have no time for that now Phae, we must concentrate on defending ourselves' insisted Xin who was directing the shield energies back against Taotie, while weighing up their escape options.

'I can do this' yelled Phae insistently, suddenly sensing an opportunity that was only apparent to herself. 'Let me get it.'

'Now's not the time for heroics Phae, it's far too dangerous,' shouted Xin, his voice clear and commanding. Having been the leader of the Astraxi for so long, he was all too aware of the habit of tigers to behave like a loose cannon!

'Don't be ridiculous Xin. We can't let them take it' said Phae. Having found it, she was reluctant to lose the Cup of Souls into the hands of Evil.

'This is not the time for an argument Phae, remember your training.' Xin was angry at her, while directing the shield's combined energies to counter the thrust of the Fiends' dark weapons, which were pushing against the shield, tearing small rifts of darkness like a void of nothingness in its glowing energy shell. Xin was using his hands to physically manipulate the shield back into shape.

But in Phae's mind a clear plan of how to snatch the Cup of Souls had presented itself and she was going to take it. She would summon her celestial companion Xantix the Star Tiger, to join the fight. 'I'll get it, while they're distracted' said Phae with more than a hint of determination in her voice.

'For once in your life Phae, calm down and listen to Xin!' bellowed the normally relaxed Eduardo, the Snake Warrior.

Back in the Perpetual Motion Café, Eduardo was always a bit of a loner, very intelligent but softly spoken, some would have described him as a bit of an 'Emo.' He was naturally charming, but in a slightly hypnotic way and had the remarkable ability to blend in or disappear invisibly into a background. The seriousness of their current situation now raised Eduardo to a whole new level of anxiousness that they hadn't seen before in this normally ice-cool and charming character.

But Phae's mind was already made up. 'No, I will do this!' she insisted.

Taking her amulet she turned its dial, all the way to its end point aligning the tiger symbol with the Astraxi rune. Bright, fast moving circular shafts of light appeared from the vault's ceiling, which merged into a single silvery ray bursting through the roof of the chamber as Phae's celestial companion Xantix the Star Tiger emerged, landing in the space behind the two Fiends.

Xantix' appearance was that of a very large tiger, but her fur was coloured in silvery hues, like starlight. Xantix' body glowed with translucent celestial energy, but she was as solid and terrifying as a real tiger in tooth and claw.

Xantix roared ferociously, baring her fangs. Being from the celestial plane, she didn't have the limitations of mortal creatures when faced with the undead and so was not intimidated by them or their deathly weapons. As the two Fiends momentarily backed off, Phae raced towards the shelves, heading for the Cup of Souls. But by leaving the star shield, Phae had weakened its collective protective power.

'Jeez, Tiger trouble again!' quipped Ben nervously, breathing out sharply with a sense of resignation as he held his position behind the now weaker star shield.

While Hundun parried the attacks of Xantix' mighty paws, Taotie continued to batter the star shield with his sword, each blow causing sparks to discharge from it, disrupting the protective energy patterns coruscating across its surface. More cracks and dark holes appeared in the flowing light, deadly voids of deep foreboding, which were then filled once more with light as the shield recovered under Xin's manipulation.

Hundun's attention was now completely taken up defending himself against the Star Tiger, which was just what Phae had planned, to allow her to move quickly and acquire the Cup.

'I got it' shouted Phae, as she grabbed the Cup of Souls. But Hundun stepped up his attack on Xantix, pushing the creature back with the flat of his unholy sword. Energy flashed and sparks of silver and blackness fizzled as the weapon of the dead clashed with and reacted against Xantix' celestial energy.

Realising his attack was getting nowhere, Taotie turned away from the group under the shield and charged Phae, but Phae reacted instinctively, throwing up her Shield of Harmony to protect herself from Taotie's flesh mortifying, undead touch.

Phae's shield was created with energy drawn from the Plane of Harmony and consisted of two sheets of red and blue light drawn together in a flattened spiral disc shape. She held it in her right hand, attempting to keep the Fiend and his dire sword at bay.

Now that both Fiends were engaged, Xin moved forward to find space to use some of his own magic that he knew would be effective against the undead. The situation was looking disastrous for the Astraxi. Eduardo was being overcome by the physical effort of holding the shield together and Phae was only just managing to hold off Taotie while crouching behind her own shield.

As Taotie intensified his attack on the lone Tiger Warrior, Eleni was becoming increasingly alarmed by the danger her friend was in. She launched herself forward through the star shield calling 'I've got your back Phae'

Eleni was truly magnificent as the fully transformed Dragon Warrior. Her impressive physique was sealed in gleaming Dragon scale armour from head to toe, and she was crowned with a spined helmet reminiscent of the legendary Star Dragon, Adraxa. She raised her head defiantly and her eyes blazed with fiery anger as she hurled herself at Taotie.

But Taotie was ready for this ill-judged attack. Two long, vicious looking spikes burst up on the surface of his shield and turning he smashed them straight into the Dragon Warrior's armoured breastplate.

Xin gasped, and time stood agonisingly still as Eleni's mouth opened emitting an ear shattering scream before her body was transformed into a burst of vivid blue flame, which flickered violently for a moment before collapsing in on itself like an imploding star, disappearing into the darkness.

As Eleni's shriek faded from the chamber, her Dragon amulet dropped noisily to the floor, but the DragonStone ring that she had been wearing on her finger, simply floated in the air for a moment before it too disappeared in a flash of topaz light. Ciara let out a desperate cry. 'Nooooooo. Eleni!'

A hideous smile grew across Taotie's distorted features as he relished the destruction of the brave Dragon Warrior. Eleni's soul would be added to the millions he had taken over the centuries. 'Be ready to join your friend in eternal darkness and torment, Tiger Warrior' he hissed malevolently.

Utterly bewildered by the terrible fate of her friend, Phae fell back under her shield with tears running down her face. Cold fear gripped her as she struggled to move, once more succumbing weakly to the *'Bane'* magic of the Fiends. The remaining Astraxi were now tiring as their reserves of both physical and star energy had been drained under the pressure of maintaining the shield.

Hundun was still engaged in his battle with Xantix and as one would expect of such an experienced warrior, Xin knew that this was the moment not to collapse but to take the initiative. He raised his hand and with a clear voice called out an incantation in the ancient Astrellian tongue, '*Fornat e foreïs.*'

Out of the darkness a ghostly translucent shape, in the form of a giant hand about a metre and a half in height, appeared in front of the star shield and floated towards Taotie. As Xin curled his fingers and tightened his fist, so the phantom hand grabbed the Fiend, lifting him off the ground and holding him firm, preventing him from finishing off Phae. The effort of lifting Taotie was a massive strain on Xin's own body, but he had much strength in reserve.

With Taotie immobilised, Xin now raised his other hand and spoke another incantation in ancient Astrellian, '*Hundun, Yoshara Kalente.*' Hundun's vile form wavered for a moment and collapsed into itself with a ghastly howl and a strange flash not of light, but of darkness that resulted from him being sucked out of the room and banished back to his native Plane of the Undead.

But being so close to Hundun, Xantix was also caught up in Xin's dismissal spell and disappeared in a burst of light that seemed to perfectly balance the dark void left behind by Hundun.

With Taotie firmly in the grip of Xin's Hand of Power, one might have felt the Astraxi could now escape their terrible predicament. But an unexpected volley of blaster shots sliced through the air ricocheting off the walls and the star shield. A group of cyber-demons appeared from another entrance to the chamber, providing covering fire for Tanielka, Princess of Darkness as she stepped into the room her pulsed energy weapon raised in anticipation. The Princess was a striking young woman clad in close fitting black scale armour that was as modern in its materials as the armour of the Astraxi was ancient. Her piercing green eyes and pale high cheek bones were set in a way best described as 'elfin.'

'Take them and release my Lord Taotie' she directed the cyber-demons.

The cyber-demons stepped forward as ordered, weapons raised. As Taotie writhed Xin called out to Ciara breathlessly, 'Ciara, make a distraction. Do it now!'

Inspired by Xin's words, Ciara snapped out of her battle-weary stupor and responded with her own ancient incantation '*Signa Macareis*,' whereupon a horde of large and very aggressive mandrill monkeys suddenly poured into the chamber from every possible entrance, causing a massive distraction as they ran riot, poking their blue and red muzzles into everything, spilling pots, statues, artefacts, scrolls and cyber-demons everywhere. While chaos raged around them, Eduardo used his snake lore to blend into the wall and slipping around the edge of the melee grabbed Eleni's Dragon amulet from the floor before retreating once more under the cover of the shield.

Xin stepped forward, his fists clenched and his eyes grim, but the cyber-demons grinned widely and fired another volley of laser-green shots at the star shield stopping him in his tracks.

The shots were absorbed by the shield which turned the blaster energy from green to gold. The cyber-demons, a bizarre fusion of armour, machinery, and magical creature, stood and observed this effect unsure how to proceed as the shield now seemed stronger than before.

'Warriors to me' commanded Xin and the small group rallied back to him, drawing the shield more tightly around themselves, but Phae was still exposed, protecting herself from blaster shots with her Shield of Harmony.

Reaching down, The Princess retrieved a small dagger from a sheath lashed to her ankle before nimbly leaping into the space next to Phae. 'You're mine, Tiger girl,' she whispered cruelly, but Phae was too fast for her and acrobatically rolled away from the thrusting blade.

From inside the star shield, Ash the Stag Warrior now engaged his own superpower, which allowed him to move and control inanimate objects.

Uttering '*Benjay Extero*' he directed his powers at a large marble statue of the Bull Warrior's celestial companion Dexmane, standing nobly nearby.

The marble statue's cold, hard figure was instantly transformed into a hot blooded, dangerous beast, rearing its head, pawing, and stamping at the ground. It leaped from its plinth, charging at Princess Tanielka its wide nostrils snorting clouds of steam.

Springing into the air with cat-like reflexes Tanielka landed on the back of the roaring ox statue, and plunged her small blade into its neck, causing it to instantly shatter into thousands of tiny pieces of marble.

As clouds of dust and smoke filled the air, Phae rolled out and dived back under the protection of the star shield. Xin looked her angrily in the eye, but sadness and remorse filled Phae's face. After all of this she was empty handed, the Cup of Souls remained on the floor next to Taotie who remained in the firm grip of the spectral hand.

Time was running out and Xin knew that before long the effort involved in mounting such a prolonged defence would cause his young team to tire further, dangerously weakening their shield. 'Let's get out of here.' Xin was clear, retreat was the only option.

'What about Eleni' shouted Ben as the cyber-demons unleashed another laser-green volley of blaster shots.

'There's nothing we can do for her now' replied Xin grimly. He edged them all backwards, in the direction of the tunnel through which they had entered the chamber. Ciara continued to direct her illusory mandrill troupe to attack the cyber-demons, who couldn't understand why their blasters were ineffective against the shrieking baboons relentlessly running rings around them and taunting them by waving their colourful bottoms!

Moving quickly, Xin directed the group to escape up the stairs, back through their original entrance point. As they passed into the open doorway, once more he used his sorcery, uttering the words '*Tura Timar*' in ancient Astrellian. The magical wall that he had removed earlier, returned shimmering from whichever plane of existence it had been sent to, closing the gap, and stopping the Princess and her cyber-demons from following them, despite their best efforts to blast it to smithereens.

Having been released from the grip of Xin's spectral hand, Taotie was now examining the Cup of Souls. He was ancient enough to read and fully understand the meaning of the symbols roughly incised on its surface. As he studied the Cup, the symbols began to melt away, and its rough clay surface became smooth and green, returning to its normal polished jade finish. The two simple handles morphed into the shape of carved dragon heads, whose tails looped and intertwined around the bottom of the bowl.

Finding themselves exhausted outside in the palace gardens, Xin directed the Astraxi back to their transport, which was parked nearby. Grave expressions were etched across the faces of the young warriors as they raced back to the vehicle.

The difficult silence that followed as they sped away in the big old hover-car which served as the Astraxi's crew vehicle was broken by Ciara.

'It's all your fault' she cried; her bitterness directed at Phae. 'Eleni's dead and we didn't get the Cup of Souls. You messed up, and now she's gone. How are you going to live with that?' she continued, thrusting her hand under her freckled chin.

But Phae just stared down at her hands, unable to speak, her lips fused together in shame and self-loathing which caused a nausea deep in the pit of her stomach.

Eduardo maintained his usual external emotional detachment, his distant gaze peering out from underneath his long green tinged fringe, but inside too he was seriously mixed up. Ash fidgeted in his seat, not knowing how to express his feelings, if he were even able to understand the feelings inside his highly logical brain, but he was very aware of the gravity of what had just happened. That's why he preferred not to get too closely involved in any action if he could help it. On the other hand, Ben's heart was ready to burst, and he let forth a huge emotional sigh.

Phae sat stony faced on the bench back seat of the car. She knew too well that her tigerish impulsiveness had cost Eleni her life and seriously endangered her friends. As she looked down at her clenched hands, tears filled her eyes, her body shaking with silent remorse. A tiger's first instinct is to protect, but instead in her haste to win the prize, she had recklessly endangered her friends.

Arriving back at the Perpetual Motion Café they sat in silence around a circular table with a pot of green tea. After pouring everyone a cup, Xin put his arm around Phae's shoulder in a fatherly way. 'It's a terrible tragedy Phae, but you mustn't blame yourself for what happened to Eleni. She knew the risks of being a member of the Astraxi. It's my fault not yours. If anything, I should take the blame for exposing you all to such danger. We weren't prepared. I should have planned better. I don't know how I could have let this happen.' Xin paced up and down the room angry at himself.

'After four thousand years I must be losing my touch.' Xin's face was full of regret and anger at himself, and he continued to pace up and down, touching his forehead as if that would help make things better.

Phae felt the warmth of reassurance in Xin's softly spoken words, and she raised her head once more to find the old man looking sad, but stoic in his emotions.

'Don't take Eleni's death on your shoulders alone, Phae. We will all have to help each other to get over this.' He turned to the group of downcast young people sitting around, not knowing what to do with themselves. 'Listen everyone, let's get some food and some rest and we'll talk about it in the morning. Astraxi, be strong!'

'Astraxi, be strong' answered the others, but with little conviction in their words. The team of young Warriors had been cut from six to five. How would they cope without the strength and power of a Dragon Warrior to support them?

CHAPTER 2
A Boy In Trouble

The day after the unfortunate events beneath the palace was a public holiday in the city of Astrapolis and many of the citizens were out enjoying the warm sunshine in the wide-open spaces.

Astrapolis was the capital of the modern state of Astrellion, a country of eighty-million people and was situated at the mouth of a river, with a wide natural harbour. Over many centuries, it had become a great trading port, a conduit for goods such as fine silks and spices flowing from the empires in the East, to the feudal kingdoms of the West, with other commodities going in the opposite direction. More recently it had become one of the world's great cities, place where business, science and culture flourished.

An observer from another universe might imagine there's a time warp operating in one small quarter of the city just off the central boulevard. Surrounding this area are the highly ordered, gleaming glass towers of Astrapolis' business district but inside lies the more traditional heart of old Astrapolis, whose ancient walled courtyards are huddled together in a haphazard mix, woven together in a maze of almost indistinguishable back alleys, rickety gated enclosures, small shops, and tiny cottages.

The truth is that most people love the past, they love the feeling that they are rooted to something much deeper, older, and longer lasting than mere mortal lifespans. This gives them not only a feeling of belonging, but of continuity of their own existence, a sort of immortality of connectedness, which includes the passing of wisdom and valuable skills through the generations.

On any afternoon in the narrow streets, you would find stalls selling fabulously embroidered silk garments, or shops selling a thousand varieties of spices, art galleries and hawkers selling food, trinkets, toys, gadgets, or souvenirs to passers-by.

Locals could move with ease from the modern, twenty-second century city to the old town and vice versa, without giving the huge contrast between the two a second thought. Hover trams and aerial taxis filled the skies of the new city, while in the old town at ground level people often still pushed their goods around on hand carts.

Many ancient villages had been absorbed as the city grew, but some pockets of quirky old buildings remained. In one dusty corner, a rickety two storey villa stood surrounded by a carefully tended garden of flowers and fresh vegetables the size of two of tennis courts. This villa was the home of Nico and his Great Aunt Cass.

Nico was described as 'difficult' by most of the adults he knew; teachers, social workers, and policemen, but in Nico's opinion this was simply because most adults couldn't possibly understand him, as they were either too slow or too stupid to realise just how amazing he really was (in his own modest opinion!).

When he was actually in school, Nico was an exceptional student, whose grasp of subjects was lightning fast, but his weakness was that his gift of intelligence was more than counter-balanced by an overwhelming tendency to extreme laziness!

Despite this, there were two things that he did lavish time and attention upon: his skateboarding skills and his appearance. Nico dressed like a typical street kid but had his own kind of cool and everything about his appearance had to be just right, especially his hair.

Many young people quite correctly believe themselves to be special or different in some way, and feel misunderstood by adults, but Nico had this in spades and an attitude problem to go with it, particularly where figures of authority were concerned. His school reports described him as short tempered and intolerant of others, but he was popular with his peers and surprisingly resourceful, even though he mostly enjoyed spending time on his own.

The only person in Astrapolis, and perhaps even the entire world, who had any power or influence over Nico was his elderly Great Aunt Cass. Somewhere behind her wise and very wrinkled smile she had a deep understanding of the way his mind worked, which was remarkable for a little old lady. She knew that Nico was not really a bad person, just misguided and it was her job to try and keep him on the straight and narrow.

'Young man, you'll either end up as President of Astrellion, or you'll end up in jail,' was the phrase that she wheeled out at moments when he was testing her patience to the limits.

'Nico, before you go out with that skateboard of yours, I want you to finish weeding the vegetable patch,' said Aunt Cass, using her commanding tone of voice that seemed so much louder in Nico's ears than it would to anyone else's.

'Oh, come on Aunt Cass. The sun's out, the vegetable patch can wait, I've got things to do,' replied Nico.

'Yes, you have got things to do, pulling the weeds out, sweeping the yard, tidying your room, doing your homework... Need I go on? I will not have you wasting your time, when there's so much you could help me with here,' she retorted, the pitch of her voice rising. Nico knew that as the pitch of her voice rose, the more trouble he would find himself in if he didn't comply, so reluctantly he followed her outside and picked up the hoe.

She now spoke to him softly, sensing that he was actually going to comply with her commands. 'First finish weeding the lettuce and the onions, then I want you to turn the soil over here, so I can plant some more vegetables tomorrow.'

'Yeah, whatever makes you happy Aunt Cass' he said with an air of resignation, while turning his head to the sun to feel its heat on his face. As she walked away, Nico started picking carefully at the weeds between the lettuces, regarding each one as a foe in a game that he was playing out in his mind. He was the great Imperial star-general, fighting off an army of invading space-weeds and his hoe was the energy weapon giving him to power to vanquish all alien weed forms from his quadrant of the galaxy. 'Ha ha, take that you green intruders!'

For a short while this battle for control of the intergalactic lettuce patch amused him, but when his phone buzzed in his pocket his dream quickly dissipated, and he found himself back on planet Earth, standing in the rich brown soil of his Aunt's vegetable patch.

On his screen he could see that some of his friends were gathering at the skate-park in central Astrapolis. He didn't take too much time thinking about it before he dropped the hoe, grabbed his skateboard from the garden shed and whizzed off towards the hover-bus stop, destination Astrapolis Central Park.

While riding the hover-bus through the broad streets of the leafy suburbs and into the city centre, Nico thought about his parents, which made him feel very sad and more than a little hollow. It had been about ten years since his parents had separated.

His mother came from a relatively modest background and had worked hard to develop a successful career in international banking. This allowed her to travel the world, landing an assignment in Astrapolis, where she met Nico's father, who worked as the Marketing Director for a multi-national sportswear brand. They were both charismatic and creative characters, and the chemistry between them was instantaneous. It was a short, high-octane courtship that saw them married within just six months of meeting.

But their demanding jobs often kept them apart and the fire of their romance faded almost as quickly as it had been kindled. Eventually, they went through a protracted and acrimonious divorce, which affected Nico deeply. He became a pawn in their ongoing marital conflict, which at first made him upset, but then it made him angry, intolerant, and disruptive. That was when authority figures became a real problem for him.

Having been a straight 'A' student at school, he dropped studying and applied himself to the one thing that he enjoyed most, and which made him popular with the other kids at school — his skateboard.

If Nico loved anything it was his board, because while he was riding it, he felt like a surfer, perched on a wave in space and time which he shaped with his mind. Sometimes he really felt he was floating through the air and as he sped past people, he had the feeling that somehow time ran more slowly for them, which was pretty cool as it meant he was always the first to react in situations.

While he was on the board no-one could prevent him from doing pretty much whatever he wanted. The slow-motion world of ordinary people would never catch him while he rode his mind wave.

He lived with his father in Astrapolis for a while but started mixing with the wrong kids. He would get into street fights, sometimes stealing from shops and occasionally using his weird ability to start fires out of nothing, just to have some fun. Fire would sometimes appear around his fingertips, but there was no source of ignition, it was like the flames were part of him and he could summon them at will. He tended to keep that ability secret for obvious reasons, not wanting to become the subject of scientific investigation and people in white coats with probes and other uncomfortable tools of a surgical nature.

After being arrested many times, he was destined for juvenile detention, but his mother agreed to take Nico to live in England, to see if this would help change his downward trajectory. But Nico hated London and he was soon returned to Astrapolis, but this time into the care of Great Aunt Cass.

Nico quickly returned to his bad habits, but Aunt Cass – his paternal grandfather's sister, had a way of dealing with wayward boys. Nico was not impressed at being 'farmed out' as he called it, but in Aunt Cass he found someone who stood up to him, was actually a bit scary and demanded he followed her strict house rules. Even his most precious possession — his skateboard — had to be stored in the outside shed.

Looking back, Nico couldn't help but blame himself for all that had happened to him. Somehow, he felt responsible for his parents' divorce and the fact that he no longer lived with either of them, just increased his overall sense of resentment and emptiness.

It was true that Nico was the main source of their disagreement, but it wasn't his fault. It was partially down to his father's family heritage, which brought with it the potential of an interesting but very dangerous destiny for her young son. His mother resented this fate for her precious boy and the peril in which it may put him if it were to come true.

At least with his pals at the skate park he had some sense of camaraderie and belonging. Nico's hover-bus soon arrived at the bust stop next to a junk shop at the edge of the old town. As Nico stepped off the bus, in the window of the junk shop, an old man was placing on display a ring shaped like a silver dragon with a topaz stone held in its claws. Yesterday the ring had unexpectedly materialised out of thin air and dropped on to his desk.

Sadness filled the old man's eyes, as he knew that for the ring to appear in this way, something very tragic must have happened to its owner. Usually, the ring would be handed back to him when the owner retired from the role to which the ring was connected.

As Nico passed the shop, the topaz stone in the ring started to glow with a clear blue light, which surprised the old man,

'So soon' he muttered to himself and turned away from the window to return to his desk. What Nico didn't know was that very soon he and this ring would be bound up in a great adventure.

Strolling confidently into the park, Nico very quickly weighed up the scene around him and where he would find his entertainment for the day. Broad avenues criss-crossed the park, perfect highways for a Grand Master Skateboarder. He threw down his board and very quickly was performing gravity defying stunts, narrowly avoiding people and their dogs, but in a deft manner that showed complete mastery of his trajectory. He appeared to almost float at times, with perfect balance, gliding past people while performing humorous pranks, such as stealing a balloon from a small child and placing it in the hands of an old lady.

On his way to the skate park, he decided to head to the ice cream stall for a free snack. As he approached it, he fixed his eyes on a large cone which was having 'sprinkles' applied to it. Just as the vendor was about to hand over the cone to his client, a small blonde girl with her hair in cute bunches, Nico flashed past and grabbed the ice cream without any hesitation or deviation in his movement.

'Hey, you little punk' called out the angry ice cream vendor.

Nico looked him in the eye with an expression of splendid indifference, as if to say, 'Well what are you going to do about it?' and wheeled around the stall coming to a dead stop while licking the ice cream. Turning to two policemen with bicycles the vendor gesticulated angrily in Nico's direction.

'That's him! That's the little punk who keeps stealing my ice creams.'

As the two policemen jumped on their bikes and set off to catch him, Nico coolly hopped back on his board still licking the ice cream, a broad smile running across his face. He was relishing the chase already. As an expert at evasive manoeuvres, he knew they would struggle to catch him in the crowded boulevards.

On the East side of the park a teenage gang, The Tiger Sharks, was hanging out by a scruffy coffee bar, playing loud music from a boom-box and generally being anti-social, including making rude comments to passers-by. Gus, their leader, was playing cards when one of the sharks spotted Nico with the bicycle police in tow.

'Hey Gus,' he interrupted.

'What is it? I'm winning here,' retorted Gus, in the slow, pained manner of speech used by a bully before he strikes out.

'It's that spindly kid on his board' came the nervous reply.

Gus didn't even bother to lift his eyes from the cards, 'So what, get rid of him.'

'Gus, you really need to take a look.' By now Nico was only fifty metres away, bearing down on the card game fast, with the police still a distance behind him. Nico had swallowed the last of the ice cream, thrown away the empty cone and now had his eyes fixed on the card game, and the piles of coins and cash arranged around the table.

Panic broke out amongst the card players just as Nico swerved at the last minute, leaving the bicycle police and the card players locked on collision course. Chairs, bikes, and bodies scattered everywhere, as Nico calmly swivelled, rode back into the scene, and scooped up the stake money scattered on the floor, before turning to the non-plussed gang leader Gus and swiping the Tiger Sharks baseball cap off his head.

Picking himself off the floor, the bicycle cop sergeant surveyed the scene and turned to Gus. 'Hey Gus, gambling in the park again. Tut tut… naughty boy!'

'It's just a little game amongst friends. Ain't harmin' no-one,' pleaded Gus, while Nico retreated to a safe distance.

'You know the law Gus, no gambling in public. Gonna have to take you and your friends in. Jones, call for backup.' The junior police office spoke into his radio as the cuffs went on Gus, who looked up to see Nico laughing and flicking the broad brim of the Tiger Sharks baseball cap he had just acquired, before he skated off into the distance.

'You're dog food kid! I'll find you' he snarled as the cuffs tightened on his wrists. 'Ow take it easy.'

'OK, that's enough now Gus' The sergeant was assertive, knowing that Gus could be difficult to handle.

Nico decided that he should leave the park until the heat died down and headed back towards the old town, gently propelling himself forward with slow deliberate strokes. He needed somewhere to hide as the bicycle police would surely continue their search for him. As he passed the old antique shop again, something in the window caught his eye. The ring shaped like a coiled dragon with a topaz stone in its claws was pulsing with a pale blue light, which Nico found hypnotic. He struggled to avert his gaze from it and after looking around to see who was watching, entered the shop to take a closer look.

The battered sign above the large window read 'Gilmane's Old Curiosity Shop' in a very old-fashioned hand painted style of sign writing. Inside were a collection of odd items and bric-a-brac from centuries before. Mysterious tools and peculiar clockwork machines that had no obvious purpose littered the shelves, amongst piles of old books, stuffed animals, pottery and works of art.

Nico quietly opened the panelled wooden door with its brass lever handle and slid in stealthily, not realising that the owner of the store, was quietly observing him from behind a large old leather-bound book.

Gilmane was a very, very old man, dressed in silken robes decorated with mystical symbols, in the style of the old Kingdom of Astrellion, On his head was the matching pork pie hat of a high-ranking court official. He sported a neatly trimmed goatee beard and moustache and had enormous eyebrows that some might believe to be a distinctly different life form, possibly a species of hairy caterpillar living symbiotically with him on his forehead! Nico moved quietly towards the window display drawn by the pale blue glow of the topaz stone.

Gilmane picked up a pair of old spectacles on a stalk, with solid brass frames and thick crystalline lenses, and peered through them giving him a slightly 'steampunk' look. '*Pambe desi tolaris*,' muttered the old man under his breath. To Gilmane's eyes alone, superimposed translucently over Nico's body by the spell, was the clothing of a Dragon Warrior.

Dragon scale armour, gauntlets and boots decorated with dragon claws, and a helmet featuring the distinctive spines, fangs, and fire breathing nostrils that you would expect of a dragon surrounded Nico who was totally unaware of the spell.

Gilmane could also detect powerful magic in the young man, more than he had seen in such a long time. Tugging his moustache, Gilmane muttered to himself 'Looks like the prophecy may be about to come true!'

He unfurled a small piece of parchment and a brush magically lifted itself out of its stand. The brush hovered briefly, before writing a few rune-like symbols in broad strokes on the sheet. The text then melted away until it was completely invisible. Gilmane stepped out from behind his desk, appearing to be searching his bookshelves and unaware of the young man.

Strange sounds filled Nico's head as he advanced towards the pulsing stone, including the voices of the many previous owners of the artefact calling across the years. Nervously he looked around, and feeling he was still unobserved, he picked up the stone, which started to glow with an even greater intensity.

'Whoa, pretty cool!' he whispered to himself in the vivid blue light. Staring into the stone he could now see the source of the sounds in his head, dragons dancing in the air, patterns of waves, snowstorms, lightning bolts, and jets of fire. Merging in and out of these were the smiling faces of many past Dragon Warriors, the last of which cried out to him in terror, startling Nico into knocking over a pile of old scrolls.

'Put that down!' commanded Gilmane sharply as he approached Nico, who for once did as he was commanded setting the ring down on the bench as the strange visions in the ring had disturbed his normally clear thinking. Nico wasn't looking for a confrontation with the old man and being in a bit of a panic he started to pick up the scrolls that he had knocked to the floor. But crimson flames suddenly ignited around his fingertips, quickly eating into the bone-dry papyrus, and causing it to catch fire.

'No, not now...' he whispered to himself as the flames grew stronger, shaking and blowing on his fingers to try and stop the fire. Despite his best efforts to put the fire out with a piece of cloth, the scrolls were now completely engulfed in flames and the old-fashioned brass bell of the shop's fire alarm started ringing loudly. Cold water spouted out in torrents from the overhead sprinklers and in the confusion, Nico grabbed the silver ring before running past Gilmane and out of the door.

Watching the young thief escape on his skateboard, Gilmane laughed out loud and waved his hands like a sorcerer to dismiss the flames. This new Dragon certainly had spirit, he thought, and with another magical gesture from his hands he sent the parchment with its invisible inscription flying out of the door and following Nico down the street.

As Nico steered his skateboard past the road signs and other street furniture, the parchment flew above his head as if it were following him. He tried to grab it as it circled around, seemingly playing a game with him, darting back and forth, but he couldn't catch it. The parchment then continued its progress down the street, and paused for a moment, seeming to beckon him to follow. Nico stuck the ring in his shirt pocket and pushed harder on his skateboard to follow the mysterious flying parchment. But at the corner he suddenly found himself facing the bicycle police again and turned to retreat quickly down an alley, knocking over some dustbins to block their pursuit, and diving behind some sacks of rubbish for cover.

The parchment followed him down the alley and started buzzing around his head like a large, demented moth around a candle flame. Worried that it might attract the attention of the bicycle police he tried to swat it with a piece of wood, but it was quick and just like an insect it made an annoying buzzing sound.

After a few seconds of thrashing around he made a direct strike hitting the parchment cleanly and launching it into the air. The mysterious message floated high above him for a moment before whizzing off down the street towards the rear entrance of the Perpetual Motion Café and entered it through a small open window.

Inside the café, Xin had been preparing vegetables when the parchment settled on the bench before him. He picked the message up and as he unfolded it the invisible text re-appeared on the page. 'Be ready for the Dragon!'

'So soon!' exclaimed Xin to himself with complete surprise. He spoke into a small intercom mounted on the wall, 'I will need your help, quickly.'

A few moments later Nico edged out from behind the sacks of rubbish and decided that the bicycle police had probably given up their manhunt. He dusted himself down and decided to follow the weird flying object into the café to see if he could figure out what it was.

As Nico approached the café, he was shocked to find himself confronted by a large tiger. It was no ordinary tiger that was facing him, because rather than having the usual orange and brown tiger-striped camouflage on its body, it was essentially monochrome, being in shades of silvery grey rather than brown. Its stripes seemed to glow with energy, is if it were made from something more than just ordinary earthly matter, and the light coming from its body seeming to twinkle like starlight. The tiger advanced on him and made a low growling sound while baring its huge fangs. Nico was rooted to the spot, too terrified to make his escape.

Stopping only inches from his face, the tiger looked him up and down slowly, before turning its attention to the blue glow in Nico's shirt pocket. As the tiger sniffed the fabric of his shirt, Nico pulled out the ring and the tiger stared into the pale blue light as if it understood its deeper significance.

Nico was about to take his chance to escape from becoming a tiger sized meal, when a large monkey suddenly dropped to the ground beside him and grabbed the ring from his fingers. The monkey was similarly as monochrome as the tiger in its colouring and had the same twinkling energy coming from its fur.

Without thinking Nico called out 'Hey, that's mine!'

'No, it is not,' replied the monkey.

'I'll think you'll find it is!' he responded and quick as a flash, Nico grabbed the ring back from the monkey before running through the front door of the café, shoving the ring back in his pocket and hiding in a booth. Xin observed the young man from behind the counter for a while with his ageless eyes and spotted the blue glow in the young man's shirt pocket.

Outside the bicycle cops paused, still looking for Nico the ice cream thief. He observed them discretely through the lattice work in the window, hardly daring even to breathe. Unknown to them, he was not just an ice cream thief, he was now also a jewel thief which magnified the level of his misdemeanour into something very serious indeed. Prison was the most likely outcome if they caught him. Seizing the opportunity to intervene, Xin vaulted over the counter with amazing agility for someone of his apparent age 'Can I help you, young man?' he asked.

'Sshh! Erm, yeah. I'll have some sweet chilli noodles or whatever,' said Nico. But Xin just stared at him, tilting his head, waiting for the nervous customer to say something more revealing, which is often what happens when you let someone else do the talking. Nico obliged, 'You'll never believe this, but I just saw a huge grey tiger and a talking monkey outside,' continued Nico.

'Well, maybe you should come and choose something from the kitchen instead.' Xin turned the sign on the door to read 'CLOSED' and grabbing Nico swiftly by his shirt collar and belt, he picked him up and frogmarched him into the kitchen, where two girls were standing, secretly watching the events through the door. One was tall and slim with long dark hair in a ponytail and had the most amazing eyes, while the other was much younger and smaller with a shock of wavy red hair and a very pale, almost marble like complexion infused with hundreds of delicate freckles.

They stifled their laughter through their hands as Nico struggled in Xin's firm grip, finding the situation quite comical, whereas Nico was starting to panic thinking he was being put under a citizens' arrest and soon would be handed over to the bicycle cops.

'Hey!' he called out as Xin pushed him firmly through the kitchen and into a small storeroom with the two girls following behind.

The walls of the dimly lit storeroom were lined with shelves loaded with sauce bottles, cooking oils, bags of ingredients, sets of chopsticks, woks and pots, knives, napkins, cardboard take away cartons and everything that you might normally expect in a café storeroom. Scarily there was a set of very sharp looking knives and meat cleavers hanging on the wall.

He scanned the small gloomy room with its yellowy light. There was no other visible exit to the storeroom he noted, while trying to plan possible escape routes.

'Hey, what are you doing with me?' he called out loud, now being sure he was in some sort of trap. 'Don't you know there's a law against kidnapping people.'

'Chilli Prawn Dim Sum, coming up!' replied Xin in a strangely expressive and comic way, which just seemed random and bizarre to Nico, but to the two girls this sounded even funnier, and they tried very hard but failed to suppress their amusement. The younger girl was struggling to hold it in, but instead produced a series of sniggers that reverberated down her nostrils like a snorting animal.

'What alien planet are you on, you crazy old man?' Nico was now getting quite rattled and squirmed harder against the old man's firm grip.

'Sometimes I just like to say a few magic words, although they're not always strictly necessary!' Xin was quietly enjoying meeting the new Dragon for the first time, and it was more interesting since Nico had no idea what was about to happen to him.

Xin had been the master of so many people's destinies over the last four thousand years, a role that suited him and which he enjoyed. He had long since lost count of how many Celestial Warriors had passed through his care, but it was certainly many thousands, and yet somehow this one was different, a bit more special. A spindly kid, with a penchant for trouble and a very loose interpretation of the rules regarding the ownership of personal property didn't strike him as prime Dragon material, but Gilmane had sent his instruction and the DragonStone ring was glowing in Nico's pocket. What more proof did he need?

Xin spun Nico around by his shoulders before twisting his arm into his back to restrain him and pushed him back through the very same door by which they had entered the storeroom. To his total surprise Nico found himself entering what looked like a small bare prison cell with a simple table and chair, a barred window and a savage looking dog.

'What the...? Where was the Café they had just been standing in?' he asked himself.

The large dog stepped towards him growling angrily, sniffing the air in front of Nico, and paying particular interest to the ring in his pocket. The wolf-like dog was also monochrome in its colouring and had the same glowing appearance to its coat as the tiger and the talking monkey Nico had encountered outside. It looked like a guard dog with a strong muscular body and a potentially nasty bite from the look of its sharp white teeth.

'SSHH! Nice doggie' Nico called, but the dog continued to growl more aggressively. Terrified, Nico tried to back off and turn to run, but found himself still being held by the old man. 'Stop it you freaks, let me out of here' He swung his skateboard at them wildly, while looking for the exit.

'*Fornat e Foreïs*' called Xin and the large ghostly hand appeared, wrapping itself around Nico, who writhed as it lifted him into the air. At the same time the DragonStone lifted itself out of Nico's pocket and floated into Xin's outstretched palm. 'I see we have a thief in our midst.'

'What's going on? Who are you people and what is this place?' Nico was struggling hard to break from the grip of the Hand of Power.

'That's not important right now' said Xin as he turned over his other palm and wiggled his fingers. The money that Nico had taken from the gang now emerged from another of Nico's pockets and floated into Xin's open palm. 'It seems you've had quite a profitable day, young man.'

'That's mine!' insisted Nico.

'So you're a liar and a thief too. That's a very slippery slope you're on young man. Such as shame, as you would appear to have some considerable potential.' Xin placed the money and the ring on the table. He then directed the spectral hand to place Nico carefully in the chair next to it.

'Let me outta here, or I'll… I'll call the cops' Nico understood the futility of that desperate statement as it left his lips.

'Go ahead, and I'll turn in the security footage from Gilmane's store' replied Xin with the confident authority of someone who was used to dealing with troublesome teenagers.

'How do you know about that?' Nico countered. On a screen on the wall of the cell, a security camera video of Nico stealing the ring was playing in a repeating loop. The defiance on Nico's face ebbed away as he realised that he had been well and truly caught this time and recognising Nico's apparent capitulation, Xin dismissed the Hand of Power leaving Nico free to move. But with his sharp wits Nico was always ready to turn a situation back to his advantage.

Like a wild animal and before anyone else had time to react, Nico made a grab for the money, jumping from the chair to make his escape, but Xin was expecting this and despite his age was surprisingly fast and grabbed Nico's wrist forcing him to the floor.

'Hmm, I think Gilmane was right about this one' he observed to himself. Nico gasped in pain before finally giving in to the old man.

Releasing Nico's wrist Xin picked up a small circular amulet made of concentric rings, decorated with ancient symbols and runes with a dragon at its centre. He attached the amulet to a wide leather strap and fitted it to Nico's left wrist, then turned the outermost ring one click to the right.

'Listen to me very carefully,' he said looking the young man firmly in the eye as a stream of fine glowing particles of light emerged from the amulet flowing towards Nico's face, drawing his mind from the harsh consciousness of the prison cell into another place, a realm of something that was soft and dreamlike, but was neither sleep nor a dream and was not of this earthly plane.

CHAPTER 3
Making Contact With The Past

As Nico felt himself slipping out of physical existence into this plane of pure thought, there was no material substance, no space he could reach into. No up, no down. No in and no out. Nor front and no back. No sense of time or space. Not even a void. How could this be? Where was he?

A stream of images appeared before him, starting with familiar scenes of his Great Aunt Cass and his parents, but very quickly winding backwards through time and history. A blur of ancient warriors, magical beasts, complex machines, lethal weapons, vast armies, noble kings, savage demons, and fiery dragons filled his consciousness in rapid succession. It was almost as if the entire history of the world was being played out in one intense video stream. None of this made any sense, he was just some street kid, how could this possibly be happening to him. All he could do was sit back and take in the show, which actually turned out to be a history lesson. The history of the Astraxi of Astrellion.

As the visions slowed down, Nico found himself in open countryside staring across a vast grassy plain that stretched to the horizon. An army of fifty-thousand demons or more was gathered. At the head of the demon army, four hideous figures on horseback waved their swords, urging the savage creatures forward. Nico was starting to feel panic welling up in his stomach when he heard a disembodied voice speak. It was the voice of Xin.

'Four thousand years ago was a time of peace in the land of Astrellion, until the emergence of the Four Fiends and their evil hordes'

He was whisked away once more feeling as if he had disappeared down a trap door, but as the movement stopped Nico suddenly found himself in a king's throne room, surrounded by guards, courtiers and advisors in elegant robes and costumes. The highly ornate room was resplendent in the works of art and science, the intellectual treasures of an enlightened and wealthy nation. King Theokeis, a charismatic and intelligent man in his sixties was on his feet making a commanding speech to his court.

'In the face of the growing threats to our borders, using our best skills and magic we will create a group of mighty Celestial Warriors to defend the land'

Once more Nico found himself accelerating away through darkness, this time to an apothecary in a high tower, where the king's chief wizard was at work forging amulets from precious metals and gemstones. Nico recognised the old man with his silken robes, long grey pointed beard, moustaches, and crazy eyebrows as Gilmane, the owner of the junk shop from where he had stolen the ring.

'Totally weird. How did he get here?' Nico muttered to himself while ignoring the irony of that statement.

Beside the glowing forge was a large circular table, decorated with runes, astronomical, elemental, and magical symbols, arranged in concentric rings. This Wizard's table was also sub-divided into various sectors, each division representing a constellation or asterism from the night sky.

Xin's voice rang out in Nico's head once more 'The King's Chief Wizard, Gilmane forged powerful amulets infused with the energy of the celestial plane, to be given to his most loyal servants.'

As the wizard raised his hand to the sky, the stars of the constellation representing Draco the Dragon twinkled even more brightly than usual. Using his magic Gilmane pulled beams of starlight down from each of Draco's stars diverting the beams through a series of crystals and lenses, which focused the rays on to an amulet placed in the Dragon sector of the Wizard's table. As the starlight infused the gemstones set inside the amulet, a young man stepped forward and using a small blade he cut the heel of his hand and dropped a small amount of his blood into the centre spot of the Dragon amulet. A cloud of glowing points of light emerged from the amulet as Gilmane carefully assembled the top cover of the magical device. Then once again, Nico felt himself following the magical cloud of glowing lights and into another, much larger space outside the palace.

In the centre of the large ceremonial plaza in the grounds of the Royal palace, a group of men and women in identical robes of red and gold were lined up before an ornate throne upon which the king was sitting, with a most serious expression on his face. It was just after sunset and as twilight faded from the darkening sky, bright constellations and patterns of stars appeared in the deep inky blue over their heads. Vast cauldrons of flame illuminated the tall columns of the temple before which they stood in two rows in the flickering red light. Many hundreds of citizens of Astrapolis had gathered to watch the initiation ceremony of the Astraxi.

Standing to the right of the king, Nico recognised the old man with the shaved head who had just trapped him in the café.

'Off the scale weirdness,' he breathed to himself. Nico was beginning to panic again and felt a bit sick. Had he been drugged? What did these crazy people want with him? What did these visions mean?

The men and women of the Astraxi had been selected for their many qualities, not just as warriors, but for their intelligence, wisdom, strength, or other skills such as healing or leadership. The king rose from this throne and fixed an amulet to the wrist of each of the Astraxi. The King's Chief wizard Gilmane produced two ornate glass vials, one containing a red liquid and the other blue, which were shaped in such a way that they could be fitted together to form a single bottle with two necks.

Gilmane separated the vials and poured some of the liquid from each into a simple crystal chalice, putting in slightly more of the red potion than of the blue. He offered the chalice in turn to each of the Astraxi warriors, who took a small sip of the potion. Once more Nico heard Xin's voice in his head.

'These amulets and the sacred Potion of Eternity transformed the people into legendary warriors with the power to summon energy from the celestial plane.'

Nico looked on in awe as the Astraxi turned the dials of their amulets. The ceremonial robes on their bodies were quickly transformed into magical armour beautifully adorned with images of fabulous creatures. During the transformation a layer of star energy briefly enveloped their bodies, which shimmered with light and power. Nico recognised the man he had seen in Gilmane's apothecary adding a drop of his blood to the amulet during its forging. The breast plate of the man's armour was emblazoned with a magnificent flying dragon breathing flames.

The Dragon warrior turned his gaze to the night sky and called the name 'Adraxa.' Above him, the stars of the Dragon constellation merged into a moving shape made of starlight, which descended from the sky while morphing into a huge silvery dragon that landed next to the warrior. Nico remained transfixed as he watched more celestial creatures being summoned from the skies by the other Warriors.

The Dragon warrior now turned to look Nico straight in the eye and to his great surprise the Warrior spoke directly to him. 'Nico, my child, now is your time. You will be the greatest Dragon Warrior that ever lived, the Dragon Mage.'

A rush of emotion ran from Nico's stomach to his feet and then across every inch of his flesh in a huge tingling sensation as if every nerve ending in his body was reacting in agreement with those words. Somehow, he felt his very soul had been exposed to the Warrior, but at the same time he felt a connection to the man that he couldn't explain, a feeling of close kinship, warmth, trust, and something even stranger — love, like the tender love of a grandparent. But Nico wasn't used to having emotional bonds with adults and in terror his conscious mind withdrew quickly, falling back into the darkness from which he had first arrived. Where would the next part of this strange dream take him?

CHAPTER 4
Back To Reality

Nico woke up in a small, crowded space with a warm, familiar smell to it. As he blinked and rubbed his eyes peering into the blurry light, the sense of panic in his head was once more ready to be converted into a fight or flight reflex.

'What…!' he exclaimed and sat up rapidly, ready to run. But the first thing to come into focus was the wrinkled little face of his Great Aunt Cass, with her lips tightly pursed and her eyes narrowed with both annoyance and concern for the young man. That expression usually meant that the eighty-year-old was ready to tear more than just a strip off him. But instead of confronting him with difficult questions, she looked him over, in an almost medical way as if to inspect him for signs of damage or illness, then turned away with a sigh and continued to make breakfast.

Questions flashed though his confused mind. How did he get here? Were the weird visions he had of Star Dragons and ancient wizards just an elaborate dream? Was any of it real, or had he been drugged?

Some of the money Nico stole from the gang fell from his pocket, the roll of notes landing softly and bouncing across the wooden floor. Nico, still reeling from his strange visions, looked around nervously as Aunt Cass watched him, silently stirring her pot of oatmeal.

'Umm, Aunt Cass…' said Nico as he shuffled on the edge of the sofa trying to get his bearings.

'Yes, that's me!' she replied in a slow but firm way that simultaneously expressed her authority and her dissatisfaction with him. 'You've been conspicuous by your absence young man.'

Nico gathered up the money in one hand, while still clutching his forehead and feeling very groggy, dropping it into the cookie jar where Aunt Cass kept a little money for the general housekeeping. 'I made some money skateboarding. A competition in the park.'

'Every little helps' she replied, not being entirely convinced by his explanation. She nodded at the DragonStone ring on his finger. 'That ring's nice. Where'd you get it?' Caught slightly on the hop, Nico wasn't sure what to say next.

'Er, this thing. I found it in the park.'

Aunt Cass stopped the slow stirring of the oatmeal and looked directly at him, 'Why do you always have to lie to me Nico? I always know when you're lying because it's written all over your face.' Nico knew this to be true. His mouth could try to speak lies but more often than not his heart wasn't really in it. He couldn't even convince himself of these simple falsehoods and therefore it was easy to detect when he was lying. Despite his bad behaviour, he was really an honest person hiding underneath his thin shell of bad-boy pretence.

'In the end all these lies will get you precisely nowhere,' she continued.

'I'm not lying,' he lied, again without true conviction. 'Were you up when I got home last night?' Nico tried to change the subject as he became interested in the prospect of a warm breakfast.

'I went to bed early.' Aunt Cass ladled a big steaming portion of oatmeal into a bowl and poured some honey on to it, before putting it on the bench in front of Nico, who just stared into the bowl blankly as other thoughts entered his mind. He shook his head in disbelief as he remembered the events of the day before and looked at the topaz ring on his finger.

'It seemed so real. I must have fallen off the board and hit my head or something. Bizzaro!'

'Eat!' Aunt Cass thrust the oatmeal into his hands. 'Then instead of just playing around on your skateboard all day, try doing something useful, like your homework for example. A wise man once said, a little sacrifice now will be repaid many times over in the future.'

Nico wasn't enjoying the lecture, and despite knowing himself to be in the wrong, his short temper snapped back at her like a reflex reaction, something that he had learned through many years of confrontation with adults or people in authority.

'You're not my mother, and I don't do homework' he said sharply but also quite casually as he had taunted his aunt with this many times before.

'Neither am I your father, but I promised them both that I would take good care of you for now.' She furrowed her brow making the wrinkles even deeper to add more force to her words, 'Now be a good boy, eat your oats and do your homework' and she ushered him away with her hands not wishing to prolong the argument.

Nico made a 'whatever' gesture and picked up a spoon while heading off towards his bedroom, which was in the attic space. Settling on his bed amongst his disordered possessions, he ate hungrily before falling back on the covers and staring up at the ceiling. He pulled the DragonStone ring off his finger and stared deeply into the topaz gem which once more glowed with a pale blue iridescent fire. His body froze as the visions came back to him, but this time they were inside the stone rather than in his head. He saw a young woman in Dragon armour in a dark underground chamber, with a group of people, including the strange bald man he met yesterday. They appeared to be in grave danger.

When a bony hand thrust a barbed shield into the woman's breastplate, Nico heard a piercing scream, which caused him to jump up on the bed and he felt a sharp pain in his chest as if an icy dagger had penetrated through to his heart.

He was woken from this vision by Aunt Cass, who was calling from downstairs. 'Nico, get down here now. You've got a visitor.'

Nico bounded down the full flight of stairs in just three steps, but almost fell over with shock when he saw the strange old bald man from the café in the living room with his Aunt. Instinctively Nico tried to make a run for it, but quick as a flash Xin blocked his path and with a flick of his wrist remotely locked the door. 'Not so fast,' said Xin.

'Leave me alone, you crazy old man' shouted Nico defensively. To escape Xin's intense stare, he turned to Aunt Cass for support.

'This gentleman's told me all about it' she said in a low but firm voice, embarrassed, but angry.

'He's lying. I didn't do anything' replied Nico defiantly.

'Well, what do you call that then?' Aunt Cass pointed to the ring in Nico's hand. 'Give it back, now.' After a moment's hesitation as he weighed up his options, Nico sullenly offered it to Xin, his eyes looking at the floor to avoid the old man's gaze. Xin took the ring without any hesitation.

'What am I to do with you, young man?' sighed Aunt Cass.

'Just cut the lectures Aunt Cass' Nico was about to break into an argument with the old lady when Xin interjected.

'Leave your Aunt out of this Nico, it's all down to you, and you know it.' Nico stared idly at his feet, bursting to speak out, but he knew he was well and truly busted.

A wry smile broke out on Xin's face. 'Look, it's not all that bad. Maybe you should call in tomorrow and have those noodles you asked for last time you were in the Café. Freshly cooked of course, on the house. Then we can sort this matter out properly. Just ask for Xin' said the old man to Nico as he bowed deeply to Great Aunt Cass in an old-fashioned gesture of respect and with that, he left the house, unlocking the door with the reverse of his earlier wrist-flicking gesture.

Nico stared at the door blankly, surprised at being offered food instead of punishment. His head was now buzzing with questions about the events of yesterday that maybe the old man could answer.

CHAPTER 5
The Next Dragon

The following day, inside the Perpetual Motion Café, Xin was preparing fresh noodle dough for the daily service as Phae arrived carrying a basket filled with fresh herbs and mushrooms which she had foraged from the forests on the edge of the city.

Phae often visited the forest to re-connect with nature and to get the city out her system. She was a lover of wilderness and had an affinity with the natural world. Phae had been the Astraxi's Tiger Warrior for six years having joined the group after her parents had been tragically killed in a house fire while she was staying with friends. Xin had taken her in, knowing her family's long history of connections to the Astraxi and recognising not only his responsibility to care for her, but to train her in the special skills and powers that all Tiger Warriors had wielded since the creation of the Astraxi.

Tigers are noble beasts, strong and proud, but also of short temper and occasionally prone to reckless acts, believing that their power and fortitude is enough for them to succeed when danger threatens. Phae was no different in this respect to the many generations of Tiger Warriors that had gone before her, but fortunately Xin had seen enough Tigers to be able to predict their capricious habits and to harness their amazing strengths. Phae was indeed a strong young woman, worthy of her inheritance.

A natural athlete, Phae could walk and run all day if she had to, without pause and was physically much stronger than she appeared. But despite her tendency to be impetuous, Phae was also a fierce defender of her group, loyal and always ready to rush to the aid of any of her companions without any consideration for her own safety.

'I gathered a few things while I was out meditating. These mushrooms are my favourite and I love the way you prepare them' She placed the basket on the kitchen surface where Xin was preparing his ingredients.

'Thank you Phae, they'll do nicely' He waved his hands over the basket and spoke the words to summon his invisible assistant, '*Masfina Mataris.*' While he continued stretching the noodle dough, an invisible pair of hands lined up Phae's foraged items on the bench, rejecting to the bin anything that may be damaged or inedible in some way. The mushrooms and herbs then dropped themselves into the sink, and were washed, before jumping back out and landing under a set of sharp knives that cut, cleaned, and sliced them perfectly then sorted them into bowls. It was exactly as if an invisible sous-chef were there to assist Xin.

Phae spotted the DragonStone on the bench nearby but didn't want to discuss it. 'Can't you get your magical assistant to prepare the noodles too?' asked Phae to distract the conversation.

'Oh, it's never the same Phae,' Xin joked while raising his own hands, 'these hands have prepared so many noodles over the years. This, is where the magic really is!' He grinned and cracked his knuckles causing Phae to wince. But Phae had something else on her mind and Xin could tell it was eating her up from the inside. 'What is it Phae?' he asked.

'What do you think Taotie will do with the Cup of Souls?' she asked quietly.

'I expect he will use it to enhance his power,' replied Xin, concentrating on stretching his noodles to get them to the perfect thickness. Phae was edgy, the events under the Royal Palace had been haunting her and the walk in the forest hadn't totally helped clear her mind the way it would do normally because of the gravity of what had happened. It would take much more than a few strolls through the forest to erase her pain and regret, if at all.

'I was absolutely sure I could get it, you know' she whispered sadly.

'You know that the Fiends thrive on human suffering, that's how and why they exist. And now Eleni is part of that.' He paused with sadness in his eyes. 'I'm sorry I didn't mean to lay that on you in quite that way. Hopefully you have learned from this, that you should be more careful in future and follow your training.' Xin was holding in his emotions, and although he had seen members of the Astraxi come and go in more tragic circumstances, Eleni's death had hit him hard as it was so unexpected and unnecessary.

'I'm not the only person who's broken the rules around here' retorted Phae defensively.

'Yes, and I have spent the last four thousand years regretting that.' Xin suddenly put down the noodle dough and groaned and winced in pain, bending double and clutching his shoulder.

'Xin?' Phae was concerned, for the old man. 'I am sorry I didn't mean anything by that…'

Xin pulled back his collar to reveal a nasty looking scar along his shoulder, a jagged claw mark, which he rubbed to ease the pain.

'A scar from a battle many years ago. I haven't felt that pain for a very long time.' He turned back to the noodles. 'That pain always helps to remind me that even though some things such as the sun and moon are eternal and indestructible, I am not. Nor will I ever be. I may be immortal, but even I can be extinguished.' Xin's expression was regretful.

Phae had never seen Xin in this emotional state. 'What do you fear Xin? Your own destruction, or is there something worse than that?'

'I fear not for myself, but for those who rely on me, those for whom I swore an oath to guide and to protect. Many have envied my immortality, but it comes at a great cost. The pain of accumulated experience... So many memories of joy, of suffering and so much sacrifice.' He turned to Phae, with a look of grimness on his face. 'It is a great burden, sometimes too great. But here I am.' It was unusual for Xin to bare his innermost feelings in this way, but it showed that he understood Phae's predicament.

'I feel your pain too Xin.' said Phae.

'I know' he replied. 'That empathy is one of your very special and most endearing qualities Phae.' As he held her gently by both shoulders, he noticed that the DragonStone had suddenly started to glow a vivid blue.

'Looks like we're about to get a visitor' he said wiping away the tears that had formed in her eyes.

Outside, as Nico approached the Perpetual Motion Cafe a knot formed in his stomach that felt a bit like the twisted möbius strips of neon fixed to the roof of the small squat building. He looked through the windows really wondering whether he should go in, but he could see Xin and Phae at the bench and decided he had nothing to lose.

He swung the door open like a gunslinger and in an attempt to exude confidence he swaggered towards the counter, where recognised Phae. She smiled sweetly, but more out of amusement at his crude and awkward display of fake self-confidence. Nico however read her reaction as one of approval, but before he could speak, he was stopped in his tracks by Xin's words.

'So, you came back Nico. Right then, as promised first let's sort you out with some noodles.' Xin stopped stretching the noodle dough and reached for a bowl to serve up some ramen soup, while the magical assistant continued to prepare the other ingredients.

'How do you do that?' Nico asked, with a puzzled expression, pointing at the knives as the invisible assistant continued chopping and sorting things into piles.

'It's just a little labour-saving trick that I've been practicing for a while' Xin said to Phae with a wink. He put down the bowl of fresh noodle soup on the counter next to the DragonStone. But as Nico reached for the soup bowl, a meat cleaver slammed down on the chopping board next to his hand burying itself deep enough in the wood for the blade to stand upright. Nico withdrew his hand and almost fell backwards at the shock. He checked his wrist and yes, his hand was still attached to it!

'Four thousand years ago, a thief would have had his hand chopped off for stealing this.' Xin picked up the DragonStone, but Nico recovered his cool and picked up the bowl. 'But we're more civilised about dealing with petty crime these days, I am very pleased to say.'

Nico picked up some chopsticks and started to move the noodles around the bowl. 'Would you just stop freaking me out, man. Last night I had some weird dreams about the past? And what about those crazy animals in the street?'

'Yesterday, you entered a shop belonging to a very old friend of mine and took something very valuable.' Xin continued holding the ring aloft as if to judge Nico's reactions.

'I thought we had established that at my Aunt's. Nothing new to see here buster!' Nico continued in his barbed tone of feigned hurt. 'So why did you want to see me, just to play games?'

Xin thrust the ring in front of Nico. 'This ring Nico; this is the DragonStone. Why did you steal it from Gilmane's shop?' Xin demanded.

'It was in the window, it seemed like it was talking to me or something, and I kind of just had to have it, I don't know,' replied Nico. 'What's that got do with anything anyway?' Nico was now rudely talking through a mouthful of noodles and Phae was starting to get irritated at his childish display of arrogance.

'Didn't your mother tell you never to speak with your mouth full?' interjected Phae. Nico just swallowed and started slurping at the delicious soup in a deliberately obnoxious way.

He tilted his head and replied, 'I never knew my mother long enough to have that lesson' thinking that this easy lie would disarm Phae, which it did as he sucked a particularly long and wet noodle through his lips with a smack and a splash of sauce.

Phae realised that Nico was starting to back up towards the door as a possible escape route and stepped in behind to block him. Xin spoke to distract Nico and hold his attention.

'Gilmane thinks you're a Dragon Warrior. Possibly even a Dragon Mage.' said Xin approaching Nico with intent firmly in his eyes.

Nico was incredulous. 'Dragon Mage, what are you on about? Are you nuts old guy or maybe you've been smoking something herbal that you probably shouldn't!?' Xin shook his head, he'd seen it many times before, he knew that Nico's rudeness was just a defensive ploy!

'Let me prove it to you. You can do a special little trick yourself, can't you Nico?' Xin took the soup bowl from Nico's hands and placed it on the bench.

'Hey, I'm still working on that' said Nico as Xin grabbed his empty right hand and squeezed his palm firmly. Small, crimson-coloured flames shot out from Nico's fingertips. 'How did you know about that?' said Nico, surprised at Xin's knowledge of his secret.

Phae's eyes opened wide as the flames grew stronger and Nico noticed for the first time, her vivid, amber-coloured eyes. Totally captivated, he forgot about the old man squeezing flames from his hands, and just stared right into Phae's eyes transfixed by their striking golden splendour.

Staring back, she flared her beautiful eyes even wider as if in annoyance or anger, 'Will you stop staring at me like you're some sort of moron!' she snapped, and Nico quickly turned his head away, embarrassed by his open-mouthed stare.

'Ouch, be careful, you're hurting me,' but the more Nico complained the more vivid the orange, yellow and crimson red flames grew from his fingertips. Xin charred a slip of rice paper in the flames until it ignited and was reduced to a large hot flake of black carbon. Satisfied with what he had seen, Xin released Nico's hand and the flames faded quickly away. Nico nonchalantly picked up the bowl and continued his annoying slurping of the noodles.

'Typical Dragon arrogance if I might say so,' said Xin with a sigh. 'But maybe Gilmane is on to something!' He reached for the Dragon amulet, which he had kept nearby especially for this moment, held it in the centre of his palm with his fingers and activated it. Soft glowing points of light emerged from its surface and drifted slowly towards Nico heading for his eyes. He dodged out of the way, batting at the lights as if they were annoying insects as their phosphorescent glow illuminated his face.

"Hey, you're putting me off my noodles!' complained Nico.

Xin released his fingers from the amulet, which flew from his palm at speed towards Nico as if it had been catapulted. Nico managed to catch it in one hand but spilled soup down his t-shirt in the process. 'Oh man, this was clean on!' he moaned and reached for a serviette to wipe off the soup.

Xin didn't really care about Nico's sartorial elegance, or lack of it. 'So, it appears that both the DragonStone and the Dragon amulet agree that you truly are the next Dragon Warrior. That's settled then, you must begin your training.'

'This can't be real? It's another trick. I'm not your Dragon Fire Warrior Mage thing, or whatever you said, I am just a nothing kid from nowhere.'

'No, you're much more than that. It's in your blood Nico and this amulet was forged with a drop of blood from its first owner, your ancestor. Did you not see it in your vision when we first met?' Xin scanned Nico's face for a reaction and Nico nodded to accept that he had seen something of that description in his vision, but he was still convinced he was being scammed.

'The amulet knows you are descended from the original Dragon Warrior, and it also knows you are the person who is most worthy to wield its power.' Xin sighed, 'Although I sometimes wonder where these modern blood lines are going.

Yet here we are!' Xin had a fond connection to the past believing that it was somehow better, even though in fact it wasn't.

'The proof is there; you saw it for yourself. It's in your blood. Going back over four thousand years to the very beginning. Which means that this really does belong to you now. Go on, take it.' Xin handed the DragonStone to Nico, but Nico was a little wary of accepting it.

'So, the last time I looked at this I had this strange dream, and you guys were in it, and there was a woman in armour, but then something terrible happened to her and she disappeared in a flash of flame.' Phae started to look uncomfortable.

Xin spoke gravely, 'The woman you saw in the vision was the last person to possess the Dragon amulet before you. Your distant cousin Eleni.'

'What cousin...? I don't have any cousins?' replied Nico tersely as if this statement proved he was being lied to.

'Like you, Eleni had the blood of the original Dragon Warrior. That same blood that is flowing in here.' Xin pointed to Nico's heart. 'Now it's down to you. You must carry on where Eleni left off.'

Nico was becoming agitated as he really didn't like being told what he must do and was once more looking to escape. 'Well, thanks for asking, but no thanks. This is crazy. I have no cousins and I'm not the descendent of some great Dragon Warrior.'

Phae intervened, 'Believe it Nico. You've seen the proof. You have the fire within you. Just like Eleni.' She looked down as a shadow of sadness passed over her face, 'I was there when she died.'

'It doesn't seem like this is a job that people retire from. Alive anyway,' said Nico.

'The evil we are fighting could and will destroy the world given half a chance. But if you fight with us, the world has a better chance of surviving,' responded Xin.

'You say we, but I still don't know why you're talking to me about fighting? I'm a kid that rides skateboards. Like you said, a thief. A good for nothing nobody.' Nico was in complete denial of Xin's revelations and arguments, and as much as he desperately wanted to belong and be part of the group, the thought of these people somehow depending on him to do amazing things, just made him want to run away and disappear into a dark corner somewhere.

Xin sat Nico down at a table 'You're better than that, but you have to be prepared to work at it.'

'Those stories you told me, the first time I was here, about the king and the Astraxi. I thought it was just a dream,' replied Nico.

'Sometimes even I wish it were so,' replied Xin.

Nico toyed with the amulet, 'So what do you expect me to do, Xin?'

'I only wanted to inspire you to join us. I cannot make your decisions, that's down to you,' replied Xin.

After a short pause for thought Nico got up and slammed both the amulet and the DragonStone on the table.

'Nah! It all sounds a bit dangerous. See ya' later, and thanks for the noodles!' he said before exiting the café carrying his skateboard. Phae and Xin were left staring at each other in bemusement at the young man's sudden about-face. But Xin was not overly concerned or surprised by Nico's reaction. This was the typical response of someone with a simultaneous sense of both self-confidence and self-doubt, which is actually very common.

'Don't worry, he'll be back, I am sure of it. Come on Phae, let's see what I can do with those mushrooms of yours,' said Xin who smiled as he went back to his kitchen.

As Nico entered the street, he felt a sense of relief that people weren't going to have to rely on him for anything. Responsibility was something he actively avoided as it just led to worse complications when he inevitably failed to come up with the goods. But as he hopped on his board and glided down the street, he felt a growing sense of regret that he was missing a real opportunity to show people that there was much more to him than some spindly kid that could do breath-taking tricks on a skateboard. Becoming a Dragon Warrior sounded pretty cool but considering what had happened to the woman in the vision, he'd rather be chancing his luck on the streets with the gangs, than disintegrating in a dungeon somewhere. He headed back to his Aunt's place seeking the security it held for him. Her villa and his skateboard were all he truly had in the world right now.

CHAPTER 6
The Empire of Darkness

Beyond the heavily guarded northern border of the modern state of Astrellion, lies a country known as Golteria, which is almost but not quite as old as Astrellion. Golteria was also founded around four thousand years ago but not by King Theokeis. It was founded by Cyax, Theokeis first-born son and has been in a perpetual state of war with Astrellion ever since.

Cyax was a particularly dangerous and evil man. As the commander of Astrellion's army, he had a well-deserved reputation for ruthlessness and ruling with a rod of iron, or a blade of steel. He was also known for having a very short temper and a lack of tolerance for any kind of weakness on the part of his soldiers or other staff. But he was nevertheless a highly accomplished warrior in his own right, being quick, accurate, and extremely lethal. Mercy was not in his vocabulary. Cyax was the master of most kinds of weapons and martial arts and this set of qualities inspired both fear and respect from his soldiers in equal measure.

His arrogance was limitless, his assumption was that as first-born son of the King he would always hold the highest positions in court and the armed forces before inheriting the throne for himself one day. But Theokeis began to worry about the darker side of Cyax' personality, which often affected the wisdom of his decision making and the harsh judgements and punishments he meted out to soldiers that had failed in their duty.

So, when selecting the people that would become the first members of the Astraxi of Astrellion, Cyax naturally assumed that he would get the job of leading this elite force. But instead Theokeis chose his younger son Cyrus, whom he believed to be a more reasoned and humane character, with the wisdom and fairness of judgement that his brother lacked. Theokeis worried that if Cyax were ever to be given the great power of the Astraxi to command at his will, the risks to life and liberty would simply be too great.

When Theokeis announced that Cyrus had been chosen to lead the Astraxi, Cyax was enraged, but he was clever enough not to show this anger publicly to his father or his brother. During the initiation ceremony Theokeis invested Cyrus as the first Stag Warrior of the Astraxi, but a few months later during a hunting expedition, Cyax angrily confronted his brother and took the Stag amulet from him, before mercilessly kicking him off a high cliff to his death. Cyax' terrible crime wasn't detected at first and soon after he took Cyrus's beautiful widow Tan Iskai, to be his own wife.

A year later she bore him a child, a girl whom they named Tan Elliae. But Tan Iskai had already given Cyrus a son, Laius, who would naturally be next in line to inherit the Stag amulet. This indeed was demonstrated when Laius successfully took the amulet test, to which Cyax reacted furiously, having hoped to retain it for himself.

Eventually Cyax' lust for power and hatred of the Astraxi led him to steal the sacred Potion of Eternity which is the root of their strength and celestial powers. Greedily, he overdosed on both parts of the potion causing a burning pain to rip through him, transforming his body and corrupting his soul. But the mix and high dose of potions had an unexpected effect on Cyax.

Whilst Xin and his companion mentor had been given a measured blend of the two potions, granting them immortality but not the full strength and potency of the Astraxi warriors, Cyax had consumed large amounts of both potions, which had the effect of making him not just immortal, but seemingly indestructible. Some wise scholars later suggested that this property of Cyax' immortality was actually a direct consequence of the creation of the Astraxi, as the universe demanded a counterbalance of evil to the Astraxi's creation as a force for good.

In the madness and lust for vengeance that now engulfed his mind, Cyax attempted to overthrow the King in a coup but was subdued by the Astraxi. Theokeis decided to show mercy on his remaining son, in the hope that he could eventually be redeemed. Until he atoned for the sin of fratricide, Cyax was disinherited by Theokeis and sent into exile.

Arriving in the lands to the northeast of Astrellion, Cyax soon formed an alliance with the Four Fiends, the dreaded undead sorcerer kings from the ancient and long-lost empires to the East. Cyax then raised his own armies and working with other kingdoms who were hostile to Astrellion, led successful military campaigns against his father's army whose defensive tactics he originally designed himself, making it easy for him to predict their next moves. Cyax captured vast territories and their people, subjugating them to his terror, before deciding to consolidate his gains by founding the country known as Golteria. From his fortified lair in the mountains, Cyax could then prepare his final assault on Astrellion to take his birth right, the Royal throne, whilst crushing the Astraxi and neutralising their power for ever.

It soon became widely believed in Golteria that Cyax was in fact a god, not just because of his apparent invincibility on the battlefield, but also for the fact that his father Theokeis was believed by some to be one of the legendary gods involved in bringing the people out from the chaos that existed after the creation of humankind and leading them into civilisation. Theokeis neither confirmed nor denied this story, and so the legend continued. As such, Golteria's capital city of Golterion became the centre for a personality cult for the worship of Cyax as the King of Darkness and a vast monastery was built, dedicated to this new religion.

Growing up at first in Astrellion, Tan Elliae turned out to be very much more the child of her father than of her mother. She trained as a warrior, rebelling against her grandfather and half-brother Laius, and eventually turned her back on Astrellion to support Cyax in his claim for the throne. In reward Cyax dubbed her Tan Elliae, the first Princess of the dark Empire of Golteria. She became the founding mother of a matriarchal line of ruling princesses that still existed four thousand years later, power being passed from first born female to first born female over the centuries.

Tan Elliae did not inherit her father's immortality, but she had inherited his lust for power and cruelty. Her daughters and all their subsequent daughters were highly trained in the martial arts, deadly warrior princesses committed to continuing the struggle against the Astraxi and to help Cyax regain his lost birth right.

Many wars followed, but despite his best efforts Cyax could not overthrow the King's Guard while they were supported by the Astraxi. Thousands of years later, the emergence of the Five Weapons of Elemental Power, combined with a deadly power struggle within the Astraxi and an act of treachery against the King, gave Cyax his best opportunity for victory as he embarked on what would later be known as the Great battle of Astrellion.

Cyax shattered the Great Gate of the citadel using the elemental magic of the Blade of Astrellion, and all appeared lost until the re-appearance of the greatest Dragon Warrior the world had ever seen, Drakeidis the Magnificent. In Astrellion's direst hour of need, Drakeidis swooped down to the palace gates riding on the back of Adraxa the Star Dragon, who grabbed Cyax firmly in her powerful claws, and bore him up into the skies.

Royal scouts last saw the Star Dragon disappear into the Western Mountains of Astrellion, but Drakeidis never revealed to anyone (not even Xin or his companion Cally) where he had taken Cyax, or what he had done with him, and Cyax was never seen again, his existence eventually becoming almost a matter of myth and folklore. Having lost their key general, the armies of the Four Fiends collapsed back to Golteria in a great and devastating rout, leaving Astrellion to prosper once more in peace.

The quantity of potions Cyax had stolen and consumed had made his body totally indestructible and therefore it was inevitable that at some point he would escape from the prison in which he had been left by Drakeidis. Patiently the ruling Princesses of Golteria rebuilt his empire and maintained their armed forces, ready for the day that Cyax returned to them, to continue the war against Astrellion.

And that day was soon to be upon them. As Xin felt pain in the old, deep, scar that Cyax had left on his shoulder during the Great Battle, a team of climate scientists were exploring a remote glacier in the Western Astrellian Mountains. They were drilling ice cores to establish the changes in air pollution over recent centuries and to map the change in the shape of the glacier over time, when one of them detected an object buried deep below the surface. For some reason unknown to the scientists the ice had become thinner at this point than elsewhere on the glacier, and within time the object would eventually have become exposed to the air of its own accord. The scientists decided to take a closer look and after carefully excavating around the object they could see what appeared to be the frozen body of a man in black armour.

'Oh man, just look at this' said a scientist who was carefully chipping at the edges of the ice, so as not to damage the remarkable find.

'How did he get buried all the way up here?' said one of the others. They peered at the body to try and discern any clues as to his identity or origin.

'Fascinating!' said the lead scientist as he studied the frozen form. 'He's perfectly preserved. That armour looks medieval, or maybe even older. We should really call in the archaeologists in case we damage it.'

He was about to get on the radio when the sharp sound of cracking stopped him dead. Suddenly a fist burst through the ice shattering it and revealing the upper body of the frozen warrior, who seemed to have miraculously returned into life. The pale flesh of his face ran with rivulets of melt water, while shards of ice still clung to his long, dark braided hair. He shook his upper torso and arms, breaking away the ice from his helmet. Steam rose from his armour, but his legs were still firmly embedded in the ice up to his midriff. The scientists looked on in surprise and amazement as the warrior brushed away the ice from his cloak, while struggling to release his lower body.

'Stop staring you fools and get me out of this' commanded the ancient warrior. The scientists looked at each other, not really being able to comprehend what was happening, but one of them reached for an ice axe and started chipping around the warrior's legs. The figure spoke again, but this time with malice in his voice.

'Pathetic mortals,' he glowered. The scientists didn't have a moment to think as a powerful explosion blew them off the glacier and sent them tumbling towards the valley below, triggering a massive avalanche. Impervious to the cries of the scientists, the figure stepped out from his ice-prison and although he was still very stiff from his twelve-hundred-year incarceration, he climbed on to the pile of snow left by the scientists' excavations, to survey his glacial dominion. He breathed the freezing cold air deeply, savouring every fresh gulp into his lungs before letting out a shattering roar that caused further avalanches in the high peaks that surrounded him.

'No time to waste,' thought Cyax to himself as he strode off down the glacier towards the valley bottom.

CHAPTER 7
A Vision Comes True

On the same day that Nico turned down Xin's invitation to join the Astraxi, Princess Tanielka's motorcade was heading back to the citadel that was her ancestral seat of power. Roads had been cleared of traffic to allow her car and armed escort to pass unimpeded. Riding in the back of her armoured limousine she sat perfectly poised, as if every muscle in her body was at its optimum fitness and she was prepared for a fight to break out at any moment.

Within her pale complexion, long dark hair and very high cheekbones, her green eyes had an almost cat like setting, giving the impression of emotional detachment, which was actually a very accurate description and was a common personality trait amongst Golteria's ruling princesses. She particularly enjoyed toying with the minds of people over whom she had absolute power, like a cat with a mouse.

As all the rulers of Golteria before her, Tanielka was raised as a warrior princess. She always wore a visible weapon as well as having something of a small and exquisitely lethal nature concealed on her person, for those unexpected events such as assassination attempts, that occasionally happen to absolute rulers. Following her mother's untimely death, Tanielka had now assumed her official duties as ruler of Golteria and was returning from her mother's state funeral.

Golterion's citadel was a large, brutal fortification surrounded by the modern city, its thick, straight walls built from white stone with medieval battlements that towered over the surrounding boulevards and a grid of streets full of bustling traffic. The modern city had been built entirely for practical considerations not for architectural or aesthetic beauty, its functional offices and accommodation blocks poking up like bony fingers through the industrial smog that often enveloped the region, as if grasping at the clean air above.

Waiting with a large entourage at the entrance to the ancient monastery in the centre of the citadel was Tanielka's first minister of government, Fong.

A vampire who had been around since the time when Cyax last walked the earth, Fong was the master of self-preservation. Over twelve hundred years old, he was a cunning and astute politician, always careful with his words, fawning and obsequious when it was to his advantage, but treacherous once anyone's back was turned. Fong's appearance was that of a skeletally thin, pale man with a waxy complexion of about average height.

Above his narrow shoulders he had a long thin neck with a protruding larynx, upon which his narrow head was perched. He had probably been a relatively handsome man before he joined the undead, with well-formed cheekbones and a strong chin. His lips were thin and very pale as befits a vampire and sitting upon his large, but surprisingly noble nose was a pair of blue tinted spectacles with round lenses and a thin frame made from a silvery metal. Crowning his head, he had very long but lank dark hair, centre parted and falling loosely over his shoulders, which were usually clad in a dark jacket of either leather, or on more ceremonial occasions black silk and a loose white shirt.

The motorcade pulled up to the grand ceremonial entrance of the Monastery and guards ran to open the door for their mistress, who stepped out without even vaguely acknowledging their existence. The entourage quickly knelt obsequiously to demonstrate their respect for their ruler, respect which was enforced by terror. Fong gave a long sweeping bow as she walked up the steps.

'My sincerest condolences for your loss, your highness.' Tanielka didn't stop to reply but continued walking into the monastery at speed, her face looking forwards with a look of total disdain. The guards and Fong rushed to follow her as she made her way up to her private quarters.

She entered through the heavy mahogany double doors into the high-ceilinged room which was her office and paused by the circular Wizard's table in the centre of the room. A personal assistant helped her off with her long black cloak of the finest, most supple leather lined with a rich dark red silk, but as she paused to remove her gloves, she felt a deep tremor within her body. Unaccustomed as she was to any kind of ill health or physical weakness, she was briefly taken aback by this sensation. But its effect was overwhelming, causing her to gasp and reach for the table, stumbling slightly.

A heavy darkness flooded into her field of vision starting from the edges, like a photographic vignette until she was momentarily enveloped in a blackness, which then erupted into an intense vision of a fist shattering through a wall of ice and an explosion, followed by a thick cloud of steam. As the steam dissipated, it revealed a dark figure in armour silhouetted grimly against the sheet of ice and snow surrounded by mountains. She could see and recognised the man's face but couldn't quite understand the vision she was having, or why she was having it.

Fearing that her mistress may fall and injure herself Tanielka's personal assistant spoke, 'Princess?'

As her eyesight faded back in, Tanielka snapped back into the room, hesitating to speak as she struggled to evaluate the vision. 'Leave me, I am fine.' Internally she battled to regain her perfect composure, not wishing to show any signs of physical weakness to her servant or anyone else. There was a knock at the door, and Fong stepped in with his usual low bow.

'Princess. A moment?' His senses immediately alerted him that something unusual was going on and he quickly ushered the Princess' assistant out through the door, slamming it shut. Tanielka didn't respond, still contemplating the vision in her head while staring silently into the distance.

'Now that you are our Supreme Ruler, there are some important matters of State that I must discuss with you, my Princess,' he said with an air of self-importance.

'Oh really' replied the Princess quietly. 'and what would be so important right now Fong?'

'As you know, before her 'unfortunate accident,' your mother was trying to make peace with Astrellion...' But before he could finish his sentence, she interrupted him angrily.

'Her attempts at making peace with Astrellion were unfortunate. But her accident was not.' Tanielka paused, darkness was once more filling her field of view from the edges. Fong moved closer, feigning concern while looking into her eyes and watching her facial expression change from clarity to confusion, to a look of fear, or was it excitement? 'Very interesting' he thought to himself. 'Matricide is an unpleasant crime, even for a Princess of Darkness, I wonder if she is now feeling some regrets?' The possibility of detecting a potential weakness in the princess' personality intrigued him.

'My Princess is everything all right?' not pushing too hard, to avoid one of her explosive outbursts of temper.

As she struggled against the mental weight of the visions filling her mind, Tanielka managed to utter just two words, which she repeated. 'He's back!... He's back!' Pulling herself together she turned her gaze towards the enormous mural decorating one wall of the chamber, which was a depiction of the Great Battle, with Cyax at its centre, smashing down the main gate of the city with the Blade of Astrellion. Fong followed her gaze to the mural, with curiosity.

'Cyax; he's back amongst us once more,' she said calmly. Fong was initially unsure how to react to this revelation.

'How? He has been lost for twelve centuries since he was taken by the Star Worm. We know not where. Long have we searched for him. How can you be sure he is back?'

'His soul reached out to me. He's in the Western Mountains, on a great river of ice.' Adrenaline surged through her veins as the enormity and excitement of what might happen next was starting to sink in.

'Find him Fong!' she shouted. Fong started to make a long elaborate bow, one of his respectful, exiting the room sorts of bow, sweeping his right hand low and walking backwards towards the doors, which also meant he would be aware of and ready for any object or weapon being hurled at him. Tanielka shrieked at him in anger 'Now Fong!' sending him scurrying away.

Tanielka turned back to the mural and studied the beautiful painting of Cyax in his glory, surrounded by hordes of vicious morgai demons, with the vanquished Astrellians lying shattered and dying at his feet.

Fong quickly headed for the military compound behind the Monastery and requisitioned one of the fleet of cybernetic scouting aircraft belonging to the Golterian air force stationed there. The craft was a bizarre blend of the biological, the magical and modern science.

Over a long period Golteria's sorcerer scientists had successfully developed a means of enhancing the demonic creatures that lived in their lands with modern scientific technology to create these hybrids. Despite their bizarre construction these cyber-craft were efficient flying machines, as the part of them which was a living magical creature could harness forces that were beyond the reach of ordinary aeronautical engineers.

The flight deck consisted of a glass bubble blended into the body of a large lizard-like demon, whose scaly body supported the rest of the fuselage with its shoulders and backbone. The head of the creature formed the nose of the aircraft, just below the pilot's position, facing the direction of flight with a large bulging red eye either side of the glass bubble. Its flared, scaly nostrils were at the very tip of the nose, just above its wide lizard mouth that was filled with sharp teeth and long fangs.

Attached to the rear were two engines for forward propulsion, one on either side by the tail structure which resembled that of a lionfish, a series of spines webbed together with flesh. Below the body of the cyber-craft were four squat lizard legs with razor sharp claws on which it stood. Folded away into the sides of the lizard demon were another set of spines, which when unfurled provided a webbed wing-like structure. The majority of the cyber-craft's fuselage was coated in the sort of grey scales normally found on demon hide, which reflected the ambient light with an iridescent sheen, making them less visible against the skies and providing a kind of camouflage.

Fong climbed into the passenger seat and the pilot engaged the controls before the part creature, part aircraft unfurled its webbed wings. After taking a few steps it launched itself into the air, before climbing surprisingly quickly.

Neither Fong nor the pilot were the sort of people who enjoyed or practised small talk, and they remained mostly silent until almost an hour later, as they approached the glacier, the pilot spotted a figure dressed in black walking across the ice.

'Mr. Fong! Over there, sir.' Fong felt a nervousness creeping over him as they flew up the glacier towards the figure. His previous relationship with Cyax had been complicated to say the least, having begun in an act of great personal treachery against the King, just before the Great Battle. Fong had been an ambitious, but middle ranking official in the government, who was seduced by the offer of immortality and a position of great power within an empire which would be under the rule of Cyax after the war.

Working in very close proximity with Cyax and the Four Fiends had slowly sapped his life force leaving him the pale shell of a human being. The vampire immortality, which was eventually bestowed upon him, was not the reward that Fong believed he had been promised in return for his betrayal of his King and he became the pale shadow of a bitter and tortured soul. When Cyax was captured, none of that mattered anymore and Fong was forced to flee to Golteria to escape punishment by the king.

Being very resourceful, Fong re-established himself at the Golterian court as an advisor to the Princess in her efforts to discover the fate of her master after he was taken away from the battle in the claws of Adraxa the Star Dragon.

He soon found a home and a new purpose to his existence. Ever wary of his physical fragility in the dangerous and unpredictable court of the Princess, Fong's deviousness kept him safe from potential attack by his enemies in the court. At the same time, he quietly sucked dry the souls of others around him to feed the incessant hunger that constantly gnawed at him from inside.

Now, the return of Cyax presented a very dangerous threat not just to his position but his actual existence. He had seen may princesses come and go, but Cyax was an entirely different matter altogether, and he had better tread very carefully indeed.

From the ground Cyax looked up in curiosity as the strange demon-lizard-bird-machine headed towards him. It looked a bit like a dragon, but not a kind of dragon he had ever seen before. As the pilot landed the cyber-craft Fong instructed him, 'Don't land too close Captain, and keep the engines running. We might need to get out quickly.' The cyber-craft banked steeply as the pilot made it ready for landing. The part demonic beast, part machine flexed its wings and landed surprisingly gracefully, almost vertically like a parachutist, requiring very little room, and stopping after a few short steps from its lizard legs.

Fong stepped carefully on to the ice and approached Cyax warily, bowing low in his most obsequious manner. 'My Lord, welcome back. Her highness Princess Tanielka sends her warmest felicitations at your return and is awaiting your arrival back in the Monastery.'

Cyax hadn't expected to see his old servant arrive in quite such a manner and scrutinised Fong's appearance intensely. 'Fong!' he said, with a long slow delivery and a patronising tone of mock pleasure in his voice. 'Still undead, I see! How long has it been?'

'Twelve centuries my Lord,' Fong remained bowed at the waist.

'Well, we'd better not waste any more time then,' said Cyax as he strode towards the cyber-craft and leapt aboard with Fong running to catch up with him.

Taking his seat in the front, Fong spoke to the pilot, 'Take us back Captain, as quickly as you can and inform Her Highness Princess Tanielka of our imminent return with her Master.' The pilot nodded and nudged the cyber-craft forward while applying extra power from the engines. As the craft's lizard legs took a few hurried steps forward, it spread its wings wide and rose sharply into the air.

They turned and passed back over the glacier where Cyax had been imprisoned for many centuries. For a short while, Cyax surveyed his broken prison cell and remembered his arrival on the glacier. After being picked up in Adraxa's claws he had been carried there hanging beneath the Star Dragon, while Drakeidis, Dragon Mage of the Astraxi rode on the creature's back. Later, while hovering over the glacier, Adraxa's hot fiery dragon breath melted a hole deep in the ice before she dropped Cyax in and sealed the hole shut with the icy, freezing version of her dragon breath.

Being entombed in the deep cold rapidly slowed Cyax' metabolism, freezing his magical powers, and leaving him physically paralysed, literally frozen solid. But the bitter cold could not shut down Cyax' evil mind. In twelve hundred years you can come up with many schemes to destroy your enemies, and so he did, but Fong's arrival in this strange living flying machine had caused him to dismiss most of them in an instant.

Not being familiar with any kind of technology, Cyax became absorbed by the screens with moving maps and controls being used by the pilot. What sort of strange new power was this and how could he use it? And what of his enemies, the Astraxi, did they still exist? He needed to learn more but decided that now was not the time to interrogate

Fong, who would most probably lie to him anyway. He would wait until he was back in the Monastery and speak to the Princess, his descendant, his own living flesh and blood. But he needed to know if she was continuing the fight for his cause and whether he could trust her? Many such thoughts spiralled around inside his head, so he sat back in his seat, deciding for now just to enjoy the ride and take control later.

CHAPTER 8
The Return Of Cyax

As the cyber-craft made the turn on to its final approach into the military airfield inside the citadel, Cyax looked upon the city of Golterion with wonder. For over three thousand years he had walked the earth, before being frozen into the ice, but in the twelve hundred years that followed the world had changed out of all recognition. A city of bright lights and towering spires upon which were mounted huge visual displays bearing state propaganda messages, wishing a long life and prosperity to the new Princess Tanielka.

Her beautiful young face beamed out from the screens with a saintly, benevolent smile, which was the total opposite of the reality of her ruthless personality.

'Moving paintings?' thought Cyax to himself, 'I wonder what other new magic awaits?' There was a familiar look to those large green eyes in their elfin setting, and Cyax was reassured that his legacy was indeed continuing, but at the same time he resolved to act fast and assume immediate control over everything.

The cyber-craft made another of its short but steep landings in front of the military air terminal, where a collection of high-ranking officials and an honour guard of cyber-demons were gathered. As they disembarked from the cyber-craft Fong directed Cyax to an official vehicle, the door of which was being held open by a man in ceremonial uniform. Fong said nothing, just bowing and knowing that anything he did say about the present state of things in Golteria could trigger a sudden and violent response from his master. Best to allow the Princess to make that mistake.

Everything that Tanielka knew of Cyax was the stuff of the legends that she had been taught as a child. Cyax was pretty much a god-like figure to his people as indeed the daily worship in the Monastery praying for his safe return continued. His blood flowed in her veins, but she wasn't prepared for what would happen if he actually did come back. It was a pretty sure bet for most of the Princesses that had ruled Golteria in the last twelve hundred years, that they would never ever see him return in the flesh, but now here he was, all too real and very dangerous.

The official car drew up outside the ceremonial entrance to the Monastery, and as a guard opened Cyax' door he stepped on to the red carpet that had been laid and was flanked by the rows of cyber-demons in the honour guard. Cyax chose to ignore the gathering of deeply bowing strangers and strode purposefully through the cloisters heading for the Great Hall.

As he arrived in the high-ceilinged chamber with its murals and tapestries dedicated to military triumph, he paused to look at the scene before him. The room was very familiar but standing in the centre was a striking young woman with the same face and emerald eyes as depicted on the screens perched on the city's tall buildings.

She was dressed in black leather styled like a close-fitting suit of armour with technological enhancements around her shoulders, collar, and wrists. Strapped to her back she carried an ornately decorated, curved ceremonial sword while on her head she wore a simple but well-crafted platinum band with an inset diamond at the front, which was the state crown she had inherited from her mother. Surrounding her was a group of people standing in a semi-circle split in two with a gap that revealed the large granite plinth on which stood the throne of Golteria. Cyax' own throne awaited him, but this was not the throne he craved.

Her hands clenched by her sides, the Princess observed him carefully, not showing the slightest hint of pleasure, fear, or any other emotion to her ancestor. She dropped to one knee and the assembled crowd quickly followed her gesture as one. 'My Lord, my King' she spoke loudly and clearly, without hesitation and with her head bowed.

Cyax strode toward her, his face stern. 'Stand up, Princess' he commanded. Tanielka rose to her feet to approach Cyax, but against all protocol she reached out and touched him on his face. Her hand recoiled briefly as it was freezing cold to the touch, and he looked her in the eye unwaveringly. 'You are Tanielka, blood of my blood?'

Fong stepped forward from behind Cyax. 'Yes, my Lord. Princess Tanielka has recently inherited the title due to the untimely death of her mother.'

'I didn't ask you Fong.' Cyax rasped glaring at the vampire, who quickly withdrew realising his potentially fatal error.

'My Lord, your blood flows strongly in my veins. It is an honour finally to be in your presence,' replied the Princess. She looked down at her feet in a gesture of modesty and subservience. Tension was growing silently in the audience who were still down on one knee.

Cyax raised the index finger of his right hand, on the end of which was a very sharp looking fingernail, claw like in its form. He pushed it hard into the soft flesh under Tanielka's pale but strong chin, raising her gaze into his eyes so that he could look within to search her soul. He recognised a kindred spirit in the emerald eyes and as he did so, he swiftly disarmed her with his other hand, drawing her ornamental sword from its scabbard.

Tanielka remained ice-cool, but her mind raced with strategies for self-preservation should the situation suddenly turn nasty. Continuing to hold her on his fingertip, Cyax twirled the sword in his hand before pausing to examine the forged steel blade's exquisite decorations.

'I know this sword. Good!' he nodded in approval. He withdrew his fingertip from under her chin but then quickly relieved her of the small dagger she had hidden in the armour covering her forearm. Tanielka's head dropped momentarily, and she pursed her lips in self-anger at being easily caught out in this way, but she proudly lifted her chin once more and re-engaged Cyax' gaze as he inspected the fine, small blade.

'So young, yet so deadly' Cyax purred, as he returned her weapons with a faint smile. He turned to the vampire who was still bowing low. 'Fong has a history of treachery. You should be most careful of him, Princess.'

Fong raised his head slightly while remaining on one knee, 'Though many things have changed over the centuries my Lord, I remain the humble servant of you and all your descendants.'

Tanielka spoke to raise the subject on everyone's mind 'My Lord, we continue the fight for your legacy.'

'Are the Astraxi not yet destroyed?' enquired Cyax.

'No, my Lord, six remain. The others have been unaccounted for since the Great Battle,' she replied.

'And what of the wretched traitor Xin?' Cyax demanded with distaste on his lips.

'He still resists us,' replied the Princess boldly, being acutely aware that no progress had been made in defeating the

Astraxi despite twelve hundred years having passed. Cyax stood in silent contemplation for a moment'

'Stand!' he commanded, his deep voice still reverberating throughout the room, as the crowd got to their feet. Cyax ascended the plinth and turned to speak to the crowd, with the throne behind him.

'Hear me now. After twelve hundred years I have returned to reclaim my birth right. While they are weakened, now is our opportunity to wipe out the Astraxi for ever. Then I, Cyax, first born son of Theokeis, and his only true heir will take the Throne of Astrellion.'

'All hail Cyax, the one true King of Astrellion' proclaimed Fong loudly.

'Cyax be praised, the saviour of Astrellion' replied the crowd and the Princess as Cyax seated himself in his throne for the first time in many centuries. He stretched out his hands and spoke an incantation in an ancient magical tongue, not heard in Golteria for many years. '*Karothia: Yoshara Finsun!*'

The room darkened, as if someone had dimmed the lights, and a rush of cold air caused the huge drapes suspended around the windows to flap against their ties. Panic gripped the crowd as the huge mahogany doors at the end of the hall crashed open, blown into the room by a fast moving thick grey cloud of smoke. A ripple of terror flowed through the audience as four hideous figures condensed out of the smoke directly in front of Cyax.

Apart from their recent appearance under the palace ruins, The Four Fiends, Hundun, Qiongqi, Taotie and Taowu had not been seen in Golterion since the Great Battle. They were the spirits of four evil rulers who were born in a time even older than Astrellion itself. So terrible had been their corruption and so wicked their crimes against humanity that their physical bodies had transmuted into another state, neither living nor dead and that their souls were bound to remain this way until the end of time itself.

Their physical forms were strangely undefined, having no clear edge, and shimmering as they were connected to two different realms — the material plane and the plane of negative existence. Their faces were covered in a pale parchment-like flesh, stretched across their faces, greenish in hue and textured with arcane symbols and each of them carried an evil looking sword. Atop their black armour each wore a long cloak which rippled and floated blown by an unearthly breeze.

The Fiends had been constant allies of Cyax since his original treachery against his father, recognising in him a means to get the thing they craved, the suffering of humanity, for it was on this negative energy that they fed and sustained themselves. Human misery was usually very easy to come by, just create conflict between people and it would soon follow.

Taotie moved to the front of the group and addressed Cyax in a deep but dispassionate tone, 'Your Majesty, once more you grace us with your presence. May we enquire as to your intentions?'

Cyax responded to Taotie 'My body was frozen, but for twelve hundred years my soul has been burning for revenge.'

Cyax displayed no fear in the presence of the Fiends, unlike the assembled crowd. After initially shielding her eyes Tanielka could not resist looking upon all four of the Fiends for the first time. To most people they were the monsters of legend and childish nightmares. Now they were here, would they seek to re-form their alliance with her master once more?

For a moment the Four Fiends seemed to enter a conversation that only they could hear, but then Taotie stretched out his arms as if to welcome Cyax back to the group. 'Once more we the Four stand ready to give our support to your noble cause' he hissed and bowed.

'So many times have we stood together my friends. But now this is our time, the enemy has never been so weak, and we will prevail' replied Cyax.

Taotie nodded in approval, 'Indeed your majesty, and we have acquired something that may help in your quest. In the vaults of the Palace, we recently encountered Xin and the six of the Astraxi.'

'And...?' Cyax was curious.

'We destroyed the Dragon and took this.' Taotie pulled aside his cloak and from a small pouch presented the Cup of Souls. 'A precious gift, which we offer in celebration of your return.'

Cyax rose from his throne and approached Taotie who offered the Cup to him. He examined it carefully before asking another question, 'Excellent. And did you also retrieve the Dragon amulet?'

'That we did not, but we trust that your majesty will honour our previous agreement and use this gift wisely' replied the Fiend.

Cyax continued to examine the Cup of Souls, 'Once Astrellion is reclaimed, I am sure there will be more than enough human misery to satisfy your needs. Tell me, after the Great Battle, what became of the other four weapons of elemental power?'

Fong was first to speak, 'The Shield of Fire and the Blade of Astrellion were lost to us your majesty. The thief Gilmane stole the DragonStone, and the Master of Wands still wields the Wand of Xylos, in the Forest City.'

Addressing the Fiends, Cyax spoke again, 'My friends, once more we must unite the five elemental weapons and use their combined power to defeat our enemies. First, I will take the Wand of Xylos, but you will seek and bring to me the Blade and the Shield. The DragonStone I shall acquire later, by other means.'

Once more The Fiends looked at each other appearing to have some sort of unheard conversation before Taotie turned back to Cyax saying 'As you wish your majesty.' The room was filled once more with a sudden rush of chilled air and with an ear-splitting howl the Four left in the same way in which they had arrived.

Cyax turned to his descendant and gave his first order. 'It's time we paid the Master a visit. Princess, make preparations, now.' Tanielka hadn't expected she would be engaging in open conflict so soon after her accession. Her mother had strayed from her sworn purpose by seeking to normalise diplomatic relations with the government of Astrellion and end thousands of years of war, a decision that had ultimately cost her life. Tanielka was not going to make the same mistake. The Princess nodded obediently to her master and left the room to start planning a raid on the Forest Folk.

CHAPTER 9
Back To Bad Habits

Ignoring his Aunt's instruction to stay home and do his homework, Nico had decided to go back to the park. In truth he had enjoyed disrupting the gang's card game, which had led to him stealing the topaz ring from the old man's junk shop and then the weird encounter with the crazy old dude in the café. It had been an interesting day for once!

Having turned Xin down for the chance to become a member of his strange group, Nico was now having some regrets about it. For most of his life Nico had been ordered around by people including his parents, social workers, and his aunt, all of which had led him to withdraw and just rely on himself. He didn't need other people's structures, and if he wanted company, he could always find it, but he had to admit to himself that he was intrigued. Intrigued by not just the strange powers the Astraxi could call upon, but also by the possibility of making some interesting new friends. He always knew he was special, and now perhaps he had the chance to prove it. What did the old guy say? 'You are a Dragon Warrior. Or maybe even the Dragon Mage' Fear of missing out was a powerful pull for Nico!

As he passed near to the play park, where kids were enjoying playing on the swings in the sunshine, he spotted the ice-cream vendor who was as usual serving a small crowd of eager customers. 'Time for another free ice-cream.' He smiled and jumped onto his board, kicking off hard with his foot and shifting his body weight subtly to give him the perfect interception trajectory for a frozen dessert.

His eyes were fully focused on his prize, a sugar cone piled high with raspberry ripple ice cream and chocolate sauce, which was about to be handed to a small, very excited boy. But Nico wasn't aware that the vendor had laid a plan to thwart him.

'I got you this time, you little punk!' muttered the vendor quietly to himself as he saw Nico approaching.

Nico confidently swooped in on the perfect attack vector shaped by his super-spatially aware mind, but he didn't notice the vendor take a last-minute short step to one side. Just as Nico stretched out his hand to snatch away the ice cream, the vendor kicked over a small piece of wood right in front of his skateboard. With a mighty crash Nico was yanked out of his slow-motion skateboarding universe and went flying through an empty table and chairs before stopping in a painful heap at the feet of a bicycle cop.

'That's him, that's him! That's the little punk that keeps stealing my ice cream. Arrest him now!' shouted the vendor, whose face had turned a vivid shade of puce, exactly the same colour as the strawberry syrup bottle on his stall. The vendor jumped up and down, pointing his finger in a state of extreme agitation.

The bicycle cop bent over and picked the slightly dazed Nico off the floor, with a firm grip to stop him from escaping and scooped up the skateboard with his other hand. 'OK sonny let's see what your folks have to say about this,' he said to Nico in his most officious tone of voice.

While being frogmarched towards a waiting police car, Nico felt no fear of any sanctions, just a sense of boredom with the process of being grounded. His aunt would make a lot of noise and stomp around the house, slamming doors like she always does, making threats and such, but he knew she was powerless to punish him.

He could pretty much do as he liked. But being caught by the police stealing ice creams from little boys didn't make him feel good and if anything, when he thought about it, it only contributed to his sense of emptiness. If success in life was measured by one's ability to make life difficult for little old ladies and to make small boys cry, then he was destined for greatness. But it was a pathetic future he was facing and deep inside he knew it. Maybe that's why he kept thinking about the café as he peered through the window from the back of the police car that was taking him home.

The police car pulled up in front of the small, traditional villa where he lived with Aunt Cass and Nico got out of the car with the bicycle cop's hand resting firmly on his shoulder. They walked up the path to the front door, but Nico didn't need his key as he could see that the door was off the latch.

'Strange, why would she leave the door open?' he thought to himself, and he pushed the door wide, stopping to pet his aunt's cat Sooty, which was waiting in the hall. The black cat with a white patch on its breast purred and arched her back before making several short sharp miaows that left you in no doubt, she was both hungry and pleased to see him.

'OK scuzzball, I'll get you something in a minute,' Nico said as he rubbed the old cat's ears which just made her purr even more strongly.

As Nico and the cop entered the living room, they could see Aunt Cass lying on the couch, which faced away from the door, seemingly asleep. Nico hesitated, but the cop coughed and nudged him a step forward.

'Er, I've got something to tell you Aunt Cass, …erm, looks like I messed up again.' But Nico sensed something wasn't right. 'Aunt Cass?' he called to her with a hint of trepidation in his voice as he approached the couch.

He walked closer to Aunt Cass and gently shook her shoulder, but she didn't respond. Instead, her arm slipped slowly off her chest and dangled loosely over the edge of the couch. Nico's body shuddered as he realised that the old lady was dead. He knelt down to look at her and although it seemed at first as if she had passed away quietly, there was something odd about her face. An expression of terror was etched across the open eyes and gaping mouth of her grey lifeless visage, as if something or someone had literally scared her to death. Nico recoiled in horror.

The bicycle cop, suddenly waking up to the situation, stepped in ahead of Nico and touched Aunt Cass' neck to check for a pulse. 'Just a minute kid' he said to Nico, pushing him aside. But there was neither breath, nor a heartbeat in her wrist and the policeman reached for his radio. 'Better send an ambulance over here right now and call social services. Realising that she had been dead for a while the policeman put her cold hand back across her chest and turning to Nico he said, 'Sorry kid, she's gone. Don't worry, we'll get you some help.'

Nico's entire world had just been wrenched away from him, and he was now enveloped by a numb nothingness. He simply didn't know what to do with himself, such was the total shock he was experiencing.

'Why do I always lose everybody?' he shouted angrily and dropped himself into a chair, drawing up his knees to his chin with a distant look in his eyes. The policeman tried to comfort him, but he was unresponsive, a grim look spreading across his face, which he hid in his knees.

Gently shaking Nico out of his waking nightmare, the policeman said, 'Better go pack a bag kid, we'll find you somewhere safe to stay for a while, until we figure out what's best for you.'

Nico went slowly upstairs to his attic bedroom. Light rain was now making a pattering sound on the skylight window above him, and he was illuminated by the faint light of the streetlights outside. He sat on his bed in the darkness to contemplate his fate.

'What would happen now? Would they put him in a children's home, would they contact his folks? Maybe he could escape and live on the streets, then he wouldn't have to answer to anyone.' He sighed and picked up a bag, which he started to fill with clothes.

When he came back downstairs, the paramedics were already taking Aunt Cass away in a black bag on a trolley. Though the bag was large, Aunt Cass was tiny and filled only a small part of it, the rest hanging limply over the sides of the trolley. Just this morning, despite her small stature, his aunt had been a very big presence in his life, but now she seemed small and insignificant.

This made Nico feel very sad indeed, because she was significant, if only to him. He heard the familiar sound of his aunt's cat wailing, she must be hungry, because she was always hungry! A man from the local animal shelter was taking Sooty away in a box and this made Nico realise that now he too would find himself living a very different life, a thought which brought back his insecurities.

Outside Nico watched the paramedics load the body into the ambulance, just as the social worker arrived in her car. The policeman directed her towards Nico, who had withdrawn back to the internal safety of his thousand-yard stare. But as he zoned out of the real world someone caught his eye. Next to the crowd of neighbours gathered in the street was the girl he had seen at the café, the one with the extraordinary amber eyes. She was with the other younger girl, the one with the flame red hair and a definite look of mischief on her face. They were gesturing to him and mouthing some words, 'Come here,' they appeared to be saying. He looked around and saw the social worker approaching him from the opposite direction,

'Come with me young man, we need to get you somewhere safe' she said taking his arm. Nico looked back to Phae and the other girl, when Phae whispered in the other girl's ear. The smaller girl laughed and raised a circular amulet attached to her wrist by a leather strap, very similar to the one Nico had been offered at the Perpetual Motion Café the day before.

As she turned the dial, a large mandrill monkey appeared out of nowhere and ran through the crowd towards the social worker. Startled people jumped out of the way of this aggressive creature which bared its long white fangs at them. The red-haired girl then cast a 'confusion and panic' spell in the ancient magical language of Astrellion '*Extralis!*'

Screams and irrational panic spread like wildfire through the crowd, who ran in all directions as if terrified for their lives. The spell also worked on the social worker who had already released Nico.

Phae grabbed Nico by the arm, 'C'mon' she shouted and shook him, waking him from his trance like state. He blinked for a moment and then started to run with Phae, automatically, without thinking for himself. Maybe the panic spell had caught him too.

The policeman, who was made of stronger stuff, and was trying to calm the crowd spotted Nico running and was about to give chase when the monkey leapt up and stole his hat and baton.

'Hey, give me those back' he cried chasing the beast down the street as Nico and Phae ran towards the other girl, who was now roaring with laughter at the mayhem she had created with her illusions.

The three of them escaped into a nearby side street, when Nico pulled the girls back. 'Where are we going?' he said.

'The place you need to be' replied Phae. Nico could tell she was serious, and he was certainly not going to go and live in a children's home if he had any choice in the matter. Phae pulled his hand, which he stubbornly withdrew in his usual resistance against any form of authority, well-meaning or not.

'Come on, this is for your own good' she insisted and grabbed his hand again, squeezing it hard, but flames came out from his fingertips, and she was forced to let go. 'Ow... hey! Don't do that!' she shouted as she rubbed her slightly scorched fingertips angrily.

'Sorry, I can't help it,' he said, a smile returning briefly to his face. Thinking once more about escape, Nico turned around only to find the other girl blocking the road and flanked by a troupe of monkeys, who were mocking him, pulling faces, and generally making very rude gestures.

'Stop playing games with me,' Nico was starting to get rattled.

'This isn't a game' said the red headed girl forcefully.

'Oh, I think it is. But the rules seem pretty random to me.' Nico asserted himself physically in an attempt to intimidate the girl, pushing her back into the troupe of monkeys.

'I told you it isn't a game, aren't you listening?' Ciara's eyes blazed with anger as she held her ground and pushed him back.

'So, what's the weird stunt you're pulling with the monkeys?' As he faced up to Ciara once more, the monkeys started to bray, running up and beating their chests at him in a very aggressive manner.

'What's wrong with you? Maybe you need your eyes testing as well as your head, stupid!' Ciara jabbed Nico hard in the centre of his chest, making him fall back slightly.

Phae stepped in to take the heat out of the situation, 'Ciara, that's enough!' She took Nico's hand once more, but this time more softly. 'Come with us Nico, we only want to help.'

'Now I get it, you're working for the creepy old dude in the café. What a whacko!' Nico was showing a bit of bravado, but only because his life on the streets had conditioned him to do that when he was stressed or in danger. It was a bluff in reality.

'Don't be ridiculous. There's nothing creepy about him, wake up you idiot!' exclaimed Ciara, full of indignation at this insult to Xin. Nico just shrugged his shoulders dismissing her claim.

'Look Nico, I'll show you what's going on' said Phae softly and nodding to her companion. 'Ciara, lose the monkeys.' Ciara turned the dial of her amulet, which made a loud click before the entire troupe of monkeys disappeared in a flash of light.

Nico quickly withdrew his hand. Something registered in his mind, unlocking possibilities had previously rejected or misunderstood. He was being offered something very special here and they really seemed to want him. But he also realised that he was being given an opportunity, and instead of rejecting it, maybe this time he should take it. With his aunt gone he knew that perhaps the time to stop running away from life had finally arrived.

'That thing with the monkeys was totally awesome, by the way' he said nonchalantly. 'Why didn't you show me that in the first place?' Nico slung has bag over his shoulder and threw down his board, trundling effortlessly down the street, leaving the two girls looking at each other in surprise at his sudden about turn. 'What are you waiting for?' he shouted back at them as they started running after him.

'He's going to be difficult, this new Dragon' said Ciara to Phae as they chased him down the street.

'I kind of like him,' replied Phae, 'he's got attitude.'

'That's Dragons for you, always a bit too full of themselves! A bit like Tigers!' Ciara was ready to duck as she knew this would provoke a swipe from her friend.

'Cheeky little Monkey' teased Phae in response. The girls laughed and pushed each other playfully as they turned into the next street where Nico was waiting outside the Perpetual Motion Café. The sign on the door read 'CLOSED' but Phae pushed the door open and as they entered a bell chimed with a loud, crystal-clear ping, like that of a pair of perfectly pitched finger cymbals.

As they entered, Nico spotted something he hadn't seen last time he was in the café. On a shelf in a prominent position was a kinetic sculpture shaped like a spinning wheel with spokes that were curved back on themselves. In the space between each of the spokes was a small metal ball that moved along a groove in one spoke before falling on to the spoke below as the wheel turned around. The effect was such that it appeared the wheel would turn for ever, driven by the weight of the metal balls as they fell to the lower spokes. Nico was briefly intrigued by this device, until Phae yanked him away.

She led him behind the service counter towards the wooden door at the back of the shop and they entered the small dingy storeroom with no other exit. Nico was starting to feel a bit nervous again, was this another trap, or was he about to become the main ingredient of the next service? Or were they going to throw him back into the prison cell where had been questioned about the ring and the cash he had taken from the gang. Before he could react, Phae spoke, 'Shall I say the magic words?'

Ciara giggled, sensing the stiffening unease in Nico's posture. 'If you must' she replied.

Phae raised her arms in a sweeping comic gesture, like that of a cheesy circus conjuring act, then drew a deep theatrical breath and threw her arms open wide. In a dramatic voice, quavering with laughter she delivered the magic words 'Chilli prawn dim sum. Coming up!'

She grabbed Nico by the shoulders, spun him around and thrust him back through the same door, except that he didn't emerge back into either the café's kitchen or the prison cell, he was somewhere completely different.

Stumbling forward, Nico almost fell into a large, darkened room that looked more like the control centre of a space agency or a military installation. Around the walls were screens and displays that showed live video feeds from all over the world. Other screens and holographic displays showed real time information coming in from sources such as satellites tracking weather patterns, animal movements, air traffic, and transport systems. One with the grand title 'Space Weather' was even counting the flow of charged particles that was causing a beautiful auroral display over northern Canada. He stood for a while, unable to comprehend how he had gone from being in a small café, to finding himself in a command and control centre. But if he had thought the day had been a bit of a weird game, things were about to get a lot stranger!

CHAPTER 10
A New Team Member

Standing by one bank of screens, Xin was studying what looked like a set of satellite images of mountains, glaciers, and the capital city of the neighbouring country of Golteria. Next to Xin was a neat and precise looking man, who looked young, maybe in his early 20's but who might have been older. It was hard to tell, perhaps it was the way he dressed or just the lack of any beard or facial hair.

The man was spinning a computer track ball rapidly, scrolling through many images and scanning them very quickly as if trying to find a clue to something, but at a speed where it was surely impossible for any normal person to discern any fine detail. This was Ash, the Stag Warrior of the Astraxi, shrewd and quick witted. Ash was also the technical genius behind the Astraxi's operations.

The reason why he was scanning so many images so quickly was quite simply because he could. His senses were so sharp, his mind so fast, and his eyesight so keen that things which were a blur to other people were quickly absorbed by Ash and locked into his photographic memory for analysis later if necessary. Like Nico's skateboarding, when Ash was in his own mind space, the rest of the world seemed to slow down, which accounted for his amazing reaction speed. Xin was absorbed by what was on the screens and had not noticed Nico falling through the door.

'I am sure that's probably where Drakeidis took him.' Xin said as he stared at a map of the great glacier.

'If I do this, I can show you what the glacier looked like twelve hundred years ago and predict roughly where Drakeidis would most likely have buried Cyax.' Ash pressed some keyboard buttons and scrolled a set of pull-down menus which tracked his eye movements, before an animation overlaid itself on the satellite views of the glacier. As is normal with glaciers the ice had moved steadily down the valley and the glacier had retreated in some areas and grown in others, but Ash's clever programming had allowed them to wind back time and estimate how far Cyax' icy prison would have moved. 'If he buried Cyax up near the top, then that position has now probably moved about 3 km down the valley closer to the end of the glacier. Drakeidis didn't know that glaciers move slowly, and I think it was only a matter of time before Cyax broke free,' observed Ash with the confidence of someone whose intellectual rigour was unquestionable.

In the next picture that Ash brought up Xin pointed to the crater where the ice had been blasted away by Cyax and a Golterian cyber-transport that had landed nearby. 'Looks like we may already be too late' said Xin with a heavy emotion in his voice, borne out of the experience of many centuries of conflict with Cyax.

Apart from Drakeidis and the celestial dragon, Adraxa, no other being had been present during the imprisonment of Cyax deep under the surface of the glacier, a secret which Drakeidis had considered necessary to prevent Cyax' heirs or followers from finding and releasing him. Afterwards Drakeidis gave up his role as the Dragon Mage and disappeared into obscurity taking this very dangerous piece of information with him. But Xin had received word from one of his eagle familiars living in the mountains that the Star Dragon had indeed passed through the high peaks heading towards the glacier. Xin hoped that with Cyax gone and his whereabouts unknown, the world would get a respite from the terror, so that he and the Astraxi could heal the damage that Cyax' malice had caused. But now that period of peace appeared to be coming to an end and Cyax was once more, free to work his evil on the world.

'That Golterian transport, can you analyse the figure standing next to it for me? See if you can enhance the detail' Xin gestured to the small figures boarding the cyber-craft.

'Sure thing boss!' replied Ash, but they were distracted as Phae cleared her throat loudly and stepped forward.

Xin had become aware of the commotion caused by Nico's appearance at the door but couldn't ignore the images appearing on Ash's screens. As he turned to face the three young people waiting for him, his expression was grim. Nico fidgeted, remembering his previous scary trips to this establishment, as well as his highly impertinent refusal to get involved with the Astraxi. Now here he was once more, face to face with the angry bald old man, but whose facial expression suddenly became warmer and more genial.

He spoke to the young man sympathetically, 'I was sorry to hear about your aunt, Nico.'

'How does everybody know about that?' replied Nico looking out into the control centre where the teams of analysts had stopped their work to observe the new arrival.

'We know things, we see things in many different ways.' Xin could sense Nico's vulnerability at this moment and realised that with careful words he may be able to persuade the potential young Dragon to join the group, but if he got it wrong, they may need to start looking for another Dragon, and that could take a long time, years even. Xin gestured for Nico to take a seat at the circular Wizard's Table in the centre of the room and sat down next to him saying nothing to allow the young man the space to express himself.

'She was all I had left. I haven't got anybody else. I haven't seen my parents for years.' Nico was becoming introspective, which is not a characteristic you might normally expect from a Dragon Mage! Before Nico could withdraw back into his thousand-yard stare, Xin took the initiative to reassure him.

'We can be your family Nico, if you want to stay,' he said with an air of calm sincerity. Xin had mentored many thousands of Warriors over the four millennia since King Theokeis handed him the task and had learned to deal with some very diverse personalities in that time. His best tactic was patience, after all when you've been doing something for four thousand years, there's no need to be in a rush, especially when a little more time could bring great benefits.

'Are you sure I can be part of this… like really?' Nico was still overwhelmed by the room with its amazing technology and the teams of people working there. He had never belonged to a group before, always preferring to stay on the outside in case some sort of commitment might be necessary, so this was in many respects a new experience for him, and he wasn't finding it easy.

'I would say so Nico,' said Xin, 'you've got what it takes, and deep down inside you know it. It'll be my job to bring out the Dragon in you!'

Inside Nico was starting to fizz with a mix of emotions but worked hard to contain himself and retain his air of coolness, 'I suppose I could give it a go, just for a while to see what it's like.'

Xin put his hand on Nico's shoulder, 'OK Nico, as you wish, but remember there'll always be a place for you here.

First, I think you will need to get to know everyone. Eduardo, would you like to start?'

In the centre of the room, a teenage boy sitting at a console shifted slightly in his chair and smiled. In the blink of an eye Eduardo vanished, melting into his surroundings before re-appearing in the chair next to Nico.

Nico was taken back by this disappearing act and shrank back slightly in his chair, but on the scale of the general weirdness he had recently encountered he simply thought to himself 'Well, whatever!'

Eduardo was stylishly dressed, but in a slightly gothic way with jet black hair that was cut to fall forward and partially obscure one of his pale green eyes. He was intelligent and softly spoken, but as a Snake Warrior was often misunderstood by some and seen as sly by others, which was not normally his intention. His subtle emotional intelligence and his occasional reticence or hiding in the background were not a way of being devious but rather a natural form of self-defence, the opposite of the naked aggression used by some warriors.

'Hey Nico' said the young man in a teasing manner, and with a subtle smirk on his lips he stared deeply into Nico's eyes. The stare was intense and intimidating, without as much as a blink, but Nico couldn't look away, he was transfixed, almost paralysed. Ciara nudged Phae and they smiled at each other knowing what Eduardo was doing.

'Eduardo is our Snake Warrior' said Xin and was careful not to break Eduardo's hold over Nico, who was now unable to move, due to the powerful Snake lore being used on him.

'You know that ring you have, the DragonStone?' Eduardo spoke in a very persuasive, almost hypnotic tone. Even the others standing nearby were finding it hard not to fall under his influence.

'Y, Y, Yes...?' stuttered Nico, now becoming aware of the growing control that Eduardo had over both his mind and his body. It was as if subtle tentacles were spreading through and surrounding his conscious mind, binding, and squeezing it into a submissive mode.

'Well, Ciara's always loved topaz jewellery, it matches her pale blue eyes. Maybe you should give it to her.' Ciara giggled, she always loved a little bit of mischief, and this was right up her street.

'After all, like the monkey told you, it's not really yours anyway, is it?' Ciara added, joining in Eduardo's game.

Nico's hand started to move, but Nico was not in control of it, and the others could see the struggle going on behind Nico's eyes to wrest back control! His hand trembled but worked its way slowly towards his shirt pocket from which came the faint blue glow of the DragonStone. Nico's eyes looked down helplessly as his own hand opened the button on the pocket to remove the ring.

Ciara was loving the spectacle and stepped forward to receive the ring with a huge beam on her face, while beads of sweat broke out on Nico's forehead. She took the ring from his trembling, outstretched hand and slipped it on to her finger, admiring the beautiful blue stone in its setting, being gripped by the claws of a platinum dragon.

By now Nico's whole body was shaking when he shouted, 'Make it stop!'

'All right that's enough Eduardo, you can let him go now,' said Xin shaking his head. Eduardo calmly reached for the Snake amulet on his wrist and reset it to its 'off' position. As he did so Nico slumped back in his chair, released from his hypnosis as the thought-tentacles withdrew their pressure from his brain. He composed himself quickly and snatched the ring back from Ciara, who was still enjoying the fun.

'Oh, Nico, it looked so much prettier on my finger than yours' she said feigning hurt at having to give up the ring. Light-hearted amusement broke out amongst the people gathered in the room.

'Your lack of will power Nico, that's something we'll need to work on,' said Xin shaking his head but with a reassuring smile and moved swiftly on to introduce another member of the Astraxi.

'You've already met Ciara the Monkey Warrior and Phae the Tiger Warrior, so now meet Ben the Dog Warrior.'

'Dingo Warrior more like it!' was Ciara's smart response.

Ben, whose heritage came from Australia's First Peoples, was the youngest in the group. He had a smooth brown complexion and the sort of curly mop of hair that you would expect of someone, who had spent much of his time surfing on sun-kissed beaches.

'Woof woof!' joked Ben amiably as Ciara patted him on the head and ruffled his hair in a patronising way.

'Good boy, would you like a biscuit' she teased, before Ben turned and licked her on the face like a friendly dog. 'Ugh! You're just so gross Ben' she snapped, wiping the drool from her cheek. A wide, satisfied grin spread across Ben's face revealing his perfect white teeth.

'No worries, any time me darlin!' he said mocking her Irish accent and ruffling her ginger locks in return, much to her annoyance and the amusement of the others.

'I am not sure that after this performance Nico will still want to join the group, but maybe Ash will set a better example of how a member of the Astraxi should behave with strangers!' said Xin with a sigh.

Ash stepped out from the console where he had been seated and walked forward with his hand outstretched to shake Nico's in an awkward and very formal way.

Ash was actually much older than the other members of the Astraxi, having been taken in by Xin twenty years ago when he was just a small boy, after his parents were killed in a car crash. They had both been professors at the local university and Ash was an engineering, science, and computer technology prodigy.

Ash was continuing to shake Nico's hand, not being quite sure when to stop, when he spoke tautly, 'Ash, Stag Warrior. At your service.' Nico withdrew his hand and Ash looked down awkwardly avoiding Nico's gaze.

Xin spoke to break the silence, 'Ash is a direct descendent of Cyrus, second son of Theokeis, the first ever Stag Warrior.'

'It must be great to be able trace your family back so far,' said Nico.

Ash was a little introspective, not really sure what Nico meant by this, 'It is interesting, from a historical perspective, but that's all,' he replied curtly as if to imply that he was an individual in his own merit and not merely the product of his ancestors.

Nico hadn't quite understood the meaning of this comment and so he moved on to a much more casual, small talk type of question, 'So, what do you do around here then?' asked Nico.

Ash suddenly became more engaged with this line of enquiry, which allowed him to talk about the things that really interest and excite him. 'I run the technical side of our operations, computer systems, and things like that. I'll get you access to some pretty cool tech if you like'

Ash suddenly became enthusiastic and gestured towards the large screens on the walls, which brought up images and data feeds from sources all over Astrellion and other parts of the world.

'Pretty smart!' said Nico as he re-seated himself at the Wizard's table. Looking around, he realised that there were symbols for many Warriors other than just the Dragon. He was able to identify the Tiger, Monkey, Stag, Snake, Dog, Winged Horse, Goat, Eagle, Bull, Wolf, and a few others. But there only appeared to be six Astraxi Warriors here if he counted himself.

'Looking at this table I get the feeling that there are supposed to be many more Astraxi than we currently have in the room' he said to Xin. 'Where are the others?'

'Well, that's a long and complicated story, but the Great Battle of Astrellion brought about some pretty big changes to the Astraxi...' Xin was just about to continue when Ash interrupted him in a very blunt and slightly agitated manner.

'Xin, giving Nico a history lesson is all very well and good, but we should really finish reviewing those satellite images.'

'You're right Ash. It's a story probably best left until I've got plenty of time to tell it properly. We've got more pressing matters right now.' Xin got to his feet and followed Ash back to the console they had been sitting at when Nico arrived.

CHAPTER 11
An Away Mission

Nico shuffled in his chair, not really knowing what to do next. Everyone else returned to their duties, but he didn't have any duties, well not yet anyway, so he decided to have a look at what the fuss was all about. Back at Ash's console, Xin was studying closely the enhanced images of the figures on the glacier.

'Who is that?' enquired Nico pointing to the large dark figure at the centre of the image, whose face was partially obscured by the camera angle and deep shadows.

'Cyax?' speculated Phae. She had never seen him, but a big part of the training that all new members of the Astraxi took was to prepare them for his return, and included the history of his many misdeeds, wars, and tyrannies. The Library of the Astraxi contained many volumes dedicated to him and how to fight him, his strengths, and his weaknesses. Sadly, his weaknesses were few, and they all knew this, which was why they were constantly reminded by Xin that together as a group, they were always stronger.

'I'm afraid that it almost certainly is Cyax, Phae.' 'This is the dark day that I have feared for many centuries,' said Xin with resignation in his voice.

Ash swivelled his trackball and pointed to another figure standing near the cyber-transport. 'Who do you think that is then?' he asked Xin. As Ash zoomed into the picture, the 3D image enhancer revealed a pale, gaunt figure, who was bowing deeply.

Xin looked closer still at the screen, 'It's Fong. He would only go to such a desolate place if it was of the utmost importance. That's it then, it must be Cyax. We need to prepare, quickly.'

'Just as well we have a new Dragon on the team' said Phae.

'Cyax won't waste any time waiting for us to train our new Dragon. Ash, bring up some information about the Five Weapons of Elemental Power.'

Ash quietly spun his trackball once more with one hand and with the other threw a gesture towards a bank of holo-screens lining the wall and bringing up five windows of information.

'I'd like you all to study these five objects' said Xin.

'The artefacts were created many centuries ago by master weapon smiths, who channelled energy from the elemental planes of Water, Earth, Fire, Wood, and Metal. Each artefact was endowed with incredible power based on its elemental source' continued Xin.

On another screen was information about the Lore of Elemental Energy, a five-pointed star, which showed how the artefacts worked either in conjunction with each other or would counteract each other in a series of hierarchies. Water quenches Fire, Fire melts Metal, Metal chops Wood, Wood parts Earth, Earth dams Water etc. The opposite generative effects are Water nourishes Wood, Wood feeds Fire, Fire creates Earth, Earth bears Metal, Metal collects Water and so on.

'Study this carefully' said Xin with more than his usual gravity.

'It looks a bit like a game of rock-paper-scissors, but with five objects instead of three' observed Nico.

'Yes, that's one way of looking at it. But the most frightening implication is that a powerful enough Mage such as Cyax, could combine the five into one single elemental super-weapon'

The young Warriors were already familiar with two of the elemental weapons, the Cup of Souls, which they had tried to retrieve from under the Palace and the DragonStone, which was still glowing in Nico's shirt pocket. Nico was speechless as he read the details of the incredible properties of his small topaz ring scrolling down the screen: The ability to control weather, create ice storms, lightning, whirlwinds, blizzards, purify water and enhance all other forms of Dragon power, including walls of fire and flying! 'Whoa!' thought Nico 'Unbelievable and totally unreal!'

He turned to Xin and pointed at his pocket, mouthing words like 'Really? What the...?' Xin just nodded and shrugged his shoulders in acknowledgement, while everyone else soaked up the information.

Xin interrupted the buzz of chatter that had broken out in the room, 'The last time these artefacts fell into Cyax' hands we almost lost everything, the city, the King, the people, the land and even the Astraxi were divided.

Phae was next to speak, 'What do you think the Fiends will do with the Cup of Souls, and what about the other items? Where are they now?'

'The Fiends will probably hand the Cup over to Cyax. As far as I know the Shield of Fire and the Blade of Astrellion are still lost somewhere, hidden deep and out of sight. Thanks to Nico we know the precise whereabouts of the DragonStone, and the Master in the Forest still has the Wand of Xylos. If Cyax were to take possession of the other artefacts it could be catastrophic, just as it was during the Great Battle of Astrellion.' said Xin, solemnly.

Phae chipped in with her abundant enthusiasm and sense of purpose, 'Well what are we waiting for. We are the Astraxi. We should do something about that. Right?!' The others were stirred into a semi-convinced, murmuring agreement, as the scale of such a task hadn't quite sunk in.

Xin stood up to address them, 'Phae's right. We must act fast to make sure the Wand is secure, and then we need to track down the other missing artefacts before it's too late.' He turned to Ash sharply, 'Ash, prepare Cygnus for an away mission to Dendropol.'

'Aye aye captain' replied Ash with just a hint of enthusiasm. He was quietly pleased that the team were off on an away mission, which would give him the chance to test Cygnus' new systems in a real operational situation.

Cygnus was the Astraxi's principal long-range mode of transport. She was essentially a flying boat, but not in the style of the elegant transports that crossed the oceans in the twentieth century. Cygnus was a sleek, highly advanced aircraft that could just as easily land on water or a runway. Not only was Cygnus beautiful in design, she was the most advanced craft of her type in the world, and most of her greatest innovations had been designed personally by Ash.

Still being unsure what to do with himself, Nico decided he should just go with the flow and followed Phae out of the control room down to the underground shuttle bay that would take them to the Port of Astrapolis where Cygnus was moored.

As the others left the room, Xin took Eduardo to one side, 'I have a separate assignment for you, Eduardo. Go to

Golterion, hide in the walls of the Monastery, and find out what you can about Cyax. I want you to be our eyes and ears in there! Ash will track your movements. Good luck and be very careful.'

'Don't worry about me, I'll be fine. See you when you get back from Dendropol.' replied Eduardo with a nod. He powered up his Snake amulet and melted into the background.

Xin stepped into the shuttle bay where the others were waiting, 'OK everyone, let's go.'

Nico was still a bit awkwardly unsure of himself and had to be dragged inside the shuttle by Ciara. 'Are you coming, or do you always look that stupid, Dragon Warrior?!' she teased. Inside there was a brief health and safety announcement about standing clear of the automatic doors, before they slid shut, then slid open again, having got jammed on Nico's skateboard.

'Stand Clear of the Doors Please' said the cool computer voice once more.

'Oops! Sozz everybody!' Nico grinned sheepishly and withdrew his board close to his body while everyone stared at him.

'Why don't you leave your board here for now Nico? You can pick it up later when we get back,' said Xin, as he pressed the button to override the doors. Nico stepped out for a moment and carefully put his board near a control console then stepped back into the shuttle just as the doors were closing. 'Sorry, sorry!' he whispered, slightly embarrassed.

Lights flashed past the windows for what seemed like many minutes, but it was in fact a very short trip on the magnetically levitated shuttle, which shot through the underground vacuum tube at great speed. After a rapid, but smooth deceleration the shuttle stopped on a platform in the harbour next to Cygnus. They got out and walked along the jetty to enter the ship, just ahead of the wing.

As with all flying boats, Cygnus' bow was sculpted to plough smoothly through the waves. Her wings were situated towards the rear of the fuselage, curving out from the top of the hull, down towards the water. At the end of each wing was a retractable float to provide stability when at sea. Two tail fins sat above the thrusters that provided her forward propulsion and once airborne, Cygnus could flex her wings into a flat platform that gave her a swan-like shape to anyone viewing her from the ground.

Nico stood back for a moment on the quayside and looked up and down the vessel, with its smooth aerodynamic curves and seamless construction. He still couldn't quite believe he was part of this team of amazing people, and his nagging impostor syndrome began creeping up on him again, with the effect of slowing him down and making him appear uneasy.

Phae sensed his edgy mood, which as a Tiger was one of her strengths. She could read emotions easily, particularly when they were out of balance and causing the person involved to suffer anxiety. She put her hand on his shoulder to reassure him, 'Come on Dragon boy, you're going to love it on board. Why don't you go ride with the pilot?' With a nod Ash gestured to Nico to follow him upstairs.

They climbed up through Cygnus' spotlessly clean white interior, with its smooth walls that connected to the floors and ceilings with curved joints rather than sharp angles. When Nico touched the walls, he didn't get the sense that they were made of metal like he would have expected, because they weren't cold to the touch. Occasionally the walls would become transparent with large screens displaying either flight information, the world outside, or sometimes just a beautiful and calming work of visual art.

As Nico followed Ash into Cygnus' flight deck area, he was surprised by the lack of buttons, dials, and switches that one would normally find on a flight deck. Instead, the whole interior appeared to be made of curved smooth dark matt finished surfaces with backlit information displays. In the centre, facing the front window were two very comfortable looking pilot's chairs, each of which had a conventional flight control column. Between the seats were a few levers and buttons mostly coloured black or grey and a small panel that was covered in black and yellow stripes. At the back were two folding seats for observers and even more of the translucent matt black surfaces.

Ash sat in the pilot's chair on the left and invited Nico to take the right-hand chair. 'Go on, take a seat. Make yourself at home,' said Ash. As Nico settled into the co-pilot's seat, Ash made a wide sweeping gesture with both of his arms, like an orchestral conductor or a stage magician. But there was no magic here, just technology. The flight deck was programmed to respond to Ash's physical gestures and as he drew his hands into his body, Nico could hear the satisfying sound of systems powering up, indicated by a series of musical tones and a gentle humming that increased in pitch, while the holographic flight control and computer displays flickered into life.

Ash put on his headset and made an announcement on the ship wide comms system, 'This is Captain Ash speaking from the flight deck, I'd like to welcome you all aboard Cygnus today for our flight to the Forest City of Dendropol. We expect to arrive in just over two hours, so fasten your seat belts and prepare for take-off, Captain Ash and his crew wishing you a pleasant flight.'

Ash turned to the main display in front of the flight deck windscreen. A holographic face had appeared in the centre and was listening to Ash's announcement. The face was animated in a way that made it seem more human than any computer-generated character that Nico had ever seen before. It seemed to have genuine facial expressions that made it look as if it were a real person who was being projected from a remote camera in a studio somewhere else. The feminine face appeared friendly, with a subtle and contented smile and an air of confident intelligence. 'Mira, load up the fight plan for Dendropol,' commanded Ash.

'Confirmed Ash. All systems set to manual, you have control,' responded the hologram.

'Perfect, let's go' replied Ash, who with a series of small hand gestures engaged the ships manoeuvring thrusters to take Cygnus out of her berth. The ship moved slowly sideways from the jetty before turning towards the mouth of the Astrellion River estuary and gliding slowly past the small fishing boats and pleasure craft going about their business. Some people in kayaks paused to watch the flying boat pass between the long twin piers that protected the Port of Astrapolis.

Once Cygnus was in open water, Ash spoke to everyone again, 'Time to make sure you're fully buckled up people, here we go!' Ash put his hand over the holographic throttle display and gently eased it to full power. With her flight engines roaring, Cygnus gained speed quickly, which surprised Nico for such a large vessel.

There wasn't much buffeting from the sea as Ash pulled back on his control stick and edged Cygnus' nose upwards into the skies. The flying boat lifted herself off the sea and climbed very steeply. As Nico looked through the side window, he could see the starboard wing bending and stretching to form a flat aerodynamic shape. Smooth acceleration pushed him firmly back into his seat. He had flown in aircraft before, when he was younger and travelling with his parents, but this felt more like being in a fighter jet than a passenger plane.

Ash levelled Cygnus off into cruising altitude as Nico studied the myriad displays across the consoles indicating the ship's technical condition, navigational information, and many systems that he couldn't figure out by just looking.

'This is just so totally awesome Ash' said Nico coolly. He couldn't take his eyes off the ever-changing displays. 'How does a ship become a plane and fly so easily? It's like there's no effort involved.'

Having been responsible for much of her design, Ash was very proud of Cygnus and was keen to show her off to anyone that showed even the slightest bit of interest. He had harnessed fundamental physics, engineering, computing, and materials science to achieve the ship's maximum potential.

'I won't go into all of the mathematics of it right now, but when Dr. Klara Oberdorf of the Max Planck Institute in Munich, published her Quantum Theory of Spacetime in 2046, as well as explaining the true relationship between inertial and gravitational mass, some rather exciting solutions emerged from her equations of universal quantum entanglement. The possibility of negative gravitational mass was one of them. It was like the moment when, early in the twentieth century, solutions of the Dirac equation appeared to predict the possibility of negative energy, which of course later turned out to be anti-matter, a new and unexpected property of the universe.'

Nico looked at Ash totally bamboozled, as if he were speaking an alien language. Ash continued, 'But things are rarely that simple. So, to be able to use anti-gravity to make the ship fly, we need a containment field to fix the balance of inertial forces and provide lift. Then we need to have a dampening field surrounding that to cancel out the possibility of spacetime distortion effects, like closed time like loops for example. We wouldn't want that would we?'

Ash's question was rhetorical, and he turned to his companion to judge his response, but Nico was confused and could feel his mind fogging over, so he asked a question with a more obvious answer.

'What do all of these controls do?'

'As well as the anti-gravity drive, the ship has conventional fanjet engines. This system controls the main fusion reactor, and this is the defensive cloaking system.' Ash flipped open a yellow and black cross-hatched cover in the centre console, revealing a large red mushroom shaped push button which in Nico's mind was calling out to him 'Push me!' but instead he pushed the thought out of his mind, although it was very tempting.

'Never touch that button Nico!' said Ash with a faint smile on his face. Ash was playing a little private game with Nico, to see how long he would go before temptation made him touch it.

'And this... this is Mira, my closest companion.' Ash pointed to the holographic face that had been closely following his descriptions, and she smiled warmly as she was introduced.

'Welcome aboard Nico! I hope you are enjoying your trip aboard Cygnus today.'

'It's been pretty mind-blowing so far thanks!' replied Nico.

Being very keen to complete his description of the ship's systems, Ash continued his speech. 'Mira has one thousand and twenty-four quantum computer cores, all working in parallel, moderated by an algorithmic delta function that synchronises the data output and corrects quantum errors.'

'Of course it does!' said Nico with a hint of irony in his voice that wasn't recognised by Ash. They hadn't noticed that Ciara and Ben had joined them on the flight deck, sitting down in the jump seats behind.

'Yada-yada. Don't let him geek you out with technobabble! Come down to the rec room with me and Ben' said Ciara.

Ash sat up abruptly in his seat. He didn't really know how to deal with loud and mouthy characters like Ciara but wasn't too concerned that his audience was about to be taken away from him, preferring to get on with monitoring the flight in his usual diligent fashion.

'Good, that means I can get some work done. Mira, let's run a diagnostic test of the holo-emitters while we're in cruise.'

'Confirmed Ash,' replied Mira, as the others left the bridge and Ash buried himself deep in computer sub-routines.

Ben, Ciara, and Nico descended through three decks deep into the centre of the ship and entered Cygnus' mess room where Phae and Xin were already seated at a table. The room was a rectangular space, with some comfortable chairs, a small library of books, a table football game, and a kitchen across one wall.

Xin generally didn't cook for the Astraxi on the ship, preferring to let Mira's automated systems take care of that. But everyone agreed that despite having a library of the best recipes and techniques in the world, Mira's food just seemed to lack something. Not that it was bad or inedible, maybe it was because Mira didn't have taste buds of her own to sample the food.

Nico felt it was time to get to understand this new world he had joined, 'So what's the crack with these amulets and the super-powers and stuff like that?' he asked.

As often was the case, Phae was first to react. 'Training Nico. Years of training, practice, and hard work. Discipline too, you have to be very careful when you use your amulet.'

'That's a bit rich coming from you!' was Ciara's provocative response.

'I always know what I am doing, unlike some!' Phae clearly understood Ciara's taunt.

'I'm not sure about that' Ben was certainly on side with Ciara, but as ever she didn't really care who she was teasing.

'Yeah, maybe Nico will run and hide in a cupboard like Ben did, when Xin told him about his powers!' Ciara continued.

'I did not run and hide,' insisted Ben dropping his usual laid-back style, being slightly ashamed about what the new team member would think of him. Tension, a bit like a close sibling rivalry existed between Ciara and Ben.

Ciara didn't really care about this as Ben was big enough to look after himself, but she was keen to demonstrate to Nico how an amulet is used and to show off a bit of Monkey Lore at the same time. Ciara's tendency to be a bit spikey with people was partially down to the fact that as a younger member of the team she felt she had to work harder to get people to take her seriously, but she also had something of a 'devil may care' spirit.

'Let me show you. If you activate it, you can get a little bit of celestial energy going, like this.' Ciara squeezed the amulet and a stream of fine, glowing light particles emerged from the centre. She spoke the spell '*Makhareis*' and a perfect, but illusory replica of Ciara shimmered into existence standing right next to her.

The replica of Ciara held up her amulet and turned the dial. The real Ciara continued to speak, 'Then if you turn it, you change into a Warrior.' Ornate armour in leather, reinforced with metal, and complete with a helmet morphed around the body of Ciara's replica. The armour was ancient in its style and designed for hand-to-hand combat but beautifully decorated with the patterns and runes of ancient Astrellion, as well as the symbol of the Monkey Warrior in the centre of the breastplate.

'Turn the dial all the way to the rune and you can summon your celestial companion, the creature that your Lore comes from.' As the replica Ciara turned her amulet fully to the right, there was a ripple of light in the ceiling and out of this appeared the Celestial Monkey, whose body shimmered with starlight.

The creature stalked the room and paused recognising Nico from their previous encounter shaking its head in disapproval before peering intensely into his eyes from a very close distance.

Nico shrank back, thinking that this was an aggressive move on the part of the star creature, but maybe it was more that the Monkey was intrigued by being in the presence of the new Dragon Warrior and was trying to find something behind his eyes that would either prove or disprove it. This spindly kid could well turn out to be the most powerful Warrior the world had ever seen. The creature started to cackle at the thought of it, whooping with laughter, which unnerved Nico even more.

'This is Raxalas, the Star Monkey. My amulet draws its power from him. If things get tough, I can summon Raxalas for help,' said the real Ciara. 'That's pretty much it.'

She turned the amulet back to its starting position and the illusory Ciara disappeared, as did Raxalas who vanished through a shimmering beam of starlight.

'That looks easy enough' declared Nico confidently and picked up his amulet.

Mira broke in from one of the holographic screens nearby, 'Fire extinguisher systems fully available and on standby Xin!' she said with her usual calm efficiency.

Xin quickly grabbed the Dragon amulet from Nico's hand before he could activate it. 'No, not here Nico' he insisted.

'I thought you said I was the Dragon Warrior and that I should get some training.' Nico was really keen to get started and was a bit put out by Xin's actions.

'It might look easy Nico but risking a fire on board Cygnus while we're in flight isn't a very good idea. You've no idea how dangerous Dragon power can be. You do need to learn, Nico, but there's a time and a place for everything.'

'As I said, years of training and self-discipline!' added Phae with an ironic smile. Ciara rolled her eyes and shook her head once more in disbelief at what the Tiger Warrior said about self-discipline.

'See you, you're just so full of something!' snapped Ciara at Phae.

'This is not the time for bickering! Everyone get prepared for the away mission. Now!' ordered Xin, his voice was firm, and it was clear from his facial expression that he expected orders to be followed to the letter. 'Just because the Forest realm of Dendraxia is friendly territory, that doesn't mean we shouldn't be fully prepared and ready for action.'

'What should I do Xin?' asked Nico, who felt like he needed to be doing something to help but didn't have the faintest idea where to start.

'Just stick within the group and you'll be fine. Today your role is that of an observer, and we'll get round to your training as soon as we return.' Nico silently accepted Xin's words and headed back to the flight deck so he could observe Cygnus landing in Dendropol.

CHAPTER 12
The Wand Of Xylos

For many centuries the verdant land of the Forest Folk in the southern province known as Dendraxia, had been one of a number of smaller realms within greater Astrellion. The Dasofilaxi were very famous for their prowess in the manipulation of the elemental power of wood. The most skilled practitioner of this lore appointed by the ruler of Dendraxia was known as the Master of Wands.

From his seat in the flight deck, Nico observed Ash making a fully manual approach to the capital city of Dendraxia, which was known as Dendropol. Ash seemed to enjoy the technical processes of being a pilot, with its many formal routines and almost religious and ritualistic attention to fine detail.

As they passed over the lush sub-tropical forest, Nico could see a vast city, but quite unlike any city he had ever seen before. It seemed to Nico that it was almost impossible to work out where the forest ended and where the city began. All the human-made infrastructure both new and old, blended perfectly into the natural world.

There were no huge tower blocks, but accommodation and office buildings seemed fused to the tree trunks that formed part of their built structure. The Dasofilaxi had used their command over the element of wood to grow trees that were many times bigger than in any other part of the world. Their thick trunks were as wide as the tower blocks in other cities, and they had strong sweeping branches to match. The city's original defensive wall had been made from a vast ring of enormous trees whose heavy trunks had merged together and were almost impenetrable by invaders.

More recently other materials such as graphene, glass, steel, stone, and concrete had been integrated with the trees in a harmonious blend of plant life and human-made structures. Even the city's elevated metro system sat on top of rows of sculpted tree trunks that supported the stations, rails, and train carriages.

Ash had decided that it would be a shame not to take the opportunity to land Cygnus on the vast lake by the city, rather than making a conventional landing at the airport.

Nico could see The Master of Wands' official residence, a tall wooden, pagoda-like structure near to a long pier at the water's edge. As they made their final turn, Ash reconfigured Cygnus from her swan-like aircraft shape back into her flying boat configuration with the wing tips flexing back downwards. Then with great precision Ash landed Cygnus softly on the smooth water of the lake, slowing her down to a more sedate speed before taking her inshore to the end of the pier, where they could disembark.

The Dendraxian Minister for External Affairs was waiting to greet them formally, as the Astraxi had been involved in the defence of the land on many occasions in the past. The Astrellian ambassador was also present with a small honour guard of soldiers clad in the leather uniforms of the Forest Kingdom's armed forces. A small fleet of vehicles drove them towards the pagoda for their discussion with The Master of Wands, about the security of the Wand of Xylos, and to warn him of the threat posed by Cyax.

From the information provided by Ash, the group had learned that the Wand is not the sort of small handheld stick you might expect to be used by an orthodox witch or wizard. It is physically a much larger object, more akin to a quarterstaff or a rod. It's a long, thin, ebony cylinder about a metre in length and about five centimetres thick. It has no visible markings, although some high-level users would say they can see the symbol of Eternal Peace hidden in the wood grain by its maker.

More important than its use as a mere weapon of combat are the Wand's special properties, available in lesser or greater quantities depending on the skill of its wielder or their knowledge of elemental wood lore. The Wand was created for one of the great Queens of the Forest, Autonoë, by her master weapon smith and lore master Xylos.

Autonoë was a great leader of the forest folk, loyal to the Astrellian King and their alliance, but she was equally aware of her responsibility to defend her own borders and she instructed Xylos to create a weapon that was most relevant and useful within the woodland environment.

Xylos took on this commission with relish pouring all his vast knowledge and that of many others into creating something that appeared harmless enough to the untrained eye but was endowed with a vast range of awesome powers that could be used for good or indeed evil. It was the true embodiment of the natural magic of the forest. As a reward Xylos was the first person to be endowed by Autonoë with the title Master of Wands.

For example, if the Wand is inserted into earth, the user can summon plant roots, creepers, trees, branches in fact pretty much any type of woody vegetation, which can be used to entangle an enemy. It is even possible to take command of whole trees to use as weapons. But it is also a very effective weapon when used in close combat, inflicting damage that goes deeper than simple wounds. Besides its destructive abilities, the Wand also has very strong healing properties particularly, where plant life or agriculture are concerned, with the power to revive barren lands.

As the official motorcade completed the short drive from the jetty, Nico got a proper look at the ornamental pagoda that was their destination. It was an entirely wooden construction, thirty metres wide at the base, rising to a height of around sixty metres in ten octagonal stages, each one slightly narrower than the one below.

Entering at the ground floor, they went through a pair of wooden doors, and climbed a short flight of stairs leading up to the exquisitely decorated main entrance to the ceremonial chamber. Wood panelling covered every wall of the high-ceilinged room. Marquetry inlays in many different coloured woods, depicted past kings, queens, and scenes from the history of the Dasofilaxi.

The Astraxi were ushered through the chamber's main door into an open space, where they were prevented from going any further by a group of guards armed with staves.

Directly in front of where the Astraxi were being held, was a throne, which was fashioned from many intertwined tree stems. Fanning out from behind the seat was a living canopy of oak leaves.

The Master of Wands was seated with a serious expression on his face, like someone waiting for bad news. Next to the Master and floating freely in the air above a carved wooden plinth, was the Wand of Xylos, making its usual gentle humming sound. Occasionally the note coming from the Wand wavered slightly, as if to indicate some subtle disharmony. Xin noticed this but wasn't unduly concerned.

The Master was a tall, willowy man with long limbs and very long twig-like fingers. His almost tree-like frame was as lean and muscular as you might expect of a gymnast or an acrobat. He was dressed in a more ornate version of the armour worn by his soldiers, a rich brown leather suit fitting his body closely, but jointed to give him freedom of movement. The leather suit's breastplate was sculpted with patterns of intertwined leaves, and he wore a golden necklace fashioned from links in the form of oak leaves. His long hair flowed over the cloak that was fastened at his shoulders.

After a lengthy and almost painful silence staring at the group, the Master of Wands dismissed the guards which were still holding back the Astraxi.

With a low respectful bow, Xin approached the throne and acknowledged his host. 'Master'

'Master Xin. What brings the Astraxi to Dendropol after such a long absence and with such haste?' The Master crossed his arms as if to express some surprise and disdain at the decision of Astrellion's famed warriors to pay him a visit at short notice.

Xin was diplomatic in his response, 'It is always a pleasure to visit the fair lands of the Dasofilaxi, Master. Although my visits have been infrequent in recent times, the city seems more beautiful than ever.'

'Anyone who keeps the ability to see beauty never grows old, my friend,' replied the Master graciously, in response to which Xin made another deep and respectful bow. 'But I am sure you didn't come here just to exchange pleasantries.'

'Master, I must speak with you about the Wand of Xylos, I have concerns about its security...' Xin was about to reveal what he knew about the possible return of Cyax to Golteria, when the Master interrupted him.

'Oh, I see. Now that Cyax has returned you're suddenly worried about our security arrangements, are you?' He paused as the room remained silent, only for the echo of his rich voice that reverberated from the wooden panels. 'I heard about the Cup of Souls. You didn't manage to keep that very secure.'

There was an edge to The Master's speech which came as a surprise to Xin who thought of him as a friend and equal.

He was wrong footed by the Master's confrontational stance, because in the past the two men had always been on the best of terms, serving a common cause to protect their lands and the people.

Xin replied politely, not seeking to inflame the unexpected tension in the room, 'The Fiends caught us in a trap, so it's vital that we secure the other weapons of elemental power, in case they…'

The Master cut him off again angrily, 'In case they what?' His face grimaced as he leaned forward to face Xin and make his point even more strongly.

'In case they fall into the wrong hands' Xin maintained his dignity, while trying to work out where the conversation was going.

'The definition of who would happen to be "the wrong hands" has always been a matter of opinion, or perspective wouldn't you say, Xin'? The Master sat back on his throne while evaluating the group of young warriors gathered in front of him. A pale looking girl, a spindly teenager, a nerdy man shuffling at the back of the group and a surfer boy, they didn't strike him as warrior material, but the young woman with the long hair looked as if she definitely had some fight in her. The Master pondered the possible strengths and weaknesses of this group of Astraxi for a moment, drumming his fingers on his throne.

Xin began to suspect something was wrong but couldn't quite put his finger on it. 'I haven't come here to discuss politics Master. Cyax has escaped, so we must presume that he will continue where he left off. And that means he will attempt to acquire all five of the elemental weapons, including the Wand of Xylos. It must be made safe, immediately!'

With a look of resignation on his face, the Master of Wands replied in a more regretful tone 'Well, I am sorry my old friend, but it seems you might have just missed your chance to do that!'

As he finished speaking, two doors either side of the room slid open and two squads of cyber-demons burst in, armed and ready for action, their weapons pointed at the Astraxi. They quickly surrounded the chamber blocking every available exit.

The cyber-demons were a slightly random collection of soldiers. Not every cyber-demon was ever quite the same.

This was because each one had a different set of electro-mechanical implants embedded into their demon physiology. But there was a common style to the wires, cabling, and components encased in their mechanised armour.

Apart from that they also varied by the type of demon underneath the armoured suits, being variously water-demon, fire-demon, ice-demon or mountain-demon and many other species of demon. Two things were consistent about cyber-demons, their hatred of humans and their loyalty to the rulers of Golteria. Other than that, they weren't best known for their intelligence or prowess on the battlefield, but when they worked together in sufficient numbers, they were extremely persistent and dangerous.

Last through the door came Tanielka, Princess of Darkness, striding in confidently with a look of great satisfaction on her face. She carried a handgun sized pulsed energy weapon, which she trained on Xin. She hadn't reckoned that during her next encounter with the Astraxi, she would so easily gain the upper hand. Fong followed her in, but stayed near the exit in case things got out of hand

The young Warriors were totally caught out by this surprise invasion, but instinctively grouped themselves into a defensive circle in the centre of the room. Xin pushed Nico into the middle as he had no training and was therefore the most vulnerable member of the group.

Nico was used to getting himself into a little bit of trouble from time to time, but this was so many levels above his experience that he just stood rooted to the spot staring at the array of guns pointed at him. The Astraxi gripped their amulets waiting for the order from Xin. Even Phae was sticking strictly to her training and the agreed protocols in the face of such overwhelming odds.

'Once again you're too late Xin. Slowing down in your old age? I suggest that you all surrender and hand over your amulets, now,' purred Tanielka as she confidently faced her ancestor's old adversary.

Xin pondered for a moment. Had the Master betrayed them to the Golterians or was he also a prisoner of the Princess? Knowing that he was caught in a very dangerous position, Xin tried to appeal to reason.

'Princess. Wasn't your late mother about to sign a peace treaty with Astrellion? This doesn't strike me as a very peaceful thing to do.' But Xin's appeal to Tanielka for diplomacy was short lived as the door slid open once more and Cyax strode into the room.

'Peace is no longer on the agenda' growled Cyax as he took his place next to Tanielka.

'Cyax!' The word sprung from Xin's mouth in a reflex action. He hadn't anticipated that Cyax would move quite so fast. Maybe the Princess was right, all these years without such a powerful adversary to keep him sharp, must have blunted his senses to the extent that he had walked his young team straight into a well-planned trap. Now they would have to pay a high price for his lack of foresight.

The Wand of Xylos had been floating in the air, humming with its dis-harmonious tone, but now the sound coming from it had a deeper, more strident quality, a threatening pitch, almost as if two closely matching notes were competing and producing a resonance that was painful to the ear. In this musical conflict, the battle for the Wand had already begun.

Cyax taunted his old adversary, gently at first 'Xin, you've barely changed in the twelve hundred years since your Dragon Warrior and his wormlike friend sealed me in the ice.' He directed his gaze at the young Warriors and raised his voice, in a sneering manner.

'I see they don't make Astraxi Warriors like they used to. They seem...' he twisted his face in mock disdain, '...smaller? What's the matter Xin, can't you find any grown-ups to play with anymore!'

One of the guards stationed by the Wand saw an opportunity and grabbing the Wand launched an attack on Cyax. But Cyax had not forgotten the skills that had once made him the commander of his father's army and he swiftly overpowered his attacker before taking the Wand from his hand.

Cyax swivelled like a dancer and putting his full body weight behind it, smashed the Wand into the midriff of the guard, who sank to his knees. As he did so a look of terror shot across the guard's face as his whole body was consumed in a burst of blinding light which quickly shrank back to a tiny point before disappearing completely. The guard had been despatched to another plane of existence.

With a look of total contempt on her face, Phae was ready to dive in, but Xin anticipated her impetuous reaction and restrained her, 'Phae, wait. Cyax is much more dangerous than Taotie' and being reminded of her previous disastrous encounter with Evil, Phae stepped back. Xin drew his short sword and stepped forward towards Cyax.

'The world's changed Cyax, or are you still too blinded by hatred to see that. You're just not relevant anymore,' he said firmly. 'Why don't you just give up?'

Cyax laughed, 'Me? Not relevant? I see you still have your sense of irony Xin. If anything, my return actually gives you relevance and a reason for your own existence. For without me, why do you even need to exist!'

Cyax' attention was drawn to the faint blue glow in Nico's shirt pocket. 'Today it looks like I am going to acquire two elemental weapons for the price of one.' He pointed the Wand at Nico and uttered the single word '*Sagaris*' his *Bane* spell. Nico felt his stomach fall through his feet, and he collapsed to his knees. Never in his short life had he known such terror. But Xin seized the moment and with his short sword he hacked off the hand with which Cyax was holding the Wand. It clattered to the floor, the hand still gripping it.

'Star shield now' he commanded his small group. Cyax stood still, momentarily surprised at being out manoeuvred himself. The Astraxi simultaneously operated their amulets into their defensive mode and were quickly enveloped by a magical shield of energy. Moving in the surface of the shimmering golden energy field were small points of light, like stars which would occasionally merge to form the recognisable asterisms of the Warriors' celestial companions.

'Being on ice for a while has slowed you down Cyax!' It was now Xin's turn to taunt his adversary. But even as Xin spoke, the severed hand on the floor faded away before miraculously re-appearing on the end of Cyax' wrist.

'You'll have to try harder than that!' Cyax sneered as he swept up the Wand from the floor. Reacting to a gesture from the Princess, the cyber-demons launched a volley of weapon fire against the star shield, which both absorbed and deflected the blasts.

Inside the shield, Nico was still struggling with his fear but was managing to get a grip of himself and had staggered to his feet again. This was exactly what he had been trying to avoid when he earlier turned down the chance of a place in the Astraxi. It was way too dangerous, but for now he just needed to survive.

The Master of Wands reacted to the weapons fire by reaching for the staff that was slung over his shoulder. As he did so his face and hands took on the texture and appearance of tree bark, which was a form of armour used by the Forest Folk. Leaping over a wooden barrier, he swiftly engaged two of the cyber-demons using his staff, smashing them to the ground.

Realising that a fight was about to break out, Fong decided on his usual survival tactic of retreat, but found his exit blocked by one of the guards. Fong was determined not to be in the room when things got really nasty, so he shoved his hand into the guard's face and using his vampire powers brutally sucked the life energy out of the man, whose face turned grey in terror as he collapsed, leaving the way clear for Fong's escape.

Meanwhile Tanielka launched herself into hand-to-hand combat with the Master's guards, using her martial arts skills to tackle more than one at a time, jumping, spinning, and kicking her way through the soldiers.

The Astraxi were held fast, maintaining their protective star shield under a barrage of fire. Meanwhile the Master had taken on another cyber-demon, holding it in a head lock.

'*Talo arego*' he said. Small patches of rust grew on the cyber-demon's metal armour, which quickly merged together, before the whole suit disintegrated into a pile of red-orange dust leaving the creature almost naked and vulnerable to a knockout blow from the Master's staff.

Despite his fear, Nico decided he needed to try and help. After all what's the point of being the Dragon Mage if you can't help your companions in their time of need. He could summon fire from his fingertips without any effort, so maybe he could use the amulet to do something more useful. He squeezed the dial, but nothing happened. He tried again, but it just didn't respond. Maybe it had a safety catch? It seemed totally useless, which was also how he also felt about himself at that moment. What was the strange expression his aunt used to say about him? 'Nico, you're about as much use as a chocolate fireguard!'

Cyax raised the Wand aloft with both hands and struck one end firmly into the floor, which shook violently like an earthquake. A ripple spread across the surface and roots sprouted out from where the Wand had struck the floor, slowly at first but then more quickly. Thick curling, woody shoots, long strangling brambles with sharp thorns, and creeping vines surged out and spread towards the Astraxi. Strong leafy tendrils curled and wound their way around the edges of the star shield, picking at it trying to find a way underneath.

Xin was alarmed and knew he needed to find a way to thwart the vegetation before it cut through and engulfed them all. They needed to do something without compromising the protective shield.

Cyax detected weakness in the group. It was blindingly obvious, the untrained boy in the middle, the one with the DragonStone in his pocket, was there for the taking. Cyax focused his thoughts to use mind control on the young Dragon.

Nico had already been too easily manipulated by Eduardo when he handed over the ring to Ciara. Cyax had also detected his openness to suggestion and weak mental defences. Nico found himself involuntarily reaching for his pocket and drawing out the ring with its topaz stone. A deep, commanding voice entered his head. 'Water. Think water Nico'

Nico repeated the words out loud, 'Water. Think water Nico' and as he did so water poured out from the palms of his hands running towards the tendrils curling under the edge of the star shield.

Cyax fully understood the reinforcing effect of elemental water to that of wood. The twisting tendrils now tore more vigorously at the star shield, fraying its edges and causing the Warriors to react and concentrate their energy in those areas. Phae struggled to maintain her discipline, but Xin knew how to react.

He grabbed the DragonStone and shouted at the young man, 'Nico. Cyax has got inside your head. If you keep bringing water, it will only make things worse. Think fire instead!'

Nico snapped out of his trance, 'Think Fire. Think Fire, Think Fire' he repeated the words like a mantra, and the water flow dried up. A thin flicker of flame appeared around his fingertips and as he continued to repeat the mantra, a flash fire burst forwards from his hands, singeing the woody invasion.

The blackened vegetation withdrew rapidly, allowing the Warriors to stabilise the weakening star shield against the volley of shots being fired by the cyber-demons.

Phae had decided that enough was enough and summoning her Tiger Warrior armour, dived out of the star shield. She charged impetuously at Tanielka, but the Princess cleverly used Phae's own momentum against her, leaving her sprawling on the floor.

Tanielka sprouted a set of sharp claws from her fingertips and was ready to strike deep, when Nico launched himself out of the star shield to defend Phae. The Princess was distracted for just enough time to give Phae the chance to recover into a defensive stance with her Shield of Harmony.

While Nico was trying to decide what to do next, a guard attacked Cyax from behind. Cyax turned and struck the guard with the Wand, using another of the special properties of the great weapon. The guard froze in mid movement as a smooth, polished wooden finish spread rapidly across his flesh and his clothing, which was different to the protective bark armour that the Master was wearing.

The guard had been turned into a wooden statute, a perfectly carved replica of himself, frozen solid in motion. Cyax raised his hand and uttered another spell, '*Dimensis!*' The wooden statue suddenly exploded into a million fragments which struck anyone standing within a five-metre radius, including Nico. His arms and face stung where the splinters hit him.

'Little worm. Are you ready for turning?' asked Cyax of the young Dragon Warrior. Nico was out of ideas, so once more grabbed his amulet and squeezed it hard. To his total surprise a torrent of fire gushed out from his hands like a flame thrower, catching Cyax' long black cloak and engulfing him in a blazing inferno as if someone had poured petrol on him and thrown in a match.

Nico was rocked to the floor by the explosive flash fire, but this gave Phae a chance to trap Tanielka in her Shield of Harmony. As Tanielka tried to draw her weapon, she found it impossibly heavy and immovable. Her legs felt like lead, and she was anchored to the spot, powerless until the magic faded away.

Phae used the moment to drag Nico back under the star shield which was immediately boosted by the additional power of their two amulets. Xin knew that they needed to get out fast.

'It's time we got out of here. Over there.' He nodded to one of the exits that was now clear of cyber-demons. 'Once we get through the door, run back to the ship.'

Cyax was distracted by the fire that was raging on his cloak, but the Wand was unaffected by the flames. Raising the Wand over his head he chanted '*Soto extro.*' Water drained out of the Wand, like a shower head, instantly quenching the flames that were engulfing him.

'Xin. I'll cover you' called the Master of Wands as he cleared the last of the cyber-demons facing him. The Astraxi moved as a group, backing away from Cyax towards the exit, as the Master climbed the high walls of the room in an almost spider-like manner, quickly reaching a balcony overlooking the chamber.

Nico's flash fire had quickly spread around the room. Flames were shooting up the walls, gorging themselves on the rich, dry, and heavily varnished old timbers. Despite his indestructible and immortal body, Cyax could still feel the heat and the pain of the flames, which were cutting him off from his quarry. As Cyax moved to pursue the Astraxi, the Master drew an imaginary line between him and the young people, chanting the Dasofilaxi spell, '*Morar e komani.*'

A stout and impenetrable wall of spiky hawthorn grew rapidly out of the floor, cutting off Cyax' pursuit with a barrier of thickly woven, thorny branches. In anger Cyax raised the Wand of Xylos, not to destroy the hedge, but to direct its power against the hedge's creator. But it was too late, the Master was already leaving the scene.

He melded his body into the wooden structure of the pagoda, which was a risky strategy since the building was on fire and if it collapsed, he would be destroyed with it. As his body finished merging with the wood, for a brief moment, all that was visible of the Master of Wands was his smile etched into the grain of a wooden panel before he vanished completely.

With a roar of anger, Cyax smashed the Wand of Xylos into the ground, causing the whole pagoda to shake. A series of gut-wrenching creaks, followed by a terminal-sounding crack, signified that a major structural part of the building had given way. With a shudder, the entire Pagoda crumbled to the ground, burying Cyax under its blazing timbers. Surely nobody, not even Cyax could survive such a disaster?

CHAPTER 13
Escape

The Astraxi had only just exited the burning building in time to save themselves when it collapsed. They dropped their defensive star shield and ran for their lives in the direction of the jetty.

Each of them, except for Nico, had transformed into their full celestial warrior mode, which covered them in the protective magical armour of the Astraxi. Gilmane had intended the armour to protect against bladed weapons and sorcery, but it seemed also to give protection against the modern blaster weapons of the cyber-demons.

As they ran for their lives, the five more experienced Warriors and Xin formed a protective ring around the very vulnerable Nico, who as yet did not know how to call up the protection of his own armour. He had so much blood pumping through his veins, he thought his heart might burst, but despite the serious danger, he felt a surge of exhilaration, an adrenaline rush.

Maybe this dangerous lifestyle might work out, if he didn't get himself killed before he got a chance to start his training. Such was the thrill of it all that he started to think about the things he might be able to do,

'If only I had my skateboard' he called to Xin with a smile. As the immortal parried blaster shots with his small round shield, he shook his head and smiled to himself. These young kids never ceased to amaze him, even after four thousand years. They were all so different, yet so very similar and so brave, but with ordinary human weaknesses of mind and body. He often wondered why it was always this way with the Astraxi, but he concluded that there was strength in everyone, if they had the opportunity to let it rise to the surface.

Without warning, a squad of cyber-demons blocked the path in front of them. Everyone other than Nico, knew exactly what to do. Phae didn't need the slightest persuasion to launch herself into a fight to protect her colleagues. She leaped forward with Xin to tackle the cyber-demons head on.

While the others maintained a defensive formation around Nico, he saw a side of Phae that was completely unexpected. Her movement and dexterity were almost superhuman as she spun, jumped, and somersaulted her way around the comparatively static cyber-demons, striking them down with devastating punches and kick-boxing movements.

Despite their success, it was apparent that the Astraxi were at risk of being overwhelmed by the cyber-demons that were streaming towards them in greater numbers. Ash grabbed his communicator, 'Mira, power up all systems ready for automatic take off, and be prepared to repel boarders!'

'Confirmed' was Mira's short and assured response, as Ash summoned his own Lore from his amulet. On the way to meet the Master they had passed several large ceremonial statues of previous Kings and Queens of the Forest Folk lined up along the ceremonial driveway. He focused his attention on a group of statues and held his hands out towards them palms first. His fingers curled slightly, almost like he was trying to grip something, but in fact he was bringing the statues to life, like a series of marionettes under his control.

With a flick of his wrists, he released the statues, which now were obeying his command to defend the group '*Extero*'

In his mind Ash imagined the statues attacking the cyber-demons. The sculptures jumped from their plinths and engaged the attackers, swatting them to the floor with their heavy stone limbs. But more powerful weapons were being brought in and one by one the statues were blown to smithereens by cannon fire.

Things were starting to look desperate, as even more cyber-demons and Golterian troops appeared from all sides. The trunk of a very large tree next to the Astraxi started to bend near its roots. Bulges moved through the bark of the tree and merged into the shape of a wooden man, who stepped out of the tree trunk and stood in front of them. The wooden man morphed into the Master of Wands. He truly was a great master of the Lore of the forest, and after leaving the pagoda, had travelled through the trees before emerging in front of the Astraxi Warriors.

He spoke to Xin, 'I am sorry about what happened back there, old friend. They got here an hour before you did and took us by surprise. Let me help you escape from here now.'

The Master drew a rod, a little smaller than the Wand of Xylos from his harness. The Rod of Trees was made from many layers of different types of wood, twisted together in a spiral form to create a slender cylindrical shape. It had silver insect shapes inlaid into its shaft and both ends had a silver cap which was finely decorated with patterns of interlocking leaves.

'*Tocaro*' he called as he raised the Rod in his right hand.

Xin knew what was coming and urged his companions on, lest they get caught up in the Master's spell. 'Thank you Master. Everyone. Run for the ship, as fast as you can.'

They needed no persuading for as they stood watching the Master, hundreds of giant insects, centipedes, scorpions, and beetles erupted from the soil, being directed towards the advancing cyber-demons by the movements of his raised rod of power.

The attackers were smothered and overwhelmed by hundreds of disgusting slimy, multi-legged giant vermin, which penetrated the crevices of their armour, biting and burrowing into their cyber-enhancements causing mechanical systems and weapons failure for many of the attackers. Some of the cyber-demons exploded or burst into flames as fuel leaks were ignited by fizzing sparks from broken electrical circuits.

The group made it to the jetty with many cyber-demons still in pursuit, but Mira was ready with Cygnus' own blaster weapons locking guns on and repelling the boarders that Ash had warned her about. As they raced in through the side hatch, Ash pressed the button to seal the door and called out firmly 'Get us out of here Mira.'

A view screen in front of the exhausted Warriors burst into life with Mira's familiar face responding in her usual calm and concise manner 'Evacuation Protocol Confirmed!' The group were still trying to get their breath when the ship lurched to one side scattering them to the floor, as Mira engaged Cygnus' bow thrusters to manoeuvre the ship away from the jetty.

Xin switched the view screen to an external view, where could see the hordes of cyber-demons taking cover from Mira's automatic blaster fire, which used enhanced pattern recognition to find its targets, flattening them with a barrage of rapid shots. Ash stood up first, 'I need to get to the bridge,' and ran towards the stairs that would take him up to the flight deck.

'I want all of you to head for the central hub. Get strapped in because I am sure they won't let us go without a fight. I'll be up on the bridge with Ash,' said Xin.

But Nico had other ideas, wherever Xin was going, whatever he was doing, he wanted to be there. If he was going to learn anything about being one of the Astraxi, this old guy was the one to teach him. He had spent so much of his life so far, just meandering around aimlessly and now he wanted to seize the moment and not waste another second. He followed Xin up the stairs and into the flight deck, taking one of the rear seats as Xin strapped himself into the co-pilot's chair. Cygnus rose smoothly into the air under Ash's masterful pilot skills. 'Here we go!' he said coolly.

They were barely a hundred metres above the surface of the lake when an explosion just off the starboard wing followed by a volley of pulsed energy shots caused Cygnus to shake violently. 'Countermeasures now, Mira' called Ash with only the slightest hint of tension in his voice, despite knowing that the ship was at its most vulnerable during take-off. 'Countermeasures Confirmed!' replied the AI computer as she deployed numerous electronic and physical devices against whoever was attacking the ship. Ash took the intercom, 'We're under attack from a squadron of Golterian cyber-fighters, brace for evasive manoeuvres.'

The ship started to weave and turn violently as Ash's eyes darted across the multiple display screens to evaluate the number and trajectory of the cyber-fighters attacking them. He didn't need the ship's computer to inform him as his sharp intellect could calculate the intentions of the pilots in the other aircraft. Ash was used to playing speed chess with multiple players and was almost always victorious. 'Shields up Mira. You take over the flight controls while I deal with the weapons.'

'Shields Confirmed Ash, I have the flight control systems, you have weapons and tactical' The ship turned suddenly to avoid a missile which shot past the port side wing. 'That was close' said Xin wincing as he surveyed the sky for the source of the missile.

A flight of four fighter aircraft was pursing them and had split into two groups of two, but none of this concerned Ash as he pulled a second weapons control stick from the console. He was naturally ambidextrous and had trained himself to be able to track multiple targets simultaneously by operating each hand independently. Nico was fascinated by this as Ash locked his rear weapons using his left hand on one group of fighters that was lining up on Cygnus' tail while tracking the other group with his right hand.

Seconds later the group on Cygnus' rear were going down in flames having been roasted by the rear-mounted laser cannon, leaving Ash with just the remaining pair to take out. With his left hand now spare, he engaged a bank of holo-switches, launching a collection of high-speed drone weapons that raced towards the remaining attackers under his guidance.

A holographic tactical display showed the scene in three dimensions and Ash used his hand like a conductor to guide the weapons into a spot just ahead of the attacking aircraft, where they were destroyed in a devastating explosion.

'How do you know how to do that?' Nico asked, but Ash wasn't sure of Nico's exact line of enquiry, so he simply responded, 'Do what Nico?'

'Do all of those things at the same time. You know, use both hands to do different things.'

'It's a bit like being a musician Nico. With enough practice you can train yourself to do a number of things simultaneously by simply following your instincts.' Ash reached for the red button between the two pilot seats and spoke into the intercom. 'Activating the cloak everyone, hopefully we can have a smoother ride home'

'I thought that button was never to be touched,' said Nico.

'Even Ash has a sense of humour Nico' said Xin with a smile. As Ash pushed the button anyone outside the ship would have seen Cygnus vanish into thin air, as the ship's cloaking device rendered it invisible to just about any kind of detection except perhaps for extra-planar or magical methods. Cloaking put a very high demand on the ship's power systems, so Ash normally engaged it only when he was confident that he was in control of the situation.

Sensing this to be the case Xin gave his order 'Thank you Ash. Mira, set a course for the forward operating base, where we can try and take stock of what just happened.'

"Course Confirmed!' came the standard affirmation from Mira once more. Nico was impressed by the efficiency of the pilot, the ship, and the way they worked together but he couldn't resist making a teasing observation.

'Your talking computer isn't exactly very talkative, Ash' Nico quipped.

'Just like the pilot! They're a bit of a double act!' added Xin adding to Nico's humorous observation.

'Mira and I have a very close understanding of each other.' Ash's response was a little edgy, and Nico felt it wouldn't be wise to push the pilot on this right now, so he changed the subject.

'So how come you're so good with all of this tech stuff?' At first Ash didn't answer, just checking the head up displays and adjusting the ship's systems.

'My folks were research scientists, at the University of Astrellion, so I kind of grew up with it' said Ash in a matter-of-fact way, to make it sound as if anyone could have achieved such things, which was not the case as Ash's IQ was speculated to be well off the scale of most minds, although it had never formally been measured.

'So how did you end up here, working with Xin?' asked Nico.

'One day we were driving to a chess tournament. I don't really remember what happened, but our car was in a crash with a lorry, and they were killed. Somehow I survived.' For just a brief moment, and with a subtlety that could easily have been missed, Ash appeared to be battling with his emotions, but he quickly stifled them and returned to examining the flight plan making small adjustments to Mira's recommended route.

'After I left hospital, I was taken in by Professor Snow. She was very old, but very kind. She showed me a lot of cool stuff, quantum super-computers, materials science, and things like that. And while I focused on that, it stopped me thinking about what happened to my parents. Then one day Xin turned up, so here I am.'

'Ash's modesty hides the fact that he is actually responsible for most of what makes this ship work.' Xin's remark made it very clear, just in what high esteem he held Ash, who despite his quiet logical manner was a very important member of the team.

Nico thought about this for a while as he relaxed back into his seat. You didn't necessarily have to be a hero to be a member of the Astraxi, it was the combination of personalities, skills and teamwork that gave the group its strength. He had seen all of this in action in the last couple of hours, so the question for him was, what would be his contribution to the group? He tried to think of the skills he had, but other than being a bit of a wizard on a skateboard, he couldn't come up with much else. He hadn't much of a track record in school or in sports or anything else and was worried that with so little to offer he might get found out as some sort of a Dragon Warrior impostor, despite having passed the amulet test.

'Well, I suppose I've got my work cut out if I want to be a useful part of this team' he whispered quietly to himself as he stared out of the window and stifled a bit of a yawn. He had realised just how exhausted he was, and now that the adrenaline had stopped flowing, his teenage body had decided to slow him down to recover from the day's exertions. His head lolled on his shoulder and his mouth hung open wide.

Xin climbed out of the co-pilot's chair and pressed a button on the side of Nico's seat, which gently reclined into a position more suitable for sleep. A cushion softly pushed Nico's head into a position less likely to give him neck pain when he woke up. 'Sleep well young Dragon,' he said quietly, 'Tomorrow is going to be a very big day.'

CHAPTER 14
Out Of The Shadows

The Pagoda on the lake had been highly vulnerable to destruction by fire because once it was burning, its octagonal tower structure and internal staircases made it behave like a chimney, and as it got hotter and hotter it drew in air even faster, intensifying the heat and the flames to the point where even some metal objects would be melted beyond recognition.

This raging inferno would have incinerated any normal mortal creature caught within the flaming timbers, but Cyax was neither normal, nor was he mortal, nor could he be absolutely destroyed. There would be no reports of his body having been found later in the smouldering ashes and blackened timbers, and neither would anyone find the Wand of Xylos, which being a powerful magical object would survive any earthly fire such as this. Only specific types of extra-planar fire would have any chance of damaging the Wand, the sort of blaze that could be produced by the Shield of Fire or from the mouth of a Star Dragon, for example.

As the Master of Wands directed his guards against the last few remaining cyber-demons, he could hear the flames roaring with an even greater intensity than before, sucking increasing amounts of oxygen into the fire storm. A large number of flaming timbers were suddenly hurled skywards and into the surroundings, causing the Master to take cover as a cloud of thick black smoke shaped like a giant panther burst upwards from the centre of the fire. In its jaws the smoke-panther held the Wand of Xylos, as it launched itself into the sky and disappeared into the night. Cyax was making a spectacular escape from the inferno.

To say that the Master was having a very challenging day, was perhaps the greatest understatement you could make. It had started with the surprise arrival of Cyax and Tanielka who took members of his family and the government as hostages and forced him into the charade of his discussion with Xin about securing the Wand. Just as the situation had turned back to his advantage with the Astraxi making their successful escape, he then watched his prized artefact being carried away by the most evil incarnation. He felt not only a great sense of loss, but also a deep foreboding.

Cyax now had two of the five elemental weapons and using his great skills as a Mage he would probably very soon track down and acquire the last two missing artefacts, the Blade of Astrellion and the Shield of Fire. Then that left only the DragonStone, which was still in the possession of a spindly looking kid, who would probably snap in two if Cyax pushed him hard enough. Was that kid really the new Dragon Mage? It hardly seemed credible. Things were looking bleak, but all was not yet lost if the Dasofilaxi and the Astrellians could combine their forces behind the Astraxi.

Meanwhile The Princess had managed to escape from Phae's Shield of Harmony and the Pagoda just before its collapse. Flying back to the city of Golterion with Fong in one of her military transports, she was disturbed at the lack of any reports of her master's fate. Although she knew well the legend of his invulnerability, no-one except perhaps Fong had ever witnessed this in action, that was until they saw Cyax' giant smoke-panther rising into the air while their transport aircraft was taking off.

After returning to Golterion, Tanielka retired to her private chambers in the main central tower of the Monastery complex which had been Cyax' original fortress built at the time of the foundation of the city. The room was grand and opulently furnished with fine antique furniture, works of art, and other remarkable objects having been the personal accommodation of all the ruling Princesses for many centuries. Weapons and trophies of past wars, conquests, and victories against the armies of Astrellion were either fixed to the walls or displayed on mounts. Swords, shields, and elegant suits of armour all captured from the unlucky foes of her ancestors, who had succumbed to the Golterian armies. There were even a few trophies from vanquished members of the Astraxi, in particular the helmet of a very unfortunate Monkey Warrior. But what she really wanted, and what no-one had ever managed to capture was a Tiger amulet.

She was brushing her hair in a mirror and paused to inspect a scratch on her cheek inflicted by Phae during their fight. This Tiger Warrior was starting to get under her skin, and the mark on her face, even though it was just a small scratch irritated her. She would have her revenge on the Tiger just as soon as the opportunity arose and then maybe she would be able to take her amulet too. As Cyax' heir and being also a descendent of Theokeis, she would have the ability to use the device, maybe not as well as its owner, the hereditary Tiger Warrior, but nevertheless it would increase her already great power.

She was startled by an icy cold hand placed on her shoulder. An intense shiver ran up her spine and as she reached for her concealed weapon, she realised that she had been caught off guard by Fong, but she recovered quickly pressing the blade sharply into his neck without breaking the flesh. He had entered the room silently as he often did, but being a vampire, he had no reflection in her mirror and therefore she had not been aware of his stealthy approach.

'A successful mission, Princess' he spoke in a slightly choked manner with the tip of the blade pressing on his windpipe. Tanielka looked down at his hand on her shoulder, then up at his eyes and he realised his error of being over-familiar. He removed his hand quickly before Tanielka withdrew the dagger and slipped it back into its concealed sheath.

'No thanks to you, Fong,' said Tanielka as she continued to brush her hair.

But in a very deliberate move, Fong overcame his apprehension, snatched the brush from Tanielka's hand and carefully continued the brushing of her hair. The strokes were long, hard, and deliberate, slightly hostile, and not the most pleasant experience for the Princess.

'As you know, I leave combat to the experts Princess. My skills are more subtle, but just as effective.' Fong had been the centre of many plots and intrigues during his centuries of existence, mostly in support of the regime, but these often served his own needs and treacherous ambitions.

'Beware Fong. Cyax will see your hiding in the shadows as a sign of weakness,' she warned him, with a hint of menace in her voice, while maintaining a dignified air under his slow brush strokes.

'He knows my strengths Princess, and I have served him well in the past.' Fong was raising the temperature of their conversation because with Cyax' return, he needed to re-define his position within the hierarchy of power in Golteria. He returned her gaze coldly and paused the brushing 'But you

Princess, you must also ask yourself — do you add strength, or do you bring weakness to his cause?' For Cyax, blood is not necessarily thicker than water. He could easily dispose of you, just as he did his brother, and just as you did with your own mother. Your sister may be more worthy in his opinion.'

Shocked by Fong's insolence Tanielka rose to her feet to challenge him, 'I'm not playing your mind games Fong, get out of here now!' But Fong was prepared for an immediate violent response from the Princess and disappeared into the air as a cloud of thin grey vapour.

Angry and frustrated by Fong's reading of the truth of her new situation, where absolute power now rested not with her but in the hands of Cyax, Tanielka flew into a rage sweeping away the brushes in front of her and smashing the mirror.

Like all the hereditary princesses of the last twelve centuries, she had patiently awaited her master's inevitable return, but now that he was here, she felt not just elation, but also fear and vulnerability. This was unexpected. The rulers of Golteria had always been ruthless, it was in their genes and a steely determination was necessary to maintain their hard grip on power.

She resolved not to let Fong scare her into dropping her guard and showing weakness in front of Cyax. The vampire was once more playing his long-term power politics and she was not about to become his next victim. She would need either to be vigilant or ready to strike first.

CHAPTER 15
The Library Of The Astraxi

The Astraxi's forward operating base was a substantial military facility shared with the Astrellian air force in the north of the country. It was situated on an island set in a spectacular river delta that was fringed by steep jagged peaks like the scattered teeth of a giant reptile.

Cygnus could either land on the water or use the conventional runway on the island base, which was what Ash opted to do on this occasion. On one part of the base were all the aircraft and maintenance facilities of a modern defensive air force and on the opposite side were the Astraxi's own buildings and installations.

The most significant building on this side was a large protective hangar for Cygnus when she was undergoing maintenance or repairs as the result of damage caused during operations. A large staff of technical personnel and engineers assisted Ash in his work. Xin also maintained a staff of analysts supporting the Astraxi by studying data feeds and satellite information and providing intelligence that might reveal a threat to Astrellion and its allied states.

Xin had just finished his de-briefing with the Astraxi, in which they discussed the seriousness of the situation in a world that was once more threatened by a resurgent Cyax.

It was a difficult discussion, full of regret and self-analysis of their recent failures. The last few weeks had not been good for the Astraxi, they had lost their Dragon warrior Eleni, they had lost the Cup of Souls to the Fiends and now they had lost the Wand of Xylos to Cyax. Could things possibly get worse?

Yes, was the emphatic answer, things would get a whole lot worse if Cyax were to acquire the other three weapons. The one positive thing that had happened was that they had already found their new Dragon Warrior and once Nico had completed his training, he would substantially reinforce the Astraxi with his incredible abilities.

Training a Dragon Warrior is normally a very long process, being both complex and dangerous. Xin would usually introduce a new Dragon to the lore slowly and give her or him plenty of time to absorb the lessons, harness and acquire the special skills and fine control that are an important part of wielding the Dragon amulet and its celestial energy.

But the events of the last few weeks had changed everything. With Cyax' successes there came a great urgency to bring Dragon power back to the group and since Nico was potentially a Dragon Mage by virtue of a prophecy, then he could turn out to be a very potent warrior indeed. Xin was also acutely aware that doing things in a rush often led to mistakes, and in the heat of an Astraxi operation, mistakes could be fatal. There was no margin for error.

As they left the central hub, Xin beckoned Nico over. 'Come with me Nico, I'd like to show you around' They left the futuristic main headquarters building with its amazing white curved architecture, solar panels, and large glass windows. There were no straight lines and the structure seemed to flow like several drops of liquid fused to form a group of giant snowballs. As they walked across the hard standing, Nico watched Astrellian air force trainer aircraft practicing their landing and take-off skills on the main runway.

'It's time you started your training Nico' said Xin directing him towards another building, which stood close to the hangar where Cygnus was being thoroughly checked over following her engagement with the Golterian fighter aircraft the day before.

'I thought I did pretty much OK yesterday' was Nico's positive response.

'I'm afraid that pretty much OK isn't good enough and will probably get you killed, young Dragon. Or get all of us killed. You were lucky. We were all very lucky.'

Nico's enthusiastic bubble was slightly deflated by this harsh analysis of his performance, but he was determined to make his point. 'Maybe I am lucky, and that's not such a bad thing' said Nico making a positive of his actions in the pagoda.

'The problem with luck Nico, is that it's random and you can't control it. Cyax is very powerful, but trained and experienced Astraxi Warriors armed with amulets are always a match for him, especially when working together as a team.' Xin was serious about this. Experience had taught him that discipline and teamwork were essential, and that luck would often let you down just when you needed it most.

'What's his next move Xin?' asked Nico.

'On his own he won't be able to defeat the Astraxi, this has been shown many times in the past. But if his power is enhanced by acquiring some of the amulets and the five elemental weapons, he will be unstoppable.'

Xin entered the smaller building next to Cygnus' hangar and led Nico towards an elevator. 'Come Nico. Deep below this base is our most precious resource.' They entered the small steel box with its display screens and Xin pressed the button to descend.

'Where are we going?' asked Nico, but Xin remained silent to get the maximum impact of what he was about to reveal. After quite a long but fast descent the elevator stopped and the doors opened to reveal a large circular room, with a very high ceiling supported by wide columns decorated in red and gold.

As Nico stepped out of the elevator, he could see tunnels heading off radially from the central area. Above each tunnel hung the insignia of one of the Astraxi, indicating that it was either the Tiger tunnel or the Snake tunnel, and so forth. On the walls between the tunnels were racks containing books, scrolls, unusual weapons, and strange artefacts, presumably magical but Nico was inexperienced in sorcery and couldn't tell by just looking and for that matter what would a magical object look like anyway? Silk banners painted with the heraldic insignia of armies long gone were hung on walls alongside preserved suits of armour in most of the different styles worn in the last four thousand years.

The room also served as a giant real time planetarium. Its deep night blue hemispherical ceiling was painted with fantastic celestial creatures in silver. Many crystal lamps floated in the air below the ceiling, glowing brightly and illuminating the chamber. The lamps varied in size, brightness and colour and were arranged in such a way that an experienced astronomer would quickly recognise familiar patterns of stars in their layout.

Viewed as a whole, the lamps represented the same stars that made up the major constellations or asterisms that were in the skies over Astrellion at that moment and just like those stars, they transited across the ceiling, just as an astronomer would expect with the passage of time.

Also passing through the astral vault were five larger illuminated objects representing the five major planets, which also represent the five elements. These followed the line in the sky that all astronomers, ancient and modern would recognise as the plane of the ecliptic and like the star lamps, only the planets directly in the sky over Astrellion at any given moment were visible in the sky vault.

The sun was not represented in this display except that the ceiling was a noticeably paler blue in Astrellion's daytime, but a large silver orb representing the moon was also present in the planetarium whenever it would be visible in Astrellion. The silver orb also showed the current phase of the moon ranging from darkness for a new moon to a boldly glowing full moon.

As Nico stood gazing around himself trying to make sense of the amazing surroundings, he could see that this part of the complex was very different in its style to the hyper-modern structures at the surface, distinctly old school and very reminiscent of Gilmane's old curiosity shop, but much more tidy, less dusty, and well organised with the feeling of an ancient academy.

'This is the Library of the Astraxi.' said Xin, his voice echoing around the vast hall. 'Inside these tunnels is kept all of the accumulated knowledge of the Astraxi. It's stored deep beneath the mountain to protect it. Every spell, every martial arts move, every tactic, every journal and every device ever invented by the Astraxi has been recorded and stored in this library, so that future generations can access the knowledge, wisdom, and skills of their predecessors.'

In the centre of the room was a large circular table, a Wizard's table similar to the one that Nico had first seen in the operations room below the Perpetual Motion Café, with its radial segments and concentric rings containing strange markings, runes, and pictograms, as well as representations of the planets and major constellations.

Nico was curious and headed over to the table for a closer look. At the outer edge of each of the segments of the table there was a large book. Six of the books were open at a blank page and the others were closed. Above each open book floating in mid-air, was a quill pen poised as if it were being held by an invisible hand ready to start writing. The other books were all closed with the quill pen on a stand next to a silver inkwell as if waiting for a story to write.

The first book Nico looked at was for the Stag Warrior Ash, which was open about 50 pages in from its start. The quill pen hovered gently in the air near the last entry on the page, which Nico could see was beautifully inscribed with an account of the mission to the Dendropol, when they tried to secure the Wand of Xylos. It described Ash's heroic actions, the lore he used to animate the statues and his successful piloting of Cygnus back to base, all illustrated with animated images of the events, like short films.

Nico flicked the book back to the front pages and found descriptions of Ash's early days in the Astraxi as a rookie Warrior and of his many contributions as a technologist and engineer working on the development of Cygnus.

Xin explained to Nico that these books were there to record the activities and works of the Astraxi without them actively having to be at the table to write it themselves. None of the quill pens were scribing at that moment but were ready to record should some notable event be taking place. Each completed book would later be added to the library as a source of reference in the future and to keep an historical record of the Astraxi.

'How do they work Xin? Is it magic?' asked Nico.

'It's quite simple really when you know how Nico,' laughed Xin. 'There's no magic as such, it's just that these pens are controlled by a set of invisible assistants in another plane of the universe, the Plane of Destiny in fact. They can see events in our plane and translate that into images and writing on the pages, without even being here. I have visited them many times to offer them my gratitude and that of the Astraxi.'

He paused as if reflecting on something. 'It's actually quite an odd place, as they seem to be able to see all the possible outcomes of events throughout the many planes of the universe, which can be quite confusing, scary, or inspiring, depending on your point of view. Ash once told me that a physicist called Everett came up with a similar idea in the middle of the twentieth century. Funny how science sometimes imitates real life!' he said with a wry smile.

Nico thought about this for a moment but was intrigued to read what had been written about him so far and walked over to the Dragon book to take a look. He was surprised to find that there was already a page with a short family history and a family tree that connected him to Eleni via a great uncle who was himself closely connected to Great Aunt Cass. 'So that explains it, Aunt Cass probably knew all along' he thought to himself and wondered why he had never heard of these people that were so closely related to him.

Maybe that's just the way some families work out, losing touch with each other because they're just too busy doing their own things, having their own problems, and just trying to get by. Eventually it's too late and they are lost to one other, which Nico thought was a bit sad as he had often dreamed of being part of a large and lively extended family, and now here it was in front of him on the written page.

Further down the page began the description of his own history within the Astraxi. It wasn't very flattering. It started by describing him as a liar, petty thief and minor criminal who stole the DragonStone from Gilmane and struggled to understand his own potential.

Under a heading entitled 'The incident of The Wand of Xylos' it described his failed attempts to use his amulet in Dendropol, his lack of mental strength in the face of Cyax and his shocking lack of control of his dragon lore, while starting the devastating fire that caused the collapse and total destruction of the precious and exquisite wooden pagoda, which was a highly prized part of the forest people's cultural heritage.

'Harsh, but probably fair' he thought to himself. 'You could have done so much better!' was something that was regularly said to him by his teachers.

At that moment he also realised that the next blank page would be his chance to change direction and build his reputation. If things worked out, those following pages could be filled with the heroic deeds of Nico, the greatest ever Dragon Mage. But that would require actual heroic deeds, effort and focus from him, and that was the sort of hard work he usually sought to avoid, preferring to base his life on the skilled wastrel's principle of getting maximum reward for minimum effort, also known as the path of least resistance.

This would be a big change of style for him and there would be nowhere to run and hide as a member of this team. But he knew that for the first time in his life people would be there to support him when he had problems, and this was the major difference for him going forward.

The floating quill pen twitched in front of his face as if urging him to do something amazing that it could write about. Instead, Nico moved over to look at one of the other closed books, in the segment of the Winged Horse Warrior. He opened the cover, but the pages inside were blank.

'I guess these must be the books for the lost Warriors of the Astraxi because there's nothing recorded,' he said to Xin, who nodded in agreement.

'The books are waiting for the time when they are returned to active service. Our search for them is on-going.' Xin turned and made a sweeping gesture,

'The things here in the centre of the room are mostly just curiosities, objects that were found or were created by a Warrior to test a new fighting technique or a way of using their amulet's celestial power.'

Nico walked over to a display of objects near the elevator that had brought them into the library. He picked up a small wooden box decorated with brass and mother of pearl inlays. The inlays on top of the box seemed to get narrower and narrower until the one at the centre was little more than a dot as if you were peering into a long tunnel. He opened the lid to have a look. Inside, the box's wooden interior did indeed appear to stretch away to infinity and darkness as if it were hundreds of metres deep.

He couldn't resist putting his hand in, and his eyes opened wide as his entire arm disappeared into the box up to his shoulder, without reaching the bottom or coming out of the other side. A harsh chattering sound, like voices or whispers that had been sliced up and stitched back together with their own echoes came from inside the box, growing in intensity, while a sharp gust of air blew Nico's hair backward giving him a distinct sense of vertigo. He withdrew his arm in a hurry and slammed the box shut.

Such was his curiosity though, that when he slowly re-opened the box, it appeared to be just a normal small, decorative wooden object about fifteen centimetres deep inside. He then thrust his fingers inside on to the wooden surface, he confirmed that the bottom was now indeed solid. 'Bizarro!' he muttered to himself.

Xin took the box out of Nico's hands, 'Be careful before putting your hand into a box like this Nico, you never know what you'll find, or where it might take you.' Xin reopened the box and dug around inside with his forearm before wincing and then dragging out a creature by the scruff of its neck. A small, but very savage reptilian with bulging eyes and way more teeth than should be able to fit inside its mouth, was trying its best to grab and bite Xin's fingers and wrist.

'Hmm, a bog-demon, I wonder who left that in there? Better send it back where it belongs.' He put down the box and waved his hand at the snarling creature which was writhing in the grip of his other hand and uttered the spell to send the creature back to its native plane. '*Yognam: Yoshara kalente*' The creature appeared to recede into itself in a blur that ended with a small burst of light. Xin set off walking at quite a pace leaving the young man behind, 'Come on Nico. Let's go and have a look around the Dragon library.'

He led an enthused Nico over to the tunnel above which was hanging the Dragon emblem. 'This collection is the entire history and wisdom of Dragons over the last four thousand years. More than six hundred Dragons have contributed to it,' said Xin. Nico looked into the tunnel which he guessed was maybe a hundred metres long and lined with randomly sized shelves.

Many of the shelves contained books bound in leather that looked like scaly dragon skin, but there were mechanical devices in display cases as well. The library was neither ordered by subject nor was it alphabetical, but the books were arranged in sections under the name of the Dragon who had made the contribution to that part of the library and was therefore chronological.

At the start of each new section was a portrait of the said Dragon usually in the midst of some noble deed. Right at the front of the tunnel were the works and histories of the most recent Dragon Warriors. Nico recognised the portrait of Eleni as the girl he had seen being attacked as he peered into the visions inside the DragonStone. She was portrayed as a beautiful Dragon warrior, heroically defending her colleagues from the Fiends, but although the image was inspiring, it disturbed Nico as Eleni's fate was a reminder of how dangerous his life was about to become.

'It's the girl I saw in the vision, in the stone, isn't it,' said Nico.

'Yes Nico. Eleni's loss was an unexpected and entirely preventable tragedy' confirmed Xin sadly. 'But the good news is that you're here now!' and the sadness lifted from his face as he patted the young man on his shoulder.

Xin led him deeper into the tunnel passing various collections arranged neatly by the portraits of other previous Warriors, which also indicated the years when they served. Some of them had served the Astraxi for decades, but others had a surprisingly short term of service, even down to a few months.

'Do you have to die before you can leave the Astraxi?' It was the question that Nico had been burning to ask for ages.

'It is the nature of our work that there are inevitably some casualties, but no Nico, you don't have to die to leave the Astraxi. Most Warriors eventually leave to follow other paths in their lives or destinies and usually it's a personal decision made by that individual' replied Xin.

They paused for a moment in the dimly lit tunnel and Nico looked at more of the Dragon portraits in the collection. Their faces all felt somehow familiar to him, as perhaps they should because if the legend were correct, then he was a direct blood relative of all of them, with their single common ancestor being the very first Dragon Warrior.

Where they did look different was in their clothing and the scenes in which they were portrayed. The particular section, where they had stopped was from the period about seven hundred years ago and the portraits showed people in medieval costume, with old castles and towns as the backdrop.

From some of the portraits Nico could see that not all the Dragons were fighters or had faced great peril, and some of them had the look of studious academics pursuing Dragon Lore as a technical subject, to expand their abilities and special powers. Others were more statesman like, diplomats and orators with scrolls, or addressing large gatherings of people. It wasn't all about fighting, but generally the portraits showed a Dragon succeeding at something or being a great leader. '

Hmm, the pressure's definitely on to achieve something' thought Nico to himself. As a novice, the scale of the deeds recorded in the library was already intimidating him, and the weight of that realisation was starting to hang heavily on his shoulders. Eventually he let out a deep sigh, which Xin recognised as the moment when the magnitude of the task had sunk fully into Nico's mind. Time now to inspire the new Dragon to take up the challenge.

'This room will be the making of you Nico. Spend time in here and you will soon acquire the skills and Lore of your ancestors. Your power comes from the celestial plane, but by studying these books and with enough practice, you have the potential to use that power to become a truly great Dragon.'

'But where do you start? I mean look at it, it's way too much to handle.' Nico felt he was facing a mountain that was impossible to climb.

'Don't worry about that. The library already knows what you know, what you don't know, what you know you need to know, what you don't know you need to know, and in which order you need to know it!' said Xin cryptically. Nico tried to work out what he had just been told, but it was way too confusing.

Xin waved his hand at a polished brass and wood bookshelf ladder which was floating by the racks on one side of the tunnel. The ladder moved towards them at speed stopping just in front of Nico, who was urged to climb on to the second step by Xin, who then hopped on to the step below him. The ladder shot off at such speed down the tunnel that Nico had to grip the handrails very tightly to stop himself from falling off. The books and shelves merged into a colourful blur as he shot past them with his hair flapping in his face. After a few seconds the ladder came to a rapid, but smooth halt under a very impressive portrait that stood at the head of a very large section of books and magical objects.

'Interesting!' exclaimed Xin.

'What do you mean, interesting?' said Nico.

'I just meant that it's interesting that the library has brought you here before anywhere else' explained Xin.

'Who's that?' Nico pointed to the portrait of a handsome young man in his early twenties riding the back of the celestial dragon Adraxa, while plucking Cyax out from the centre of an intense battle'

'That Nico, is Drakeidis, the greatest Dragon Mage who ever lived' said Xin with reverence in his voice, 'Well, until now maybe! Climb up and see what the library has put in your reading list.'

Nico climbed up four rungs of the ladder that took him to a much wider shelf at the top, just as a dragon hide lined book slid out from the shelves and placed itself in front of him on the collecting shelf at the top of the ladder. But Nico didn't have time to examine the book as the bookshelf ladder had already decided it was time to look somewhere else.

It hurtled at great speed towards the very deepest part of the tunnel where it stopped under the portrait of the original Dragon Warrior Takareis, Nico's ancestor who had spoken to him in the vision when he first met Xin.

'Hey, I recognise this dude!' The man in the painting had the same noble gaze that Nico remembered from his visions below the Perpetual Motion Café and anyone looking at the painting could not help but to be captivated by his powerful eyes.

The painting illustrated Cyax being held in chains by the Dragon warrior after his betrayal of King Theokeis just before his banishment for the murder of his brother. A smaller and much slimmer volume slid out from the shelves and placed itself at the top of the ladder. The animated front cover illustration showed water flowing, which quickly turned into ice before being evaporated by a breath of fire and then condensing back to flowing water once more. It looked more like a physics or chemistry textbook in that respect. A small handbook covered by a scene of dragons dancing through the skies also slid onto the pile.

Once more the ladder shot back at breakneck speed towards the middle of the library, where it located an ornate volume whose binding was decorated with images in silver leaf and encrusted with small topaz stones. With another great jerk the ladder now hurtled back to the entrance of the tunnel forcing Nico to hang on tightly once more.

As the ladder came to a rapid halt, Nico gathered up the books and jumped to the floor following Xin back into the central hall where they sat down at a large mahogany desk.

'Let's see what you've got here then. Hmm, Fire, Water, and Ice – How to harness the most essential elements, for first level Dragons. The DragonStone, A User Manual for

Beginners, Volume 1, by Gilmane the Great. Flight Briefing for Dragons part one, and Drakeidis the Magnificent – An Illustrated History, Parts I & II.'

Nico started to leaf through the copy of Fire, Water, and Ice with its illustrated descriptions of basic Dragon lore involving the use and control of heat and cold and the manipulation of water, steam, fire, and ice that would allow him to be able to take control of the weather should he so desire.

Just like the books he had examined on the Wizard's table, the illustrations alongside the text were animated showing Nico how to wield his powers. He would never have guessed that most of it turned out to be a state of mind. Whatever he imagined, the power would flow through his amulet and allow him to summon things from other parts of the universe and other planes of existence.

Whatever his internal thoughts could focus upon could be delivered if he were clear enough in his mind. The difficulty was being able to channel those thoughts when confronted by a range of distractions, such as being in the midst of a raging battle and facing the most evil person that ever walked the earth who is also trying to destroy you! That was where learning to control his mind would come in useful.

Like a musician he would have to learn to make different parts of his conscious and sub-conscious mind work together in the real physical world, to create whatever spell or effect he had in mind. Like plucking multiple strings on a guitar with the fingers of one hand, while selecting the correct finger positions on the neck with the other to achieve either harmony or discord. But instead of channelling the music on a sheet of paper, Nico would be directing the celestial energy of the Dragon constellation and moving real physical objects between planes of existence.

'This is amazing!' Nico was totally engrossed in the book in a way that no book had ever engaged him in his life.

'I think you should study the history of Drakeidis most carefully' advised Xin.

'Why, how would that help me? Surely I just need to learn how to do it?' Nico was sceptical simply because he didn't want to spend time studying some piece of ancient history when he could be learning to unleash his powers.

'Drakeidis was certainly magnificent in many ways, but in others he was not. Being a Dragon isn't just about wielding power. You need to have the wisdom to use it correctly and if you read that book, hopefully you will learn from his mistakes, of which there were many, and then maybe you won't repeat them.'

Nico could see from his face that Xin was serious, and he picked up the book. Its cover was illustrated with an animation of a group of Warriors arguing with another group about something and from their facial expressions it looked pretty serious. This was a bolt out of the blue for Nico because he had naively believed that the Astraxi had always been a closely bonded fellowship, but clearly there had been some serious strife in the past, centred around the Dragon Mage Drakeidis.

'What did he do that was so terrible Xin?'

'It's not an easy subject to discuss, but with great power comes great responsibility, always. Drakeidis started his career in the Astraxi as quite a young man, a bit younger than you as it happens. He was clever and learned rapidly and his abilities were way beyond anything I had seen before. But as his lore and his power grew, sadly for us, so did his arrogance.'

Xin was finding it difficult to cope with the bad memories of that period, but he continued. 'Let's just say for now, he did a lot of things that he regretted later, things that didn't need to happen, things that played right into the hands of Evil.'

'But in the end, he defeated Cyax, didn't he?' Nico was puzzled that such a great Dragon could do anything wrong.

'Yes, but before that he had become a danger to everyone else. Once he realised this he exiled himself to the mountains before any more damage could be done, but this only weakened the Astraxi further. Eventually when Cyax attacked Astrapolis in the Great Battle of Astrellion, the folly of Drakeidis' behaviour was brought fully into focus, and he returned just in time to save the city, before burying Cyax in the glacier.'

Nico was about to ask a whole load of questions about Drakeidis, but Xin decided to change the subject

'Nico, before you bury your head in these books, why don't we start with something more practical. Let's give you a chance to see what you can do with that Dragon amulet, but this time in a more controlled situation.'

Nico's eyes lit up. This was just what he had been waiting for. 'Nice one Xin, I can't wait to give it a try!'

CHAPTER 16
How To Train Your Dragon Warrior!

Xin sent out a message instructing everyone to assemble on a concrete pad near the main laboratory building. It was another of the giant snowball meets a giant ball of mercury sort of buildings which were common on the site. A set of huge curving windows revealed an internal structure of walkways, elevators, escalators, and stairwells. Behind these were the laboratories and workshops where the most brilliant minds were creating new science that to some people, particularly Xin, was indistinguishable from magic.

When Xin was educated over four thousand years ago, there was little science or technology that was much more advanced than the forging of weapons and tools from fire and stones. A few people such as the King understood astronomy and mathematics, but when Xin went to school, he was taught that the entire universe was made from five basic elements all stirred up with a splash of celestial energy.

Now there were well over a hundred elements, or so Ash had once told him, but he never felt the need to understand the detail of the ins and outs of chemistry or physics. As long as the lore of the five elements still worked and there were Warriors to train, he still had a clear purpose. Ash was more than capable of dealing with the science and technology on his own.

Ciara, Ben, Ash and Phae were waiting in the open concrete hard standing area as Nico and Xin arrived. Two fire tenders were also parked nearby, and a fireman was distributing shiny silver protective suits and boots to the others.

'You look like a bunch of oven ready chickens in those suits!' teased Nico. He had no real idea what was about to happen, but it was clear that there was a considerable amount of danger for the bystanders. Or was it just Health and Safety being over-cautious? Fire hoses had already been deployed and the perimeter taped off, to keep people safely outside the danger zone.

'We had better all stand well back behind this line' Xin warned the others. 'Mira, inform the Fire Chief we're ready to start.'

'That is Confirmed Xin. The fire team is standing by,' replied the cool computer voice of Mira. Except for Nico they all moved behind a line of hover traffic cones that had been laid out by the Health and Safety department with tape between them that said DANGER in large block letters on a black and yellow background.

'OK Nico, you can try the amulet now, but remember what I said, stay calm, take it nice and easy and whatever happens, try not to lose control.'

Nico on the other hand, was so excited about trying out his new powers that a certain amount of typical Dragon bravado was already starting to come to the surface, the type of self-confident swagger that was so predictable and could be so annoying to others. In his mind, because the amulet had chosen him as the most worthy person to wield, it then there should be no problem. Watch and learn little people and be in awe of the mightiest Dragon Warrior the world had ever seen, well since Drakeidis at least.

Nico activated the amulet and the usual stream of fine glowing particles of light emerged from the centre of the disc, but as he cautiously turned the dial nothing else happened. Nothing at all. The other Warriors just looked on silently, waiting for something to happen.

Nico became conscious of their staring at him, so feeling an acute attack of peer pressure mixed with impatience, he started to twist it randomly backwards and forwards as if it were broken and this rapid dialling would fix it.

Without warning a jet of flames burst out of the amulet towards his friends who were quickly forced to retreat a few steps. As quickly as they started, the flames disappeared again, and then something peculiar started to happen to Nico's physical form. Parts of his body were flashing in out of existence and being temporarily replaced by other things. His forearm acquired a layer of dragon scale armour, his right foot became a giant claw, and a Dragon Warrior's helmet appeared on his head before disappearing again leaving him with a very nasty case of helmet hair. Knowing just how much care Nico put into his appearance, particularly his hair, the others and especially Ciara the Monkey Warrior, found this hilarious,

'That's the best laugh I've had in ages' she giggled as he self-consciously straightened his locks, but she was forced to flee as another unexpected jet of flame from Nico melted the plastic tape they were standing behind.

The mix of embarrassment and rising anxiousness at his inability to access or control his Dragon Lore was starting to bring back Nico's teenage uncertainties about himself and a little bit of impostor syndrome. Watching his colleagues so easily use their amulets at Dendropol had seemed so effortless to him. Now at the moment when he desperately wanted to be part of the team, he was showing no aptitude whatsoever.

'Try turning it off and then turning it back on again,' said Ash. Nico wasn't sure what he meant, not realising that Ash was trying to be funny in a computer nerd sort of way.

Nico turned the dial hard to the right resulting in a column of flame shooting out from his hand along the ground into a pile of tyres nearby. They lit up like a torch, being incinerated as if they were soaked in petrol. The ferocious burst shocked Nico and he fell to the floor on the seat of his pants before fully returning to his normal non-Dragon Warrior human shape. As the fire chief stepped forward to douse the flaming tyres a wisp of acrid blue smoke from the burning rubber was drawn up Nico's nose causing him to sneeze, but this was no ordinary human sneeze, it was a Dragon sneeze.

Jets of flame shot down Nico's nostrils and out of his mouth re-igniting the tyres and engulfing both Nico and the chief in a massive fireball. Fortunately, the fire chief's personal protective equipment had a full Dragon-proof fire safety rating, and he was quickly doused by his colleagues in a thick foamy fire-retardant liquid for good measure.

Nico remained seated on the cracked and blackened concrete quite shocked, but weirdly elated by the celestial energy that had just been released through his body via the Dragon amulet. 'Hey. How come I'm not burnt?' he asked.

'Duh! You're a Dragon Warrior stupid! You're flameproof, you idiot! But we're not, so be more careful next time!' shouted Ciara who had been standing uncomfortably close to the hover-cones when they were torched by Nico. The devices now looked like so much molten pizza cheese with embedded circuitry sticking out.

At first Nico thought this performance was disastrous, but Xin was not worried. He had seen many new Dragons try their magic for the first time and the range of outcomes was very variable. Some Dragons got it immediately, with the full flame thrower effect, but others started with just tiny wisps of flame and needed time to build up the skill. Nico's power was very impressive, but his lack of control made him dangerous to everyone.

Xin spoke to Nico patiently, 'Concentrate Nico, take it very easy, slow down, let the celestial energy flow through you, and use your thoughts to control its direction. But whatever happens, stay calm. Start by imagining you are the Dragon Warrior.'

Nico picked himself up and reached for the amulet again. It had reset itself to the 'off' position. He took a deep breath and activated it, this time turning it just a few clicks and more slowly. It was his hands he noticed changing first. A pair of armoured gauntlets appeared growing around his wrists, followed by red and gold dragon scale armour that started to cover his arms up and over his shoulders. Leather boots delicately inlaid with a rampant dragon design appeared on his feet as his legs and torso were also being covered by the dragon scales. The suit of armour was completed by shoulder and knee protection with a skirt arrangement to protect him from his waist to his thighs and an ornate breastplate featuring an inlaid design based on the Star Dragon Adraxa. Finally, he was topped off with a magnificent helmet decorated with the heads of two fierce dragons converging in fire and ice and with impressive and dangerous looking spines on top. He stood just looking at the armour for a while until Phae broke the silence.

'Have you ever seen anything quite like that. You look amazing Nico' she exclaimed. For Nico, receiving a compliment from a girl like Phae was a rare thing. Despite his good looks, he wasn't always confident with girls and tended to be a bit shy until he got to know them better. He blushed and hung his head looking at his feet while trying to decide how best to respond, a moment that wasn't lost on Ciara.

'Your face now matches the colour of your armour!' she jibed at him sarcastically.

'That's enough Ciara,' snapped Xin, 'don't break his concentration. We'll work on controlling the energy flow. Clear your mind and imagine what you want to do.'

Nico composed himself once more, closed his eyes and blew out his cheeks, exhaling deeply. 'OK, I'm ready Xin.'

'I want you to burn those bales of hay. But don't get carried away!' Xin pointed to a group of hay bales that had been placed on the concrete behind Nico, in a place that was far enough away to be safe for the others. Nico turned and remembered his little trick of producing flames from his fingertips. 'I guess that must be how it works' he thought to himself and raised his right hand. Orange and yellow flames licked around his palm. Flicking his wrist outwards he pointed his palm towards the hay releasing a plume of fire like a flame thrower into the dry straw, which ignited immediately.

'That's more like it' he thought to himself, but the flames on his hand faltered and died, while he struggled to maintain enough concentration.

Xin was interested to see just what this new Dragon warrior was capable of and given the escalating situation with Cyax, decided to take this test much further than he might normally attempt at such an early stage of training.

'The next thing I want to do is to introduce you to your companion creature from the Celestial plane, the Star Dragon Adraxa. She is the source of your power and has been the companion of every Dragon Warrior since the creation of the Astraxi. You saw her in your vision quest when we first met.'

'There may be times when you need help and because you are bound to her by the power of the Celestial plane, then you can open a portal into that realm and bring her through. Just turn your amulet dial all the way to the final position with the dragon rune and she will appear. Simple!'

Xin was insistent, but Nico was a bit scared at the thought of summoning such a powerful and dangerous beast. 'Isn't that the dragon that buried Cyax in the ice?'

'Yes, the very same. But don't be afraid, she doesn't bite! Well, actually she does bite, but don't worry she probably won't bite you, young Dragon!' Xin's face broke into a smirk as he tried to stop himself from laughing at his own jokes.

'OK then, here we go' said Nico as he turned the dial slowly, click by click to its end stop, opposite the dragon rune.

With the sound of the final click still ringing in his ears a point of light appeared next to Nico, growing rapidly from its own centre. Rays of bright starlight burst out from this point in the same way as sunlight appears from behind a dark cloud. A shadow inside the light source expanded and came into sharp focus as the starlight beams faded away revealing the magnificent creature that is Adraxa.

Not being of this earthly plane, Adraxa's glorious dragon body seemed to shimmer as if she were made of some unearthly material. Xin might have suggested concentrated starlight, and he probably would have been right.

The Star Dragon drew her body up high, dwarfing the young Dragon Warrior that had just summoned her and studied him carefully for a moment, looking his spindly limbs up and down to assess Nico's physical qualities.

Adraxa turned to Xin, 'Hmm, if you don't mind me saying Xin, Dragon Warriors seem to be made of much less warrior material these days.' Nico was a bit crestfallen by this assessment of his stature.

Xin quickly spoke up in Nico's defence, 'You should know better than to judge a book by its cover my friend. This young man has many hidden properties. He will prove very worthy given time.'

Adraxa raised her head and then leaned her long neck downwards, positioning her huge head next to Nico's. Great spines spread out like a mane, or a crown from the back of her head and she stared directly into Nico's eyes. Nico shrank back nervously at first but couldn't resist reaching out his hand to touch the creature's beautiful shimmering dragon scales. She seemed solid enough and as the two looked into each other's eyes, Nico heard a rich velvety voice inside his head,

'Go on Nico. Climb up on my back and I'll take you for a ride.'

The Star Dragon lowered her neck further and Nico grabbed one of the spines around her head to haul himself up on to her back.

'Hold tight!' came the velvety voice once more as Adraxa launched herself skywards in an almost vertical trajectory. Nico wasn't expecting such speed as the dragon's flying ability was more to do with Dragon lore than any sort of aeronautical engineering, but he clung on tight and soon they were in level flight circling the base.

Down below Xin and the others stood and stared as the Star Dragon soared over their heads. Nico's Dragon Warrior armour protected him from the cold of the air rushing around them and as he grew in confidence, he lifted his upper body off the dragon's neck and adopted a more natural riding position.

'Take me down over the lake' he said and soon after they were gliding just above the surface of the water at speed, inches above the crests of the waves. Nico had to hang on tightly once more as the dragon suddenly surged higher to avoid colliding with some ducks flying in close formation.

'Take me back to the hay bales. Let's attack them,' he commanded his companion, and sure enough Adraxa turned tightly, speeding back at ground level towards the still smouldering piles of straw. Instinctively the Star Dragon turned away from the bales at the last moment, as Nico concentrated on summoning his dragon fire. In mid-turn, at the closest point to the target, he launched a jet of flames from his hand that hit the bales dead centre, and so intensely that they seemed to explode with energy. It seemed to those watching, that Nico and Adraxa both understood what they needed of each other, no conversation or explanation was needed. It was a kind of telepathy.

Nico had just learned that all the years of becoming a skateboard wizard were going to pay off, big time. His natural ability to glide through situations on four wheels translated perfectly into riding the back of a dragon. Moreover, he could simultaneously use his other skills. He felt his perception of time somehow slowed down, allowing him to concentrate his mind. Except that this time instead of stealing an ice cream from a small child, he had become an aerial flamethrower amongst many other things!

Self-confidence was now starting to flow rapidly through his mind, and he turned to take an aerial bow from the assembled crowd, who applauded him rapturously while Ben leaped up and down blowing loud piercing whistles through his teeth. 'Good on yer, Nico lad!' he roared while slapping his thigh.

Laughing now and gaining in confidence, Nico took Adraxa higher into the sky to perform aerial stunts, while weaving jets of fire and trails of smoke in the air.

'He's definitely a Dragon, a total show-off!' Ciara was starting to get fed up with Nico's antics but resisted the temptation to intervene and take him down a peg or two, at least for now anyway.

'No showboating Nico, you can't keep that up for long.' Xin shouted up at him, as he was well aware of the limitations of the human body when channelling celestial energies, especially for an inexperienced Astraxi Warrior. But Nico ignored him, soaring even higher and replicated some of his favourite skateboarding moves across the sky and around the buildings. The way his mind instinctively sculpted his skateboard trajectories also worked for his dragon flying manoeuvres. When he let the movement flow naturally, that was when it worked best, and if he paused to think about it, that's when it became clunky and less smooth. He was elated. Not for a long time had he felt such freedom and a sense of self-worth.

No sooner had he completed another high-speed circuit of Xin's laboratory, than something started to go wrong. He felt a wave of fatigue sweep across his entire body and his magnificent red and gold dragon scale armour disappeared abruptly. He sensed that he was in real trouble, flying too high and if he were to fall off, the resulting impact with the ground would certainly be terminal. He clung on to the Star Dragon with what little strength he had left, while trying to maintain his cool demeanour for the sake of appearances.

On the ground the rest of the Astraxi were unaware that Nico was struggling. In the middle of yet another tight turn his grip finally failed, his hands slipping off the spines he had been clinging on to. As the others looked on in horror, Phae reached for her Tiger amulet, while Nico tumbled out of the sky, to his certain death.

'*Tolar to candiso*' the spell came effortlessly from her lips as she transformed into the Tiger warrior. Nico closed his eyes as he plummeted, expecting the inevitable hard, final landing that would end his short life in an amalgam of blood, shattered bones, and crushed flesh.

To his great surprise he found himself decelerating until he was almost floating, like a feather blown out from a soft pillow, drifting gently earthwards.

Tiger Lore works around the principle of providing balance to the effects of sorcery, elemental energy, or even natural phenomena such as light and shade, and in this case gravity. Phae sprinted across the concrete and with a small leap plucked the featherweight Nico from the air, landing cleanly on her feet with him in her arms.

He had gone from being Dragon Master of the Skies to falling like a sack of potatoes.

'Phew, that was close,' he said, massively understating the danger of the situation from which he had been rescued by Phae.

'You overdid it,' said Xin, 'you need to be more careful Nico.'

'You were showing off and it went wrong more like it' replied Ciara acidly while Phae still had Nico in her arms.

'Maybe you should put him down now!' Ciara added with a raised eyebrow. Phae reacted and almost dropped Nico to the ground, embarrassed by Ciara's suggestion of some sort of affinity with the young dragon.

'Thanks Phae, but I really had it all under control,' said Nico without a hint of irony, as he stepped away from her, trying to find his composure and cover up his awkwardness.

Already smouldering with anger from Ciara's barbed observation, Phae rolled her eyes and snapped at Nico in disgust,

'Typical Dragon arrogance! A little gratitude would be nice!' She glared at him, her lips pursed, fists clenched and her amber eyes burning into him furiously.

Nico was taken aback by Phae's reaction but wasn't ready to acknowledge his mistake and not knowing what to say, just stood there trying his best to look cool. After staring at him for a moment hoping for some reaction or at least an acknowledgement or word of thanks for her quick intervention, Phae couldn't contain her temper any longer. Irritated by both Ciara and Nico's behaviour she lost control,

'Sometimes I wonder why I bother,' she said tersely while the others fidgeted, waiting for the scary, angry, man-eating version of the Tiger to be break loose. Instead, with a massive exhalation of frustration, Phae turned and stormed off in the direction of the accommodation blocks.

As usual Xin was the first to break the tension, 'Don't worry, she'll calm down and forget about it soon enough. You know it takes enormous energy Nico, to do all those things at the same time. Like any physical skill you need to build it up and learn to conserve your strength, otherwise you'll come crashing down again.'

Ben patted Nico firmly on the back. 'Oh man that was something else. Just watching you made me hungry!'

'You are always hungry!' Ciara was once more successful in getting the last word, which was something that really mattered to her. As one of the younger members of the group she didn't want the others to think she could just be pushed around or ordered about like some younger sibling or even worse than that ignored. Sometimes she was funny, but other times she was just irritating, which was why Phae had lost her temper.

'Come on then, let's get some lunch' said Xin herding the group together towards the accommodation blocks, where they would find Phae waiting in the small kitchen that he used to feed his team when their morale needed boosting.

Once more Nico heard the velvety voice in his head 'Farewell young Dragon, no doubt I will be seeing you soon.' As the dragon spoke, he looked upwards to see beams of starlight sparkle and carry her back to the celestial plane, where she usually lived. Nico stood and watched as the light faded.

By the time lunch was served, Phae had mostly forgotten about the argument with Nico and was musing over what she had seen the young man do that afternoon. It was impressive, more so than her own faltering early attempts at Tiger power. He was a bit younger than her and often she regarded boys as immature fools, but Nico had a certain charisma, something in his smile and his manner that she thought was cute and maybe even a little cool at the same time. He could sometimes be a little juvenile, but then again that's true of most teenage boys and grown men. She liked him, but more like a little brother than anything else.

Nico had been thinking about his ham-fisted response and lack of gratitude after Phae's intervention and joined her at the table to offer some sort of apology for his ingratitude.

'Phae, erm, I just wanted to say thanks, for… er, well what you did. I mean, you know… If I can return the favour some time… I'll be watching your back.'

But unfortunately for him, he didn't understand Phae's tigerish sensitivities, and all he managed to do was to quickly re-ignite her anger. Phae cut him off quickly and brutally,

'Honestly, do you really think I need you to watch my back. You can barely look after yourself!' and with that she stood up leaving Nico alone, staring at his lunch in contemplation of the tiger-sized strip she had torn off him. Being a super-hero it would appear had other dangers, particularly when it came to understanding the others.

CHAPTER 17
The Cup Of Souls

After his dramatic escape from the inferno that engulfed the Pagoda in Dendropol, Cyax returned to the citadel in Golterion. The skies over the Monastery darkened to the slate grey shade of an approaching thunderstorm, before a large panther-shaped cloud burst from it, descending at great speed into the central courtyard, throwing up dust and gravel in its wake. Almost as quickly as it arrived, the black cloud condensed into the solid figure of Cyax, with a mighty crack of thunder, but without the usual flash of lightning.

Cyax stood for a moment. He was, as he would have expected, completely unharmed and unmarked by being caught in the collapse of the Pagoda. With the Wand of Xylos now his to wield at will, he also planned to make use of his gift from the Four Fiends, the Cup of Souls. With two of the Five Weapons of Elemental Power now in his possession, he felt that the tide of this latest war against Astrellion was already turning in his favour.

In his previous battles with the Astrellian armies, he had united the forces of the Four Fiends with those of the various warlords, whose lands bordered the Kingdom. But these strange modern nation states, or republics, did not face their enemies in the same way. The warlords and their armies had long since vanished along with the ancient kingdoms of The Four Fiends.

A new kind of international order had brought peace to many lands, and although hostilities between Astrellion and Golteria had never formally ended, Cyax still needed to be able to summon sufficient warriors to support his plans for invasion. Fortunately, the Cup of Souls would provide a very potent solution.

While his colleagues were failing in their attempt to prevent the Wand from falling into Cyax' hands, Eduardo had followed Xin's orders to head north and infiltrate the Monastery, which was easily achieved as the three most dangerous characters were in Dendropol.

The various guards and CCTV monitors around the complex were no match for Eduardo's stealthy skills of disguise and he slipped into the heart of the citadel undetected. He spent his time there well, changing his appearance to gain the confidence of soldiers, imitating officials, and charming others to learn details of the plans to organise and execute the invasion of Astrellion. All this information he was feeding back to Ash in the command centre at the Astraxi's forward operating base while Nico was learning about his new Dragon skills.

Despite being a very young man, Eduardo was very comfortable in his role within the Astraxi. The power came to him easily and he used it in a skilful way that gave him confidence when working in dangerous situations. Normally Eduardo appeared cool, if slightly remote, but friendly and charming when you got to know him better. His emo-style green-tinged long fringe of dark hair that flopped forwards over one eye, gave people the signal that he was a bit shy but also approachable at the same time. This mission in the Dark City of Golterion was the sort of mission that Eduardo enjoyed most, a chance to work on his own.

The only thing he regretted about not going to Dendropol with the others was that he wouldn't have a chance to go back to the place where he had lived when he was a young boy, before his parents went missing. Being lovers of culture and archaeology, they had left Eduardo at his boarding school while travelling on an expedition to study South American indigenous tribal art. Sadly their aircraft went missing in a remote part of the rainforest, and although it was later discovered that they had survived the wreck, they both succumbed to their injuries before rescue teams could arrive.

By virtue of the power of the Wizard's table, Xin became aware that the young orphan was destined to become the next Snake Warrior of the Astraxi. One of Eduardo's close relatives took care of him for a short while, until Xin took him into the group and began his training in the Library of The Astraxi. It wasn't long before he showed great promise, using his skills to charm and entertain his new colleagues. Now he found himself in the very much less hospitable circumstances of Golterion City.

Having witnessed Cyax' dramatic arrival in the citadel at first hand and with Tanielka and Fong also having returned from Dendropol, Eduardo needed to be extra careful in his secret surveillance activities. This dangerous trio were much more capable than the soldiers whose minds he had been manipulating so easily, and their combined powers put him at a much greater risk of detection, capture, and whatever else they may do to him if he were caught. He shivered at the thought of it but remained focused on his task.

Later, using his '*Power of Suggestion*' Eduardo learned from one guard that Cyax was planning a special demonstration of the elemental power of the Cup of Souls in the main central courtyard, and despite the heightened danger he knew he should try to get himself in as close to this event as possible. Maybe after that it would be sensible to escape back to Astrellion and re-join the Astraxi.

During his brief stay Eduardo had found himself a safe hiding space in a residential part of the citadel that was little used, having once been the living quarters of some of Golteria's most senior government officials. To get to the central courtyard he would need to travel undetected, so his choice was to use either the low-risk tactic of simply being stealthy and blending into the surroundings, taking the opportunity to move when there was nobody around. Or more dangerously he could use his Snake Lore and move quickly, but risk running into a '*Detect Magic*' spell which may have been set as a kind of low-level security alarm or trap for a careless sorcerer. This was the sorcerer's equivalent of a trip wire.

Taking the riskier option would save time, so he decided to use his skills to move more quickly and hope not to be detected in the process. The choice of which of his skills to use was also two-fold, either to '*Disguise*' himself as some sort of Golterian guard or official, or to '*Shadow Walk*' to the courtyard. He decided that to '*Shadow Walk*' was probably the best option, given that he could disappear unseen into the gloomy darkness of the monastery's tunnels and passageways, moving rapidly via the shadows, before reappearing elsewhere and it would not involve any risky interaction with the Golterians.

He activated his amulet and stepped into the shadow cast by a door at the entrance to a corridor that would take him towards the heart of the citadel complex. Merging into the shadow he found himself in a strange twilight world, which seemed to be the inverse of normal lighting conditions, a bit like a photographic negative, with the same low contrast feel, flat and two dimensional. Since shadows are two dimensional then this should perhaps not have been a surprise.

To Eduardo's eyes areas of darkness now appeared light, so he could navigate easily to the next usable patch of shadow.

Eduardo's plan seemed to be the right choice, as within ten minutes he had made his way unseen past various guard posts and other groups of soldiers, via a network of intersecting shadows. The time of day helped too, as it was late in the afternoon and the shadows were getting longer, offering more options to the shadow-walker. He emerged into a dim, shady tunnel leading off the central courtyard in good time, as the courtyard was still being prepared for the event, but as he was about to blend himself into the back wall of the square courtyard, he was challenged by a Golterian guard.

'Who goes there?' shouted the soldier with his weapon raised. Eduardo maintained his cool, hoping that the soldier was just another of the weak-willed types he had met earlier. In his head Eduardo imagined himself as a colonel in the Golterian army and projected this thought pattern directly into the eyes of the soldier, who as Eduardo had hoped, put up zero resistance to the mind-warping power directed at him. Eduardo knew that attack was the best form of defence, any hesitation could prove fatal.

'Soldier, stand to attention when you address an officer, and what happened to your salute, I'll have you sent down for this' With his mind now totally immersed in Eduardo's charm, the soldier shuffled nervously and snapped to attention, 'Sir, yes sir!' he shouted before flashing a salute to Eduardo, who still had his gaze fixed firmly into the soldier's eyes.

'That's better,' said Eduardo with more than enough conviction to help carry off the effect. But as good as he was, Eduardo was not yet powerful enough a Snake Warrior to perform the *'suggestion'* charm on more than one person at a time. So, he had to think fast to get rid of this guy before they were discovered by another guard.

'Report to the guard room. I'll deal with you later.' The soldier nodded his head and flashed another salute before rushing off, his face twisted in anticipation of the harsh sort of discipline regularly meted out by Golterian officers to their subordinates.

Eduardo exhaled a deep sigh of relief and gripping his amulet tightly, he merged his physical shape into the stonework of the rear wall of the central courtyard. In this large space none of the guards on the surrounding towers would detect the ripple in the wall's texture as he moved his camouflaged body across it. Eventually he found a recess behind a large buttress in the wall in which he should be able to hide while watching Cyax' demonstration of the power of the Cup. He didn't have to wait long.

Cyax strode confidently into the courtyard from the entrance used by the leaders and high-level dignitaries. He was followed closely by Princess Tanielka and Fong, who in turn were followed by a collection of army generals, guards, and cabinet ministers of the state of Golteria. A platoon of cyber-demons had already lined themselves up in two rows near a ceremonial stage that had been erected in the centre of the courtyard. Other lower-level military and governmental officials were gathered either side of the stage to witness the power of the Cup of Souls for the first time in twelve hundred years. While the high-level observers took their seats on the upper part of the stage, Cyax remained on a lower part, a point from which he could be observed by everyone including Eduardo. Feeling very vulnerable indeed, Eduardo added a '*Non-Detection*' spell to his camouflage as a belt and braces measure.

To the Princess, Fong appeared to be in a state of nervous distraction. Something was bothering him. Tanielka thought that since he knew what Cyax was planning, having seen him use powerful weapons in the past, then the memories of that experience were making him feel a little edgy.

'Princess, if I may be excused for a moment,' he said as he headed off the stage and into the courtyard. Cyax seemed unconcerned at Fong's sudden departure. But Fong's unease grew as he left the stage. He had a feeling that energy other than Cyax' was at work that day, so he decided to walk the perimeter wall to see if that either dispelled his anxiousness or revealed an intruder.

Eduardo, still in his camouflaged state, was switching on his com-pad's camera to relay an encrypted video feed back to Ash when Cyax spoke.

'Bring the prisoner to me,' he commanded. A very unhappy looking man was brought forward in shackles. He was one of the Forest Folk, a guard in the service of the Master of Wands who had been captured during the engagement at the Pagoda. The man was pushed on to the stage by a cyber-demon and shuffled forward, his chains clanking, to a position just in front of Cyax, who looked at him closely in his emotionless cat-like manner. This unfortunate man was just the latest in a long line of the victims of Cyax. As he stared at his feet, he just hoped that whatever was about to happen to him would be swift and painless.

While continuing to glower at the prisoner, Cyax held out his hand and an attendant presented him the Cup of Souls, which had remained in its undisguised state since being presented to him. Nothing in its design suggested anything about what it was about to be used for. The smooth jade surface bore no clues or inscriptions, and the two dragons carved into handles with their tails entwined around the Cup's base, implied no special kind of dragon power and were perhaps a simple adornment given by the Cup's creator to hide the blandness of the powerful artefact's design.

Cyax wasn't interested in the aesthetics of the Cup either. His purpose was clear, he would use the power of the Cup to create the army he would need to conquer Astrellion. The crowd and Eduardo looked on silently, their eyes moving between the prisoner and the Cup. First Cyax drew in a long, deep breath and then exhaled over the top of the Cup, like someone cooling a hot drink, while maintaining his gaze on the prisoner's face.

A deep resonant sound like a bass pan pipe, came from the Cup as if to indicate it had been activated. A wide look of terror appeared in the eyes of the prisoner as he felt something being tugged from deep within him. From his open mouth a cloud of grey vapour was drawn towards the Cup. The prisoner panicked and tried to react to this but was powerless to prevent his life-energy being dragged from his body.

The grey vapour poured over the rim and into the Cup forming a swirling vortex, while drawing more of the nebulous vapour from the prisoner. The cloud condensed into a silvery, mercury-like liquid, inside the Cup, but the shimmering fluid had an energetic current flowing through it, causing it to churn around.

With a spasmodic heave from his body, the last of the grey vapour left the prisoner's mouth and he collapsed to his knees, being held up only by the shackles binding him. Ever since the moment when he had stolen the Potion of Eternity, Cyax had understood how to corrupt the life force of other beings to his own ends. Eduardo watched this scene in terror. For him sorcery was generally used for a good reason, either in self-defence or to help others, but not today.

Cyax kicked the lifeless body over with his boot and stepped over it to leave the stage and stand on the rough, earthen surface of the parade ground. Looking into the bowl the silvery fluid was still churning around, occasionally coalescing into something resembling the anguished face of the dead prisoner.

Cyax felt a deep satisfaction, the power of the Cup was working just as he remembered. He dipped his fingers into the silvery liquid and pulled out a few drops, which he scattered on the loose soil beneath his feet. He repeated this action again many times, placing the silver drops in different spots in front of the stage and watched them being absorbed into the earth.

He handed the Cup back to his attendant and raised his arms like a priest invoking a deity and uttered a spell in the ancient language of Astrellion, '*Morgai: Yoshara Finsun.*'

In the places where the drops had landed, the earth stirred as the elemental power of the Cup set to work. Scaly fingers clawed their way up through the soil, shifting the earth aside, to allow the heads and shoulders of the snarling demonic creatures to follow, emerging into the daylight. It didn't take the twenty beasts long to fully remove themselves from the earth in which Cyax had created them. They were the size of a small adult human and covered with a grey-brown clay-like flesh. Their deep-set yellow eyes had a look of intense savagery, while their mouths were filled with needle like fangs. On their hands long fingernails formed vicious looking claws.

The Morgai demons looked around themselves, trying to understand where they were, what was their purpose and who had summoned them. Exactly who was their master? In the moment, they stood like a pack of wolves, snarling, and poised, waiting for their leader to give them the sign to unleash the raw evil contained in their bodies.

The shocked crowd looked on as the Morgai leered back at them growling, nobody was really sure what was going to happen next, but the audience were very worried that these beasts would turn on them and a murmur of panic went around as people started looking for the quickest route to safety.

Calmly Cyax raised his arm and pointed to the platoon of cyber-demons who had remained at their position near the stage.

'Attack' he ordered, and the Morgai turned rabidly on the surprised cyber-demons who weren't ready for this assault. Blades and blaster weapons aren't much use when you have steely claws and needle like teeth tearing at your body armour and instinctively seeking the vital blood vessels in your neck. The cyber-demons were easily overwhelmed. Tanielka was fascinated and found it difficult to take her eyes off the scene,

'My Lord, the Morgai are most impressive.'

'Stop' called Cyax and without hesitation the Morgai broke off their attack on the platoon of cyber-demons, some of which had suffered mortal injuries while others were left lying on the ground with deep and nasty flesh wounds. A team of medics, who were standing by expecting a quiet afternoon, soon found themselves with an unexpected major medical incident on their hands.

Opposite the stage, Fong was continuing his walk around the perimeter of the parade ground. He had seen the Morgai at work during the Great Battle of Astrellion and did not need to be reminded of their effectiveness as a fighting force or their loyalty to the person who had summoned them from the earth. The creatures had an innate hatred of the living, especially humans, but even as a member of the undead, they were great a risk to him. His unease was still growing as he approached the buttress where Eduardo had concealed himself.

Something there caught his attention, a slight shimmer in the surface of the stones in the wall, a tiny refraction of the light that was almost imperceptible. Fong realised he was looking at the heat signature of the body warmth of a person or creature, which is how vampires usually detect invisibility in other beings.

Fong figured that he was probably twenty metres or so behind the potential invisible intruder and most likely had not been seen approaching. Using a '*Blink*' spell to improve his chance of surprising the intruder, he silently disappeared and re-appeared in almost the same instant, right behind the shimmering shape. He muttered the spell '*Intara*' under his breath, to break the invisibility and grabbed the person that was suddenly revealed, by the back of the neck.

Eduardo was unable to defend himself as he had been utterly caught out by Fong's surprise attack and instantly succumbed to Fong's '*Freezing touch*' which is one of the principal weapons of vampires against the living.

Eduardo fell weakly to his knees with Fong's grip firmly on his neck, the long fingernails digging into his skin. Fong recognised the Snake amulet and the com-pad relaying live video back to Ash. There was no doubt in his mind whom he had caught. He stamped on the com-pad smashing it to pieces and severing its data link to the Astraxi.

'My Lord. I have the Snake Warrior' Fong called out to Cyax and the crowd, who had started to recover from the grisly carnage they had just witnessed, As the Morgai waited for the next command from their master, Cyax strode over to Fong, picked Eduardo up with one hand, then tore the Snake amulet from his wrist. In his usual feline manner, he studied his captive before barking an order to a nearby guard.

'Lock him up, he'll be useful to us later.' Whatever Cyax had in mind for Eduardo, it wouldn't be pleasant. Without his amulet he was powerless, just a teenage kid with a long, floppy fringe and some very stylish clothing, but he hoped that Ash was aware of what had just happened, and that rescue would come soon. Eduardo felt his energy being drained. Vampire magic, probably. Fong, most likely!

Princess Tanielka joined Cyax and Fong, as Eduardo was dragged away in a semi-conscious state. Cyax' continuing run of success was starting to lift his mood, two elemental Weapons of Power and now he had the Snake Warrior complete with the Snake amulet.

Deep inside the Princess also felt a surge of excitement. Before she murderously removed her mother from the Golterian throne, Tanielka had already made her own plans to take the war back to Astrellion. It would have been very difficult and very costly in terms of resources, but as the ruling Princess of the Dark Empire of Golteria, it was what she was trained for and destined to do.

Now with the two elemental Weapons and the ability to raise an army of Morgai, in a very short period Cyax had lifted the Dark Empire's power to a whole new level. Together they were invincible and perhaps Cyax' quest for the return of his birth right was now within easy reach.

CHAPTER 18
The Calm Before The Storm

Nico had taken Xin's advice and was spending more time studying than he had ever done in his life. He had temporarily abandoned his skateboard in favour of the texts that the Library of the Astraxi's magical ladder was throwing at him as he whizzed up and down the dragon tunnel gripping its brass handrails. Quite a pile had built up on his reading desk and the more he read, the more he became wrapped up in Dragon lore. He could see the magical connections that previous Dragons had made and how they had built upon the work of the Dragons that had gone before them.

His thirst for knowledge had become almost addictive, as Nico found true purpose in his life for the first time ever. If Great Aunt Cass could see him now, she might have assumed that he was up to some trick to win her favour, but he wished that she could have been here to see that he had changed direction for the better.

Maybe she was watching him from somewhere because who knows what happens when a person passes away. The thought of Aunt Cass looking down on him made him feel better and even more determined to do his Dragon homework and practice his skills.

Maybe even his parents might be proud of him at this moment, but he still wasn't ready to get over the feelings of rejection he had where they were concerned. That part of his personality was neatly packaged away for the time being, until he had made something of himself and could impress them and make them regret having let go of him into Aunt Cass' care.

Today's book of choice was by an early Dragon in the history of the Astraxi, who was known as the Snow Dragon. It mostly concerned the Dragon lore that allows transformation of liquid water into other states or modes such as ice, snow, steam, clouds, mist, fog, and the myriad other ways in which water behaves naturally. It is a very basic but useful Dragon skill and can be used defensively either to create diversions, obscure your position, or slow down opponents.

In the reading room with Nico were Ciara and Ben, but when Nico started throwing droplets of water into the air and turning them into small flurries of snowflakes, they couldn't help but join in the fun. Ben chased the snowflakes trying to catch them in the air and watching them melt in his hands, before shaking off the water and running after more. His laughter quickly became infectious, so Nico made bigger flurries with larger amounts of water.

Ben was panting with excitement like a small dog that had discovered a new game. Being from a warm part of Australia it was highly unlikely that Ben had ever seen much, if any snow in his lifetime.

'This is great, I love this stuff!'

Nico filled a glass from a large pitcher and threw the water into the air above Ben's head. In Nico's mind he imagined snow, but much more snow than he had imagined before. Ben didn't have time to move out of the way as a massive dump of snow accompanied by a howling blizzard engulfed him from head to toe like a snowman.

There was a moment of silence before Ben burst out from the pile of snow laughing, with an enormous grin on his face, brushing the meltwater from his eyes and shaking his long hair to release the flakes.

'Make some more! Let's build a snowman.' Ben tried to gather up the snow, but Ciara decided to start a snowball fight instead. Whack! She hit Ben right in the face. But this was just sport for Ben, and he leaped forward to scrub Ciara's face with a handful of snow.

For once facing up to the responsibility for his actions, Nico felt it was his duty to re-establish order before things got out of hand. 'OK, that's enough. We don't want Xin to catch us throwing wet snow around all these old books.' He raised his hand and concentrating once more on the transformation of water into another state, he reduced the snow on the floor to pools of water and clouds of vapour. 'Oh man, I was enjoying that' complained Ben.

But Nico had something else on his mind. After his initial acceptance of all the exciting new things that were happening to him within the Astraxi, questions were forming in Nico's mind for which he would need answers. Questions like, how did the others join the group, what about their families and what was Xin's part in all of this?

'Ben, I meant to ask you something. How did you end up here, all the way from Australia? Haven't you got family there?'

Ben stopped brushing the snow from his clothes and his shaggy hair. He looked down at his feet for a moment while he tried to find the right words to tell the story of personal tragedy that had brought him into the Astraxi.

'Not much to say really. I never really knew my Dad. He often came and went without much in the way of an explanation. My mom never knew when he would turn up and he would never say where he had been or what he had been doing for months on end. Once when he came back, he seemed pretty shook up, as if he had got badly hurt or spooked by something. He had some nasty looking bruises, but he just covered them up and refused to answer any questions, saying he had fallen over and that he would be fine.'

'Last time I saw him, he patted me on the head and told me to be good for my mom and then he told our old sheepdog Rex to take good care of me. What seemed strange to me at the time was that the dog seemed to understand him.'

'Anyway, I never saw him again, but a few days later someone broke into our house, they were looking for something and started beating my mother up. Then they threatened to hurt me if she didn't tell them. But they just kept punching her asking where it was and eventually one of them hit her so hard that she fell and hit her head on the corner of the coffee table, and she didn't get up again.'

'Rex stepped in to protect me and I ran away as fast as I could and hid out in the bush. A few days later I got picked up by the local police and when I went to the station there was Xin.

He told me that neither of my folks would be coming back and that he would be taking care of me from now on. To be honest, I just didn't know what to think or do, so I went along with him. He seemed very kind and later he told me that my Dad was the Dog Warrior and that it was the Golterians who had been looking for his amulet, when they broke into our house. Then he brought me to Astrapolis and the Perpetual Motion Café, and you can guess the rest.' Ben turned away from the others. He didn't want to say any more as his big brown eyes misted over.

'Sorry I asked' said Nico sympathetically, when Ben turned back with a broad smile on his face.

'And here I am now, covered in snow!' he grinned, having shaken off the bad memories and returning to his usual waggy-tail humour.

'Oh yeah, sorry! Look, I was just wanting to get to know you guys a bit better. It seems that all of us were out on our own until Xin came along.'

'That's pretty much the way it is for all of us' added Ben with a shrug. It was true that the various members of the Astraxi were all young people, who had somehow become displaced, either by bad luck, or by losing their parents, or in Nico's case by being opted out of his family.

Nico wasn't sure if it was some weird property of the amulets or Xin's interventions that led to the Astraxi being a bunch of lost kids with nowhere to go and nothing to lose. And if they have nothing to lose, what does that mean for each of them? Were the Astraxi simply disposable pawns in a much larger battle? That thought disturbed him. He would have to ask Xin about that, hopefully the old man would be honest with him.

Ciara wasn't ready to start discussing her past with Nico, not here and now and decided it was time to have some fun using her own powers, which would also provide a distraction from this topic of conversation.

'Ben, if you like snow, then watch this!' She activated her amulet and waved her hands while imagining a snow scene in her head.

Nico and Ben stood in amazement, as the whole reading room started to fill with snow piling up in heaps on the tables and chairs, on the wooden floor and lining the display cabinets. It was as if an artist was using a brush to paint frost and snow across the scene stroke by stroke.

After a few seconds the scene was complete, the reading room had become a winter wonderland. Ben's eyes opened wide, and he rushed towards a pile of snow throwing himself in enthusiastically.

'Waaaaay!' he shouted. But as Ben hit the snow with a hard thud, he was left reeling backwards in pain gripping his midriff.

'Gotcha!' Ciara's eyes were lit up with mischievous joy and as she started to laugh the snowy scene melted back to reality, as if it had never been there. Such was the power of Ciara's illusion of snow, that Ben and Nico were totally convinced it was real.

'I hate it when you do that!' Ben was very angry. As much as he was generally a happy-go-lucky sort of character, the one thing that really upset him was when someone tricked him. His canine instincts of loyalty and working with his pack made him particularly sensitive to betrayal, even if it was just for fun.

To make matters worse, Ciara pointed her fingers out of the top of her head like a dog's ears and started to make barking noises.

'You're such a dingo Ben!' she teased. But as Ben launched himself at her to take his revenge, Xin, Phae and Ash entered the room.

'Nice to see you're all using your time constructively!' Xin shot a sharp glance at Ciara who immediately returned to her desk. He knew that if trouble broke out, it was almost always Ciara who was at the heart of it, either trying to make herself noticed by the others or just exercising her monkeyish mischievousness.

Despite her penchant for tomfoolery, Ciara was a good team player, but Ben needed to stop being manipulated by Ciara into situations that would always get him into trouble. His affable nature made him too easy a target for Ciara's mischief making, and she couldn't resist winding him up.

Xin often thought he should write a book on personality traits in people, because with four thousand years of managing the Astraxi's various foibles, he considered himself to be something of an expert in the human condition. It would be a very long book, if he ever wrote it. Xin gathered them around an unoccupied reading table.

'We think we've figured out a way to find the other two missing weapons of power. Phae will help me demonstrate.'

Phae produced an object about twelve centimetres in diameter that looked like a large pocket watch. It was fashioned from a pale precious metal, probably platinum and the upper surface was engraved with a yin-yang symbol surrounded by five rampant flying dragons chasing each other's tails. As it opened, the upper metal surface split into five segments which retracted into the shell in a spiralling motion.

Underneath the inner workings were protected by a glass cover that also retracted into the shell but in a very strange fashion. A hole appeared in the centre of the glass which spread out towards the edge until it disappeared completely, exposing the inside to the air. An amazingly intricate set of moving parts, cogs, wheels, pointers, glowing lights, and rotating discs were thus revealed.

In the same style as the Wizard's table, there were concentric rings etched with runes and magical symbols. In other parts of the device, it was possible to identify recognisable patterns of stars, the sun, the moon, and the five major planets Mercury, Venus, Mars, Jupiter, and Saturn. Some of the object's components were solid, while others seemed to be made from a glowing, ethereal sort of light which flickered and flowed around the dial.

'For those of you that haven't seen it before, this is the Sun-Moon device. One of the most interesting magical objects known to humankind, although some wizards find it a bit simple and pedestrian, and lacking in imagination, or so I am told. Invented by King Theokeis himself, apparently, although he never admitted this to me directly,' said Xin cradling the object in his palms.

As they examined the Sun-Moon, the wheels, and highly decorated dials spun in random patters, like a crazy kind of astrological timepiece that had a broken mainspring. The Sun-Moon had no other external fittings, such as a winder and appeared to have no means of power, other than two intertwined gemstones at its centre that were pulsing with red and blue light.

Xin made one of his more rhetorical observations, 'Nico, I see you have the DragonStone' Nico nodded in agreement as the ring glowed on his finger.

'Right then. Phae I'd like you to use the Sun-Moon to locate the DragonStone, but don't let the fact that you already know where it is, influence your control over the device.'

Phae turned a small thumbwheel that adjusted a pointer to indicate the planet Mercury, which is associated with the element of water. She then moved two of the concentric rings to line up a rune representing magic weapons, with another ancient Astrellian pictographic symbol representing the word '*place*' The one thing which she didn't need to physically adjust was the question in her mind 'Where is the DragonStone?'

For a high-level user like Phae, the Sun-Moon device can be used telepathically without any physical intervention, and because Phae's Tiger lore is based on bringing balance and harmony to the world, then she is very much in tune with the magical object created by Theokeis.

Cogs whirled and concentric rings rotated into new positions to indicate constellations and their positions relative to the planets. A glowing pointer appeared in the centre of the dial, like that in a magnetic compass and lined itself up in the direction of Nico. Two other smaller subsidiary pointers also aligned themselves in the direction of the young Dragon.

'Pass me the DragonStone Nico' asked Xin. Nico pulled the ring off his finger and threw it to his mentor. Xin caught the ring without any hesitation and the pointers of the Sun-Moon re-aligned themselves to point at Xin as he was now the bearer of the ring.

Phae spoke to explain to the others, 'So we can use the Sun-Moon like a kind of compass, but to find elemental weapons like the Blade of Astrellion and the Shield of Fire.'

"Yes, but the Sun-Moon can be used for a few other things too, like restoring order back to nature where it has been put in a state of disorder, which might help us in a battle with Cyax' added Xin.

'That's easy to demonstrate' He said throwing the ring back to Nico. Once more the pointers followed the trajectory of the DragonStone. 'Nico, you've been reading up about elementals. Do you think you could create a water elemental for me?'

Nico wasn't expecting to be called into any sort of demonstration of his lore, but Xin's request was a chance for him to show that he was taking his role very seriously indeed. He put the ring back on his finger and peered inside the soft glow of the topaz stone to find what he needed.

The ring had already read his thoughts and the image that formed from the swirling clouds within, was that of a small humanoid figure made from water. He transferred his gaze from the ring to the jug of water he had been using in his snow-making experiments and continued to picture the elemental in his mind.

The remaining water in the jug started to move, slowly at first, drawing itself up into a pinnacle in its centre. Then the pinnacle tore itself away from the rest of the water, before popping into a small humanoid shape that threw itself over the rim of the jug and landed with a slight splash on the table. Any loose droplets shaken off by the fall quickly rolled back and were absorbed by the humanoid figure, a water elemental, which stood quietly waiting for a command from its maker Nico.

Nico was fascinated that his powers had worked so well and was at a loss for words, peering through the elemental's body which distorted the light passing through it, as water naturally does due to its refractive index. But since it wasn't being commanded to perform any tasks, the elemental decided to explore the table, collapsing into a small rolling wave of water, sloshing around for a while, and then morphing back into a humanoid shape about twenty centimetres tall.

In her usual inquisitive manner Ciara decided she wanted to test the little figure by putting first a finger, and then the whole of her hand through its body, but the water flowed around her skin and reformed its shape elsewhere.

'Now watch what happens when we use the Sun-Moon' said Xin as he picked up the device and re-set its controls. First, he set the planet dial for Saturn and twisted the concentric rings to align the runes for the element of water, living beings and sorcery.

'So, the device is now set to harmonise with water elementals, but if we add the moon into the situation, then this happens' Xin lined up the moon with one of the thumbwheels and splosh, the elemental collapsed into a puddle of water on the table.

Ciara looked a little sad that her new toy wasn't playing any more. 'What did you do to it Xin?' she asked.

'The elemental's positive energy comes from water, I neutralised it with negative energies from the Sun-Moon. The natural balance of almost anything can be altered or restored by the Sun-Moon. In much the same way as Phae's Tiger lore works.' Xin handed the device back to Phae.

'So, what do we do now, Xin?' asked Phae.

'See if you can locate the Shield of Fire' he replied.

Phae used the thumbwheel to select the element of fire using the planet Mars but wasn't quite sure what to do next and gave Xin one of those enquiring looks that asks a question without needing any words to be spoken, and assumes the other person knows what you are thinking.

'Now add the sun to it, align the runes for magical weapons and '*place*' then let's see what comes out' said Xin in reply to Phae's silent question. Once again, the lights, gears and cogs of the device started spinning and other wheels shifted around indicating new patterns of stars, planets, and the phase of the moon.

The central arrow turned to new position, the direction of which was hard to define as they were deep below the surface of the earth in the reading room of the library. The other two pointers aligned themselves differently, indicating some sort of connected information that was not clear to an inexperienced user of the device. Phae was baffled by what she saw, not being able to discern any clues from the information being displayed.

Ash however, had recognised some of the patterns in the alignments of the pointers and other parts of the display. He asked a question out loud for the computer to answer,

'Mira, can you give us the location based on the polar co-ordinates encoded on the device?'

Without a moment's hesitation Mira responded, 'Yes Ash. That location is in Western Australia. North by northwest of Perth.'

'Good, save those co-ordinates Mira. Now Phae, dial in Venus to try and find the Blade of Astrellion.' said Ash. Phae turned the thumbwheel once more and set the device for the element of metal, which is governed by Venus, but nothing happened. The device didn't respond to her request and Phae stared at the device willing it to do something.

'Have you broken it, or does it need new batteries' teased Ciara. Ash reached over and took the device to get a closer look. 'It just stopped working' said Phae as if to clarify that she hadn't broken it, even though nobody would have suggested that was the case despite Ciara's comment. Ash examined the settings closely before suddenly handing it back to Phae.

'Nah, it's working just fine' he said, 'Test it on Nico again.' Phae re-set the controls for the DragonStone once more and the device immediately pointed to him. 'Turn it back to Venus again' said Ash confident that he had solved the problem without revealing his thinking to anyone else, because it was very obvious to him, while the others were mystified.

After Phae reset the device for the Shield of Fire it returned to its previous configuration with the same pattern of dials, pointers, and celestial objects.

'It's obvious, isn't it?' said Ash looking around at the blank faces, who were reluctant or too embarrassed to admit that they hadn't solved the puzzle for themselves. Xin cleared his throat and raised his eyebrows to Ash who fortunately knew Xin well enough to realise this meant that he needed to explain himself better.

'OK, I'll spell it out then. Both objects are in exactly the same place, Western Australia it would appear.'

Ben suddenly became animated at the thought of a trip to the land of Oz. 'Aah, looks like we'll have to go down under. Maybe we can get some surfing in too, while were on!'

Xin shook his head and rolled his eyes as the rest of the group burst into spontaneous laughter at Ben's first thought being about chasing some waves, never mind the fact that two highly dangerous magical weapons were hidden somewhere. Ben had already planned his leisure time and mentally packed his surfboard alongside his sunscreen.

At first, he was a bit put out by his friends' reaction, but there was no disguising his enthusiasm at the prospect of getting in the surf.

'What's the matter with you guys? You're such a bunch of stiffs!' But soon he realised that they were laughing with him rather than at him, and Ben's usual fun-loving nature returned with a bit of light-hearted pushing around.

'We'll need to move fast. Ash, when will Cygnus be ready for an away mission?' asked Xin.

'The repairs to the damage we took escaping from Dendropol are complete, there's just a few new software updates going in, so we should be good to go in the morning,' replied Ash in his matter-of-fact way of dealing with technology.

'Good. Listen everybody, be packed and ready to go. Report to the hub at 06 hundred tomorrow morning for a pre-flight briefing.' As the group dispersed Xin took Ash to one side.

'Ash, have you heard anything from Eduardo recently?' Xin was worried about the sudden end of transmissions from the Snake Warrior.

'Nothing since when the feed was cut off, Xin. I've got an alarm on his frequency, so if anything comes through, I will know straight away, and I'll contact you.'

Ash was already on the case and had Mira's advanced AI systems scanning video, audio, and text feeds from numerous sources at the same time to try and get any clues as to his condition.

'He really should have checked in by now,' said Xin, 'I've got a bad feeling about this. Keep me informed if anything changes.'

'Affirmative, Xin. I am on it.' Ash replied in his understated manner and headed off to the control centre to conduct more scans and data analysis.

Losing the Snake warrior to Cyax could be a serious problem if Cyax were to take control of his amulet and his powers.

CHAPTER 19
A Warrior Turns

After his successful demonstration of the power of the Cup of Souls, Cyax' focus was switched to the unhappy new prisoner he had acquired, Eduardo the Snake Warrior. It was a surprise to him that Xin had sent the young man alone on such a dangerous mission, and this reinforced the idea in his mind that despite their victory at the Great Battle of Astrellion, the Astraxi had never really recovered from the damage he had inflicted upon them that day.

He had been so close to victory, with the city on its knees, his armies running triumphantly through the streets, looting, and burning, despoiling everything in their sight. The King's Guard had been totally defeated by Cyax' superior tactics and his use of the weapons of elemental power. It was only the intervention of the Dragon Mage Drakeidis and the Star Dragon Adraxa that had caused his defeat and imprisonment in the glacier.

Now the Astraxi were reduced to a force of just six and judging by their appearance alone, they were six rather weak looking young people. Whatever had happened to the great warriors that had previously filled the ranks of the Astraxi, against whom he had to put up a real fight? Why was Xin training youths to do a job that had been the preserve of people with more experience of life?

He knew that the amulets were instrumental in selecting new Warriors, but what had changed the pool of possible recruits, what had so diminished them all? Maybe after four thousand years the blood lines had weakened so much that the amulets struggled to find suitable candidates. The celestial magic was still strong but maybe the human component was no longer as strong as it used to be. He concluded that this may be the factor that would finally tip the balance of power in his favour and secure victory.

Cyax considered this for a while and decided he would go and take a look for himself. One thing he would not do, was to underestimate either Xin or the captured Snake Warrior in all of this.

Well trained Celestial Warriors are always a formidable challenge, but with the Snake in his captivity another factor had shifted the balance of power slightly in Cyax' favour.

Golteria had a very clear legal code, where prisoners such as Eduardo were concerned. People might expect this 'miserable Astrellian spy' to be tried and most likely executed. But despite being intensely evil to the core of his being, some elements of civilised, almost law-abiding behaviour persisted in Cyax' personality. This included the need for a due process of law, even if the intent of that law was to support and justify his evil deeds. One might have described Cyax' character therefore as Lawful Evil.

The justice system in Golteria was designed to work entirely in the favour of the state. Random killing for the sake of it was not usually Cyax' way, he usually needed some justification when it came to deciding whom to kill, when or how, and for criminal cases a formal charge sheet had to exist. This could be a simple as defining the prisoner as an 'Enemy of the state of Golteria.'

The Golterian legal system automatically assumed guilt before innocence, which ensured that the burden of proving their own innocence was laid upon the accused. A trial wasn't always necessary if Cyax believed the evidence laid before him was sufficient to condemn the prisoner for whatever charge had been laid.

He did sometimes allow trial by combat for his own entertainment, but this was rarely chosen by prisoners, who knew how it would end, without much hope of winning. Some would take their chance in combat with Cyax' chosen champion, to get it all over with quickly. Anyone who entered these dungeons as a prisoner had a very high probability of never being seen again. This was the situation in which Eduardo now found himself, as he sat in his cold, dark cell.

Cyax took the spiral staircase built into the monastery's tower descending into the ancient dungeons where he had kept many thousands of wretched prisoners in the past. The small cells were hewn out from the base rock upon which the citadel stood. There was no comfort to be found here deep inside the cold stone walls and floors.

Torches illuminated each cell door that he passed, but he noticed that the current regime seemed to keep fewer prisoners than he would have expected. Maybe this too was a sign of weakness, perhaps like the Astraxi, the modern Golterians were also less formidable these days. Cyax was not a man to forgive any real or alleged transgressions and keeping his dungeons full was a good way of using terror to ensure loyalty amongst his subjects.

Power struggles in the ranks of Golteria were very common and usually deadly, as it was widely believed that anyone who had been successful in enhancing his or her position by using underhand tactics, should be rewarded, and encouraged as it kept people on their toes. The downside of this was that every now and again a purge would take place that would put honest people in the dungeons and deplete the country of some of its best minds. Maybe this was why there were fewer prisoners in modern times, but Cyax did not understand this.

When he reached the most secure level of the dungeon complex, Cyax spoke to the gaoler. 'Take me to the Snake Warrior, I wish to interrogate him personally.' The gaoler nodded and gathering up the cell door's electronic keys he indicated to Cyax to follow him. As they stood at the door, the gaoler nervously tried to open it using the electronic tag, but with no success. Panic fogged his mind as he started to imagine what Cyax might do to him if he failed to open the door quickly.

After a few tense seconds Cyax pushed the gaoler to one side and raised his gauntleted fist. The gaoler flinched expecting a fatal blow, but as he dropped to his knees, Cyax smashed the lock and kicked the door open. With another firm kick Cyax sent the gaoler sprawling over the floor, after which he crawled back to his post.

Cyax entered the room, where a pale and haggard looking Eduardo was hunched up on his bed. He pulled up the cell's rickety chair and set it next to the roughly finished bare wooden table in the centre of the room.

'Sit' he commanded. Eduardo lifted himself slowly off his bed and settled into the chair while Cyax continued to stand, studying the teenager carefully.

This boy didn't conform to any of Cyax' usual expectations of a great warrior. He was not small, but neither did he appear physically powerful in any way, but then again as a Snake Warrior his role was not necessarily about his prowess in combat.

He would most likely be using his powers and his skills of stealth, disguise, and mind control to affect events in any kind of conflict.

None of that really mattered right now as the question foremost in Cyax' mind was what he should do with the young man, what advantage could he gain from this situation? He could just kill him and take the Snake amulet for himself, or he may be able to use the boy to further his own ends, either as a hostage or maybe something even more useful than that. He drew up the other chair in the cell, sat down opposite Eduardo and drew the Snake amulet from his pocket.

'This amulet, I suppose that in the few years you've been using it, you haven't experienced the full range of its powers?' Cyax looked directly at Eduardo menacingly and turned the dial to the right, but nothing happened. Eduardo wasn't quite sure how to react, he knew that Cyax had some ability to use the amulets because of his consuming of the Potion of Eternity, but that was where his knowledge ended.

Without Cyax as a regular enemy, the Astraxi's training in such situations was in many ways incomplete, compared with previous eras when he had ravaged Astrellion, and the risk of capture of a Warrior or loss of an amulet was much higher.

Eduardo remained silent feeling that there was little he could say that would change his fate and looked down at his hands, while hiding his eyes behind his long fringe to try and retain some mental distance between himself and Cyax. He may not have his amulet, but he still understood how his mind could be manipulated and was trying to avoid being drawn by Cyax into revealing the secrets of the Astraxi's operations.

He withdrew further into his own mind space, an internal fortress behind which he hoped to defend himself mentally and retain control of his thoughts. He dispelled all thoughts of his friends and his life in the Astraxi, locking them into sealed, hidden compartments and cleared his mind of everything else, leaving a void that even if it were invaded, there would be nothing for the invader to read.

Cyax contemplated the silent young man before turning the outer amulet ring once more, but this time to the left and grabbed Eduardo's wrist while speaking an incantation in the ancient magical language of Astrellion:

Sinar, til xorin disexeis
Sinar, kai en guerro, Eduardo
Komaneis en mando si terro
Sinar, kai en guerro, Cyax

The amulet became active in Cyax' hand, as the glowing particles of magic flowed out from the snake image at the centre. The lights flowed through the air, as if guided along invisible lines of force between the amulet and Eduardo. Within seconds Eduardo was surrounded by the glowing lights. Snake scales rippled across his skin until eventually he was entirely covered by them.

The glowing particles then gathered around Cyax, whose features also started to ripple with snake scales. Eduardo struggled with the transformation, as it broke down his mental fortress, knocking out many of the sealed secret compartments and laying his thoughts bare to Cyax, who now appeared in his mind, overwhelming his personality.

Cyax released his grip on Eduardo's wrist, and the young man slumped briefly to the table gasping for breath and shuddering after the effort of trying to keep Cyax out of his mind.

Most of Eduardo's defences were easily smashed to pieces by Cyax' mental battering ram but he didn't make it all the way through to the carefully disguised final cell. Eduardo was defending his own essential self, by hiding behind one of the smooth bricks in the walls that made up the complex maze he had built inside his mind. But it didn't matter that the essence of Eduardo's personality was still safely hidden, Cyax had what he needed, he had control of Eduardo's lore and his knowledge.

With the Snake amulet and the Warrior to do his bidding he would be able to combine the young man's powers of disguise with his own enormous magical strength, to be able to mount an attack on the Astraxi.

After a few seconds Eduardo lifted his head off the table, pushed himself upright in his chair and staring directly at Cyax said just one simple word 'Master.'

Eduardo had been 'turned' and now the Snake Warrior was completely under Cyax' control.

A more experienced Snake Warrior may have been able to resist for longer, but Cyax figured that this young man would be no match for the brute strength of his ancient magic, and he was right.

Cyax left the cell taking Eduardo with him. He followed in a manner which was a little emotionless, lacking any spirited movement, but was essentially normal. Nothing had changed physically about Eduardo, but deep inside he was hidden in a sort of prison of the mind, to which only Cyax held the key, unable to express his own thoughts, wishes or actions in any way,

They ascended the spiral staircases to join Princess Tanielka and Fong in the large state room of the Monastery that had become the nerve centre of their plans to put Golteria on a war footing with Astrellion. Further boosted by his latest success in turning the Snake, Cyax had decided to accelerate his plans and strike the Astraxi while he had the upper hand.

'Princess, what is our state of readiness?'

'My Lord, a wing of our cyber-attack aircraft is ready and at your command, as are strike troops, cyber-demons and a squad of Morgai' she responded eagerly.

'Excellent. At first light put the Morgai into transports and we will begin the first phase of our plan. I had not quite appreciated just how weak the Astraxi had become in my absence. Now is the time to draw first blood.'

The Princess bowed her acceptance of Cyax' command with a discreet smile of satisfaction, 'All hail Cyax, the one true King of Astrellion' she called out before leaving to fulfil her master's command for another strike deep into Astrellian territory.

CHAPTER 20
Conflict Begins

Early in the morning, before they were due to embark on their away mission to locate the Shield of Fire and the Blade of Astrellion, Xin and Ash had gathered with the others in the base's central hub to discuss and review Eduardo's lack of contact and probable capture. On the screen in front of them Ash was playing back the video feed which was the last contact they had before things went silent.

'Still no sign of him and no clue as to what happened,' said Ash as he shuttled the video backwards and forwards.

'Wind the recording back further, use the AI to filter out anything that would be normal and let's look for anything that involves Cyax, Fong or the Princess with a five-second handle either side,' said Xin. Mira very quickly reduced the long video stream to one clip of Cyax' demonstration in the courtyard and Eduardo's apparent arrest by someone who had surprised him and cut the video feed. Xin didn't give anyone time to dwell on this moment.

'Ash, wind the recording back, I want to see what Cyax is up to.' The reverse double arrow button flashed on the screen and the pictures skipped backwards rapidly like a speeded-up stop-motion movie.

'Hold it right there,' Xin pointed to the screen at the moment when Cyax raised the Morgai from the earth and mercilessly set them on the cyber-demons standing nearby.

'Morgai,' said Xin, 'he's building an army. This is much worse than I had feared. Wind back further.' As the pictures skipped back to show the prisoner standing in front of Cyax, Xin asked Ash to stop once more. A freeze frame this time showed the Cup of Souls raised in Cyax' hands.

'Yes, the Cup of Souls. I suppose I should have known that Taotie would give it to Cyax. We have no more time to lose, we must leave for Australia to secure the other two weapons immediately.'

'But what about Eduardo' said Nico, who couldn't shake the thought of the Snake Warrior's capture from his mind.

'There's not much we can do for him right now. Our priority is to secure the other weapons before Cyax gets them.

Ash, prepare Cygnus for immediate departure. Everyone else gather your away mission kits and be ready to leave in thirty minutes.'

But before they could head for the exit, the mood of quiet anticipation was shattered by a series of explosions across the airfield. Alarms sounded as Astrellian military personnel ran for cover from the surprise attack.

'Mira, what's happening?' demanded Xin.

'On your screens now, we're being attacked by Golterian forces,' replied the computer, with just a hint of pre-programmed emotional tension in her voice.

They rushed for the windows but had to take cover as another explosion blew glass everywhere. A large formation of cyber-attack fighters had materialised in the skies and was attacking the base, while a group of part-machine, part-creature cyber-assault craft were landing in their typical vertical manner at the far end of the airfield disgorging troops on to the ground.

Anti-aircraft fire swung into action to defend the base, but it was too late, as the Golterian fighter aircraft strafed and destroyed them easily with their energy weapons using the element of surprise to great effect. Diving from great heights, some of the attack craft released explosive drones which swarmed across the base.

'Where did they come from Mira? How did they get past the defences?' asked Xin as he tried to decide on the best course of action.

'That is unknown Xin. Either a spy has infiltrated the base and compromised the sensors, or possibly Eduardo was coerced into providing them with a means to avoid detection,' answered Mira in a way so as not to pass judgement on the Snake Warrior.

Things were deteriorating rapidly for the desperately unprepared Astrellians. A safety protocol on board Cygnus had already activated her cloaking device and defensive shields, offering protection from the aerial assault.

"Come on, we need to get aboard Cygnus now!' shouted Xin as he led the Warriors to the flying ship. He knew that if Eduardo had been turned by Cyax, this would be a grave setback for the Astraxi.

Bounding towards the ship, Ash spoke into the small comms device on his wrist. 'Power her up Mira, all systems, route extra power to the shield generators. They won't let us go easily!'

On the concrete open spaces, they could see squads of cyber-demons racing from their ships to engage the Astrellian ground troops. One particularly large transport arrived after the others and as it settled to the ground the squad of Morgai demons created by Cyax poured out to wreak havoc on the base and spread terror amongst the defenders.

Astrellian military aircraft were being destroyed as they sat on the ground, while those that managed to scramble into the air were being hunted mercilessly by the attacking Golterian cyber-fighters.

Surrounded by fire, explosions, and wrecked vehicles the Astraxi sprinted to where Cygnus was waiting in her cloaked state, invisible to eyes and most types of technology. Ash remotely activated the ship's rear air-stair, which seemed to just drop out from under her invisibility cloak and hang in mid-air. But before they could make it to the ladder, several cyber-demons appeared and blocked their way.

Without the need for an order from Xin, the Astraxi activated their amulets and transformed into their fighting warrior mode. Xin squared up to the cyber-demon in front as Phae leaped over his head, ready to tear into the mechanised demonic creatures. She knocked one to the floor with a flying kick to its midriff and wheeled around rapidly to engage another only to find Xin already beating it into a stupor with his staff. But the dangerous creature was resilient and wasn't going to be subdued easily.

With almost zero combat experience, Nico found it hard to know what to do in this situation, things were moving so fast. With more Golterian forces heading in their direction he stood like a rabbit in the headlights for a moment, before raising the DragonStone in his hand and roasting a cyber-demon with a burst of Dragon fire.

Despite its most savage intentions, the one remaining cyber-demon was no match for a very angry Tiger Warrior, and Phae despatched it by kicking it hard into its chest and smashing its helmet open before ripping out its life support system and shoving it down the creature's throat.

'I see you're getting the hang of this now Nico!' said Phae with an approving nod of her head as she wiped the breathing fluid of the dead cyber-demon from her hands. She stood over the creature's body without the slightest sign of remorse.

'Not sure I want to pick a fight with you any time soon!' Nico half joked in response.

Meanwhile Ash had used the commotion to get himself safely aboard Cygnus and prepare for a quick getaway. A larger group of cyber-demons arrived on to the scene splitting the Astraxi into two smaller groups. Under heavy fire Phae, Ciara and Ben were split away from the others and forced to run for cover behind a small group of buildings on the edge of the airfield. Xin and Nico were driven back in the opposite direction off the base and towards the rough terrain at the centre of the island below the mountain.

Ciara was the first to react using her powers of illusion. In her mind she imagined that she, Phae, and Ben had emerged from behind the building and were running off towards the research labs. The cyber-demons were completely fooled and chased after the illusionary Astraxi, aiming volleys of blaster fire at them.

Pausing to take cover from an attack drone, Xin and Nico crouched behind a low wall. Xin reached for his communicator, 'Ash, protect Cygnus. get her out of here. We'll rendezvous later.'

'Affirmative,' acknowledged Ash and with a high-pitched whine of her engines and a rush of hot jet exhaust, Cygnus rolled forward invisibly on to the tarmac ahead of the airstrip. The huge wash of thrust from the cloaked ship knocked down a group of cyber-demons that were approaching, allowing Xin and Nico to escape through a gap in a nearby perimeter fence.

Ash didn't have much time to get airborne, as Cygnus' cloaking device couldn't hide the effects of her engines, which were blowing debris from the attack all around the airfield.

A Golterian pilot realised this must be a cloaked vessel and took his opportunity to launch a volley of missiles just as Cygnus launched into a very steep climb, using all her available power in a very short take off space. Fortunately for Ash, Mira was monitoring any potential threat and brought the ship's countermeasures into play just in time to see the missiles diverted into the ground in a massive explosion.

But other Golterian pilots saw the same opportunity and shortly afterwards many more missiles rushed towards the invisible ship, snaking through the skies at hypersonic speeds, targeting her engines' heat signature. Cygnus' countermeasures were working hard to defend her, but the attack was intense, and one missile exploded perilously close to Cygnus, scattering shrapnel across her defensive shields.

A metal fragment tore into one of the field emitters generating Cygnus' invisibility cloak. For a moment a large part of the ship flashed in and out of view as Mira tried to stabilise the cloaking field, while Ash attempted to fly his way out of trouble. Warnings, both visual and audible, were ringing insistently in the flight deck, but in his cool and logical way Ash was managing the ship's complex systems to stay in control, reinstate the cloak and avoid being shot out of the sky.

Despite Ash's best efforts, the field emitter couldn't be brought back online and a cascade effect across the other emitters took them all offline simultaneously. Cygnus was now fully visible to all attacking aircraft. Mira revealed the desperate truth of their situation in a very minimalist statement, 'Incoming. Two missiles. Cloak and shields offline.'

'OK, taking evasive manoeuvres, make sure everything's locked down.' Ash hit the throttle controls and pulled Cygnus into a seemingly effortless rapid climb by diverting the anti-gravity field. Despite her size and multi-purpose design, Cygnus was surprisingly agile in the air because of the advanced lightweight materials used in her construction and the very high power to weight ratio that her combined engines and anti-gravity system could provide. Cygnus had been designed as a clean machine, drawing her power from a compact fusion reactor and fuel cells, producing only water vapour in her exhaust. Solar power could also be generated by light sensitive structures in her body shell.

Ash rolled Cygnus hard to the right moments before another missile passed close to the starboard wing exploding and scattering another deadly cloud of fine shrapnel particles. There was no time to take stock, Ash instinctively threw Cygnus into a power dive, before rolling away once more as a second incoming missile hurtled towards them, exploding close to Cygnus' main thrusters and control surfaces.

The ship lurched and swayed as Ash battled to regain control, but the aerodynamics of Cygnus' flying surfaces were complex, and as a result of damage, the computer assisted flight controls were not fully responding as usual to Ash's input. As he battled with the joystick, the situation deteriorated rapidly with the ship falling out of the sky in a flat spin, rotating horizontally like a giant boomerang. Fortunately for Ash the axis around which the craft was spinning was roughly in line with his command position, reducing his disorientation.

Ash realised with his laser sharp mind, that despite his excellent flying skills, this was not a state he could escape from on his own. With the damage to the control surfaces unknown, and the ship not responding to his commands in the normal way, it was time to let the Artificially Intelligent Quantum Supercomputer, take control of the flight dynamics, while he defended them from incoming fire.

'Control surfaces aren't responding to manual input. You have flight control Mira, give me the weapons.'

'Confirmed. I have flight control. You have weapons control,' replied Mira in her cool professional tone.

Ash briefly looked out of the flight deck window as the mountain at the centre of the island kept flashing past his line of sight, with the sea getting closer by the second. The altimeter was counting down rapidly as they plummeted earthwards.

Cygnus shuddered once more as Mira realigned the thrusters and shocked the aircraft out of its flat spin. Ash quickly reset his console for weapons and pulled on his targeting headset, trusting his intelligent electronic colleague to calculate the best possible trajectory to defend against the enemy attack.

Mira made probability estimates based on the telemetry of all the enemy aircraft she had been tracking simultaneously. To determine their possible future vectors she adjusted the calculations using an algorithm that analysed each pilot's preferred attack pattern and then calculated a flight path that would make it as difficult as possible for the attackers to shoot them down. It would have taken a team of statistical mathematicians many weeks to do what Mira managed in a nanosecond!

'On the best current trajectory, our probability of being shot down currently stands at thirty-two-point six five percent' announced Mira.

As Ash took out another Cyber-fighter with the laser cannon, she made another announcement. "Probability of destruction now down to eighteen-point five three percent.'

'I think we can cope with those odds Mira,' said Ash calmly.

The targeting headset that Ash was wearing was the only one of its kind in existence, as he had in fact designed it for his own exclusive use. Connecting wirelessly to an implant in his skull, it fed information from Cygnus' sensors in a way that allowed him to have a fully three-hundred-and-sixty-degree view of the airspace around the ship.

A special neural connector interfaced directly with his optical cortex via a laser data link, which meant that its images were being read directly inside his head. Ash however, had had to spend many hours in training, learning firstly to interpret and understand the signals and images he was receiving from the headset and then many more learning how to deal with the immersive three-dimensional view that he had acquired.

He didn't need to turn his head to see what was happening over his shoulder, he could see targets in all directions at the same time, which was an extremely difficult skill to acquire, almost like stepping back inside yourself and looking out again with an extra pair of eyes.

If that weren't enough Ash also used two joysticks on the arms of his pilot's chair, which allowed him to operate two weapons systems at the same time, in an ambidextrous way, a skill he had acquired by simultaneously playing two characters in stereoscopic computer shoot-em-up games. The next stage of development was for him to be able to operate the weapons controller with just his mind and zero physical input, but that was still in the experimental testing phase.

For the incoming fighter aircraft, Ash's combined human-computer weapons interface was a game changer, a game which they would certainly lose. A blink of his eye was all he needed to lock weapons. Within moments he had taken out two more cyber-fighters that were coming in blind, straight out of the direction of the sun and then locked himself onto another heat-seeking missile that was targeted on

Cygnus' main thruster. With a squeeze of the trigger, Ash fried the missile with Cygnus' pulsed energy weapons before it could explode in a burst of devastating shrapnel.

Meanwhile Mira had regained full control of the aerodynamics and with a steep banking turn the ship pivoted over one wing and opened her throttles fully to escape further attack.

'Nice flying partner!' said Ash as he surveyed his 3D world for more fighters.

'Nice shooting!' replied Mira.

Ash smiled to himself. He and Mira were a close partnership. To him Mira was as much a living being as any of his colleagues in the Astraxi. She may have circuits and programming where people have flesh and bone, but that didn't matter to him, he was very attached to her. Despite his special powers and personal heritage stretching all the way back to King Theokeis, Ash preferred technology to people because of the strange, unpredictable things that happen when you get too personally involved with them.

But another explosion close to Cygnus' tail rocked the ship once more and shook Ash out of his self-congratulatory state of mind. He had relaxed for a moment and nearly got them shot down. Ash acquired the two new targets with his headset and destroyed them, but Cygnus was now losing airspeed, and one of the main thrusters was working at less than fifty percent. With smoke coming out of the back of the ship, they were sitting ducks.

'We need the cloak back up Mira. Cygnus can't take much more of this.'

'OK Ash, diverting power, trying again.'

Ash re-engaged the cloaking device, but it was only partial and the sight of such a large craft flashing in and out of sight made it even easier for the Golterians to track them.

'This isn't working. Take over the defences as well for now. Give me the core systems display in my helmet Mira.'

Streams of data and sections of computer code replaced the targeting view that he had used to shoot down their enemies. Ash was using his mind in an interactive way to manipulate and divert the data flow in the same way as he was able to operate the ship's defensive systems.

He scanned more than one set of commands at once, his nimble mind could rapidly skip across the code while looking at whole blocks of characters rather than individual words. He didn't need to read the individual strings of characters, by studying the overall shape and pattern of the data he could spot any anomalies in the core system's programming.

Ash suddenly started shouting in a way that was completely counter to his usual calm, logical self. 'Mira, the cloak. It's missing a command string!'

'Are you sure? I ran a diagnostic...' but before she could finish speaking Ash cut her off.

'This is not the time for a discussion, Mira. RE-INSERT THE LATERAL EMITTER COMMAND STRING AT LINE 20970. DO IT NOW!'

Mira didn't pause for a microsecond, 'Code Insertion Confirmed, Ash' A line of new code shot across Ash's display headset as he re-engaged his targeting mode in time to shoot down another enemy fighter.

To the unaided human eye, Cygnus shimmered briefly in the sky before appearing to evaporate like a light cloud of soft fog in a breeze. As the ship disappeared from the Golterians' means of detection, more warning alarms started to ring out on the bridge.

'Let's put Cygnus down somewhere safe, while we still can. Give me manual flight control Mira.'

'You have control Ash, Cloak and shields are back online. What do you want to do about the others?' asked Mira.

Ash understood his clear order from Xin. He knew he need to protect the ship, while also trying to help his human colleagues but getting shot down in the process wouldn't serve anyone he reasoned.

'We're not equipped to take on an entire wing of the Golterian air force on our own Mira. So, let's just stay out of trouble for now. Scan all frequencies to try and find out what's happening to the others.'

'Monitoring all comms channels and searching for a safe landing site Ash.'

As Cygnus swept away, the few remaining Astrellian fighter aircraft were losing the fight and were forced into a tactical withdrawal to save their machines for future battles, leaving the base to be overrun by the invaders.

Ash sank back into his pilot's chair to consider what had just happened. Cyax had only been free of the ice for a small number of days and already there had already been two acts of war by Golteria against the peaceful nation of Astrellion, without provocation or warning. This was just the opening act in a much bigger conflict to come. How would the Astraxi recover from a devastating attack that had split the team wide open?

CHAPTER 21
Retreat

Back on the ground Phae, Ciara, and Ben had moved from the spot where they had encountered the cyber-demons into an area of the base where they figured they might be able to join up with the Astrellian forces that were resisting the attack.

To avoid detection, they circled around the rear of the main complex hoping to be able to gain access to the command centre and take shelter from the air attack and artillery barrages. From their position they could see cyber-demons swarming around the buildings destroying things in an almost random fashion, not considering whether any of it may be of value to them later.

Some cyber-demons were using their limited magical powers to throw open locked doors and move large objects around like toys. Others were using their embedded cyber-technology such as infra-red vision or energy weapons in a more conventional approach to warfare. But because they were essentially modified magical creatures, with the chaotic nature that brings, the cyber-demons were too ill-disciplined and were just as likely to fight amongst themselves as to attack the Astrellians. The defenders used this to their advantage by confusing their enemies and springing traps on them.

Phae spotted an opportunity to make a run for the command complex, which was not yet overwhelmed by invaders. In these instances, Phae was a truly inspirational and brave leader, brimming with confidence and taking everyone with her on whatever journey she was starting. Phae didn't always know how these things would work out, but her speed of thought and belief in her own abilities and her sheer tenacity usually led to a successful outcome. This *Shield of Faith* was part of her special powers when she was using her amulet and she didn't need to cast a spell for it to be active and inspiring those around her.

Nor did she let previous failures cloud her decision making, and at this moment the tragedy of her role in Eleni's death was far from her mind. With a simple gesture she signalled her young companions to follow her, ducking down low and running at full speed towards the entrance, while taking cover behind parked vehicles. As well drilled members of the Astraxi, Ben and Ciara were perfectly synchronised with her movements and the trio made ground quickly towards the building.

But as they rounded the last piece of cover, Phae realised that she had made another potentially deadly error of judgement. The reason why the building was not under attack was that it had already been captured by the Golterians. The three warriors almost fell over each other as the door opened to reveal Tanielka flanked by two snarling Morgai and three cyber-demons. The three projected a star shield as the Princess fired a volley of shots from her raised blaster, which caused a vile green light to ripple across the shield's glowing golden surface.

'The Tiger's mine' said Tanielka relishing the chance to take on Phae personally.

The Morgai reared up to attack, hurling themselves savagely at the star shield but were burned by the powerful celestial energy as they attempted to thrust their claws through the shield's surface and retreated to their mistress' side growling with anger and frustration.

'Someone, do something clever — anything!' Phae was still reeling from the unexpected arrival of the Princess, but Ciara was already anticipating trouble and was ready for action. In training Xin constantly reminded the Warriors that they were always strongest when they worked together.

'*Agari signa Astraxas*' she cried out loud. Instantly the three cyber-demons were transformed into perfect replicas of the three Astraxi. The transformed demons were completely fooled by the illusion cast on them and started fighting amongst themselves. The Morgai didn't need an excuse for a fight and started tearing into the transformed cyber-demons anyway. Tanielka was distracted by the commotion around her, which gave Phae enough time to make the call to escape.

'Head for the escape shuttles – GO!' The three sprinted back in the direction they had come from, towards the escape pods situated by the edge of the command centre.

'Move you fools' shouted Tanielka at the group of cyber-demons involved in a savage fist fight in front of her.

Summoning her own special powers, she raised her hands and spoke the spell

'*Demeto valfare'* shattering Ciara's illusion and returning the three cyber-demons to their normal state, except that they were even more confused at what had just happened and continued their fight amongst themselves anyway.

However, the Morgai had no such problem and chased the three escaping Astraxi, bounding along using their long forearms to add more speed. Tanielka, still brandishing her energy weapon also joined the chase.

It wasn't far to the shuttles, but far enough for Ben to gain quite a lead over the others. When in his Dog Warrior state, Ben possessed the ability to run very fast indeed, as quick as or maybe even quicker than any wolf in the hunting pack that he could summon at will using his canine lore. He arrived first and leaped into a small cylindrical pod that looked like a missile that had been modified to carry a human payload rather than an explosive warhead.

'Hit the pairing button Ben' called out Phae as she followed Ciara, looking over her shoulder at the rapidly approaching Morgai, followed by Tanielka.

'Sure thing Phae!' he responded. The escape shuttles were necessarily designed to be as simple as possible, to allow anyone to use them without training. Ben hit the large red 'power up' button and the yellow pairing button next to it. This second button remotely booted-up the systems of the other shuttles standing nearby, reducing the time needed to launch.

As he strapped himself in, control screens flickered into life, and he felt the rumble of a rocket motor firing up underneath him. Two seconds later he was hurtling skywards, being pushed down into his seat as the g-forces squeezed the air out his lungs. He gasped for breath and looked out of his window to see Ciara and Phae arrive on the concrete pad below, as their pursuers were catching up with them.

Without thinking Phae lifted Ciara off the ground and dropped her into the first escape shuttle they came to.

'*Yoshimo!*' she called out and made a gesture towards their attackers, circling the palms of her hands in opposite directions and drawing a spiral shape in space.

A trail of blue light followed one hand and a trail of red light followed the other evolving into large slowly rotating spiral made up of the two energies and blocking the entrance to the shuttle launch area. The Shield of Harmony easily absorbed Tanielka's weapons fire as she blasted it repeatedly.

Ash was particularly fascinated by this magic, as he was curious about whether Tiger lore or indeed any form of sorcery, obeyed the laws of physics. Every now and again, Ash would try to engage his colleagues in a philosophical discussion about the relationship between their special abilities and laws of physics, which usually resulted in most of them leaving the room!

'Phae, I'm scared. Where's Xin?' asked Ciara as Phae strapped her young colleague into the shuttle.

'Hey, everything's gonna be all right. See you later monkey girl!' Phae activated the red and yellow buttons and the pod sealed itself shut as Phae stepped back to protect herself from the rocket exhaust that blasted it skywards.

The Morgai threw themselves at Phae's spinning force field but bounced off it as if it were a trampoline. Tanielka fired more blaster shots, but they were deflected away, ricocheting around the buildings and stationary vehicles parked near-by. She was forced her to duck to protect herself as one blast came back off a mirrored surface and took out one of the cyber-demons standing by her.

Tanielka could see that her chance to capture Phae was once again fading before her eyes. She gritted her teeth and flicked her wrists releasing her cat-claws. From the tip of each finger on both hands there appeared a razor-sharp talon, about ten centimetres in length, a weapon she and all the previous Princesses of Golteria had inherited from their ancestor Cyax.

During the creation of the Astraxi, Cyax had argued for himself to be in the group of warriors, based on his personal preference for the constellation of the panther, which was well known in ancient Astrellion. He warped Gilmane's magic when he stole the Potion of Eternity and diverted energy through his body from the Celestial Panther, which had the unexpected but not wholly unwanted effect of giving him a set of retractable panther claws. His descendants also inherited this intriguing physical phenomenon. Tanielka stood poised to thrust her talons into the force field.

'I wouldn't do that if I were you!' shouted Phae as she made her way to the next shuttle on the pad.

Tanielka glowered at Phae and thrust her claws into the Shield of Harmony hoping to disrupt it. She tore at its surface, but her claws behaved more like an electrical conductor for the energy field. Like a lightning rod in a storm, Tanielka caused the energy field to collapse in a brilliant white discharge with forks of electrical energy fizzing out and throwing her to the floor alongside the cyber-demons and Morgai.

Smoke started to come from one of the cyber-demons whose power systems had been fused by the energy blast. A look of panic went across its face as it realised that its main fuel cell had been split open. Tanielka shielded her eyes as the unfortunate creature erupted in a bright blue flame. It jumped about trying to use its hands to extinguish the fire, before throwing itself into an ornamental pond nearby.

Phae jumped into the shuttle and didn't bother to strap herself in, just punching the two buttons and hoping for the best. As the rocket motor hurled her skywards, she reached for the restraining straps, fighting the massive g-forces that were holding back her arms. With a great effort she managed to click the strap buckles in place and spoke to the shuttle's on-board computer to establish voice-command of its navigation systems.

'Pair shuttles four and five with this one as master' Confirmation messages flashed up on her screen that the other shuttles had engaged the pairing protocols and were locked to her navigation systems. As her screen brought up an array of escape options, she could see the two other shuttles containing Ben and Ciara streaking across the sky towards her.

'Where are Ash and Cygnus?' she interrogated the nav computer.

'Information on the whereabouts of Ash and Cygnus is not available at this moment' replied the computer voice.

'I need to figure out where we can go that's safe and in range until we can meet up with Ash. Bring up a map.' A series of concentric circles showing flying time and the maximum range of the shuttles appeared on the main map display.

'Take us to the Forest of Handin, we should be able to hide there for a while until Ash gets in touch.'

The nav system flashed confirming the destination, as Phae waved at her two young companions now flying in tight formation alongside her. At least they had escaped, and she had seen Cygnus evade the Golterian air force's fighters, but she had no idea what was happening to Xin or Nico. As they passed over the open countryside, she could only hope that they had managed to escape too.

CHAPTER 22
Treachery

Xin and Nico had been forced to leave the base under close pursuit, but Xin's old huntsman's tricks had enabled them to escape unharmed and thus far undetected. They were now just north of the airfield, heading up the mountain that was at the centre of the island on which the base stood. Xin hoped to get a good view of what was going on before deciding what to do next.

He had witnessed the aerial battle that Ash had fought with the Golterian fighters before escaping under the cover of his cloaking device and he had seen the three escape shuttles blast into the sky unharmed and more to the point un-pursued. His heart was settled by the fact that the ship and the four other Astraxi were probably well on their way to safety by now.

Nico was at a loss for how to deal with this situation. He had only been a member of the team for a short time and already they had twice been defeated by Cyax. He wondered if there was more that he could have done during the attack. His inexperience had got the better of him again and for now the best course of action had been to stick with Xin, which also meant that he was less likely to be captured or killed.

Sitting down on a high ledge overlooking the area, Xin silently contemplated the devastation of the base, while Nico mooched about, his hands in his pockets, unsure of what to say or do. The Golterian forces had successfully destroyed the base and were rounding up the remaining Astrellian defenders, engineers, and scientists that hadn't managed to escape.

Xin had a grim look on his face, the lines on his brow were furrowing even deeper, and his head was slightly bowed. Once again Cyax had completely outmanoeuvred him. Being without his major foe for so long must have seriously blunted his instincts. The bigger issue on his mind was what would Cyax do next? These acts of war that Cyax had perpetrated against Astrellion, a peaceable nation, should not have been such a surprise, they really should have expected and been prepared for it.

'We're beaten, it's over before I even got started' said Nico in a defeatist way, kicking random loose stones into the ravine with his baseball boots.

Xin looked up and engaged Nico directly in the eyes. 'It's never over Nico, there's always an answer. The balance of the universe is eternal. Like a pendulum it will eventually swing back to a more harmonious position.'

'What are we going to do? This is hopeless?' Nico sat down on the ledge next to Xin, who could sense that Nico's mindset was swinging back to that of the young man who a few weeks ago could see no real future for himself.

'Whatever happens Nico, you must believe in yourself and believe in your future. You have what it takes, the amulet showed you as much.'

'I never really had a family and now I'm losing this one' Nico sighed as the possibility of a brighter and better future was slipping away from him.

Xin put his hand on his shoulder, firmly and once more looked him in the eye,

'I will always be there for you, as will the others, but we need to find them and reunite as the Astraxi.' Nico seemed reassured by this and nodded in response, but as he withdrew his hand Xin suddenly turned his attention to the surroundings, scanning for something that had alerted his keen hunter's senses.

'What is it Xin' asked Nico nervously.

'*Nixas*' Xin invoked his reveal invisibility spell and to Nico's great surprise, Eduardo the Snake Warrior's physical shape was revealed in a large boulder nearby. Knowing that he had been discovered, Eduardo quickly dropped his disguise and brushed himself down before walking towards the others in a slightly nervous way.

'Eduardo! Are you OK?' Nico called out, reacting to the surprise of finding his missing colleague here in this situation.

'Yeah. I'm fine. Nasty business that.' Eduardo pointed to the base where several buildings were either smouldering or on fire. But the uncharacteristically short and emotionless response from Eduardo made Xin more suspicious about his unexpected appearance.

'How did you get here Eduardo?'

'Cyax brought me along for the ride, but I managed to slip away when the fighting kicked off.'

Xin studied him carefully for a moment. Eduardo was a master of not only controlling his own emotions, but also of controlling other people's minds and now he seemed almost puppet-like in his own actions.

'What happened at the monastery, after we lost contact with you,' asked Xin.

'Fong spotted my body heat while I was camouflaged and then I was captured.' Eduardo's words seemed straightforward enough, but Xin might have expected a little more detail from him. He seemed reluctant to say too much, which of course is what was really going on, as Cyax had control of his mind and actions.

Somewhere deep under Cyax' enchantment, Eduardo had barricaded his own personality into a safe space from which he hoped to emerge when the time was right. But he was so deeply under Cyax' spell that he couldn't force open the door that he was hiding behind. Xin was reading the subtle signs of this inner conflict in Eduardo's face, but Nico was oblivious to his friend's torment.

'What did they do to you Eduardo? Are you sure you're OK?' Xin stepped up to the young man and was considering whether he had anything in his magical repertoire that might reveal the truth, when a sinister voice interrupted him.

'Everything's going to be just fine Xin' announced Cyax in a tone that was simultaneously triumphant, sarcastic, and ironic. A small group of cyber-demons followed him into the space by the ravine where the three were standing. Nico started to panic looking for an exit, but Eduardo just stood still staring at his master, awaiting his next command. Xin, on the other hand, stood his ground firmly as his ancient foe strode up to him.

The cyber-demons raised their weapons anticipating Cyax' order to shoot, which didn't come. Instead, Cyax reached into the inside pocket of his cloak and took out four black cylinders, each about twenty-five centimetres long. Two of the cylinders had a silver cap on one end, which Nico immediately recognised as belonging to the Wand of Xylos.

Cyax held the four cylinders flat on the upturned palms of his hands. As Xin reached for his staff, which was slung over his shoulder, the four cylinders rose into the air and performed a complicated spinning move, rotating around each other until they were lined up in the correct sequence, and then assembled themselves into a single solid object. As each of the cylinders locked together the Wand began to make its usual humming sound, but with Cyax in possession, this was more like a continuous menacing growl.

'That's three times now I've caught you by surprise. You're out of practice my old servant.' Cyax picked the weapon out of the air and started to spin it, as if making a few moves to warm up for the contest with Xin, who now stood defensively.

'You see, it just goes to show how much you need me. But sadly, I am not sure I have much need for you anymore.' Cyax swivelled quickly aiming a treacherous blow directly at Nico who was totally unprepared, but the old man was ready for him and parried the blow away from the younger man. Cold fear ran through the Nico's body as he realised how close he had come to being destroyed by Cyax.

Cyax and Xin squared up to one another, circling and throwing out blows to test the other's skills and reactions. No matter how hard he tried, Xin's staff never quite made contact with the Wand, seemingly being deflected by its power, leaving a small gap between their weapons like two matching magnetic poles being forced together by hand.

Cyax took the initiative lunging hard at Xin, who raised his staff to protect himself but soon found himself buckling under the combined strength of Cyax and the energy sapping power of the Wand. He gasped as he freed himself from the pressure and rolled near to the edge of the precipice before recovering to face Cyax once more. Xin moved forward quickly to distance himself from the treacherous drop behind him, pushing back at Cyax with all his energy.

'Powerful isn't it!' mocked Cyax as he was locked in a battle of strength with Xin. He called up one of the Wand's spells '*Mantro*' and the Wand's aggressive humming grew in intensity, as Xin's staff began to vibrate in his hands. He struggled to keep a grip on it while Cyax slowly pushed him ever harder, back towards the cliff edge.

Nico was still very much a spectator to this event, but now he worried that things were not going to end well. Beads of sweat ran down the brows of both combatants. Xin's staff was now shaking intensely, and after what seemed like a minute but was probably only a few seconds, a crack appeared in the middle of this very old wooden weapon. Xin clenched his teeth and pushed harder, but as he did so the staff vibrated with even more intensity, and the crack widened until the staff snapped, forcing him to drop it with a gasp of exhaustion. Xin was unbalanced and for a moment hesitated in front of Cyax, who took his opportunity to deliver a hard blow from the Wand to Xin's midriff knocking him to the ground, breathless.

Nico was frozen to the spot, as Cyax turned to taunt him. 'What's the matter little worm? Want to burrow into the dirt where you belong?' He lunged at Nico ready to strike the young Dragon with great force, but Xin wasn't going to give in so easily and picked part of his staff off the ground, rushing in just in time to parry away the blow. The two immortals re-engaged their fight, but the Wand of Xylos was giving Cyax a great magical advantage, reinforcing his attacks with its elemental power.

He forced Xin back towards the precipice, sweeping away the remains of his staff and beating the old man rhythmically until once more Xin was on his knees by the cliff edge. Cyax raised the weapon once more calling out '*Engara*' and smashed it hard into Xin's back.

The ancient mentor of the Astraxi reeled under the blow for a moment, and as he swayed a ghostly light seemed to illuminate his body, which turned into a flowing stream of fine glowing particles that drifted away into the air. Xin hovered by the side of the ravine, unbalanced by his injuries. Satisfied that he had delivered a mortal blow to his old adversary, Cyax then cruelly kicked Xin's wavering figure over the edge and into the deep, rocky ravine, leaving a stream of the glowing lights in its wake.

'Xin, no…….!' screamed Nico in anguish as Xin's body disappeared out of sight into the depths of the chasm. Cyax now turned on him.

'Now it's time to put out your fire, little worm.'

Nico didn't stop to think. He reached for his amulet and activated it, instantly transforming himself into the Dragon warrior and blasted Cyax with a huge fireball from the palm of his hand, hurling him into some nearby bushes which caught fire.

The fury of this attack surprised Cyax, who was not protected by the magical weapon in his hand. In fact, the opposite happened as the Wand of Xylos added more intensity to the fire, as under elemental lore *Wood feeds Fire*. Cyax dropped the weapon but had enough presence of mind to summon a sharp blast of wind '*Mintaris*' to snuff out the flames as he remembered the last time the young Dragon had managed to set him on fire in the Master's Pagoda by the lake.

At the moment Xin tumbled over the cliff edge, a small sliver of gold in the shape of an oak leaf had fallen from inside his tunic and drifted towards Nico's feet unseen by Cyax. Nico quickly scooped it up without questioning what it was and was about to unleash another fireball on Cyax, when the cyber-demons let loose a volley of shots from their blasters straight at Nico.

Nico's fire-proof Dragon armour absorbed most of the energy of the blasts, but not all of it and the burning pain reminded him of the great danger that he was still in. Cyax was emerging from the smouldering ashes of the bushes he had been blown into. Nico decided that escape was his best and only option. Using his amulet he summoned his celestial companion, the Star Dragon Adraxa.

The amulet opened a portal which appeared as a burst of starlight projecting from the celestial plane, and expanded next to Nico, ferrying the amazing beast to his side. Just the mere presence and memory of the last time he met this fearsome creature, caused Cyax to pause. The last time he had seen the Star Dragon was when he had been captured in her claws and imprisoned in the glacier. Despite being indestructible, Cyax still knew fear and pain.

Nico leapt onto Adraxa's back, grabbing two of the spines behind her head and swinging a leg over the Star Dragon's neck. Adraxa made a mighty leap into the sky and Nico had to hold on with all his strength just to avoid tumbling back to earth as the cold air rushed past him.

Cyax stood and watched, powerless to prevent Nico's escape. He had not managed to take the young Dragon Warrior, the DragonStone or his amulet, but he had succeeded in finally destroying his ancient foe, Xin. Now, without their wise leader, these young warriors didn't stand a chance. Never in the past had Cyax had such a clear advantage in his struggle against the Astraxi. Victory was his to take and take it he would.

CHAPTER 23
Lost In The Forest

With the situation on board Cygnus having mostly stabilised, Mira had identified numerous possible safe landing areas for the damaged ship, where they could attempt some temporary repairs, but before that Ash was keen to find out what had happened to his colleagues.

No communications of any sort had come through from either Xin or Phae, which was unusual and very worrying. Normally while on missions the team kept in regular contact via their comm links, and in this prolonged silence Ash was starting to fear the worst.

Ash activated the multi-format comms unit which would broadcast to any available channel that his friends may be tuned into, using the Astraxi's own dedicated global network

'Anyone out there? Cygnus to Phae, Xin, Ciara, Ben, anybody? Nico? Come in!'

He stared at the console willing it to speak back to him, but all he got was silence, not even a burst of static.

'Mira, are our comms down too?'

'Yes Ash, not quite dead, but badly damaged, carrier signal strength is only about twelve percent. I am afraid that the main antenna array was taken out by one of the missiles. The number one backup was also partially damaged and is functioning with a limited set of frequencies. I believe repairs are possible using the spare parts in our on-board inventory.'

Ash frowned to himself while looking at the systems damage report that Mira was gathering on his screen. He knew every inch of the ship's engineering and computer systems, so this repair didn't particularly worry him, it would probably be a simple substitution of modular components.

A sudden lurch to the port side and a flurry of automatic alerts shattered the silence, warning Ash of problems with the main power reactor, and flight control stabilisers. The ship's structural integrity system was also failing, which diverted his attention from the much less serious communications issues.

'Hmm, we'd better fix that before the ship falls apart. The others will just have to fend for themselves for a little while longer.'

Raising both of his hands, Ash pulled up numerous holographic displays of the ship's power systems and their controls, which he could manipulate using a combination of sensors tracking his eye movements and physical gestures with his hands. This enabled him quickly to solve multiple problems at the same time. He knew exactly where to divert the ship's increasingly scarce power resources and what to shut down to save precious energy.

Any observer who didn't know him, might have thought Ash was someone with excellent physical self-awareness and timing, the sort of skills required by a dancer or an elite sportsperson. But Ash didn't have the first clue about either sports or dance. As far as Ash was concerned, if a pastime or sport required him to interact with some sort of spherical object, using a bat, stick, boot, hand, or racquet etc, then he wasn't interested.

As far as dance was concerned, he was way too self-conscious to express himself on a dance floor, not really understanding where the joy was to be found in the kind of physical movement that came from allowing yourself to be lost in the music. Yet here, without consciously thinking about it, Ash moved with confidence, speed, and agility while controlling the ship's systems with his gestures.

Another alarm sounded on the flight deck, barking its strident, ear-penetrating warning tone. While Ash and Mira solved one set of problems, others started to appear, as the ship was much more badly damaged than he had feared.

'We need to find somewhere to land before we crash!' he called out to Mira, as his usual coolness finally began to evaporate.

'Your analysis of the situation is very accurate, Ash. I have identified a viable landing site at a clearing just to starboard,' replied the computer.

'I see it. I'll take us in on manual. Make sure I've got enough power to get us down safely.'

'Confirmed Ash. You have flight control. Would you like me to prepare your ejector seat?' Mira wasn't being negative, rather being ready for all possible outcomes.

'My calculation is that we still have enough resources to get down safely, as long as nothing else goes wrong, so thank you but no!' Ash continued his preparations for a vertical landing.

Ash swiped away the tactical holo-screens and sat back into the pilot's seat. Carefully he adjusted the ship's trajectory towards the clearing identified by Mira. As alarms and warnings chimed around the flight deck, the ship shuddered and lurched through the air, but Ash was able to focus his mind on the task of achieving a safe landing, in a space barely bigger than the ship, knowing that Mira would help manage the engineering problems at the same time.

As he neared the ground, an anti-gravity stabiliser failed causing one wing to drop suddenly, but Mira diverted what little spare power they had to the force field that helped maintain the ship's physical structure and despite hitting the ground with quite a thump, Cygnus sustained no further serious damage.

Mira was quick to congratulate her colleague, 'Great flying Ash!'

'Well, if you hadn't been holding the systems together it might have been a bit less pretty!' Ash jumped out of his seat to shut down the ship's main reactor, so that he could start repairs. 'Let's see if we can get Cygnus ready for action again.' Ash was fond of both his ship and the ship's computer, a bond which was as much of an emotional tie as most people had for their closest companions or family.

A little while earlier, the three escape pods that were carrying Phae, Ciara and Ben had reached the limit of their range and Phae had guided them to a landing spot near the edge of a vast wooded area. The three touched down without any incident using the pods' automatic flight controls. With a hiss of air the glass windows of the pods opened, allowing them to climb out. As the eldest and most experienced in the group, Phae once more took control of the situation and decided that for now they should probably stay relatively close to the pods, in the hope that Ash would be able to track and rescue them.

Like Ash she was concerned about the radio silence from Xin, who like any good leader, paid close attention to the individual needs of his team members. Having tried and failed to communicate with the others they salvaged their emergency supplies and a few other useful items from the pods and Ben began to camouflage them with loose branches and ferns from the woods. But Ciara had a better idea. She reached for her amulet and with a short turn to the right powered up her illusory magic.

In her mind she imagined thick bushes and vegetation surrounding the pods. Sure enough as she stood there with her mind focused, brambles and ferns appeared to cover the small pods as if they had been left in the wild for years, rendering them invisible to anyone except those with an especially well-trained mage's eye.

'There you have it!' she announced. 'No need to drag branches out of the woods. Completely concealed.'

Phae led them deeper into the woods to find a good place to shelter. Despite being worried about her colleagues, she was relaxed as the woodland environment felt like a natural home to her and she was very much in her element. After a short walk she identified a space near a spring, with fresh clean running water. It offered good natural defences, with a small cave tucked under a mound upon which stood some thick and thorny bushes and a large oak tree.

In her usual fashion Phae took no time in coming to a decision about where to set up camp, with the assumption that the others would simply comply,

'This will do,' she whispered to herself and put her small backpack of supplies on the ground in front of the cave and turned to the others. As it happened Ben and Ciara were not in a position or in the mood to argue. Having narrowly avoided capture by Tanielka and with their hasty escape from the base, they were both unusually quiet as they processed what had just happened to them.

As he laid down his backpack, Ben's mind also turned to things more relevant to him, which in his case was to find something tasty to eat! He rummaged through his bag but only found emergency dried rations and even though these would probably be perfectly good enough for a few days, he was looking for something more interesting.

'Hey Phae! Fancy doing a little foraging in the forest for something with a bit more flavour?!' Ben's waggy-tail personality was enough to lift even the darkest spirits and the girls both smiled, infected by his enthusiasm.

'OK Ben,' replied Phae. 'Ciara, you set up camp here and gather some firewood, while Ben and I go scavenging. Let's see if we can come up with something tasty.' As the two walked off into the woods, Ciara set about gathering dry sticks to make a fire, before assembling a rudimentary stand from which she hung a cooking pot, which was part of the survival kit in her backpack.

With the aid of a little magical fire to ignite the kindling, she boiled some water and poured in some of the dried rations to make a kind of stew. The packets described it as 'Supreme of Cheese with Pasta,' but it formed a sticky, lumpy grey sludge that glued itself viscously to the base of the pan. As she added more water to try and loosen the gloopy mass from its congealed state, the others returned to the camp. Ben was absolutely bouncing with enthusiasm, clutching a small canister to his chest and a smile as wide as the Sydney harbour bridge!

'Bush tucker!' he announced and unscrewed the top of the canister to reveal a collection of large white grubs that wriggled at the bottom.

'Bugs! Seriously! I don't eat bugs.' Ciara's face was contorted with disgust.

'Add some berries, nuts, mushrooms, and herbs. That'll make it taste better,' said Phae, who presented a more wholesome, less insectivorous container of ingredients to Ciara.

Reaching into the canister, Ben pulled out a fat grub. It writhed in between his finger and thumb, and he held it in front of Ciara's perfectly formed nose, which was now wrinkled into a shape more resembling a button.

'Grubs are good. Trust me. Have you never had bush tucker Ciara?' He pushed the fat white larva closer to her face then promptly nipped off its head before dropping it into his mouth. He chewed it slowly without dropping the grin on his face, as Ciara's levels of horror went through the roof. She was convinced she was going to vomit but managed to hold on to the contents of her stomach, despite a few short and intense wretches.

Ben was loving every minute of Ciara's discomfort and turned to Phae picking the next grub from the pot and offering it to her.

'Wanna try one, stripey?' For the sake of keeping up appearances as leader and to keep the team bonded together, Phae felt obliged to eat one. She looked Ben in the eye trying hard not to reveal her total inner revulsion and plucked the fat creamy coloured grub from his fingers.

Despite appearing outwardly calm, Phae felt her stomach churning too, but she didn't want to give Ben or Ciara the satisfaction of seeing her wretch. She nipped off the grub's head and thrust it into the front of her mouth, holding it between her lips while keeping her tongue further back in her mouth so that she wouldn't have to taste it. However, the grub's fat body burst open and emptied its slimy innards down her chin.

Ben was struggling to contain his laughter as Phae first looked for a something to wipe her face. Then she pushed the mushy insides of the grub into her mouth while trying to appear cool and unflustered.

'So, what do you think of bush tucker?' he asked as she gagged slightly on swallowing the last of the grub's gooey flesh and washing it down with a huge gulp of water.

'Could do with a little seasoning!' was Phae's choked, but razor-sharp response as she dabbed at her chin with a delicate lace handkerchief that she had pulled from her pocket.

Phae's attempts to hide her discomfort from her friends, did not have the desired effect. Ciara had watched her tormented choking and rapid chewing with great amusement, and the delicate dabbing of her chin with the dainty handkerchief was the crowning moment. She exploded with laughter, almost falling off her perch. Ben couldn't contain himself any longer and let out a massive snort, before being consumed by uncontrollable sniggering.

Phae was still desperately trying to maintain her composure as the leader of the group, but it didn't last long and she too was consumed by the giggles, tears running down her cheeks.

'You got me!' she managed to speak, before breaking into laughter once more. 'It was actually completely disgusting, like the most vile thing ever imaginable!'

The stress of what had just happened to the three of them had been replaced by humour due to the comic and futile attempts of Phae to retain her professional demeanour and failing, while sticky grub innards dribbled down her chin.

But the moment didn't last long. As the laughter subsided Ciara stared into the fire below her cooking pot and once more her face sank back into sadness. She abruptly stood up, walking off into the bushes on her own, with her head down.

Phae stood up and followed Ciara, leaving Ben to stir the cooking pot, with its pasta meal that was now enhanced by the foraged herbs and mushrooms. A few metres away from their camp she found Ciara perched on a log, her head in her hands. Phae sat down next to her and pushed away Ciara's thick mop of auburn hair to reveal tears trickling down her freckled cheeks which were more flushed with pink than usual.

'Hey Ciara, what's wrong?' Phae put her arm around the distressed girl and drew her in.

'We're lost and alone in the middle of nowhere, with just a load of bugs to eat! The base is destroyed, and we've lost Ash, Xin, and Nico.' Ciara forced the words out between sobs and turned her face away from Phae, trying to cover up her sadness.

But Phae drew her in tighter. 'We've got each other. We'll always have each other. I am sure the others are just fine. They'll be out there looking for us, you'll see. Let me dab your tears away.' Phae reached once more for her lacy handkerchief and was about to dry Ciara's tears, when she remembered that it was covered in a sickly yellow larval goo.

'Oh, I'm sorry.'

Ciara let out a muffled giggle and went silent for a moment before letting out a deep sigh.

'I'm scared. I wish my mum was here.'

'Tell me about her,' said Phae, trying to help Ciara find some happy thoughts.

'Oh, She was amazing.' Ciara activated her amulet and a stream of tiny particles of light flowed from its centre towards a small rock on the ground in front of the girls. The stone's shape rippled for a moment, before it morphed into the figure of a woman with long flowing hair. Ciara stared at the figure, which smiled and held out its hands towards her as if seeking an embrace. Ciara reached out and held one of the figure's hands.

'She used to take me to the theatre with her all the time, but one day I was feeling a bit sick, so she left me with the neighbours.' The figure took a step back and the image of a small and very young Ciara appeared next to her. Phae was very quickly drawn into the images as Ciara's magical illusion started to grow into a much more detailed scene. A row of neat houses with small gardens appeared behind the two figures.

The figure representing Ciara's mother picked up the small child and carried her to the front door of one of the houses, where she handed the child over to a woman, who was surrounded by a small group her own children. Ciara's mother kissed her goodbye and waved as she walked off down the street.

'She was the best theatre actress in Ireland. So brilliant and funny. We laughed all the time.' A rippling wave of the same fine glowing lights transformed the street scene into a Victorian theatre stage with an audience. The curtains opened and Ciara's mother stepped forward and took a bow to a standing ovation from the crowd. Ciara's voice became sad once more. 'But one day she never came home'

'What happened to her,' asked Phae sensitively.

'She was crossing the street,' continued Ciara. Once more the glowing lights swept away the scene before the two girls, replacing it with the street outside the theatre. As Ciara's mother stepped into the road, a fast-moving car hurtled towards her, but just before the moment of impact the illusion turned into two bright headlights heading straight towards them and blinding their eyes.

Phae turned away and shut her eyes but as she opened them again the image was already fading away to nothing.

'The driver didn't stop and was never seen again. Nobody knows what really happened or why.'

Before Ciara's mood could turn dark once more, out of the shadows came a pack of small dogs, mostly shaggy-coated mongrels with bright eyes and wagging tails. They raced straight for Ciara and jumped up at her, licking her face and barking in excitement. Following close behind was Ben, with a big smile on his face,

'I thought you might need something to cheer you up!' he exclaimed proudly.

Ciara couldn't cope with the weight of the excited puppies, which eventually pushed her off the rock she was sitting on and completely engulfed her with their excited licking of her face and hands.

'Get them off me you idiot!' Ciara was actually enjoying the attention and it was fair to say that Ben was enjoying it too, so he let them go on a little longer before he blew a short whistle signalling the dogs to come to heel behind him.

'There's a good boy' said Ben as he knelt to pat and hug all of the small pack of local dogs that he had summoned using his celestial powers. 'So, what's the plan Phae?' he asked.

Phae didn't have to think for long to answer what she thought was a rather obvious question, with an even more obvious answer.

'The plan is, find the others, then defeat Cyax. Simple!'

Ben continued playing with the small group of dogs who were thoroughly enjoying the attention he was lavishing on then, making little yelps and barks of pleasure as he stroked their backs and played with their ears. He laughed ironically,

'Sure, no problem. Just look at us, stuck in the middle of nowhere, with no equipment and nowhere to go!'

'Until we hear from Xin, we should still try to seek out the other missing elemental weapons.' Phae was as usual shooting from the hip, pulling ideas out of thin air, but was very confident in her analysis and her thinking, which was why it was often very difficult to argue with a tiger!

'And how do you propose we get to Australia then?' Ciara was very good at pointing out the big gaps in Phae's thinking.

'Easy! First we find Ash and Cygnus.' Phae reached into her backpack and produced the Sun-Moon device. She opened the case to reveal its mechanical movements, with spinning pointers and rotating dials. At its heart the device's energy source glowed in two point-sources of red and blue light. It was hard to tell where this light came from, or what it was as, it just seemed to exist. Nothing solid or mechanical created it, just pure magic.

Phae was about to start setting the dials to find Ash, but because she was the Tiger Warrior and had used the Sun-moon before, the device had already formed a close telepathic link with her and was already reacting to her thoughts and intentions. Phae had conjured up an image of Ash in her mind, but the device already knew she wanted to find him, and the dials and settings were rotating to the required positions including pointers for the Stag constellation, the element of water, his date of birth and the planet mercury.

As the dials settled into place, the main pointer appeared and indicated a series of symbols inlaid around the edge of the outer ring. These were the precise celestial co-ordinates of Ash's position at that moment. Not all co-ordinates are earthly, so the Sun-moon can also indicate positions on other planes of existence, magical, temporal, and ethereal. Ciara and Ben looked at the pointer as it repeated its sequence of indicated symbols but failed to discern anything that made any sense.

'How are we going to read it without Mira or Ash to decipher the pattern?' asked Ciara.

'We don't need Mira or Ash,' replied Phae with a big smile. Her face was illuminated as if she had just been let into a huge secret, which indeed she had. The telepathic connection to the device was two-way, so she had no need to be able to read the symbols and interpret the order in which the pointer indicated them.

The answer simply appeared in Phae's mind, not as a spoken instruction, but more as a set of instincts that would lead her to the destination she was seeking. As she stood concentrating on the revelation inside her head and trying to convert that into real world actions, the others looked on at her mystified as to what she would do next.

'He's actually very close by!' Phae gasped in excitement. 'Let's head back to the pods.'

CHAPTER 24
What Next?

Nico gripped the horns on the back of Adraxa's head firmly as the Star Dragon carried him high above the earth through the dense darkness of the moonless night. Below him stretched vast open plains of farmland, featureless apart from an occasional road, tree, barn, or grain silo. A river snaked through the plain, but the lack of any moonlight rendered it invisible to the eye from his high vantage point. Even the highway that connected the urban areas many miles away, was hidden in the inky darkness, with small sections being illuminated by the headlights of an occasional road train or tall lamp posts in the centre of a junction.

This lack of anything earthly to look at caused Nico to turn his attention to the heavens instead. The darkness of the clear cloudless night and the lack of any human generated light pollution drew his eyes to the stars instead. There were so many stars to his night adjusted eye, that it was almost impossible to make out any structure or shapes of constellations. The Milky Way arched across the highest part of the heavenly vault through which he was soaring on the back of his celestial companion.

He remembered how he had been given a beginner's guide to astronomy by one of his Aunt Cass' friends, a kindly old gentleman who had been a schoolteacher and was trying to encourage Nico to take more interest in academic study rather than his skateboard.

From the fold out illustrated star maps which he had studied with genuine interest, he could just about remember how to use the Great Bear to find the Pole Star and that the constellation of the Little Bear that hung down from it, like a smaller version of its greater namesake. Curving around that group of circumpolar stars, almost totally surrounding them was the constellation of the Dragon - Draco, which he thought he could just about work out, tracing the stars all the way from her tail to her head.

Now fate had brought him to be riding on the back of Adraxa. Many millions or even billions of humans had probably viewed the constellation of Draco, without realising that it was a projection of the Star Dragon's presence out of the celestial plane and into the realm of the earthly universe.

Only wizards or people with access to a very particular lore would ever know or understand this point of crossover between two very different universes. The reality was that the earth and the plane in which it was embedded, intersected with other planes and that there were portals to these other realms, most of which were inaccessible or hidden from plain sight. Being a powerful Mage, Xin had the ability to see into these other realms and to summon fabulous creatures from them or banish them back to their natural habitats.

But Xin had been cruelly wrenched away from Nico by the villainy of Cyax, and as such Nico was on his own once more having to draw on his own resources. The surprise attack on the base had scattered the young warriors without any means of communication. In the event of an emergency, Xin had taught them that they should attempt to regroup at either the Astraxi's Desert Base, or the Perpetual Motion Café. But Nico's training was incomplete and so he had to come up with his own plan.

Plans, however, were the last thing on his mind. Sanctuary was something he could definitely use right now. As he raced through the skies on the back of the dragon, his body tightly gripping the silvery scales, occasionally his mind would be filled with the grief and terror of what had just seen.

How could this be happening? Xin couldn't just be kicked off a cliff by Cyax, after he had been the leader of the Astraxi for four thousand years and had survived much greater peril. That didn't make sense, but sadly for Nico it was a hard fact, one he couldn't deny, having seen it with his own eyes.

Maybe he should try and go back to the base and see if he could sneak into the Library of the Astraxi and secretly continue his studies and come out fighting. Somehow this seemed unappealing at that moment and being scared he desperately needed something familiar to cling on to, something that felt like home. So it was that the Star Dragon was taking Nico back to the only home he had known for the last few years, Aunt Cass' house.

As they approached Astrapolis, the bright glow of street lighting and the vast numbers of illuminated buildings in the city, blotted out the dimmer stars in the sky, leaving only the brighter more obvious constellations visible. Even the dragon constellation was difficult to discern as it snaked around the Polaris.

As the Star Dragon made a steep dive into Aunt Cass' back garden, Nico felt a light cool dampness on his cheek, a soft drizzly shower, but just the sort of rain that gets you wet quickly. He swung himself off the dragon's back and looked up at the empty house, which appeared abandoned even after this short time. It was remarkable to Nico what a difference human presence makes to a building. Aunt Cass' house seemed to have decayed quickly once she wasn't around to heat and light it or cook dinner and tend the garden's vegetable patch.

The windows were boarded up with large sheets of plywood roughly nailed into the frames. He rattled at the handle of the back door, but this also appeared to be nailed shut.

'Looks like I'm not welcome here anymore' he muttered to himself after he tried unsuccessfully to shoulder the door in.

Sensing that her help was no longer required, Adraxa dematerialised into a series of pinpoints of light that rapidly climbed into the sky in the direction of the Dragon constellation. Nico watched this trail of starlight feeling very grateful for the intervention by his stellar companion that had almost certainly saved him from capture or something worse by Cyax.

Walking around the side where the composting bins were kept full of grass cuttings from the lawn and weeds pulled from the flower beds, he noticed a small window to the bathroom that had been left slightly open. Jumping up on the log store next to the bins, Nico was able to get his arm inside the window and undo the catch allowing him to swing the window upwards. It was a fairly small, narrow window, but Nico was fit and slender from spending hours practicing stunts on his skateboard. He remembered that below the window on the other side, was the toilet, and if he managed to slither through the window, he would have to try not to lose control, otherwise he would be having an impromptu hair wash in the bowl below!

He reached his arms through the window and hauled his body off the top of the log store so that he was supported by his chest. Then he pulled himself in a little further so that he was now balancing on his waist with his legs sticking out of the window, still catching the soft rainfall, and soaking his jeans. He edged his body forward gently and as he lowered his head and his arms downwards his feet went upwards, like a seesaw with his hips as the pivot point.

Suddenly he sensed that he risked losing control and sliding headfirst down towards the toilet bowl that was at least a metre below him. Realising there was nothing that he could grip on to slow his descent, he levelled his body once more around his hips. There was only the smooth plaster of the wall to try and grip on to as the cistern was just out of reach. If he lost control at this point, he wouldn't just get a hair wash, he might break his neck into the bargain, by plunging headfirst into the ceramic bowl. He laughed with a little dark humour to himself at how ridiculous it would be if the much-heralded new Dragon Mage was found dead, with his head down his aunt's toilet before he could get to work fighting Cyax!

A controlled fall and a little faith in the strength of his arms versus gravity was what he concluded would get him out of this precarious and comic position with his legs still sticking horizontally out of the small window. He stretched his arms on to the smooth wall with his palms facing forward and allowed his body to slide downwards, his hands landing flat on the top of the cistern. So far so good, but now he was almost vertical, performing a handstand on top of the cistern with his feet and shins still sticking out of the window.

Nico was a bit stumped as to his next move, he hadn't really thought the problem through, as he was simply approaching it a step at a time, and each move so far had landed him in a seemingly more impossible position. Now as he hesitated, the blood drained from his body into his head, and he started to feel a bit dizzy and slightly sick.

There was no other option, he was just going to have to try and lower himself down using one arm and hope that a bit of friction would slow his fall into the ceramic bowl and its suspiciously foetid water. This was a moment when having a bit of muscle as opposed to long spindly limbs might have helped.

He lifted one hand and slapped it flat on to the front of the cistern and lowered himself with his stronger more dominant right arm while trying to maximise the friction of his body against the plaster wall. Slowly he slid downwards, reaching out to the rim of the toilet seat for support.

Inevitably the force of gravity overcame the friction of his body against the plaster wall, and he tumbled into the room, as his single arm couldn't support his weight. Flexing his body as he slid, he narrowly avoided crowning himself king of the lavatory, and landed in a heap by the wash basin, his legs tumbling to the floor behind him.

He blew out a massive sigh of relief and checked himself for cuts and bruises. Not only had he managed get in without breaking any bones, but none of his cool new friends were around to see his ridiculously comic entrance to the bathroom. Ciara would probably have died laughing if she had witnessed the scene, which resembled something from an old silent movie but without a honky-tonk pianist in accompaniment!

He picked himself up and straightened his hair in the mirror that hung over the wash basin and headed for the living room. It was dark and even though the electricity was still connected, he decided not to turn on any lights for fear of attracting attention from the neighbours. A small amount of streetlight was coming in through a gap at the top of the boarded-up window, just enough to be able to see. He lit the torch on his com-pad and started to look around.

Although the room was familiar, it appeared soul-less without Aunt Cass to bring it to life. All the things that she had gathered and displayed in the room, small items of pottery, souvenirs from holidays and gifts from family members were neatly arranged on shelves and cabinets. Nothing much of any value to anyone, except in its sentimental value to Aunt Cass.

He felt sad because in most likelihood the contents of the house would be cleared by people who would only be looking at the monetary value of the objects they could sell for a profit, leaving the rest of Aunt Cass' memories to be consigned either to land fill or to an incinerator. That would include the collection of family photographs that Aunt Cass kept on a dresser. He picked up one that showed him as a small boy with his parents in happier times, visiting a fun fair and spoke to the people in the picture as if they might hear him,

'Why is it that everyone I ever care about either leaves or is taken away?'

In the silence of his own thoughts, he dismantled the picture frame loosening the fittings on the back and removed the photograph, which he studied looking closely at the faces of his mother and his father.

'Wonder what you're doing now?' he asked them, before stuffing the picture in his shirt pocket.

He had decided that it probably wasn't a good idea to stay here. The house was probably going to get sold or redeveloped, as it was an old building that could be cleared to build something shiny and new. He headed back to the bathroom window, this time to make his exit in a more controlled manner, standing on the cistern and poking his legs through the window first, before dropping to his feet on top of the log store.

Opening the shed door, he found an old skateboard and picked it up to inspect its condition. There was a little bit of rust, but the wheels spun freely on the trucks, which still seemed to have quite a bit of spring in their suspension, despite the many hours he had spent practicing on the board.

The longboard was worn and marked, but in good shape without any serious damage. Nico felt good at being re-acquainted with his old board and closed the door heading for the street, where he dropped the board and skated off towards the centre of town. As he left the house the shadowy figure of Hundun emerged from his camouflaged hiding place. He had been spying on Nico and evaporated into a thin plume of grey smoke that followed the young man as he glided down the street.

In the short period since the attack on the Astraxi's forward operating base, a great panic had broken out in Astrapolis. The peace that had been offered by Tanielka's mother had been quickly shattered by Cyax' return from the glacier. Shop owners were boarding up their windows for fear of disorder. Citizens who could escape were already filling their cars and mobile homes to head for safer places in the South. Military vehicles were visible on the streets, something that was unheard of in peacetime and police patrols had been reinforced to try and manage the surge of people rushing out of the city.

Nico wasn't keen on being found by the authorities and kept to the back streets and alleyways as he headed further into the city. The Perpetual Motion Café was a possible refuge, if he could get past the protective spells Xin had put on the door. But there was another option. Maybe Gilmane could help him. Surely such a powerful wizard would know what he should do next and how he could find his friends again.

As he approached the Old Town, he turned into the side street where Gilmane's Old Curiosity Shop was located. He slowed his speed by making a wide sweeping turn before jumping off and flipping his board into the air, catching it, and putting it under his arm before opening the door and entering the shop.

There was a shrill jingling sound from the brass bell that hung over the door which announced his arrival. Gilmane was sitting in a chair in the middle of the shop, surrounded by old books and scrolls. An empty chair was facing him, and he pointed to the chair, gesturing Nico to sit down in it, almost as if he knew Nico was coming, which as it happens, he did.

'Sit, sit! Tell me of your adventures, young Dragon!' he commanded.

Nico lowered himself into the soft tub shaped chair which was made of smooth dark red leather and put his arms on the sides and shuffled a little in his seat while he composed his answer to Gilmane in his head.

'It's over. Xin is dead, and the Astraxi are finished. I am sure you know that already!'

'Dead? How can that be, is Xin not an immortal?' Gilmane was a little taken aback by Nico's short and blunt response, as he had expected a full description of the events that had brought him back to the shop.

'Cyax hit him with the Wand of Xylos. I saw him fall. I saw the lights leave his body.' As he summoned the painful memories, Nico started to get emotional.

'Oh! I see things too. And I know many things,' responded Gilmane with a gentle concern in his voice.

'Then you know he's dead and it's over.' Nico's blunt words resonated in his own head, and he looked away from the wizard's direct gaze.

'I cannot dispute what you saw. But I know what I feel. You know the Universe has many potential destinies Nico, some following prophecies, and others not, but which one will you follow?' This question wasn't quite what Nico was expecting. He thought Gilmane would give him some direction on what to do next or use his sorcery to reveal the fate of his friends, but instead Gilmane was asking him to make a choice. Making some sort of important decision or taking responsibility for what happens next were things that he had carefully avoided for the last few years while he lived with his aunt.

But instead of making a rational decision, Nico retreated into his old ways and slammed the DragonStone on the low table that separated the two chairs.

'You can have this back. I don't need it anymore.' He pushed the ring towards Gilmane before sinking back into his chair.

'It's not that simple Nico, you are the Dragon Warrior, and that ring is rightfully yours,' said Gilmane as the ring slid back across the table towards Nico, as if an invisible hand had pushed it. 'Now is not the time for me to take it back. You still have much work to do,' he replied firmly. Nico pushed the ring back across the table defiantly,

'Didn't you hear me, I just quit. I can't do this anymore.'

'Nico you need to stop running away from things.' This time Gilmane left the DragonStone where Nico had placed it, but he observed something strange about one of Nico's shirt pockets, which had started twitching.

'Hmm, what's that in your pocket?' he enquired.

Nico stared at Gilmane for a moment mystified, then looked down at his pocket which was making little bulging shapes as if something was trying to escape from inside. As he undid the button the gold leaf that had fallen from Xin's pocket, floated into the air, and fluttered towards Gilmane.

'Xin dropped it. I don't know what it is,' said Nico as the mage plucked it out of the air and raised his monocle to examine it in detail. Gilmane didn't really need the monocle to look at the leaf, but the monocle helped him read and understand any sorcerous properties of such objects.

'Interesting. The last time I saw this was four thousand years ago.' Gilmane held it to his ear and listened carefully. Many voices filled his head, the sounds of battle, people shouting, others crying. Some of the voices were familiar to him and he sighed deeply as he spoke to Nico.

'In the troubled history of this land, many thousands of brave warriors have died in terrible battles for just causes. Most of them left this world before their time.'

'What do you mean? What is that thing?' asked Nico.

'Their souls lie in wait, to be called once more to fight, for vengeance. All you need is the right conditions, and back they will come.' Gilmane's eyes misted over as one very familiar and dear voice spoke to him through the golden oak leaf.

'What? Do you mean like some kind of spell?' asked Nico bluntly.

'Yes, a 'spell' if you like!' Gilmane's face returned to a smile as he placed the leaf on the table and reached for a blank piece of parchment and a writing brush. He drew three characters on the sheet, shapes that Nico didn't recognise because they were from the ancient language of the wizards, who were created by Pangu when the universe was born. That language had never been read, spoken, or learned by mortals.

He folded the parchment and pushed it across the table for Nico to take along with the golden oak leaf and the DragonStone.

'You can believe me or not young man, but you still have a big part to play in this story. And the story is far from over. Great change is coming on earth and across the many planes that intersect with it.' Gilmane stroked his long moustache thoughtfully.

'I like you Nico, and therefore I seek to protect you, though I usually prefer not to intervene too much in human affairs. It gets me into trouble with the others.'

'You seem pretty involved to me!' Nico's cutting response was insensitive.

Gilmane became angry and he gripped his beard with his hand slamming his other hand down on the table.

'Enough of your prevarication! It's down to you now, young dragon. Time for you to stop behaving like one of life's victims and finally to embrace your destiny. Are you a maker of history, or are you simply a passenger in this long voyage?'

But Nico wasn't going to be pushed into anything by the wizard and jumped out of the chair.

'Sorry Gilmane, this is just too big a deal. You need to find a bigger and better hero.'

'Where are you going?' demanded Gilmane, as he stood up to face the young man.

'Nowhere!' said Nico picking up his skateboard and heading for the door. Gilmane shook his head in exasperation at the young man's defeatist attitude.

'Yes, precisely nowhere indeed! Well, we'll see about that,' whispered Gilmane to himself. 'I shouldn't interfere, but once more it seems I must.'

The brass doorbell rang its sharp chime marking Nico's exit from the shop, as Gilmane waved his hands over the parchment, ring, and the golden oak leaf while whispering the spell '*Afarensis.*' The three items magically picked themselves off the table and floated in the air briefly, before flying out the door and following Nico down the street.

As Nico jumped on his skateboard and sped off, he didn't notice the three magical objects following him and quietly tucking themselves into his pockets.

On the streets there were more signs of panic caused by the Golterian raid on the air base. Billboards flashed headlines "Golterian Forces Gathering on the Border with Astrellion" read one. 'Astrellion unprepared for war,' read another. Video clips of troop transports being loaded with cyber-demons and Morgai appeared on others, with pictures of Cyax, the Princess and Fong inspecting their armies.

Nico stopped his skateboard and watched this terrifying montage for a moment, reflecting on the fact that as one of the Astraxi, it was now his role to defend Astrellion against enemies of this sort. But what could he do against vast armies, or cyber-demons controlled by an immortal and indestructible madman like Cyax? He had only just begun his training and didn't really understand how most of it worked. He wasn't the kind of superhero that you read about in comic books; he was just a spindly street kid, who performed do a few tricks on a skateboard to impress other people when it suited him. Perhaps it was time he got out of here, then people wouldn't expect him to do heroic things and be disappointed when he failed.

For some reason that he could not explain, the idea of trying to find his parents suddenly came into his mind. Maybe it was because he had few other options unless he returned to the Astraxi. Perhaps in his mind he was trying to find security, a refuge from the coming conflict between Astrellion and Golteria. His mother was still living in London, maybe she might help him.

He reached into his pocket to get the family photograph that he had taken from Aunt Cass' house. As he drew it out, he was surprised to find the DragonStone in there with it. Gilmane must have somehow planted it back in his pocket.

Possession of the magical ring would make it harder for him to walk away from the Astraxi. Perhaps Gilmane knew that by chipping away at Nico's resistance, he would eventually accept his destiny to be the Dragon Warrior. Nico put the ring on his finger and after looking at the picture of his family once more he folded the photograph and put it back in his pocket.

He still had his amulet on the strap on his wrist. He activated it and summoned Adraxa back from the celestial plane. As the blinding burst of starlight faded, Nico grabbed one of the horns on the dragon's head and swung his body on to her back.

'What is your destination, young master?' she asked.

'I'd just like to go home to my mother for now, if that's all right with you,' was Nico's low-key response.

'When I said destination, what I really meant was, where would you like your life to take you?' replied the dragon. 'Your future, your purpose, your achievements, your legacy even.' Adraxa's question it seemed was metaphorical, as dragons often like to discuss philosophy when not otherwise engaged.

'Isn't it a bit early to be talking about legacy? That sounds a bit like the last chapter in a book. I suppose like Gilmane, you want me to stay and join the fight against Cyax?'

'I offer no advice to the Dragon Warrior, other than to remain true to yourself and your friends. Destiny is a difficult matter for humans whose lives are often short and for those whose future is obscured from them by conflicting circumstances. While you hold the Dragon amulet you still have the power to change things for good or evil. But for now, I shall grant your wish and take you to your mother. Maybe she can help you find your true purpose, we shall see.'

'How will we get there? London's thousands of miles away,' asked Nico.

'I know a short cut!' replied the Star Dragon. 'If we pass through the celestial plane, it will take very little time at all.'

'Sounds... Cosmic?' replied Nico, not really knowing what to expect.

Adraxa launched herself into the air as if she were weightless and soared up vertically. Nico held his breath and clung on to the dragon's back as the ground rapidly receded away from him, wondering how long he would be able to hang on without either freezing to death or falling off.

He needn't have worried, Adraxa raced up towards a bright star in the sky before a further rapid acceleration reduced the earthly plane around them to a narrow blur of light. Star Dragon and Dragon Warrior zoomed into the heart of the brightest star in the constellation of the Swan, known as Deneb, and entering the un-earthly realm known as the celestial plane.

CHAPTER 25
Pinned Down

Phae, Ciara and Ben were making their way back to where Ciara had magically hidden their escape pods. They hoped that they may be able to activate the comms unit of one of the pods, to see if they could reach Ash or any of the others.

'Is that a light or a reflection off something?' Overhead Phae had spotted something moving very fast, a bright light that seemed to be getting closer, but she lost sight of it because of the canopy of the forest. She led the group towards the water's edge, but the ground was swampy and boggy, the kind of mud that just gives way under your feet before flowing over the top of your shoes and inside them, soaking your socks.

Phae was still carrying the Sun-Moon device, convinced that Ash must be somewhere nearby, but she was finding it difficult to understand what the device was telling her. Pointers and dials seemed to be whirling around in all directions, almost as if the device itself was confused by the signals it was reading.

'What's wrong?' enquired Ciara.

'I don't know. I've never seen it do anything like this. I think we need to go...' Phae paused and then pointed confidently towards the river, '...That way!'

'Ugh, couldn't you find a better path?' Ciara was angry, she hated getting mud on any part of her clothing and now she was caked in it from her shins to the soles of her shoes, as if she were wearing boots made of mud!

'SSHHH!' Phae shushed Ciara, as Ben drew a zip sign across his mouth. Phae caught another glimpse of the moving light, but this time from inside the forest. She examined the Sun-Moon again but still could not understand what the strange pattern of symbols was trying to tell her. It seemed as if there were two answers to the simple question of 'Where's Ash?' that she held in her mind.

Ben had also spotted the moving light and scampered into the trees to see if he could track it.

'Heel doggy, heel!' quipped Ciara as she chased after him. Phae sighed. She had no choice but to follow them, not wishing to get separated in the dark, dense forest. Ben didn't get very far before he stopped to wait for the others, while Ciara continued to mock him by patting him on the head.

'Who's a naughty boy then!' she admonished him as if he were a wayward pet that had escaped the leash.

'Stop it Ciara' he retorted, 'this is serious.' Stealthily they moved through the undergrowth occasionally catching glimpses of the moving light which seemed to shimmer. The sound of rustling bracken stopped them dead in their tracks.

'Amulets everybody' commanded Phae and they drew themselves into a tight group to make defence easier. For a moment the rustling sound stopped, and the three looked at each other in silence but no-one dared speak. They edged forward again but the silence was broken by the terrifying roar of a large animal, as a huge stag leaped out from behind a large bush knocking Phae to the ground.

Glowing with the light of the stars, the stag slowly backed off, pointing its impressive antlers at her, leaving Phae on the ground, winded and having to be helped to her feet by Ciara. Ben used his canine hunting skills to try and contain the stag and determine if it was coming back for another try when he heard a familiar voice.

'Oh, it's just you guys' said Ash coolly, as he stepped out from the place from which the stag had first appeared.

'Ash! You... you...' gasped Phae as she tried to regain control of her breathing.

'Stag?' suggested Ash, with only a small amount of irony and a knowing glint in his eye. The celestial Stag known as Tormix, walked causally back to Ash, taking its place by his side. It stood staring at the three warriors as its coat glowed with the silvery starlight that came from the celestial plane.

'I'll get you for that later' said Phae who had now regained most of her normal breathing.

Ash wasn't sure if Phae's threat was real or a joke, so tried to dismiss her statement in his matter-of-fact way. 'Yes. Whatever... if you must, I suppose, but let's get back to Cygnus.'

Having been summoned by Ash to help him find his colleagues, the Celestial Stag sensed it was no longer required, nodded a silent acknowledgement to Ash and dematerialised in a short flash of starlight back to its native plane.

'Come on, follow me.' Ash urged his companions to follow him along the banks of the river.

'I guess your celestial companion was what caused the Sun-Moon to give me conflicting directions. It was finding two stags at the same time' said Phae. Ash simply nodded his agreement as this seemed a logical explanation for the device's unfathomable behaviour.

Ash salvaged a few components from the escape pods.

'These should help us get Cygnus' comms working again,' he said. After a few minutes tracking along the riverbank, they arrived at the clearing in the forest where Ash had landed the ship. Mira had been tracking Ash and as the group approached the ship, she lowered the rear access ramp so they could come aboard.

'Welcome back aboard Cygnus. Hot food is now available in the mess room,' announced Mira to the obvious delight of Ben.

A little later Phae was relaxing in a chair, toying with the Sun-Moon, while Ash and Ciara were sitting at a table. As usual Ben still had his head in the fridge. Ash was keen to learn about what happened after they were split up during the invasion of the base.

'So where are Xin and Nico? And is there any word from Eduardo?' he asked.

Ciara wasn't her usual effervescent self. The events of the last day had drained her self-confidence and she spoke quietly.

'We got separated after the fireworks started. Last we saw of Nico and Xin they were escaping off the base into the hills, but we were cut off by a troop of cyber-demons. We have no idea what happened to them.'

'Hopefully when I get the comms back up and running, we will be able to contact them. I did a few repairs to the ship's systems before finding you in the forest, so we're good to go and pick them up.'

Ash was about to give a full list of which parts of Cygnus were fully operational and which parts were unserviceable when Phae stood up and carried the Sun-Moon over to the table, placing it at the centre.

To the untrained eye the Sun-Moon is an extremely complex and confusing instrument, as there's always something moving. At this moment, even Phae was still having difficulty interpreting the device and she searched her innermost thoughts to see if her telepathic connection could help.

'Something's not right. It seems to indicate that there's a very strong presence of the elemental energy of wood,' said Phae, 'and I can feel it too.'

'Well, we are in a forest, if you hadn't noticed!' chipped in Ciara smugly.

'Try switching it off and switching it back on again. That usually works for most things' said Ash with a glimmer of a smile on his face.

'Oh, ha ha, very funny!' replied Phae sarcastically to Ash's attempt at humour.

Her focus went back to the device. In her head Phae could see a large white bird, like a dove perched in a tree. But as she watched a mass of twigs grew out from the branch it was standing on, trapping its feet, containing its wings, and quickly enveloping it. The bird struggled to escape the mass of wood wrapped around its body, pushing its breast against the strangling twigs, and trying to release its wings.

At the bottom of the tree Phae could see a large black cat-like predator climbing the trunk, stalking its prey, waiting for the moment to strike when the bird was trapped. The cat's eyes glowed with a malevolent green hue and for just one moment Phae felt she made telepathic contact with the creature, causing her to step away from the table in shock.

'Was it Cyax?' she thought to herself. 'It can't be. Not out here.'

On the other side of the telepathic link, Cyax understood that he had probably been detected, but no matter, he was determined to succeed and as he summoned the Lore of the Wand of Xylos it looked certain that he would.

'These readings are off the scale!' Phae closed her mind to the telepathic link and looked directly at the Sun-Moon again. The runes on the concentric dials that usually indicate the appearance of sinister energies were starting to align themselves, in a reinforcement of their message. The symbol for the moon was also aligned with Jupiter and other dials were now pointing outside the ship.

'The trees! Look at the trees!' shouted Ciara pointing through the port hole. Several huge, gnarled oak trees were uprooting themselves from the earth, slowly tearing their roots away from the soil and hauling them to the surface where they used them like long fibrous tentacles to drag their trunks towards the ship.

'Mira! Shields up!' called Ash, to protect the ship from damage as the swaying oak trees lashed the ship with their upper branches.

'Shields confirmed Ash' replied Mira as leaves came cascading down the windows with the whole ship lurching under the arboreal attack.

Cygnus made an alarming creaking noise as she were shaken around like a toy. The crew had to grip on to their seats or anything fixed to the floor to prevent themselves being thrown across the mess room. One of the trees spread its thicker lower branches across one of Cygnus' wings, pinning the ship to the forest floor.

'Mira, get us out of here!' commanded Ash. Having managed to escape the Golterian air force, he wasn't going to allow his ship to be destroyed by elemental forces beyond his control. But instead of lifting into the air with all engines humming, there was a stuttering whining noise and Cygnus remained on the ground with the trees now starting to enmesh her in their branches.

'One of the main reactor couplings has become misaligned during the hard landing, Ash. Main power will be offline until it can be put back in position.'

'Be ready to re-engage on my command.' Ash leaped out of his seat and managed to stay on his feet as the ship swayed more violently, scattering everyone else to the ground. After a short dash to the reactor room, Ash found himself amongst the array of powerful lasers making up Cygnus' fusion reactor. The harder than normal landing had caused an optical coupling to slip out of the precise alignment needed to generate the extraordinary power required to operate the ship. Without all twenty-four lasers in place and perfectly synchronised the fusion reaction wouldn't take place and the ship would not be able to lift herself into the air. He grabbed the glowing cable end, shielding his eyes against the powerful light beam and inserted it into the socket, before re-attaching the clamp that had come loose.

'Mira, run the automatic trim diagnostic for laser number eighteen and let me know when it's fully aligned.'

Mira had already anticipated this command, activating the micro-servos that would perfectly aim the laser beam on to its target. 'Automatic alignment for laser number eighteen is now confirmed Ash.'

'Let's go Mira, get us out of here.' Ash raced up the stairs to the flight deck to be ready to take manual control of the ship if required. As he strapped himself into his seat, he felt the main engine coming back online observing the thrusters coming up to maximum power and forcing the ship up against the tree branches now criss-crossing her wings.

But Cygnus was stuck. The oak trees creaked and flexed but would not yield against the push of the ship's engines and anti-gravity field. Stress gauges across the ship's hull were showing levels that were getting uncomfortably close to her design limits.

Ash scanned his instrument consoles looking for a way to divert power and exploit a weak spot in the trees' coverage of the ship, but quickly came to the same conclusion as Mira.

'We're not going anywhere without incurring serious damage to the hull.' Reluctantly Ash ran down the thrusters but left enough power on to provide resistance against the trees figuring that if he shut the engines down completely the trees would probably swamp the ship entirely and they would never be able to escape.

Phae and the others were in the meantime gathering in Cygnus' operations room, the hub that was normally the command centre when they were on away missions. In the centre of the room a holographic head was projected above the circular table. Mira's face beamed out at them as they spread out looking at the various video feeds from Cygnus' many fixed and drone cameras.

Phae had come to realise that the Sun-Moon device had a few more tricks than she had expected. It had tried to warn her of an attack but the telepathic interface to her mind gave a very metaphorical interpretation of what was about to happen. She realised that she would need to learn to interpret the visual riddles that the device fed into her mind. So, the ship was the dove, and the twigs were the animated oak trees, and the black cat could only mean one thing, Cyax!

Ben was the first to spot the invaders from a drone feed,

'Look, a group of cyber-demons coming through the trees.' But the screen went black as the cyber-demons took out the drone with a direct hit from a blaster shot. Very quickly all of Cygnus' drones were disabled, leaving them with only the ship's on-board cameras and the satellite feed. The on-board cameras were mostly blocked by the strangling oak trees, but the satellite feed was clear enough.

As ever action plans were forming quickly in Phae's mind, in her instinctive 'shoot-from-the-hip' style. How could she use the resources available to her to get a quick and positive outcome for the group? She investigated the Sun-Moon whose displays were producing even wilder oscillations of dials and stronger alignments of runes and symbols more closely associated with darker energy, or the Lore of Evil.

She remembered that Xin once advised her that the universe ultimately seeks balance and harmony, opposing forces will always settle down into a stable system and where forces were mis-matched then it was not necessarily inevitable that the strongest force would win. It was possible to use the power of a large force against itself, if a small force were applied in just the right place at the right time. He had demonstrated this in his martial-arts classes where he would show a girl like Ciara how to defeat a much larger warrior, by using the warrior's own weight against himself.

The huge force of darkness that was indicated by the Sun-Moon was almost certainly Cyax, wielding the Wand of Xylos to control the forest and trap their ship. He was using the Wand's elemental wood lore to great effect, so how could she fight back?

Thinking about the cycle of forces in elemental lore, she recalled that it was possible to either add to or diminish an elemental power, if another elemental energy could be summoned and applied in the right way. Fire energies would defeat wood but causing a large fire would also be a very risky strategy and would probably destroy their ship at the same time.

Water energies would be generative for wood making things worse, and metal would simply contain the wood energies. Earth energy would be weakened, so she was left with only one other option, to produce a directly balancing force, a kind of 'anti-wood.' This was the equivalent of putting a child of a similar weight on the opposite side of a seesaw.

'Maybe I can neutralise it,' said Phae picking up the Sun-Moon as if a flash of inspiration had suddenly gripped her. This sudden change of mood was infectious, certainly where Ben and Ash were concerned, but Ciara was more wary of her tiger companion's big bold ideas. She rolled her eyes and shook her head. '

Here we go again,' she murmured.

'What do you mean by neutralise it?' said Ben, enthusiastically seizing on Phae's possible solution to their situation.

'The Sun-Moon is more than just a fancy way of finding things. It has its own energy source and if I recall correctly, Xin said that it had been invented by King Theokeis as an instrument to bring harmony to the universe. So, I think I may be able to set it up to counteract the sorcery that is being used to animate the trees and release the ship.'

Phae started turning thumb wheels causing the concentric runed wheel to turn to a position that aligned Jupiter opposite the moon and opposite symbols indicating diminishing power.

Inside her head, she came back to the vision of the dove in the tree with the panther-like creature advancing on the bird as the branches suffocated it further. She could now see the problem. The big cat was the source of the wood-lore that caused the sprouting of more twigs and branches to strangle the dove.

She tuned the Sun-Moon to defeat the trees, and in her vision, it took on the appearance of a silver orb, like a small version of the moon hovering in space near the dove. But its effect on the cat wasn't sufficient to stop the growth of new twigs. It needed to be closer to the wood-energy source to be fully effective.

'I need to get the Sun-Moon as close to Cyax as I can manage,' she said to the others.

Ben needed no persuading to get involved, 'OK, my turn. Where do want me to put it?'

Phae wasn't sure at first about handing over this important task to the young Australian, 'But it's not safe out there!'

Ben was insistent, 'Where do I put it?'

'No, I must do it,' she argued.

The logically thinking Ash intervened to prevent an argument that in his mind was unnecessary and time wasting.

'Phae, he's quicker than you. Just set it and give it to Ben before it's too late.'

Phae knew that this was right, but she was torn between the instinct to protect her colleagues and the desire to do the job herself.

'All right. Cyax must be somewhere nearby, because he needs to be quite close to make the sorcery work.'

Ben looked through the windows to scan the area. His keen hunter's eyesight soon spotted a dark figure poised like a master puppeteer, driving the actions of the trees.

'There he is. OK, I'm ready.' He activated his amulet and transformed into the armoured shape of the Dog Warrior.

Phae spoke to him once more as he prepared to leave, 'When it's over you have to bring the Sun-Moon back. We can't let Cyax take it.' Ben nodded and disappeared through the door of the central hub.

Dropping from a hatch panel under the ship, he blew a sharp, high-pitched whistle which was at a frequency that couldn't be detected by ordinary human ears, mortal, or immortal. Running for the cover of some nearby bushes he paused for a moment to wait for the support he had summoned.

It didn't take long before he was surrounded by a wolf pack, howling with delight at being summoned. He was almost pushed over by the weight of legs jumping and pushing at his body in excitement. As well as being able to summon his celestial companion Siriaxeis from the constellation of the dog, Ben could summon a pack of earthly or extra-planar dogs to help him in his tasks.

When in Dog Warrior mode he also had the magical ability of being able to orally communicate with any type of animal. Ciara called it his "Dr Doolittle" spell, but this simple comparison belittled the real strength of this power.

Ben made a sharp barking sound to silence the pack and get their attention. Speaking in a series of short barks, growls and yelps he described the mission to place the Sun-Moon as close as possible to Cyax and activate its neutralising power. He would lead the attack by disguising himself as one of the wolf-pack as they flooded the forest floor around Cyax.

'*Caneseis*' called Ben who morphed into a large grey wolf, only distinguishable by the fact that he carried the Sun-Moon between his jaws. He sprang forward into the space in front of Cygnus followed by his pack of over fifty wolves, all howling and excited for the chase. The pack instinctively split up into groups to chase down the cyber-demons, pulling them to the ground, tearing at their wrists, disarming them by ripping out their implants, and standing over them, ears back and snarling in fury, their sharp canine teeth fully bared and ready to bite.

While the pack caused chaos amongst the guards, Ben and another group of wolves dodged blaster fire and raced towards the place from where Cyax was wielding the Wand of Xylos, directing the oak trees against Cygnus.

When he reached a point where he would be close enough but hidden from Cyax' line of sight, he transformed back into the Dog Warrior and placed the Sun-Moon gently on a tuft of moss on top of a decaying log from which was sprouting some small but vivid orange fungus. He opened the Sun-Moon's lid of sliding panels. Everything looked fine, just as Phae had set it. He transformed back into his wolf body and raced off towards the ship, followed by his companion wolves, disappearing back into the undergrowth of thick ferns and bracken.

The remaining cyber-demons were just as surprised by the rapid withdrawal of the pack as they had been by its appearance and stood looking dumbfounded, as if not really knowing what to do next.

It didn't take long for the Sun-Moon's re-balancing, or neutralising magic to take effect. First there was a kind of stasis, as the oak trees came to a gradual halt, no longer shuddering, shaking, and beating the ship with their branches. Then a web of fine white fungal filaments like spiders' webs grew rapidly up from the oak tree roots, causing the bark to shrivel away from the trunks, revealing pale amber coloured wood beneath, which cracked and dried out, turning to a shade of orange, and finally crumbling into a woody dust.

Bracket fungi and mushrooms burst out of the disintegrating trees in an extraordinary variety of colours and shapes. Tall purple ones shaped like bells. Red and white ones like the sort you would see with a garden gnome perched on top, orange ones shaped like pancakes with gills beneath and the usual common or garden type that Ben recognised he might find on top of a pizza.

'Mmm, pizza' Ben thought to himself. But his dream of lunch was broken by the sound of wood cracking and splitting apart. As the fungus overwhelmed the oaks, there wasn't enough strength left in the tree trunks to support their massive weight. Splinters of wood and branches rained down around him and his wolf-pack which retreated for safety, while Cygnus' wooden prison cracked and fell apart.

"Let's hope that's enough' Ash tested his thrusters and the remaining great oak boughs split away from the trunks as he nudged the ship higher a few centimetres at a time.

'Ben, get back here now and make sure you've got the Sun-Moon' called Phae over Ben's comms.

Cyax was unprepared for such powerful elemental lore working against his plans. He forced more of his will power into the Wand of Xylos to regain control. He knew that only the most powerful lore would be able to stop him, and it must be somewhere nearby. Stepping out from behind the crumbling oak trees he found himself facing the wolf pack, snarling, and baring their teeth. One of them leaped forward and sunk its teeth into his ankle and Cyax winced in agony, but he retaliated grabbing the creature by its neck and crushing the breath out of it, before discarding its limp body into the rest of the pack causing them to bark and howl even louder.

While Cyax was distracted Ben slipped out of the pack in wolf form and snapped up the Sun-Moon in his jaws. Cyax aimed the Wand at Ben and summoned its entanglement spell. Thick tendrils of ivy, thorny brambles and creepers surged out of the ground even as he ran. Swelling around his ankles they tripped him up and wrapped themselves tightly around all four of his paws preventing his escape and holding the wolf-pack still at the same time. The dogs were helpless, and Ben was out of ideas, surely this was the end.

As Cyax strode towards the helpless Dog warrior to finish him off and take his amulet, a familiar face morphed into the woody bark of the tree under which Ben had laid the Sun-Moon. Smiling down at Ben, was the face of the Master of Wands, superimposed in the rough surface of the gnarled tree trunk as if he were part of it. The face winked at Ben just before a tree branch swiped Cyax off his feet.

The Master whispered a spell that to human ears sounded like the rustle of a light breeze through the leaves in the forest. The roots and tendrils that were fastening Ben to the forest floor wilted, giving him a chance to escape while Cyax was pinned down by the branch.

Cyax summoned the '*true seeing*' spell which revealed to his eyes only, the full figure of the Master of Wands physically blended into the body of the tree, as if a strong spotlight placed behind the tree had exposed his body shape within. Realising he was in grave danger, the Master dematerialised, transferring his body to another tree nearby as Cyax called out the shatter spell '*Dimensis.*'

A magical explosion rocked the tree, showering the wolf-pack with millions of matchstick sized fragments of wood.

With his fast canine instincts, Ben had already seized the opportunity to escape that the Master had created for him and was racing across the forest floor back towards the ship. Cyax aimed more blasts at Ben from the Wand, attempting to drain life energy from him in the same way as which he had used the Wand to destroy Xin. But Ben was too nimble, switching his direction with ease and diving through bushes to avoid more blasts from cyber-demons, who had now got involved in the chase.

Scrambling under the trunk of the remains one of the large trees that had been pinning down the ship, Ben made a massive leap back into the cargo hold, rolling across the floor as Ash fully engaged the ship's thrusters. Cygnus lifted into the air scattering the remains of the rotten oak trees back to the ground where they crumbled into piles of orange-red dust, like so many smashed termite hills. As the ship climbed vertically at first, the downdraught from its powerful thrusters blew the dust into a thick cloud of debris obscuring it from Cyax and his guards.

'Woo-hoo that was close!' exclaimed Ben as he raced up to the flight deck to join his colleagues, full of bravado. A massive smile crossed his face from ear to ear.

'Hey Mira, how about doing the cloaky thing?' he asked the ship's computer.

'Ben, it is important that you use the correct command protocols!' replied Mira primly, slightly miffed at the young Australian's informal approach to procedure.

Ben just grinned even more. The adrenaline rush from his mission was still in full flow and he didn't really care about proper procedure anymore.

'Ahh, OK mother. Engage the cloaking sequence, pretty please!' He high fived Phae and handed over the Sun-Moon device before jumping into an unoccupied seat at the back of the flight deck and strapping himself in.

"Cloaking confirmed" replied the computer sniffily, conceding the moment to Ben's triumph.

"Let's head for the desert base, get this ship properly repaired and then see if we can find the others,' said Ash as he punched commands into the navigation system. 'We need to get this team back together.'

CHAPTER 26
The Celestial Plane

Nico's trip through the celestial plane was short as promised, but spectacular. It was a monochrome universe. Nothing around him seemed quite real. The skies were mostly a dark graphite grey, but great silver-grey clouds illuminated the land with a pale light. The landscape was mountainous with a wide silver river cutting through the centre, light twinkling off its rippling surface like the billions of sparkling stars in a galaxy. A large swan made from starlight was gliding effortlessly just over the surface of the river, while a silver eagle hung in the sky nearby as if it were riding a thermal while hunting for prey.

Most objects, trees, animals, and structures seemed to be enveloped in a shimmering light, as if they were made from the same essence as the stars. Plumes of light streaming out of the brightest stars in the sky formed arcs of energy stretching from point to point, like glowing ribbons, and curtain-like sheets of light rippled in the sky like a pale white version of the aurora borealis.

Besides Adraxa, other fantastic creatures swept through the skies. Nico saw other dragons and large fantastical beasts on the ground, recognising the celestial tiger Xantix that was Phae's companion creature. In the distance he watched a battle between a great warrior and a creature which had seven long necks and a head on the end of each one. His attention was drawn away by a great winged horse that thundered past them, its magnificent mane and tail leaving a trail of glittering starlight in its wake. Below, a celestial cat stared at them as they flew by, before it bounded across the river of stars to pursue the celestial dove.

Adraxa turned and headed straight for one of the large white energy ribbons spanning the sky. Nico closed his eyes as they entered the glowing plasma and flew towards the bright star from which it grew.

When he opened his eyes again, he found himself cruising over the River Thames. The tower blocks of the City of London shone in the night as Adraxa turned to follow the river to the West.

Minutes later Nico was climbing down from Adraxa's back on a playing field near his mother's home. He recognised the place from a visit he and Aunt Cass had made a few years ago in her attempt to maintain some sort of family bond between them all. Aunt Cass didn't believe that any amount of screen time could ever be better than a proper physical hug from your mum, so she hoped that the two would bond more easily in person.

But the visit had been a disaster. Nico's mother Emma couldn't make an easy connection with the boy. Very quickly it became apparent that Nico still harboured strong and bitter feelings of rejection that created a barrier between them, which then turned into bad behaviour on his part and frustrated anger on hers.

Now that Nico was older, he was starting to feel differently about his mother. In his heart he knew that the bond with her was real, but he wasn't sure how to overcome the protective wall he had built to insulate himself from the feelings of rejection. Now he was ready to give it another try.

As Adraxa disappeared back to the celestial plane, Nico crossed the street and walked up the stone flagged path to the front door of the classic, red-bricked Edwardian detached house, with its mock-Tudor features. He pressed the bell next to the heavy oak door and waited nervously in the cool night air, his hands fidgeting in his pockets. After a short wait the door opened revealing his mother.

'Nico?' she said in total surprise and disbelief at seeing her son standing there.

'Mum!' was the only word he could muster as all the things he wanted to say to her evaporated from his mind. He looked into her eyes and mis-read the confusion that was registered there, as a negative reaction.

Emma did hesitate for a moment, standing stiffly in the doorway. She seemed on edge, but Nico just launched himself into her arms clasping her tightly and burying his head into her shoulder. She hugged him, but he sensed the tension in her body and backed off. The truth was that Emma was desperate to hug her son, but at that moment all she wanted was for him to run away and find somewhere safe to protect himself from the evil creature that was waiting for them both inside the house.

Nico decided not to question his mother's slightly awkward response to their meeting. He had thrown himself at her as a way of trying to show that everything that had gone between them in the past was forgotten and now he just wanted them to be together as a family.

Emma was about to speak when a familiar voice came through from inside.

'Who's at the door darling? Did I hear Nico's voice? Bring him in, I'll be down in a minute?' The voice was that of Nico's father, but he was surprised to hear it, as his parents hadn't lived together for over five years. What was he doing in London?

'You'd better come in.' said Emma in a hushed voice. Nico stepped over the threshold into the ornately tiled hallway of the house and stood by the large staircase with its carved newel post in the shape of an acorn with oak leaves on the panels below. The house seemed a little dishevelled and in need of a lick of paint.

A slightly musty, dank smell like rotting wood hung faintly in the air. The hallway was weirdly lacking in light, even though the large chandelier was fully illuminated. Gloom of a mysterious grey sort filled the hallway, dampening and absorbing the light like a fog but without a misty atmosphere. The edges of the wallpaper were curling up next to the yellowing gloss white paint on the woodwork. Letters were strewn about the hall stand, unopened as if nobody really cared and a layer of fine dust coated the picture rail. It was as if the place had been neglected for quite a while.

Emma spoke to break the silence as Nico peered mystified around the hallway which he remembered as bright and airy with beautiful stained-glass panels of butterflies and tulips in the inner door.

'Gosh, when did you get so big? What are you doing here Nico? How's Aunt Cass?'

'She died. I don't know what happened. One day I went home, and the police were there. Now I'm here.' Nico hung his head, knowing that his simplistic answer would cause more detailed questions to be asked, which would be awkward.

'Nico, why didn't you call me. You shouldn't be on your own, it's not right.' Emma took her son by the shoulders and looked him earnestly in the eyes.

'I don't know, I found some new friends and I thought it would be cool to hang out with them for a while.' Nico was reluctant to talk about the Astraxi, as he knew the whole story would be too fantastic for his mother to believe him.

'What sort of friends Nico? Are you in trouble?' Now she was concerned and feeling guilty about her failure to be a mother to him and leaving him in the care of Aunt Cass.

'I'd rather not talk about it,' was Nico's tight-lipped response to this probing question. He turned away from Emma, but she turned him back to face her once more.

Emma tried to be conciliatory. 'I'm your mother Nico, I just want to help.'

'Bit late for that now, isn't it,' was Nico's stinging response, half swallowed by his emotions.

'Oh Nico, don't start that. I'm sorry. It was never easy between your father and me. You should never have got caught up in all of that.'

Before Nico could respond a figure appeared at the top of the stairs. Nico looked up to see his father standing there.

'Hey look what the cat dragged in!' said the man as he started to descend the stairs.

'Hey dad, what are you doing here?' called Nico back to him. Nico was amazed to see his father, but there was something odd about him. Somehow his eyes didn't seem right. The one thing that people always noticed about Nico's father was the character that he expressed through his eyes. Whenever he appeared in a photograph, his eyes engaged the lens in a way that most other people just couldn't achieve, which always made him the focal point of any picture.

Perhaps he should have been a model or an actor, was what Emma used to say about him when they first met. But now his eyes seemed tired and misty, with dark shadows beneath them and the intense spark of his gaze was replaced with something cold and almost sinister. Nico looked into the watery eyes and was immediately repelled by them.

'Nico, I think you should leave quickly!' said Emma as she dragged him by the arm towards the front door, but Nico was resisting, still trying to understand the situation he was in, when his father blocked the way to the door. This unnerved Nico and he suddenly sensed some sort of a weird trap but couldn't understand what his father was doing there. Was he still playing those same sad games for possession of Nico like he did during the divorce?

'Not so fast! Nico and I have some catching up to do, don't we son? You've been on quite an adventure, haven't you?' said his father in an accusatory tone as he ushered them into the living room.

'How do you know that and what's it got to do with you anyway?' said Nico defensively.

His father closed the living room door firmly behind them.

'Well, I've heard that you've been mixing with some very bad people, and that you're out of control. I saw the police reports.' A smile broke out on his face, but not a normal smile, there was something malicious about it.

Nico's sense of unease was building rapidly, 'Bad people? I don't know what you mean.'

His father's sickly smile intensified, and his eyes narrowed as if he were about to deliver something devastating, 'You've been working for a gang run by a master criminal called Xin, and you stole something very valuable.'

Emma was confused by this description of her son. Even though she knew that the creature posing as Nico's father was something of great evil that had taken control of her, she hadn't realised until now that her son was the creature's target.

'Xin's not a criminal, and I didn't steal anything!' Nico's anger was starting to surge, and he clenched his fists tightly.

'Oh!' The man raised his eyebrows in mock surprise and pointed to Nico's shirt pocket which was glowing with a familiar pale blue light. 'What's that in your pocket then?'

Nico looked down at his shirt to see the glow of the DragonStone, which Gilmane had magically planted on him. As he looked back up, the person that he had thought was his father was slowly edging towards him '

Give it to me you little thief.' His voice was dark and harsh, with more than a hint of menace.

Despite only having been in the Astraxi for a few weeks, Nico was already starting to get a feel for the world that he had been brought into when he first took the DragonStone ring from Gilmane's shop. He reached for his amulet and activated it releasing the usual fine particles of starlight as the energy from the celestial plane entered its embedded crystals, powering it up.

'You'll have to try harder than that!' he replied before transforming and casting the Dragon Warrior's hailstorm spell '*Sinaris*' at the man who suddenly lunged forward at him.

With no visible hole in the high corniced ceiling of the room in which they were all standing, a torrent of huge freezing hailstones appeared out of nowhere, engulfing the man before he could grab Nico.

The hailstones summoned by Nico, were moving with some considerable speed, almost as if they had been plucked straight out of a real thundercloud and transported directly into that living room. A fact that would have been confirmed by any knowledgeable sorcerer or practising mage. Because that's how many types of sorcery work, it's about summoning the effect or the object that you want from somewhere else, to where you are now and directing it at the target. In this case Nico was moving the hail from the centre of a massive cumulonimbus cloud directly into the room. He didn't need to know where the storm was, he just thought '*hailstorm*' as he cast the spell and imagined what would happen next.

The hailstones were huge, snowball sized lumps of ice, as hard as iron and powerful enough to smash lumps out of rock, dent the panels of a car or break through panes of toughened glass. They pounded the head and body of the man, knocking him to his knees, but he righted himself and moved swiftly to grab Emma, wrapping his forearm around her neck, and twisting her arm up behind her back to subdue her.

Nico looked on in horror as the man who resembled his father transformed into a hideous creature, the shape shifting Fiend Hundun. His face was pale and waxy, the skin stretched across his cheekbones, with ancient characters tattooed into the flesh. Hundun was now wearing the ancient decaying armour that he had worn when facing the Astraxi under the ruins of the Royal Palace, when Eleni was tragically lost.

Nico wasn't sure what he was facing at first, but when he asked Xin about what exactly had happened to his predecessor, Xin had described the Fiends and how Eleni was destroyed by one of them. He realised he was facing the same undead peril, a Lich. Now that the transformation back to his normal self was complete, Hundun cast his own spell back at Nico, '*Malexis*' the *bane* spell.

As was normal when facing such a powerful undead creature, Nico felt his spirit being sapped as the *bane* spell penetrated his mind and chilled his flesh.

'Give me the ring and the amulet and I will spare your mother.' Hundun laughed his cruellest laugh, as he watched the torment in Nico's face. The *bane* spell took hold of Nico's stomach and crushed it, almost taking his heart with it. He felt himself buckling at the knees and a black fog entered his mind, dispelling any clear or rational thoughts he had about facing up to or fighting this dreadful apparition.

He heard his mother's voice imploring him to be firm, 'Stand up Nico. Stay on your feet, Dragon warrior!'

How did she know he was the Dragon warrior? But he didn't have time to ponder this as the sound of her voice triggered inside Nico's mind the image of that first Dragon warrior, his ancestor who looked upon him and declared 'Nico, my child, now is your time. You will be the greatest Dragon that ever lived'

The inspiring memory of Takareis, the first Dragon Warrior, drove the painful sickness out of his stomach, and he found the inner strength to reply to Hundun defiantly. 'I am not afraid of you, or your master. You will release my mother now, or I will destroy you.'

'I don't think so!' hissed Hundun, who loosened his grip around Emma's throat and raised his hand pointing his forefinger at Nico. On the end of the finger was a long pointed, ugly grey fingernail tinged with flecks of green and yellow fungus. As Emma struggled against his grip, Hundun poked the hideous fingernail deep into her neck, causing her to cry out in pain.

Nico's eyes opened wide in terror, as a network of green veins spread over the skin on his mother's neck and across the rest of her body. She writhed in pain as Hundun's sinister, poisonous grin spread once more across his face.

'Mum!' shouted Nico, not really knowing what to do next, or how he could help his mother. He was still a very inexperienced member of the Astraxi and faced many years of training, even if he were to be the next great Dragon Mage.

'Get out now Nico. Run, while you still can' gasped Emma, as the green veins spread over her face, drawing the pink flush out of her cheeks, and turning them grey.

'It's your last chance. Give me the amulet and the ring and I will release her from the poison.' Hundun jabbed his forefinger in Nico's direction in a threatening manner.

'GET OFF HER!' he screamed, and gripping his amulet launched one of his most devastating spells '*Telensis.*'

Anyone standing outside of the house would have been alarmed to see a huge great whirling vortex of storm clouds a hundred metres above the house. It flashed with bright light internally for a moment before unleashing a huge, sustained bolt of forked lightning right through the tiled roof. Roof joists and tiles flew everywhere as the contents of the loft were blown into the air, by the explosive electrical power of a million volts.

Inside the house Hundun dropped Emma to the floor to defend himself, but he was too late. A second bright blue-white bolt of electricity ripped through his frame blowing off pieces of his armour and singeing his pale flesh. Nico wasn't taking any chances, he shoved the DragonStone ring onto his finger and summoned a fireball which he directed at Hundun. The Lich seemed to be illuminated from inside for a moment. He fell to the floor, with acrid smoke rising from him as he writhed in agony, his limbs flailing around the floor.

With Hundun subdued, Nico called up the spell used to dismiss such creatures back to their native plane, '*Hundun: Yoshara Kalente!*' Hundun was engulfed in a whirling vortex of starlight particles, which sucked him at speed into a void. Before the portal closed on him, Hundun let out a sickening howl, which reverberated in Nico's ears.

The room now looked as if someone had thrown not one, but many hand grenades into it. Nico turned to his mother, who was lying near to where he had blasted Hundun. 'Mum, let me get you to a doctor, quickly'

Emma was barely conscious. The disease from Hundun's fingertip was of a type that couldn't be treated by conventional medical science, only a very powerful mage healer such as the Winged Horse Warrior could possibly save her now. If only the Horse Warrior were available.

The Astraxi hadn't had a Winged Horse Warrior since the Great Battle of Astrellion, but Nico was unaware of any of this, and his focus was on saving his mother. He was the so-called great and mighty Dragon Mage, surely, he could do something to save her. He tried to sit her up, but she was too weak to support herself as Hundun's venom seeped through her veins destroying her vital organs.

'It's too late Nico, protect yourself. I'm sorry I wasn't there for you,' she said as her breathing became fainter.

'Sshh. Save your strength. I'll get help,' said Nico as he desperately tried to figure out how he could help her.

But Emma summoned the last of her strength and continued to speak to her son. 'I know all about Xin and the Astraxi. That's why your father and I fought over you. He wanted you to be aware of your heritage, but I wanted nothing of it.' She reached up and stroked his face. 'But just look at you now.'

'No, no. Don't leave me,' he called out in frustration, fear and anger while trying to take in her revelation that she had known of this potential destiny all along.

'Just believe in yourself my precious boy.' She closed her eyes, and he held her, while her breathing became shallower until it stopped. He carefully lowered her head on to the carpet and watched as her body dissolved into a layer of twinkling lights, which drifted and faded away, just like those exhaled by Xin when he was struck by the Wand of Xylos and fell over the cliff edge.

Nico stood up, shocked by what had just happened, then slumped into a large armchair to try and rationalise it all. Rain was falling through the hole in the roof and the smoke had started to clear. He thought that he should be wild with anger, but he wasn't. He was just saddened by everything that had happened to him in the last few days and took the amulet from his wrist, throwing it into a corner of the room where it clattered noisily to the floor.

'What's the point of anything anymore?' he muttered to himself. He sat with his elbows on his knees propping up his head while staring at the family photograph he had taken from Aunt Cass' dresser. Previously he was quite content to live a self-contained lifestyle, following his own personal code of conduct and pretty much pleasing himself what he did with his time, but just when he was starting to feel like he belonged somewhere, he had lost the few people that really mattered in his life. First his Aunt, then Xin and now his parents. He felt doomed to be on his own for ever.

The Dragon amulet stirred on the floor where he had thrown it, shuffling in the dust, and then suddenly it flew at him, striking him hard in the stomach. Stubbornly he threw it away again, but the amulet launched itself back at him, this time striking him on the head and falling into his lap.

'I can't do this' he whispered to himself, starting to cave into grief for his mother despite her final words to him.

With an air of deep resignation, he picked the amulet off his lap and stared into the centre of the dial, where there was a stylised representation of a powerful dragon, full of attitude and breathing fire from its mouth. But his gaze fell through the amulet into the trans-dimensional space beyond it, travelling through to another plane of existence, where he found himself being drawn into visions the same as those he saw when Xin first revealed his part in the Astraxi.

He flashed back through many images of triumphant and glorious Dragon Warriors to the scene of the ritual creation of the Astraxi at the time of King Theokeis, ending with the original Dragon warrior receiving his amulet for the first time.

In his head he could hear the voice of Gilmane, clearly as if he were speaking directly into his ear.

'It's in your blood Nico. This amulet was forged with a drop of blood from its first owner, your ancestor. It knows you are descended from the original Dragon, and it knows you are the person who is most worthy to wield its power.'

'Doesn't feel that way right now, old man,' he whispered. Nico looked at the smiling face of his mother in the photograph. He felt robbed of her and of any normal sort of a family life.

Gilmane's voice continued, 'Your mother knew of your heritage, which came through your father's bloodline, and that knowledge was the source of the conflict between them. Your mother always tried to protect you from the risks of becoming a member of the Astraxi, but your father wanted you to be ready should the day ever come'

Nico shook his head. He had had no idea of the root of this conflict in his family. Even Aunt Cass must have known about it, but nobody had bothered to tell him, probably to try and protect him.

'So that's what it was. I guess their splitting up really was to do with me. What happened to my father, Gilmane?' asked Nico.

Gilmane's reply was tinged with regret. 'It's most likely that Hundun has killed him too. Go back to the Astraxi Nico, they are your family now. You must believe in yourself and the others. Together you are strong enough to defeat Cyax. That has always been the way of the Astraxi.'

Nico was starting to realise that if the conflict between his parents was due to their knowledge that he may turn out to be the next Dragon Mage, then he might as well accept this destiny, at least for now.

'I'll do it for Xin and for them,' he said as he picked himself up, put the picture in his pocket and headed for the front door.

Nico started to wonder about the fate of his other colleagues. He had last seen Phae trying to guide the others to safety. Where were they now? Maybe he should try and join up with them if they had managed to escape from the invasion of the base. Perhaps they might have made it back to the Perpetual Motion Café? The sound of many approaching sirens suddenly woke him from this speculation, and he headed for the garden at the back of the house.

From outside he surveyed the hole in the roof caused by the lightning strike he had summoned and was momentarily awestruck by the understanding of the power he had in his hands. Maybe he really could help save the world from Cyax.

As the fire trucks parked up outside the front of the house, he summoned Adraxa who appeared with her usual flourish of ethereal star light.

'What next, Dragon Warrior?' enquired the fabulous celestial creature, her scales shimmering with star energy.

'Home,' was Nico's very short response.

With that simple instruction and with Nico on her back, Adraxa leaped back into the air entering the celestial plane with a flash of light. One of the firemen, who was unloading hoses off the truck spotted the dragon's rapid departure. He dropped his hose and turned aghast to his astounded colleagues,

'Did you see that?' The others stood and shook their heads being more concerned about checking the damaged house and rescuing anyone still trapped inside.

'It was a... a dragon, with a boy on its back!' he continued.

'Oh yes, and there's a flying pig too!' commented one of the others, at which point they all started laughing before being told by their chief in no uncertain terms to stop messing about get on with their work.

Adraxa didn't need to be told where she would find 'Home.' She already knew that Nico's home was now one hundred percent with the Astraxi, and they passed once more into the celestial plane heading back towards Astrapolis.

CHAPTER 27
Back On The Mission

While Nico was in London facing up to Hundun, the rest of the group had made it to the Astraxi's southern base to make the much-needed repairs to Cygnus, knowing that they had limited time before re-engaging with Cyax.

Phae and Ciara were searching for leads on the possible whereabouts of Nico and Xin, but Ben was spending his time learning as much as he could about the local cuisine from the base's kitchen chef. That region of Astrellion was famous for the use of particularly strong spices in its cooking, which unfortunately for his colleagues had devastating effects on Ben's digestive system.

Ciara was particularly horrified by Ben's various pungent sweaty stenches and had threatened to use a cork to solve at least one of his bodily odour problems. But without Xin to keep him in check, Ben continued his juvenile behaviour until one morning he went too far.

He walked casually into Ciara's room with the usual grin on his face, but stopped and bent forward a little, as if a sharp pain had shot through his midriff. What followed was a base animal noise that some might have compared to the sound of ripping lino! It ended with a wet sounding squelch, which left Ben looking nervous for a moment, but after shuffling slightly, he concluded that everything was OK.

'Whoa! Better out than in, I suppose mate!' said Ben with a smirk on his face.

An evil stench of partially digested vegetables blended with aromatic spices seeped through the air. Ciara wrinkled her nose and covered her mouth with her hand.

'Phew, that was close, I just managed to avoid the follow through!' Ben continued, feeling somewhat proud of his noxious prank.

'Get out you pig!' cried Ciara and immediately started beating him over the head with a hockey stick.

'I think you'll find I'm actually the Dog warrior!' quipped Ben as he ran for cover out of the room. That was the last straw and Ciara resolved to retaliate.

Later, during a security briefing with the base commander, Ben was invited up on the stage to describe his first-hand experience of the Golterian air attack on the northern base. But when he opened his mouth all that the people in the room heard was a collection of tuneful rasping noises, changing in pitch, like the sound of air being expelled from an inflated balloon, whose neck is being stretched.

Ciara had quietly activated her amulet and created the illusion that every time Ben spoke, his voice sounded like a collection of what would be politely described as bottom burps!

The scene in the briefing room quickly descended into farce as spontaneous laughter broke out amongst the officers who were normally very reserved and professional in their duties.

Ben didn't know what was going on, or why were they all laughing at him. It wasn't as if he was even attempting to tell a joke or two. In his head his own voice sounded normal, he had no idea that Ciara had spoofed him. So, while enjoying what appeared to be a promising new career as a comedian, Ben just kept on talking, pointing at the display screens, and making what he thought were intelligent observations about air cover and missile defences, but were in fact a string of parping noises with an ever-increasing comic effect on the audience.

The serious discussion about defending this base against a similar attack as the one that had destroyed the northern base quickly degenerated into wholesale sniggering and tittering, and even the General struggled to contain himself from the absurdity of it all.

Phae was extremely embarrassed by Ben's performance but soon realised what was going on and snapped at Ciara.

'What do you think you're doing Ciara! These people probably already think we're just a bunch of stupid kids, and now we're proving it to them. Stop it now!' Ciara nonchalantly tilted her head in agreement and re-set her amulet causing the various sliding trombone-like noises coming from Ben's mouth to come to a sudden stop and be replaced by his normal voice telling a joke.

'Why did the Dingo cross the road twice?' he announced to the assembled officials.

'...because he was a double crosser. Geddit?!' Ben waited for even more laughter, which didn't come as the audience recovered their composure. Phae jumped out of her seat angrily and the room suddenly went very quiet. Even Ben realised then that it wasn't necessarily just his witty oration that was causing a stir.

'I can only apologise for the juvenile behaviour of my colleagues General; can we please return to business.' She mouthed the words 'BEN SIT DOWN' in his direction and he returned to the table confused and still not understanding why everyone was laughing at him, but he had really enjoyed the attention, grinning from ear to ear in his usual canine demeanour.

'What's the big deal Phae?' he asked as he returned to his chair.

'I'll deal with you both later' said Phae in a stage whisper. Having got her revenge by making Ben look stupid, Ciara was now feeling quite relaxed about Phae's threat. 'Who put her in charge anyway?' thought Ciara to herself.

Down in the engineering area, Ash was hard at work as usual. Most of the damage to the ship was superficial and her unique style of construction made it easy to replace parts, assuming the parts were available, which often they weren't, so some had to be engineered from scratch.

A group of aeronautical technicians had disassembled the lateral emitter, which formed part of Cygnus' invisibility cloak. They were looking at the scorched electronics to see what could be repaired or salvaged. Ash was wearing a pair of magnifying glasses with a live data feed in his line of sight and a head torch as he inserted probes from his diagnostic computer to gather information about the state of the device.

He hummed and harred as the information scrolled down the display in his glasses. It didn't look good, and it was unlikely that the base would have the necessary spares to get the emitter working again. He was going to have to improvise but being a highly skilled engineer was another of his superpowers.

At the conclusion of the security briefing, Phae, Ciara and Ben made their way down to the hangar to see how things were going. Ash was still working on the lateral emitter when they arrived.

'I think we've got a problem. The lateral emitter is fried beyond repair. To fix it, I need to build a new array and EMX subassembly using the equipment at the northern base. At the minute the only choice we seem to have, is to fly without the cloaking device.'

'And take our chances out there against the Golterians, I suppose?' said Phae with an air of resignation in her voice.

Phae was dismayed by Ash's diagnosis. She was desperate to get moving and find out what had happened to their missing colleagues. Reports indicated that Astrellian forces were in the process of re-capturing the forward base, but that wouldn't solve their current problems.

The biggest priority other than finding their colleagues was still to secure the remaining weapons of elemental power. They couldn't afford to wait around, for with no shadow of a doubt, Cyax would already be seeking the weapons for himself. Maybe it was more important for them to carry out that mission before it was too late to stop him. '

What would Xin have done?' mused Phae to herself as Ash continued his technical analysis.

'Is there nothing you can do just to get it working, even if it's only a temporary fix?' she asked impatiently. Ash shook his head.

'These aren't standard components, we're going to have to make the field generators from scratch, because they're designed to match the exact geometry of Cygnus' hull. Anything I can make now will only be a partial solution leaving some gaps in our cloak.'

'We haven't got time for this.' Phae was having one of her impulsive moments, you could always tell by the expression of determination in her amber eyes.

'We can't go anywhere without it,' insisted Ash sharply putting down his data probe. 'The risks to the ship and to ourselves are too high.'

'Risks? Aren't we here to take risks? Isn't that the whole point of being a member of the Astraxi?' Phae was now getting irritated, feeling that Ash was somehow trying to thwart her.

'That is your opinion, I am simply giving you the facts on which I base mine.' Ash was firm, but unemotional in his response.

'There must be another way.' After a moment pacing up and down, Phae had a flash of inspiration. 'Have you thought about whether there's anything in our other powers that might help, by using a spell for instance?' Phae had typically come up with a left-field way approaching the problem. Ash had only looked at the repair as an engineering issue, it hadn't occurred to him that they may be able to use their lore to repair the ship, as surely magic and engineering were two completely different techniques.

'What did you have in mind?' said Ash.

'There's the '*make whole*' spell, that's part of my Tiger lore,' she suggested.

'Well, what are you waiting for?' was Ash's quick but slightly sceptical response, as he put down his test equipment.

'Well, er, first I need to know what it was like before it got damaged.' Phae realised that she knew nothing about this component, or whether her spell could actually fix it. But she usually followed her hunches, and most of the time she succeeded. A video screen called up by Ash displayed imagery of the device in detail as well as its specifications. Phae studied the screen and picked up the basics quickly.

Ash pushed the emitter into the centre of the table and stepped back as Phae powered up her amulet '*Olokliros*' she spoke, while in her head she imagined the component restored to a brand-new condition. As they looked on, the sub assembly's burned-out central processor morphed into a clean new chip mounted on a shining circuit board. The emitter nodes which had been bent into a charred, crumpled mess untangled themselves to re-form the complex array that generated the cloaking field, which protected the flying ship's upper decks.

'Remarkable!' was the only word Ash could conjure as he examined the component. It just hadn't occurred to him that magic could be brought to work alongside technology, in his mind they were two equally amazing but separate things. He plugged in his diagnostic tools and immediately lines of data filled his screen indicating 'Positive Status' for all the device's functions.

'Looks like it's running perfectly. Well done Phae!' Ash was unusually enthusiastic for once and he patted her gently on the shoulder before awkwardly withdrawing his hand back to his side. This physical contact raised a little knowing smile from Ciara, who liked to study body language, although there was often little to study with Ash! Phae broke the silence that followed.

'Well, you had better get it fitted because we need to get back on the mission as soon as we can.'

'Give me a couple of hours and I'll have all systems ready to go,' said Ash eager to have Cygnus fully operational again.

'You'll have to teach me that spell, it will save me a lot of time in the workshop!' He turned to his engineers and started to issue orders.

'While you're doing that, I am going to consult the Sun-Moon device again to see if we can get any clues about the location of Xin and Nico. We should try and find the others first, because as Xin always says, we're stronger when we work together.' Phae headed off back to the Astraxi's operations room followed by Ben and Ciara.

They sat on the edge of a replica Wizard's table, identical to the one under the Perpetual Motion Café, with all its runes and symbols. The layout of the table had some basic similarities to the layout of the Sun-Moon, but the small magical device was much more complex, with its additional pointers, dials and symbols related to the positions of stars and planets.

'I'll start by looking for Nico' said Phae as she set about turning dials and thumbwheels to represent the elemental power of water, the planet mercury, and the dragon rune. As she did so she formed a question in her mind 'Where's Nico?' which was telepathically picked up by the device and which started to align the appropriate concentric wheels and symbols.

After a few seconds the movement ceased, as the device had settled on a set of celestial co-ordinates. Mira was watching the proceedings from her usual spot at the centre of the Wizard's table and was about to announce Nico's whereabouts, when the answer appeared telepathically in Phae's mind.

'Nico has gone…'

'…Home,' said Phae.

'Astrapolis?' asked Ben.

'Yes, the Perpetual Motion Café to be precise, from those co-ordinates' continued Mira.

'I guess it's the only home he has left,' murmured Phae, as if sensing that something monumental had happened to the young man. Her tigerish instincts for protecting her family were very strong and deep inside she felt he had suffered some sort of trauma, although had no idea of the details.

'Let's hope Xin's got some food on the go when we get there' quipped Ben.

In her mind Phae formed the question about the whereabouts of Xin and as before the Sun-Moon whirred into life, but Phae had no clear answer in her mind from the device.

It was as if Xin no longer existed. As the machine stopped its movement, a series of blanks appeared in the windows. The dials and pointers set themselves to a 'zero' position. A chill ran down her spine and she examined the information on the face of the device.

'Mira, can you make anything of this? I don't really understand what it's trying to tell me'

'If I understand the readings correctly, it is telling us that Xin has entered the Plane of Negative Existence,' said Mira solemnly.

'What does that mean?' asked Ben nervously.

'It means Xin does not exist anymore,' said Mira sadly. Despite being a computer, Mira was able to be sympathetic to the emotional states of human beings and she knew the devastating effect this information would have on the Warriors.

'Are you saying Xin's dead Mira' Ben almost barked with shock at the revelation.

'I can neither confirm nor deny that assertion Ben. But the Sun-Moon appears to indicate that Xin is not in the earthly realm, nor is he in any plane of existence into which the device can see.'

The significance of Mira's words shocked the trio into silence for a moment, but it was Ciara who spoke next.

'Is there any other way you can track him down, any news reports, camera feeds, satellite data, anything!' she raised her voice in panic.

'There is one report from the Golterian State News Agency.' Mira went quiet and called up a news headline. It had a picture of Xin and the bold headline next to it read 'Master Criminal of Astrellion Terminated by our Glorious Leader!'

Phae read the first few lines of text glorifying Cyax' defeat of the Astraxi, the destruction of their base and the fate of Xin with the Wand of Xylos. Eventually she just stopped reading as the text was too upsetting to continue.

'That's settled it then. There's nothing more we can do, other than to find Nico and carry out Xin's last orders to prevent Cyax from acquiring the Blade and the Shield.'

Ciara looked downcast. If it were true that Xin was gone, how could they ever hope to deal with Cyax without his guidance? He was the only one that had ever seen him defeated. It seemed like an impossible task for a group of young people, and even if they had powerful lore at their disposal, they were without their leader and teacher.

'I wonder how Nico managed to escape if Xin didn't' asked Ben.

'I have no data on that' replied Mira quietly.

'Well, if we find Nico, then he can tell us all about it. Maybe Xin's still out there somewhere. Maybe there's some other explanation, maybe we can rescue him.' Phae's enthusiasm for the new task was running as fast as ever.

'Or maybe he's just dead! Don't you get it! D.E.A.D. - DEAD!' shouted Ciara as she dismissed the visual images being holo-projected by Mira.

There was silence once more, but Phae stood up and put her arm around Ciara.

'Come on Ciara, this isn't the end of everything. Until we know fully what happened, then there's still hope, so let's find our Dragon Warrior and get on with what we need to do. Astraxi, be strong!'

They left the room and headed back to the engineering area where they found Ash finishing his last checks. The news about Xin and Nico didn't seem to concern him, as he didn't want to be distracted from his task of getting the ship perfectly ready for action. Not one system should be at anything less than one hundred percent before leaving if he can help it.

They boarded and prepared themselves in Cygnus' central hub by reading up on the legends of the Blade of Astrellion and the Shield of Fire. Mira provided a spoken commentary which she created by combining historical texts about the weapons' makers, construction, and the specific lore that governed them, which also provided a clue to their strengths and weaknesses.

It wasn't long before Ash's professional pilot voice was heard over the ship wide intercom system, advising them to buckle up and be ready for the ride back to Astrapolis and hopefully a rendezvous with their missing colleagues.

CHAPTER 28
The Fortress Of Thanatos

For about fifty years, Cyax' mountain lair and fortress of Thanatos had been a tourist attraction. In the last century it had been lavishly restored by Princess Tanielka's great-great grandmother Tantellian. A long, crumbling, and treacherously narrow road winding through high mountain passes had been replaced by a modern highway capable of transporting construction machinery and eventually tourist buses up to the high plateau where the complex stood.

The fortress had been empty for over a thousand years in Cyax' absence and was in a bad state of repair. Most of the walls and sentry turrets that surrounded the complex were still standing solidly against the constant onslaught of weather and weeds growing in the masonry. The roof slates had become dislodged, and many rooms had suffered water damage or invasion by nesting birds, reptiles, small mammals, and the occasional passing mountain demon.

Behind the main fortress was its most striking building, Cyax' palace, a compact but impressive castle with the elaborate turrets and tiled roof you would expect in a building from this part of the world. The tiles were round in shape and overlapped each other like a perfect layer of grey dragon scales.

The palace was itself perched on top of a solitary mountain peak, almost like a spike of rock, which had had its tip sliced off to make room for the building. The building was only approachable by air or by climbing three long, steep flights of marble stairs, before crossing an elegant single span bridge that arched over a deep ravine. If you were unlucky enough to fall off, you would fall to your death on the rocks hundreds of metres below. Indeed, many of those involved in the building's construction and restoration suffered such a fate, as well as many unfortunates who had suffered the displeasure of Cyax.

Tantellian had spent much money on the repairs as an act of devotion to her ancestor, despite rising poverty in Golteria at a time of economic crisis. She lived there until her death twenty years later when she was thrown off the balcony of the palace by her own daughter, Tanusume, who had become impatient to take the throne. Unfortunately, succession by matricide was a common occurrence in the royal lineage of Golteria, which made mothers very suspicious of their own daughters, many of whom were kept under lock and key as a result.

In recent times the Princesses had preferred to rule from Golterion City, and as such the mountain palace and its surrounding fortress had become yet another shrine to the cult of Cyax, being visited by tens of thousands of pilgrims from all over the land every year.

Now that he was back in command, Cyax had removed himself and his command centre away from the Monastery complex in Golterion, back to the ancient fortress up in the mountains that overlooked the city. The nerve centre of operations was focused on a Wizard's table in the main ceremonial hall of the palace. The Princess had added many of the modern technologies used by her armed forces and so the room also housed strategic and tactical visual displays showing the state of readiness of the various forces and weapons available to them.

Cyax, Tanielka, Fong and Eduardo were gathered next to a large map of the region showing all the major cities and military installations. The map covered a large table and was enhanced by pop-up holographic displays showing the positions and sizes of armies and information on targets within striking range.

Despite being unfamiliar with modern technology, Cyax was very aware of its value to his plans to conquer Astrellion. He was easily able to engage with the tactical and strategic information, which helped him decide on his next moves. He had always been a first rate general and was often victorious against superior forces due to his ability to outthink his opponents.

The map's holographic display showed the missile bombardment of Astrapolis that had started earlier in the day. It was a tactical strike designed to scare the city's population and cause panic amongst civilians. He knew this would cause the Astrellian armed forces and politicians to divert valuable time and resources into dealing with the breakdown of law and order on the streets. Live video feeds from the city showed that this was indeed already happening.

'Princess. Are your troops ready to begin the invasion?' asked Cyax.

'Almost ready my lord. The last divisions are moving into place as you commanded.' Tanielka pointed to a holographic representation of an army moving into position at a strategic crossing on the river that separated the two countries. The image was of a group of cyber-demons supported by a smaller number of Morgai and looked like a collection of animated chess pieces.

'Good.' He turned to face the vampire, who as usual was watching quietly from the edge of the group.

'Fong. I have become aware that the Star Dragon has entered the Celestial plane, heading for Astrapolis. I want you to go there, capture the Dragon Warrior, and bring him to me with his amulet and the DragonStone ring.' Cyax' eyes glowed a more vivid green that usual as he relished the thought. 'I shall crush him and extinguish his fire for ever!' Cyax' tone was intense and menacing.

'Yes. At once my Lord.' Fong began one of his usual long obsequious bows, but Cyax grabbed him by the neck and lifted him off the ground.

'Do not fail me again Fong, like you did with the others. Undead you may be, but you can still be destroyed,' he dropped Fong back to the ground, where he stood choking for a moment, holding his crushed neck. He bowed once more, but this time in a simple gesture of obedience, walking backwards and facing Cyax at the same time, not so much out of respect but more out of fear of what Cyax would do if his back were turned.

'Eduardo, go with Fong and make sure he completes the task,' added Cyax. The Snake Warrior simply nodded his assent and took Fong by the arm dragging him from the chamber.

'Come on Fong, I think I know where he'll be heading. Let's see if we can get there before he does.' They headed off to the pad where they requisitioned a squad of cyber-demons and a transport to get them to Astrapolis as quickly as possible. Eduardo would use his Snake lore to ensure they weren't detected while entering the city.

Cyax turned back to the centre of the room and raising his hands he uttered the ancient incantation that he used to summon the Four Fiends.

'*Karothia: Yoshara Finsun.*' The space directly in front of Cyax seemed to distort as if it were being stretched like an elastic sheet. The centre of the distortion seemed pull inwards, sucking the light out of the room, and in fact the room did darken as if someone had dimmed the lights.

Papers whirled around as a cold rush of wind quickly turned into a freezing vortex. A thick fog condensed out of the chilled air as four figures were propelled into the room along rays of darkness and the Four Fiends stepped forward, bowing to Cyax. The bows were to show respect to their associate, rather than subservience, as they considered themselves at least Cyax' equal if not greater. Of the four, Taotie, Taowu and Qiongqi were their usual menacing selves, but Hundun was diminished by the physical damage wrought upon him when he encountered Nico in London.

Cyax returned the respectful bow as Taotie spoke with a rasping, hissing voice, 'You summoned us my lord?' Taotie's statement was a simple matter of fact but framed the question as to why they had been summoned.

Cyax looked at the slightly broken figure of Hundun, whose ancient armour had been scarred by Nico's fireball. Hundun's eyes had been reduced to two violet points of glowing light within his eye sockets, but they blazed brightly as Nico had only managed to weaken him, rather than to inflict any permanent damage. It would take much more than a single fireball to do that.

He looked slightly more translucent than usual, which reflected the reduction in the evil energy that held his Lich body together, but he would recover by stealing more souls from the living, if given the opportunity. Many years ago, in a very deliberate act of dark magic, a wicked king had turned himself into the horrible creature that now stood before Cyax.

Immortality was costly. Hundun and his three fellow Fiends had paid the initial asking price with their own souls and greedily accepted the consequences of using other people's souls to extend their existence for as long as they could.

'My Lord Hundun, you seem slightly, may I say, out of sorts?' enquired Cyax, with a slight mocking tone.

Hundun bowed his head and waved his bony hand dismissively,

'The Dragon's attack was potent, but I shall be restored, soon enough.'

Returning his attention to Taotie, Cyax answered the question with another, 'Since we last met what have you learned of the Shield of Fire and the Blade of Astrellion?'

As was often their manner, the Four Fiends went silent, as if in telepathic conversation with each other. They were evaluating their joint resolve to continue on this path with Cyax. The conversation was short, things were still going in the right direction and Cyax was living up to his side of the deal so far. They would continue with this plan of action.

'We have been observing the Dragon and his associates, as we believe that sooner or later, they will lead us to the two other weapons of power. When they do that, we will destroy them and bring the objects to you as agreed.' Taotie's words were delivered in a menacing style, enhanced by the rasping tone of his voice.

'My Lord Taotie, I wish you total success in your mission,' and as the echo of Cyax' words faded away, so did the ghastly apparitions of the Fiends.

CHAPTER 29
Evacuation

Nico's second trip through the Celestial Plane was no less interesting than his first. This time instead of the river of starlight with the swan gliding along it, there was a great sea of shimmering stars. Stellar dolphins were leaping out of the celestial ocean, spinning in the air, and splashing back down in a spray of starlight. A pair of large fishes swam together just under the waves dodging and weaving as if trying to stay clear of the dolphins.

Once more Nico caught sight of the celestial cat, but this time instead of watching indifferently as they passed by, the cat raised its head, as if to sniff the air. It seemed hyper-alert, as if readying itself to pounce, but it was way smaller than the dragon and presented little risk. Instead, it hopped across some of the other celestial objects trying to keep up with the dragon but had to avoid being trampled by the celestial bull.

Adraxa turned swiftly towards the land, and they approached a glittering beach made from fine silvery particles upon which the celestial ocean crashed with great curling foamy waves. Tall silvery grasses on top of the dunes wafted against the dark monochrome sky. Nico thought that the beach might be a good place to go surfing, if he could persuade Adraxa to bring him back for a holiday. Surfing on starlight, how cool would that be!

Nico couldn't understand how the Star Dragon knew where to go, but it was hardly surprising as he is a human, and not of this plane. Another turn took them straight towards another of the many ribbons of white light that rippled across the sky, arcing between points on the ground and the brighter stars. As they entered the ribbon, Nico experienced the same strange distortion of light and space, as if everything was being stretched out like the elastic on a catapult, before he was thrown back into the earthly plane.

As the visual distortion flattened out, the familiar skyline of Astrapolis opened up before Nico. But they had only been in the sky for seconds when Adraxa had to dive to avoid a missile that was streaking towards the centre of the city. Nico was stunned for a moment but managed to hang on while he worked out that he had arrived in the middle of an aerial bombardment of Astrapolis.

'Chase the missile' he instructed the Star Dragon, who duly obeyed his command and looped back to follow the Golterian weapon. Adraxa surged forward effortlessly and was soon just behind the missile's glowing rocket exhaust.

Nico reached for the DragonStone, hoping to be able to aim a fireball at the missile and knock it out of the sky, but Adraxa was already one step ahead of him as a plume of red-hot dragon breath melted the missile, causing it to explode in mid-air before it could hit its target.

Another missile was following this one and the Star Dragon swooped to chase it down, while Nico readied himself with the DragonStone. Clenching his fist, he pointed the topaz stone towards the second missile that was heading for the city's business district. In his mind he imagined plucking a ball of hot gas from the surface of a star and hurling it at the missile. The effect was just as he had imagined it. A giant ball of yellow plasma shot towards the missile blowing it to smithereens in an instant.

'Woo-hoo!' shouted Nico as he watched the burning debris drop harmlessly into the Astrellion River with an enormous splash. Seconds later the mighty Star Dragon was hovering over a street near the Perpetual Motion Café. Gently she descended while Nico slung his leg over her neck and dropped to the ground, crouching momentarily as if he had just jumped down from a high wall. Knowing that her task was over for now, the Star Dragon made her usual dazzling exit, zooming upwards through a flash of starlight overhead.

Hover transports filled the skies, taking the citizens of Astrapolis to safe places out of town where they might escape the bombardment. Smaller missiles started to flash through the air, but instead of exploding they broke open to disgorge their contents. Long, part-mechanised cyber-worms moved swiftly over the ground lashing out at people with their metal teeth. The worms resembled giant millipedes, with hundreds of jointed legs propelling the cyborg creatures' segmented bodies forward. Those that were unfortunate enough to be bitten by these monsters without seeking urgent medical help, later found themselves being consumed by nanobots released into their wounds.

Nico turned into the alley behind the Café, hoping to be able to get in the back door. Xin never mentioned anything about locking things up, and Nico supposed that there was probably some sort of magical protection on the building to keep unwanted intruders out, and he was right.

The door didn't appear to be locked and he was just about to step inside when he spotted two people cowering near the bins. It was Gus the leader of the Tiger Sharks and one of his crew. They were being stalked by two cyber-worms and found themselves trapped in a corner with the worms closing in. Using some brush handles and a piece of corrugated metal as a shield, they tried to push the cyber-worms back, but the creatures were very close and eating through their defences, tearing chunks out of the metal with their razor-sharp reinforced mandibles.

'Hey kid, do something. Help us,' pleaded Gus' sidekick.

Nico remembered that Gus had threatened to turn him into dog food next time he saw him, but that was of no consequence now. He couldn't just run away or stand by and watch what happened, he needed to help. He thought about summoning a fireball or a lightning strike, but he figured that would be too dangerous and probably incinerate Gus and his pal too.

'Ice' he thought to himself, 'That might do the job.'

He raised his hand and imagined a wall of ice enclosing the cyber-worms while calling up the spell, '*Morar Sinaro.*'

A freezing blast almost knocked him off his feet and as the snow flurry that accompanied it started to clear, a large panel of crystal-clear ice stood where the cyber-worms had been rearing up to break through Gus' remaining defences.

The ice was totally transparent, as it had been magically transported from an ice cave beneath a glacier somewhere, possibly not even from this planet, most likely from another realm where winter is the dominant season.

Frozen into the ice wall were the two cyber-worms. Their heads were just poking out of the surface, thrashing around trying to escape. Nico picked up a metal pole and with a few hard blows, smashed off their vile heads, separating them from the bodies.

Inside the heads was a mix of organic and inorganic mechanical parts, which spilled on to the ground. A pool of sticky white liquid, which had previously filled the rest of the creatures' bodies was now slowly oozing across the floor.

'Totally disgusting,' was Nico's response as he produced flames from his fingertips, which he directed at the foul cyber-remains incinerating them.

Gus and his crew member were completely thrown by what they had just seen.

'Kid, I always thought you were weird, but that was totally whacko! How'd you do that stuff? Have you got a flame thrower hidden somewhere up your sleeve?' said Gus.

Nico didn't care much for Gus, but today was probably the first time he had used his new powers to do something to help others outside the Astraxi, and it felt good.

'It's just a little trick I learned from an old man, a friend of mine,' he said trying to underplay things and not give too much away. He may have saved Gus' life, but that didn't mean he would now be his friend or best buddy.

Gus knew how to spot an opportunity and he could see one standing right in front of him in the shape of a spindly kid.

'Maybe you can help us with a few more 'tricks' like that kid. This city's freaking out right now, and tricks like that could make us a big stash. We could be big players around here. I mean really big, top of the anthill!' Gus smiled crookedly as he stood up, trying to appear friendly.

Nico was clear in himself that he didn't much like the idea of joining Gus' crew and becoming just another petty criminal under his thumb. This was the lifestyle that his aunt had predicted was coming for him if he didn't reform his ways, and he had already learned so much from Xin and the others. Even though things seemed hopeless right now, seeking solace with a group of no-hope losers like the Tiger Sharks was a definite non-starter. Nico was blunt in his response.

'I've seen what's coming, and if the things I have already seen make it here, you won't stand a chance Gus. A small-time player like you, they'll eat you alive.'

Gus was taken aback by Nico's frank response. He was used to his crew being very low down the food chain of organised crime, despite his many attempts to elevate them to a higher level of criminal notoriety.

'OK kid, you're making a mistake, because this is a serious opportunity. I heard about your aunt, so if you change your mind and you need somewhere to go, you know where to find me. And as for that stunt you pulled in the park with the cops, then I guess this makes us even, so we'll just forget that ever happened.' Gus' large figure loomed up over Nico's slight frame.

'But don't ever cross me again. UNDERSTOOD!' he growled as he leaned into Nico's personal space before laughing contemptuously.

Nico held his ground, nodded his head, and turned back to the Perpetual Motion Café as the two others made their way past the melting ice and the charred bio-mechanical remains.

Although they seemed destroyed, the cyber-worms were not quite finished. As Nico fiddled with the smashed door lock, a camera was still active on one of the frozen worm bodies and broadcasting images back to Golterion City.

Nico entered the main seating area of the café, carefully making his way past the tables, which were faintly illuminated by the light spilling in through the windows from the streetlamps outside. It was all very much as it had been left when they set off for Dendropol to visit the Master of Wands, except for one thing. The kinetic sculpture shaped like a spinning wheel with spokes that were curved back on themselves had stopped turning. Perhaps it was Xin's influence that had kept it continuously spinning, in a way that appeared to defy the laws of physics. Now that Xin was no more, there was none of his magic around to keep the device turning and maintain the illusion of perpetual motion.

A dim light glowed inside as he entered the kitchen and made his way through to the storeroom, behind which he would hopefully be able to use the magical door through to the operations room. Closing the door behind him he looked at the collection of ingredients, jars of paste, sacks of flour and disposable chopsticks that were neatly arranged as usual. If he remembered correctly, he just needed to walk back through the door to get into the operations room, but he was puzzled when this didn't happen.

'Hmm, I wonder if as well as the lights, Xin had turned the magic off too before he left,' he thought to himself. Nico was starving. There hadn't been much time to stop and eat on his frantic travels around the world and through the celestial plane fighting the Fiends and generally trying to save the world!

He grabbed a jar of pickles and ate them hungrily, then wolfed down a packet of sweet, dried fruits for dessert washing them down with a can of iced tea from the fridge. Then he noticed a large jar filled with fortune cookies. To end his meal in the traditional way of an oriental café, he unscrewed the lid of the jar and grabbed a fortune cookie.

'Wonder what's in my future today?' he asked himself as he snapped the brittle cookie open and unrolled the slip of paper inside.

'Remember the magic words Nico!' was all it said. Nico was taken aback by the personal nature of the cookie's message.

'Weird!' he said to himself, screwing up the piece of paper and throwing it into the bin. But as he sat, the memory of the fateful day when he first visited the Perpetual Motion Café came into his mind. He was standing with Xin and the two laughing girls, Phae and Ciara, when he was pushed into the operations room.

'What was it that Xin had said?' he asked himself, trying hard to remember.

'Sometimes I just like to say a few magic words. Although they're not always strictly necessary. Chilli Prawn Dim Sum Coming Up!' that's what Xin and Phae had both said just before he was bundled into the other room.

Nico put his hand on the door handle and although it felt a little odd to do so, he spoke the words 'Chilli Prawn Dim Sum Coming Up!' He pushed the door wide open and walked into the operations room where Xin had first revealed his role in the Astraxi. The lights were on, but no one was home, all the analysts and technicians had fled. The computer data and live video feeds continued to scroll down the many monitors on the walls and desks, but there was nobody to view and consider the information being delivered.

A workstation dedicated to the status of Cygnus showed Nico that the ship had been successfully repaired and was now fully operational with Ash, Phae, Ben and Ciara on board. But their whereabouts was unknown since the ship was in transit under the cover of her cloaking device. All he could do was sit back and wait until they came back online, and he could try to get a message through.

An alarm indicating that the front door was being smashed in startled him out of his thoughts and he stepped back through the storeroom and into the kitchen. Peering out from behind the fridge he could see that the front door had been torn off its hinges by a cyber-demon who was now shining a torch directly at him. Nico turned to escape through the back door, when another cyber-demon stepped in behind him with his weapon raised. More cyber-demons followed these two and Nico found himself being ushered into the middle of the café. Many bright lights were being shone through the window dazzling his eyes as two figures walked through the doorway stepping over the splintered wood, their feet crunching on the broken glass.

Nico didn't know what to do, as he was trapped with no possible escape route. He looked around, but it was hopeless, blasters were trained on him from every angle. Even if he could summon some Dragon lore he would soon be blasted, or dead, or on his way into captivity.

The two figures that had entered the room through the smoke were silhouetted by the very bright lights behind them and Nico struggled to identify their faces until one of them spoke.

'Turn off those lights' said Fong. As his eyes re-adjusted to the lower light levels, Nico recognised the other figure.

'Eduardo?' he asked, surprised to see the Snake Warrior again after their previous encounter during the attack on the base. 'What are you doing here, and who's your ugly friend with the pasty face?'

Eduardo was still very much under the mind-controlling power of Cyax, but somewhere deep inside, his real personality was still hiding, protecting him from being totally absorbed by Cyax' curse. But this inner turmoil gave Fong the time to reply first to Nico's question.

'I am here to help you, young Dragon.' The softly spoken words came slowly from the vampire's thin lips, which turned up at the ends into a half-formed, insincere smile. Nico was unaware of the power of vampires to charm their victims and weaken their will. He found Fong's words strangely reassuring, even though he found Fong physically repulsive, with his lank hair, pale waxy skin and watery eyes set behind small circular rimmed spectacles.

'You're all alone now. Your Aunt, your Master and your parents are all dead and most of your friends, except for Eduardo here, have abandoned you.' Fong's tone remained calm and somehow soothing, and Nico couldn't help doing anything other than listen.

Fong continued, 'You would make a great ally for my master, and it would not be the first time that a Dragon Warrior had fought alongside him.' Fong stepped forward and stood face to face with Nico, who shivered as he felt the vampire's cold breath on his cheek.

Fong paused for long enough to let Nico reflect on this offer and leaned even closer to the young man, right into his face, before delivering the threat that came with it.

'Equally it would not be the first time he has destroyed a Dragon Warrior. Don't make him destroy you too Nico. It would be such a waste!'

There was something in Fong's facial expression that reminded Nico of the time when he had been charmed by Eduardo into handing over the DragonStone, but this was a malign charm that somehow sickened him while remaining compelling. He struggled hard to win back control of his will from the vampire's charm and reached for his amulet but couldn't bring up enough will power to summon his lore.

'Aunt Cass told me not to trust strangers' said Nico. A sharp slap on his face from Fong startled him, the long fingernails leaving scratch marks on his cheek. The vampire's hold on his mind was firm and Nico stood motionless, not even reaching up to touch where his face had been marked. Fong had had many centuries to practice mind control over people and was particularly good at it, as a means of hunting his own preferred prey to sustain himself.

As Fong reached out to lead Nico away by the arm, a small but very angry chihuahua ran through the door barking ferociously at him.

'Stupid creature,' Fong shouted trying unsuccessfully to kick the small yappy dog out of the way, but it persisted, and the sharp yaps were enough to snap Nico out of the vampire's charm. As he regained control of his mind, a pack of other dogs burst in through the front door of the café and attacked the cyber-demons. A snarling pit bull terrier tore viciously at the ankles of the guards, while others including a boxer and several large terriers were ripping at their arms and bodies, sinking their teeth in deeply and shaking hard.

Behind Nico a familiar voice spoke, '*Lux agioteis*' It was Phae transformed into her Tiger warrior armour, she had easily disabled the two guards that were blocking the back door and was now using her tiger lore in the form of a searing light that she aimed at Fong.

A beam of the most pure, heavenly illumination shone brightly from the palm of her right hand directly into the vampire's face, which smouldered as his flesh started to burn. Fong shrieked and recoiled in pain as he turned to escape, but he was held back by Eduardo, who was still following Cyax' orders to make sure Fong didn't fail in his mission.

Nico powered up his amulet and transformed into the Dragon Warrior just as the sound of sirens and a screeching of tyres came from outside. Vehicle doors were opened and slammed shut, weapons were cocked, and blue flashing lights could be seen through the windows as an armed unit of the Astrellian Civil Guard deployed from two armoured vehicles to surround the building.

'We've got you surrounded Fong. You're outgunned and far away from home,' said Phae. 'Come with us Eduardo. You don't belong with these people. They've got you under some sort of mind-control, surely you understand that?'

Eduardo struggled in his internal mind-battle to regain control of his free will and his body, but he was buried too deeply in his own mental safe space to be able to climb from under the weight of the spell that Cyax had used to turn him. He reached for his snake amulet, but instead of transforming into the Snake Warrior, he morphed into the sinister figure of Cyax and stood laughing the other two Warriors.

Phae was not fooled into thinking that Cyax was really in the room with them, realising that Eduardo was deeply under Cyax' control. He was showing her what was really happening inside of him, by adopting the body shape of his master.

She realised that now was neither the time nor the place to attempt to break the spell on Eduardo. It would take some powerful lore to remove it, and Xin would normally have been the person to perform this. If they could get him into the Great Library of the Astraxi, then at least they could find the right text to perform the necessary ritual.

Outside Ben and Ciara were waiting for the others to make their escape. Ciara had summoned an extremely convincing illusion of the team of soldiers that were locking down the café and preventing the Golterians from escaping with Nico as their prisoner. She was working hard to maintain the pretence, and it was highly effective as long as Fong and Eduardo believed they were trapped.

Fong looked through the window at the Astrellian soldiers apparently taking cover behind their armoured cars, their weapons trained on the door.

'Come on Nico, let's go' said Phae as she took his arm and backed out through the smashed rear entrance keeping her eyes fixed on Fong for any sudden move. Eduardo stood rooted to the spot, in his disguise as Cyax. Outside they were quickly joined by Ben and Ciara and once they got around the next corner all four of them ran as fast as they had ever run in their entire lives.

Inside the café, Fong and Eduardo watched as the Astraxi made their escape, still believing they were being held at gunpoint by Astrellian soldiers. Fong was about to try and contact the commander of the soldiers outside to see if he could discuss some sort of truce and escape back to Golterion, when one of the armoured cars disappeared, along with half of the soldiers. As she ran into the distance, Ciara was no longer able to fully support the magical illusion and it was breaking down.

Realising that they had been tricked by one of Ciara's more elaborate illusions, Eduardo morphed back to his normal shape. A smarter than usual cyber-demon decided to confront the soldiers with his blaster, causing the illusion to flicker and disappear. Fong spoke to one of his cyber-demon guards.

'Track them' he ordered. The guard popped open a cover in his armour launching a small drone into the air, which flew off in the direction of the escaping Astraxi.

But Fong had slipped up when selecting his team for the mission. Cyax had planted one of his own security officers into Fong's squad and as soon as it was clear that the mission had failed, issued orders for Fong and Eduardo to be restrained and taken back to their Master. Fong hissed as the electrostatic handcuffs were applied firmly to his wrists.

Meanwhile the Astraxi were running for their lives. 'We have to rendezvous with Ash at the docks,' shouted Phae to the others.

'Won't the enemy spot a big shiny high-tech flying vessel?' quipped Nico.

'I think they'll find us first. Look we're being followed' said Ben pointing back up at the drone which was gaining ground on them.

'Cover everyone' he shouted.

'Cover where? There is no cover lame brain!' replied Ciara anxiously. Nico stopped and raised his hand with the DragonStone, unleashing a fireball like the one he had used to attack Hundun at his mother's house. The streak of orange plasma leaped out from his hand and struck the small drone head on, consuming it instantly. But the fireball continued its trajectory, striking an old wooden warehouse behind and engulfing it in flames. The dry timbers of the warehouse took fire instantly and the flames ripped across its front and over the roof in seconds.

'Overkill, I think is the word that sums up what you just did!' said Phae, 'Come on, let's keep moving, I think this fire's going to attract a lot more attention.' Nico gritted his teeth and sucked in his cheeks; he knew that he needed to learn finer control of his dragon power.

A few minutes later they arrived at the dockyard, where Ash would be waiting with Cygnus. Nico was puzzled. At the jetty he expected to see the high-tech super vessel, but all he could see was a very ordinary looking old cargo ship, rusted around the edges and in need of a decent paint job.

'Quickly, get on board' called Phae to Nico as Ciara and Ben raced up the gangplank. Nico hesitated; he wasn't sure about this old ship. Why were the others getting on board in such a hurry?

'Where's Cygnus?' asked Nico as he stood at the dockside end of the gangplank.

'This is Cygnus, you dummy!' shouted Phae as another drone appeared nearby heading towards them at speed.

'What this old tub?' he replied, still confused.

'Stop wasting time and get on board!' Phae ran down the gangplank to drag Nico on board, just in time to save him from a burst of tiny, poisoned darts fired by the drone. As they reached the end of the gangplank, Ben's head popped out from a porthole.

'Come on, quickly, get in!' Phae pulled at Nico who lost his footing and tumbled into the entrance where to his amazement he found himself inside Cygnus' interior corridors near the entrance to the mess room.

'So how come Cygnus looks like a beaten-up old boat?' A video feed to the large monitor on the wall showed the exterior of the ship as it moved away from the dockside. More drones were now following, and some were being shot out of the sky by Mira's precision targeting systems.

'Better ask Captain Ash about that' smirked Ben, 'But make sure you've got enough time for him to give you the technobabble at least twice, and even then, it won't make much sense unless you got a couple of PhD's and a brain the size of a planet!'

Nico stepped into the mess room and as he put his skateboard in a safe place, he spotted his reflection in one of the screens. He paused to straighten his thick dark hair, which had become disorderly during the chase from the Perpetual Motion Café.

'Ooh look he's got a few hairs out of place. Doesn't matter if the whole world and everyone in it is about to be fried by the forces of evil, as long as the coif looks just right!' mocked Ciara.

'Get lost Ciara,' Nico rolled his eyes, and headed upstairs for the bridge. Ash was in his usual seat surrounded by its holo-displays, streams of information on the status of the ship's systems and video feeds from around the perimeter. He was fully focused on sailing Cygnus out of the Port of Astrapolis to a point offshore where he could safely get her airborne and en route.

'Pure genius!' said Nico as he strapped himself into the co-pilot seat. 'I've missed you Ash.'

'Nice to see you too, guy with the floppy hair!' said Ash as he adjusted the ship's camouflage subroutines in the cloaking system.

'Not you as well!' groaned Nico as he sat back in his chair, pushing his hair back from over his eyes.

Ash was a bit confused by this statement, as he thought that revealing his nickname for Nico was an act of friendship, rather than the mockery that Ciara had implied. His eyes darted around the flight deck being unsure of how to react, so he settled back into his take off routine. He switched on the ship wide comms.

'This is your Captain speaking, strap in everyone and prepare for take-off.'

Once they reached a spot clear of the two long piers that protected Astrapolis' harbour, Ash reached down to the yellow and black panel situated in his centre console and flipped off the cover revealing the red button.

'Want to press the red button Nico?' asked Ash, intrigued to see how Nico would react.

'I thought you said never press the big red button,' said Nico leaning forward to look at it more closely.

It certainly looked risky with the word '**DANGER**' inscribed in bold letters. Some other text describing emergency procedures was also written in small print below, but Nico didn't stop to read this.

Instead, he put his thumb over the button and looked Ash in the eye. Ash was still studying him, trying to judge Nico's reactions. Nico didn't blink, but neither did he divert his gaze from Ash. They stared straight into each other's pupils in a kind of stand-off, until Nico detected the obvious discomfort in Ash's eyes.

'Try anything once!' and thrust his thumb hard on to the red button, pushing it into the housing. The switch didn't click, or clunk or make any noise. Instead, it felt as if it had some sort of viscous fluid behind it. When it reached the end of its slow travel, Nico felt it latch solidly into position with a click. He withdrew his hand and sat back.

Ash continued to study him and then leaned back into his chair. He had decided that the new Dragon in the group was strong willed and not afraid to take a risk involving things unknown and of course he cared a lot about how his hair looked!

There was no sinister subtext to Ash's little test, it was about helping himself to understand the people around him better and how to respond more appropriately and be a more efficient team member. Xin had spent much time taking the young Ash away from the laboratory and his studies, teaching him to work with his colleagues and not simply to exist in his own intellectual bubble.

Meanwhile the ship's external monitors showed the changes that were happening before Cygnus could re-assume her usual elegant flying shape.

The blunt shape of the disguised hull trimmed itself back into the ship's elegant profile, while other structures such as the boxy bridge and cargo handling cranes vanished into thin air. They were mostly illusions, created by the ship's holo-emitters to create realistic looking structures and making it appear like an old-fashioned cargo vessel.

'Mira, set a course to avoid the attack drone formations' Ash instructed his computer companion.

'Confirmed Ash, course is set' she purred in response.

'Engage!' he said, mimicking the captain of his favourite science fiction TV programmes of the early twenty first century.

'Tea, Earl Grey, Hot!' he muttered under his breath as he operated some more controls. Neither 'replicators' nor 'warp drive' were available in Ash's world right now, but whenever he had some spare time, he was working on both! Nico just stared, trying to fathom the quiet but complex man before him who was now totally absorbed in his flight controls.

The massive acceleration of the ship pushed Nico back in his chair as he watched the sea shoot past him at speed. Soon after he felt that sinking feeling into the bottom of his chair that indicated the ship was airborne. In a matter of minutes under the cover of the cloaking device they had swept through the swarms of Golterian cyber-drones that were surging towards Astrapolis in growing numbers. These drones were being counter-attacked by the Astrellian defensive drones that had been launched across the country, but with only partial success.

'Mira, you have control, stay on course until we've finished our discussions in the hub.'

'Confirmed Ash, I have control,' said Mira.

'Come on then Mr. Floppy Haired Dragon Warrior, we've got work to do' said Ash with a slight nod and a raised eyebrow and with that he stood up to go down below, where they were going to discuss how they might continue with Xin's plan to secure the other two weapons of power.

At that moment it felt to Nico like they were running away from trouble, leaving others to the defence of Astrellion, but the danger posed by the two remaining weapons was greater. So much had changed that they needed to reset their thinking and pull together once more. Focusing on this mission might help them re-kindle the thing that gave the Astraxi their greatest strength — teamwork.

CHAPTER 30
Regrouping

Nico followed Ash into the ship's central hub, which was its tactical control centre. In the centre of the room was a circular Wizard's table, with a seat for each of the Astraxi, but the table was not just a magical device, it was also technological and functioned as if it were an extension of the ship's computer Mira. Around the walls more screens showed the status of all sorts of parameters from flight telemetry to satellite data on the location of other ships and aircraft in the vicinity, both hostile and friendly.

Phae, Ciara and Ben were already seated and the two joined them at the table. There was a bit of an awkward silence while each of the Warriors was trying to think what to say next. Phae was about to speak when Ben butted in ahead of her to ask the question on everyone's mind.

'So what happened to Xin, Nico?'

Nico had been feeling more positive since meeting up with his colleagues, but this sharp reminder of the tragic events of a few days ago suddenly darkened his mood once more.

'Cyax killed him with the Wand, then kicked his body off the edge of a cliff into a ravine,' he replied glumly.

The others contemplated this simple but clear explanation before Phae asked another question, 'How do you know he's dead?'

Nico didn't really know what to say, he had just assumed Xin was dead. His mind returned to the scene in its full horror as Cyax mercilessly beat Xin with the Wand.

'I could see his life force leaving his body as he went over the cliff.' He pursed his lips and swallowed, trying to control his emotions. 'He died saving me from Cyax. I owe him so much.'

Nico had spent much of the last few days thinking about how he had gone from being some wayward skateboarder-kid-jewel thief to an important member of a group of Warriors in just a few weeks. It was Xin's belief in him that had kept him in the group, when so many times he just wanted to avoid any personal responsibility.

'Eduardo was there too' he added.

'Eduardo?' asked Ciara looking for more information that might put together a picture of their former colleague's condition.

'He was hiding in the rocks, he helped Cyax trap us,' said Nico.

'Is that so? Well, that explains his appearance at the Perpetual Motion Café.' Phae's voice was full of sadness at the fate of the Snake Warrior and what Cyax' mind control must be doing to him.

'It's my fault. Xin died saving my life. If I hadn't been there, he would probably have escaped.' Nico hung his head in dismay.

Phae stepped out of her chair, her natural empathy for her team members took her over to Nico to hug him compassionately, drawing his head into her shoulder. Ash and Ben didn't particularly read anything into this gesture, but Ciara noticed a subtle yielding in Nico's figure as Phae drew him closer in, but for once she checked herself and resisted the urge to break this personal moment with one of her sharp-tongued observations.

Typically, Ash was unable to read the moment's emotional balance and broke the atmosphere, 'How are we going to complete this mission without Xin?'

Phae went back to her chair and pondered for a moment

'Look there may only be five of us now, but we're still the Astraxi, the Celestial Warriors of Astrellion, and together our power is greater than his. Never forget that. He has never totally defeated the Astraxi in the past, and we're not going to let him do it now.'

Nico reminded them of their mission, 'We're doing this for Xin. With him or without him, Xin would have wanted us to find the other two weapons.'

Phae reached for the Sun-Moon device that was on the Wizard's table in front of her.

'Let's do it for Xin then. First Australia, then Cyax.' She set up the device to locate the Shield of Fire first, calling up the planet Mars and the elemental force of fire, but as usual the device was already following her intentions and other circular dials and thumbwheels started to draw up the appropriate runes and magical symbols.

'I have already interpreted those co-ordinates Phae.' said Mira interrupting. 'It's the Lancelin Sand Dunes of Western Australia. Ash, shall I set a new course?'

'Reset the co-ordinates and take us there Mira' ordered Ash, as he was technically ship's captain.

'Course correction confirmed Ash,' said Mira as the ship gently turned in the darkness and headed into the thin orange glow around the dark horizon that indicated sunrise was about to break.

'Come on everyone, let's get some rest,' said Phae as she herded the others out of the hub towards their cabins. We're going to need to be on our best game. I am sure that when we get to our destination we won't be alone!

CHAPTER 31
The Consequences Of Failure

Fong and Eduardo made their overnight return to Cyax' mountain lair in the small, stealthy cyber-transport craft. Most of the journey had been made in silence as they both understood the consequences of returning to face Cyax without the Dragon as their captive.

Eduardo was sure that Fong would attempt to discredit him in any way possible to save his vampire skin. He was entirely right in his assumption that Fong would use his experience of over twelve hundred years of treachery to make sure that it was Eduardo who took the blame for their failure.

Fong had already issued threats to the cyber-demon commander who was with them at the Perpetual Motion Café and as for the others, he knew he could either bribe or dispose of them without too much trouble.

Cyber-demons weren't like human troops who normally work as a team to protect each other's lives. They were easily bought with simple rewards of better food, promotion or better equipment and would occasionally kill each other for any slight advantage. The problem with this was that it made them ill-disciplined or self-centred in combat situations.

Since becoming a Government servant to the ruling princesses many years ago, Fong had operated as a shadowy spymaster manipulating situations, and gathering information.

His official title was Prime Minister, but he ran a web of informants that spread fear amongst otherwise loyal Golterians, as they knew any information that Fong had could be used to denounce them as 'Traitors' or 'Enemies of the Empire.' Denouncement would usually be followed by a short public show trail, before being quickly taken to the High-executioner's block. If you were really unlucky, something much more medievally unpleasant might be visited on your body, before you were eventually disposed of and fed to the guard dogs.

By running this organisation within an organisation, Fong was always able to protect his position and remove any threats to himself by appearing to work entirely for the good of the realm and the ruling Princess. Others within Fong's group also used their power to pursue personal vendettas, which only increased the sense of terror across the land, resulting in people denouncing their friends, siblings, parents and sometimes even their lovers and spouses to avoid Fong's inquisitions. It was a high stakes game for most, but the rewards were good if you could stay alive.

As they stepped off the aircraft, a group of four human guards grabbed them and forcefully escorted the two to the citadel for their audience with Cyax, to plead for their lives. There was no time to prepare any more excuses, and Cyax' personal guards wouldn't be diverted from their orders.

Perhaps for Fong, this may be the time when his luck would finally run out. Although he had clung on to his version of immortality for over a thousand years, becoming a member of the undead wasn't quite what he had bargained for when he agreed to betray his King to help Cyax in the Great Battle of Astrellion. But Cyax would argue that it was Fong who approached him first, offering access to the weapons of power and therefore any consequences of his treachery were entirely self-inflicted.

It was a combination of an ancient curse and an unholy sword of the darkest magic that had first sent Fong to the Plane of the Undead. The blade had been forged by great smith who himself had been cursed to a living death by a powerful necromancer. While travelling in the Plane of the Undead Hundun had visited the smith to acquire the sword, having been made aware of its power to disrupt mortal flesh. He did a deal with the smith that he could take the sword if he released the smith from the plane. Hundun did release him, but only by treacherously sucking the smith's soul into his phylactery.

Hundun relished the sword's special qualities, as did Cyax who had summoned Hundun to use the terrible weapon on Fong. Normally anyone killed with the blade had his or her life force dragged out of their body into the glowing violet coloured gemstone, worn by the Hundun around his neck, which was itself the root source of the Fiend's own existential energy.

But in this instance Cyax' incantation combined with a near fatal wound from the unholy blade pushed through Fong's chest, touching but not penetrating his heart, had the effect of suspending Fong's bodily functions and sending his spirit to the Plane of the Undead.

For what seemed to him like months, Fong's spirit wandered the fog-bound graveyard of the Plane of the Undead.

Ghastly expressionless figures draped in ragged shrouds wandered this grey world of broken structures, broken bodies, and broken dreams. It seemed to Fong that this was a form of hell, where he was the only sentient being amongst a world of moronic ghouls. His spirit was breaking, and he believed he would never escape, but at the point where he was ready to give into either despair or insanity or both, a beam of violet light drew him back through a portal and into the Material Plane to be reunited with his corpse in a state of un-death.

In reality, he had only been away for a few seconds, but as he gasped his first few breaths of cold air in what he thought was many months, he quickly began to doubt the value of Cyax' reward of immortality for his treachery against the King.

He had been tricked. This wasn't eternal life in the same way as Cyax, being brought about by the Potion of Eternity, it was more accurately to be described as an eternal death. He would now need to take great care of his physical body to survive, as any damage to it would heal very slowly, if at all, and he would be driven by a gnawing hunger that forced him to sacrifice others to feed himself. In this one evil activity he was always very discreet so as 'not to scare the horses' as he would say in a sick attempt at humour.

One may have thought it would have been better if Cyax had simply destroyed him, but Fong was always determined to survive at any cost, for what else did he have to lose?

Eduardo on the other hand was less concerned about how Cyax would react to failure. To all intents and purposes, he was now an additional physical instrument of Cyax' will, with some very useful powers from his amulet. Cyax would be able to wield the Snake amulet on his own, but it made more sense to have the Snake Warrior do it for him. If he killed Eduardo, he would have to use the amulet to find the next Snake Warrior, someone without the training, who would be unfamiliar with the lore and that would not be productive at all.

They crossed the ornate bridge over the ravine with its sculptures of war heroes from Golteria's past that led up to Cyax' palace. Passing through the heavy mahogany doors that were studded with shining brass domes, they entered the operations room. At the main tactical table stood Tanielka who was studying a report on a com-pad, while Cyax directed various simulations of troop engagements on the large strategic battlefield which was ranged across an enormous table.

Fong was led forward by his guards to face them, being thrown to his knees for the last few steps. 'Master, Princess,' he said before bowing respectfully, rather than his usual highly flamboyant version of the gesture, which would almost put his chin on the marble floor. Cyax didn't stop what he was doing but kept moving the military figures around the tabletop.

'Where is the Dragon, Fong?' he said as he pushed a figure of a Morgai demon across the border with Astrellion. 'Why have you not brought him to me as I instructed you?'

Fong was not normally lost for words but quickly composed himself. 'My Lord, this group of Warriors is formidable, even without Xin. I tried to reason with the Dragon, to assure him of the value of becoming your ally, but his associates arrived before we could take him. Eduardo provided little support in this unfortunate encounter, and I fear he may be turning back to the Astraxi. My cyber-demon commander will confirm this treachery in his report. I would recommend Eduardo is incarcerated before he can commit further crimes against the people of Golterion.'

Eduardo was momentarily taken aback by this tirade of lies from Fong.

'Is this true, Snake Warrior?' growled Cyax facing up to the young man.

But Eduardo remained silent and did not flinch as Cyax approached him. Cyax cast the 'true seeing' spell '*Aliethis*' and his view of Eduardo was magically altered. Eduardo now appeared to him as a figure that flickered between two states of reality, a young human and a large anthropomorphic panther standing on its hind legs.

Deep inside his mind, Eduardo could feel that the doors behind which he was concealing his personality, were being slowly peeled open, but Cyax stopped short of entering his hiding place, having concluded in his own arrogance, that Eduardo could not be turning back to the Astraxi, and that as ever Fong was lying to save his own skin.

Rage boiled up in Cyax throughout every fibre of his immortal body. He threw down the military figures and picking Fong up off the floor with one hand, hurled him across the table where he smashed into a rare and beautifully decorated white and blue porcelain vase.

It was a pile of jagged fragments and dust, in which Fong now found himself lying. He didn't feel pain in the same way as someone who is alive. Pain was just a vague numbness to his undead nerves, and indeed he was more afraid of the physical damage that he may have to live with for eternity, knowing that if he were only partially destroyed, those remaining parts of his body would live on in eternal torment.

Not one of the generals in the room stepped forward to help him get up, as they feared a similar reaction from Cyax. Fong slowly inspected himself for damage before dusting down his clothing.

'My Lord, fighting amongst ourselves will not bring the victory you so desire and so richly deserve.' Tanielka was trying to defuse the situation, but in doing so only managed to anger Cyax more.

'Do not dare to offer me your weak counsel child!' Tanielka immediately dipped her head in acceptance that she had overstepped the mark. She was already regretting not taking the chance to attack Fong and get the upper hand over his failure. She was about to do this when Cyax spoke again, but this time to the whole room of soldiers, who had already stopped to watch Fong's punishment. He spoke slowly, deliberately and with great effect on the audience.

'Four thousand years I have been waiting for this... Four thousand years waiting to reclaim my birth right... What was stolen from me then, I will take back... And I will deliver total and complete destruction to those who dare to try and stop me! I will break the Astraxi forever, and the power of the amulets will be mine, and mine alone to wield! All will lie low or kneel before me in tribute, Cyax, the one true King of Astrellion.'

Almost as one the entire room dropped to their knee in tribute, their heads bowed in submission to his authority.

Cyax walked across the room and offered a hand to Fong, lifting him out of the broken porcelain.

'Thank you master. I have learned a most valuable lesson,' Fong seemed genuinely humbled and apologetic for once, but without warning Cyax picked him up and hurled him across the table into another set of vases on the opposite side of the room.

'If you fail me again, I WILL destroy you Fong, or maybe I will return you to the Plane of the Undead. Now someone clean up this mess.'

The vases had taken most of the impact, and as a guard helped him back to his feet Fong realised that his shoulder had been dislocated in the last impact. In the twelve hundred years of trying to maintain his physical body, he had learned a few simple medical procedures and letting out a sigh of frustration he presented his limp arm to the soldier.

'Would you be so kind?' said Fong to the slightly confused soldier. 'Just take my arm, twist it and push it back in hard.' The soldier thought about it for a moment holding Fong's arm in a slightly awkward way. But he shoved the limb successfully back into place, at which Fong let out a stifled cry, before bowing and walking slowly backwards out of the room, as usual not daring to take his eyes off Cyax.

Back in his own chambers later, Eduardo's inner self carefully unlocked the first of the secret barriers in his mind that he had thrown up to prevent Cyax from completely overwhelming him. He hoped that he might be able to move against the controlling spirit and free himself, so that he could escape and return to his colleagues.

Even though he had been there, he had not directly witnessed Xin's fate in the ravine, as the images coming through his eyes were distorted by the lens of Cyax' malice, but he knew that he had played a part in that terrible crime and would struggle to explain his involvement to the others. They may never trust him again and he may need to leave the group. Whatever the future held for him now, he needed to try and regain control of his mind.

Opening the first door out of his safe space, he observed that he was back in a maze, with a shiny dark grey floor, pale green walls, and an infinite dark void over his head. He carefully made his way past various false exits and entrances but wasn't sure if he was getting anywhere at all. He could have been going around in circles but would never know how to find the way out, as it was impossible to tell without clear landmarks.

Voices whispered in his ears, but he couldn't understand what they were saying to him as the words sounded like sliced up syllables looping through an echo chamber and feeding back on themselves through his ears.

As he passed one entrance, the whispering stopped, and he checked his movement before stepping back to the last turning. A shadow appeared in the distance on a wall, the shadow of a large predatory cat. From its posture he could see that it was stalking its prey and he realised that his hidden psyche was the prey being hunted down by the beast.

Retreating down the corridor in his mind, he reached a crossroads with four possible exits, but as he stood there trying to decide which way to turn, the four passages suddenly started to recede away from him at great speed isolating him into a small, darkened square space in a shaft of light coming from over his head. With nowhere to go, he looked upwards and there behind the light source were two vivid green cat eyes staring back at him. A cruel laughter penetrated his ears and as he felt the world starting to spin, he was sucked into blackness, his mind crushed once more by Cyax' all-consuming will.

CHAPTER 32
The Lost Ship

After a brief sleep in his pilot's chair, Ash was woken by Mira. There were only three hundred kilometres to the destination, and she had started the descent. As they approached the western coast of Australia just off Lancelin, Mira adjusted the aerodynamics of Cygnus to glide the ship effortlessly just a few metres above the surface of the ocean using an aerodynamic phenomenon called the ground effect.

From any of the cabin windows, the ship almost felt like it was surfing over the deep blue waters of the Indian Ocean and in particular Ben loved the sensation of floating above the waves at speed. Pure white spray danced around the ship's hull as it was licked off the crests of the waves by the air cushion rippling the surface of the water below.

'Maybe we can get some boards and do a bit of surfing' Ben enthused at the breakfast table. 'You'll love it Nico because if you're any good at skateboarding you'll pick it up pretty quickly. It's all about balance and reading the waves'

'Let's just get to work first, and if there's time after we've recovered the weapons of power, I am sure we could all do with a bit of time off,' said Phae, trying to impose some discipline on the other members of the group.

'I am not sure I want to get out in that sun,' said Ciara with a sigh. 'It'll just burn me up.' Ciara's pale, delicate skin, meant that she often had to sit in the shade, when she was in sunnier climates other than Ireland.

'Someone just needs to turn on a light and your skin fries!' mocked Ben, whose skin bronzed naturally because of his heritage.

'High UV factor protective clothing and sunscreen is available in the ship's stores. I would recommend you all partake.' Mira's tone was unusually frank and authoritative, if not a little nannying. One of the roles at the heart of her programming was to help guide and protect the young warriors, but sometimes this just came across as making her sound like a mother hen.

'Cluck, cluck, cluck!' Ben continued in his mindset where all he did was to try and make fun of things in a light-hearted way. He wasn't being mean; it was just his sunny sense of humour and upbeat personality.

'All right Ben, calm down, this is serious. We're not the only ones who will be looking for the Sword and the Blade. You can bet we'll have company as soon as we find them. We need to stay safe and focused. Everybody goes home tonight, you hear me!'

Phae had a serious expression on her face that in Ben's mind said, 'Do not argue with the Tiger today!' so he nodded his head and got on with finishing his breakfast.

It wasn't long before Cygnus was gliding to a halt about a hundred metres offshore. There was no need for an anchor. As the ship settled into the water, Ash activated the stabilising thrusters, which were designed to keep her in that precise location accurate to a few centimetres using GPS.

'You're going to have to take the launch,' said Ash. 'I can't risk taking us any closer, the charts and the sonar are showing some nasty little reefs around here and I don't want to have to start pumping water out of the hull! I'll stay here and keep the engines warm just in case we need to get out fast. Good luck guys.'

Ben took control of a small inflatable motorboat, which slid down a chute, and guided them into the shallower turquoise waters. They jumped into knee deep water and dragged the boat on to the shore, away from the water's edge.

A sandy beach ran for miles in either direction but standing straight ahead of them were the tall, pale white dunes that made the location a popular destination for tourists. Some of the dunes were little more than small mounds of sand, but others were tens of metres high, running parallel to the seashore. Nico looked up at a large ridge of sand and wished he had a sand-board to ride down it, carving sweeping furrows into the fine white grains.

Phae was consulting the Sun-Moon. Its main indicator was pointing at a large dune, in the same way a magnetic compass finds North.

'It looks like the weapons are somewhere underneath this sand dune, but I am not sure how deeply they're buried. The elemental energy is so strong that I can feel them, even without the Sun-Moon. We must be very close.'

'Needle meet haystack!' joked Nico waving his hands in a gesture like a greeting.

'They're definitely in there somewhere' Phae was following the pointer as she walked towards a large ridge of sand, tens of metres high.

Ben was still trying to have some fun. Normally whenever he was on a beach, all he did was surf or mess around with his mates. A treasure hunt wasn't usually on the agenda.

'Can I start digging? I love digging!' and with that he raced up the hill and started throwing sand back between his legs using his hands, scooping away just like a very excitable golden retriever.

Nico on the other hand was trying to think of an easier way to shift all this sand and get the task done, so he too could have some fun on the beach. He remembered one of the books that the Library of the Astraxi had found for him, *The DragonStone, User Manual for Beginners, Volume 1 by Gilmane the Great.*

He remembered reading that the DragonStone was not just any ordinary magic ring, it had a wide range of powers that it could summon, as well as amplifying his own Dragon lore. Half of the book was about how to use the ring to summon weather effects. This included just about everything from creating a warm summer's breeze, to a raging hurricane big enough to rip up the coast of an entire continent, if you were a powerful enough mage. Something that could lift the sand off a dune and blow it somewhere else was all that was needed.

'Hey guys, I got this. I think I can summon something to cut through the sand,' he called to the others.

Nico turned to face the sea, where he could see Cygnus standing perfectly still despite the waves and tides pushing her towards the beach.

'Better not do it there, Ash won't enjoy facing a waterspout!' he smiled to himself and turned to face up the beach. He concentrated his mind and holding out the DragonStone ring ahead of him to the North he imagined whirling winds sucking water upwards from the sea.

As he opened his eyes, he could see a vortex of clouds circling around a central axis. The clouds quickly darkened, and the spinning intensified as the bottom of the rotating cloud patch stretched down to the surface of the ocean, which had also become very agitated. Then a spout rose out of the water to meet the cloud vortex and joined to it spinning in the same direction.

'Wow, what are you doing?' asked Ben.

'I'm going to bring it in to shift the sand dune, I hope!' Nico replied.

'I hope you know what you're doing' said Phae as Nico started to guide the waterspout towards the dune. But he hadn't considered that they were all standing directly in the path of the magical weather effect and as it got closer and more intense, they realised they were in serious danger.

'Run for it' shouted Ben, who bounded down the dune heading for the motor launch followed by Ciara and Phae. They dived behind a much smaller dune and took cover. Nico however, just moved slowly to the base of the dune as he pulled the waterspout towards him. By now it was a hundred meters high and squally winds were throwing up a large dust storm in its path. Out to sea the water started to froth and while observing from the flight deck of Cygnus, Ash made a call over the comms system.

'I don't know what you're doing, but I am making a tactical withdrawal until you've finished. Ash out!' He switched Cygnus' thrusters to manual and opened the throttle, guiding the ship out to a safe distance before she was thrown against the reef by the unruly sea.

Gritting his teeth and shielding his eyes against the stinging sand being blasted into his face, Nico swung his arms around, to physically drag the waterspout off the sea and into the dune. The effect on the dune was catastrophic, as it was torn apart by the vortex which ripped a massive furrow in its surface and opened the heart of the dune to the skies above. As the vortex collapsed, it dumped tonnes of airborne seawater into the centre of the dune. Rivers of mud and water oozed across the scene as the water washed away the loose sand and ran back to the sea, forming hundreds of little river deltas on the beach.

As the steamy air cleared and the water drained away, part of a large wooden ship was revealed, jutting out of the sand. From its blunt shape it seemed to be the stern end of a medieval sailing vessel. A wall of wood, forming the side of the ship was also partially revealed and on top of this there were what appeared to be some balustrades supporting a handrail around the edge.

Nico grinned. He was pleased that his plan had worked, although by the way his friends dived for cover, he thought they may not be quite so keen to see him bring in another waterspout to reveal the rest. 'The weapons have got to be in there, I reckon,' he said confidently.

Ciara was still trying to clear the wet sand that had got into her hair and was sticking to her eyelashes.

'Stand back everyone, I'm going to see if I can shift more of the sand,' Nico called to the others.

He raised the DragonStone once more, but this time he imagined a strong wind blowing up from the South and directed it at the dune. A gale force wind appeared blowing Nico off his feet and forcing him to hunker down and crouch close to the sand to prevent himself from being dragged away.

The wind formed a narrow channel that he was able to direct with his ring bearing hand, a bit like the gadget you can attach to a vacuum cleaner to blow dust around. Sharp, sandy dust swirled in the air once more scratching at his skin, but he stayed focused and was able to guide the jet of air at the sand surrounding the engulfed ship.

The blast threw plumes of sand and dust away from the dune revealing larger parts of the ship's hull. Within a few minutes Nico was exhausted and had to sit down to recover his strength, but the stern and most of the main deck had been cleared of enough sand for them to gain access to the ship. Nico sat down in the sand recovering his breath and shaking dust from his hair, nostrils, and clothes as the others climbed the dune to join him.

Phae produced some drinks from her backpack, which they shared, washing the grit from their mouths. She always liked to be able make sure her team had the things they needed to work better and maintain morale, which was often something as simple as a little food and drink.

'Got any tucker in that bag of yours?' demanded Ben. Phae shook her head knowingly and produced some energy bars from the backpack.

'No bugs this time? Chocolate would have been much nicer!' joked Ciara, even though she was very grateful for the snack.

The team climbed the rest of the way up the dune to the ship. Its timbers seemed almost perfectly preserved, the dark stained oak of its hull sitting firmly in the sand. The three masts appeared to have been broken off and this was why it had probably drifted on to the beach, where it had eventually been swallowed up by the shifting sands. They climbed the sand to a point where they would most easily be able to get aboard.

'The sailors on this ship were lucky not to get wrecked on the reef' said Nico as he stood by the vast hull.

'Or maybe they were just very good sailors,' came the voice of Ash, broadcasting from the drone which he had sent to monitor the mission. He had read about the great fleets of the past, who used to trade with many other nations and explored the oceans of the world. He realised from the quality of the ornamental detail of the woodwork around the captain's cabin, that this was probably such a ship, maybe even that of an admiral.

'Mira, can you identify this vessel from her markings,' he said.

'Yes Ash. From the carvings and the overall size, I can identify it as most likely to be the ship that belonged to Admiral Dexis that set sail after the Great Battle of Astrellion. It was officially on a mission of peace and exploration, with the primary purpose of the stellar cartography of the southern skies, and to provide important navigational data for the fleet. It was rumoured however, that as Admiral Dexis was also the Dog Warrior, then he may also have been carrying with him two of the weapons of elemental power, the Blade of Astrellion and the Shield of Fire. Nothing was ever heard of the ship, Admiral Dexis, or his crew again and they were eventually declared lost at sea by the fleet, or so the royal archives indicate.'

'So, it looks like we may have just solved that ancient mystery,' said Nico as he launched himself over the handrail on to the main deck. He was quickly followed by the others apart from Ben who was considering the implication of what Mira had just said, that Admiral Dexis was the Dog Warrior when the ship was wrecked in Australia.

'Does that mean Admiral Dexis is probably my ancestor Mira?'

'I could calculate the probability of that for you if you wish,' was Mira's enthusiastic response. 'But of course, there is the possibility that there was someone else on the ship and you both had a common ancestor that connects you by DNA to the original Dog Warrior. It's complicated after all this time, and it would be useful to have more data.'

'Tell you what, I'll just park that for now Mira, thanks!' said Ben who leaped over the rail to join the others on deck.

Most of the ship including the bow, was still buried. Rigging was scattered in tangled heaps around the deck, but there were doorways and hatches to cabins and the lower decks, which they decided to explore. Ben dug away the sand from a bulkhead, clearing the way to a door. Phae consulted the Sun-Moon again and confirmed to herself that the artefacts were somewhere behind that door. Without warning, she launched her full body weight in a flying kick. The door snapped off its hinges and broke into pieces, as the dry sand of the dune had sucked much of the moisture out of the wood, weakening it.

'You might have warned me first' said Ben as he brushed shards of broken wood from the doorway. 'It probably wasn't locked anyway!'

Ash's voice came over the drone loudspeaker again, 'This old ship is a valuable archaeological find, and you guys just want to smash it up! You're nothing more than a bunch of vandals, in my opinion!' Ash was very unhappy at the lack of any thought of conserving the ship, which was probably the only one of its type still surviving in the world. He hoped the remains could eventually be moved to the Central Museum of Astrellion.

'Don't worry, there'll be plenty left for you geeks to spend hours studying later' shouted Ciara back at the drone tartly.

'It's the future we need to save, not the past Ash' added Nico. But Phae was eager to find the artefacts quickly and get out of there. As she stepped towards the splintered wood, she activated her amulet and muttered the '*make whole*' spell '*Olokliros.*'

The broken door began to reassemble itself from the pile of fragments littering the floor. The pieces seemed to move in slow motion, randomly, although an observant person might note that they moved in almost exactly the opposite direction to that when they were shattered by Phae's foot, as if time had been reversed for that object.

'I hope you're happy now Ash!' announced Phae over the in-ear comms system. 'Let's get on with it.'

The inside of the cabin was very dark, but the DragonStone cast its pale blue light illuminating the piles of sand on the floor. Old nautical charts and navigational instruments were scattered around, as well as furniture and a few personal objects including a fine ship's decanter and some decorative porcelain. The ship appeared to have been abandoned in a hurry, but there were no signs of any human remains, so maybe they all escaped.

Following the master pointer of the Sun-Moon they descended a set of stairs into a hold. A nasty stench was hanging in the air. 'This smells pretty rank,' said Phae pinching her nose in disgust.

Ben's super-sensitive nose started to twitch, and he let out an enormous sneeze without covering his mouth.

'Smells just like a wet dog, Ben!' teased Ciara.

'I'm the one with the hyper-sensitive nose and I can assure you that a monkey's armpits smell far worse,' replied Ben with a knowing grin.

'Ben, you know, you're just completely disgusting. I'm going to teach you a lesson you won't forget, dog breath!' Ciara was about to launch herself at Ben when she realised that she was standing in something very sticky. A thick brown slime was attached to the soles of her shoes and as she lifted her feet, long strands of slime followed.

'Will you two grow up,' huffed Phae before she too realised that her feet were sticking to the floor with the same gloopy slime. It was difficult to see in the darkened cabin, so Phae powered up her amulet. '*Luxeïs*' she called, remembering the spell that Xin had used to bring light to the dungeon, applying it to an oil lamp that was hanging in the centre of the room.

But as their eyes adjusted to the eerie light spilling from the old brass lamp, they could see what was causing their feet to stick to the floor. The whole cabin was covered in slime, like that left by slugs but on a much bigger scale. Nico reached for his torch and flashed it around the room revealing a horrific creature, the likes of which none of them could ever have imagined.

In one corner of the hold was the source of the slime, a thick gelatinous mass that was translucent and pale brown in colour. At its edge the gel was just a few centimetres thick, but it increased in depth until it reached the bulkhead, where it was about half a metre thick, spreading up the wall in the same way as it covered the floor. The whole thing was about 4 metres across. Deep within the middle, there was a spherical structure about the size of a football and darker in colour than the rest, with a wrinkled surface like that of a brain or a very large raisin.

In the corner of the hold, submerged in the gelatinous mass was an old wooden trunk, like a treasure chest. Propped up against the trunk was a skeleton, its pure white bones totally cleansed of any organic material. In one hand the skeleton had a round shield with a distinctive flame design that spread out from the central boss painted in red and gold, while in its other hand was a plain metal short sword unadorned except for a small inscription near the hilt. As it caught Phae's magical light the sword glimmered and shone, its surface undamaged by the strange ooze in which it was submerged.

'It's the Blade and the Shield,' said Phae full of confidence that they had now found the two lost weapons of power. She was ready to start digging into the gelatinous mass when she was pulled back by Nico.

'Not so fast! We've got no way of knowing what that stuff is, and whoever that was. Even though he was armed with two of the most powerful weapons ever made, look what happened to him. I'll see if I can wash the gel away first.'

Nico raised his hand with the DragonStone ring and imagined flowing water running down the walls to flush away the gel. But the reverse happened. Rather than washing away the slime and ooze, the gel started to quiver and even grow a little stronger where it contacted the elemental water.

'I didn't expect that!' said Nico in surprise. Without warning several large pieces of gel launched themselves at him. The long tentacles stuck to his clothes and started dragging him towards the centre of the mass, where the brown sphere had started to pulse regularly, expanding, and contracting as if it had a heartbeat.

Nico fought back but was quickly losing the battle to stay on his feet, as his boots failed to grip in the slime. He slid ominously towards the giant amoeba's centre, slowly, a few millimetres at a time. It was clear that he couldn't stop it drawing him in with its tentacles.

'It's got Nico! Get him out!' called Ciara in terror as she grabbed his arm to try and drag him back. Ben transformed into his Dog warrior armour and used his gauntlets to tear and claw at the gel, but the amorphous creature retreated before squirting a powerful acid at him. The acid ate into his armour sending up a cloud of acrid smoke and making his lungs ache, but Phae gathered some of Nico's water into a pot and washed it off him as he leaped around like someone possessed.

'I've got an idea,' said Phae, opening the Sun-Moon's protective cover, and setting some of the dials. 'Mars, plus the Sun, plus a few other things, I think.' As she held the Sun-Moon in front of her, Nico was still fighting the tentacles drawing him firmly towards the centre of the gel, while Ciara and Ben could only look on and watch, afraid that any intervention would trigger another acid attack.

'Do something! Anything!!!' shouted Nico as his terror at being sucked into the creature increased. Phae concentrated on the Shield and as she did a ring of flame licked around its rim. The gel responded by shooting a jet of acid at Phae which she just managed to avoid, by taking a dive into the floor and getting coated in slime. The acid struck the opposite bulkhead and ate into the wood burning a hole the size of a large dinner plate in seconds. The gel didn't seem to have been damaged by the elemental flames but had grown in thickness around the shield.

Meanwhile the brown spherical nucleus pulsated more strongly as if the creature was now fully awakened, and it moved slowly through the gel towards Nico revealing more stripped white bones. Nico's panic was growing with the number of gelatinous tentacles that had now almost totally surrounded his torso locking in his arms and pulling at his legs. Not only was he now incapable of operating his amulet and summoning his dragon lore, but panic had set in clouding his ability to imagine the things he could do to help himself.

Phae had another revelation, 'I think it feeds off magic' she said, almost under her breath as if she was struggling to believe such as crazy idea.

'So, whatever you were doing, do the opposite!' Nico was now struggling to speak as the tentacles tightened around his chest trying to suffocate him.

'Moon and Venus for starters,' she said switching the device's settings 'and add a little Mercury.' She hoped that

THE FIVE ELEMENTS

her power to cause inversions of physical and elemental phenomena would work on the weapons of power.

Nico was now powerless to help himself and had dropped to the floor. The tentacles were drawing him slowly into the main body of the gel as the brown nucleus continued its migration to meet him there. It was clear that whatever had happened to the ancient sailor who last occupied that cabin, the same was about to happen to Nico unless they could stop the creature from absorbing him. His feet were now being pulled into the main body as the gel swallowed his ankles.

Phae's magical inversion on the Shield of Fire now started to work. Instead of producing flame the Shield was now doing the opposite by freezing the gel around its edges. A gap appeared around the rim and surface, where the gel was starting to solidify, shrink and withdraw into itself. Small cracks appeared in the gel where it had frozen and in reaction to this, the amorphous creature was pushing the Shield up to its surface, as if trying to spit it out.

'It doesn't like the taste of that anymore' said Ben in the hope that Phae's efforts would continue to work.

Phae's magic had a very different effect on the Blade of Astrellion, which broke free of the skeletal hand that was holding it and slipped through the gel under its own power, as if she had summoned it. The hilt of the sword pushed out through the surface of the gel but was tantalisingly out of reach as it was well within the range of the creature's acid attack.

'Leave it to me' said Ciara as she powered up her amulet and transformed into the Monkey warrior. As such she could use her special powers, but this time she wanted to draw on the additional physical skills that came with the role, the amazing gymnastics and dexterity that are second nature to monkeys.

She sprang back towards the stairs, which she used to gain some height before somersaulting back above the gel and swinging in on a pulley attached to the roof of the hold. The creature shot more acid at Ciara, but she was too quick for it as she swept past at speed, pulling the Blade out of the gel. Viscous acid scorched a hole in the ceiling, bubbling as the thick varnish coating the wood was burned away.

As she reached the other side, she deftly switched course catching on to another rope hanging down into the hold and once more swooping over the gel towards Nico. The Blade glowed faintly in her hand, a pale blue similar to the glow of the DragonStone when in Nico's presence. As she flew in, she wrapped the rope around her waist and turned herself upside down, hanging on with one hand and using the sword to hack at the gel tentacles that were still drawing Nico towards the brown nucleus.

'Be careful Ciara, I am not sure what's worse, being swallowed by this monster or being slashed to ribbons by the Blade!' said Nico still alarmed at the way Ciara was brandishing the bladed weapon.

The creature fought back by throwing out new tentacles to trap her, but Ciara was fast. The sword was mightier than the gel, as she sliced easily through the formless substance, which was instantly reabsorbed as soon as it fell back into the mass of the main body.

On her next pass across the creature, Ciara collected the Shield, which had now risen to the surface to be expelled as the gel surrounding it froze and splintered away. She threw the Shield towards Ben, who obligingly leaped into the air and caught it.

'Good frisbee skills Ben' she enthused as she landed next to him in a perfectly executed tumbling dismount from the swinging rope.

Nico was still in a very perilous position as the giant nucleus slowly approached his feet pulsating more rapidly, gearing up to dissolve the fleshy parts of his body. Green secretions appeared in the brain-like ridges of its surface.

It wouldn't be a quick death for Nico, but certainly very painful if he didn't first suffocate in the gel. Strangely he felt very calm under the circumstances. He wasn't going to let this thing absorb him, and he wasn't about to die, he was going to destroy it and having seen the effect of Phae's magical inversion on the Shield, he realised that the DragonStone could help him escape.

In his mind Nico imagined a huge Antarctic style temperature drop in the vicinity of the gel and although he couldn't raise his hand to direct his magic, the DragonStone glowed brightly on his finger, its pure blue light strongly penetrating the gel.

'Ice is twice as nice' he mused 'Time for the old freezerino!'

As the temperature inside the gel plummeted, the first thing he felt was a loosening of some of the tentacles that were wrapped around his torso and arms. Some of the smaller ones snapped off cleanly as he wriggled, while the larger ones congealed and slowed down, stiffening up and sagging away from his body. Then the area around his feet, which the nucleus was about to absorb, began to set, turning into a solid like a discoloured block of plastic.

As the gel became more viscous, the movement of the nucleus and the rate at which it pulsed also slowed. The grooves of its wrinkled surface became smoother and the whole sphere shrank. It reabsorbed the green secretions into its brown fleshy surface and now resembled a massive, dried grape. It had lost its symmetrical spherical shape, sagging under its own weight like a deflated ball, while the deepening cold ebbed its energy away.

Nico pulled himself free of the remaining limp gel tentacles and seeing that the creature was weakening, Ciara rushed in to hack at it with the Blade, chopping hardened lumps of gel out near his feet, releasing them. He sprang out of the monstrous goo, peeling off pieces of gel tentacle which he dropped to the floor and watched in disgust as they flowed slowly back to reattach themselves to the main body.

'Thanks Ciara.' said Nico with a huge exhalation of relief. He then gave Ciara a big hug, which completely took her by surprise.

She was for once lost for words at Nico's embrace. As much as she had secretly become very fond of the handsome young man with his easy manner and his luxuriant floppy hair, she didn't really know how to approach him on a personal level and was a little embarrassed to show this. She also felt that in any competition for Nico's affections Phae, who was more mature and confident in herself, would always be his first choice.

But she wasn't going to throw away the opportunity to spend a few seconds in his embrace and clung on to him tightly. After a few awkward seconds Nico stepped back from the hug and recovered his composure with a short blow out of his cheeks.

'Yeah, really, thanks Ciara,' he grunted, stepping away, having had all the breath squeezed out of him by the girl.

Phae too was surprised by this unexpected personal moment and to cover up the expanding sense of awkwardness, stepped into the space between them and took the sword from Ciara's hand, while announcing in her bossy tiger style of voice, 'All hands to the main deck! Let's get out of here.'

"Aharrr, Captain!' responded Ben in his best pirate accent. They made their way back up the stairs as the gelatinous monster pulled the rest of its slimy strands back into its main body to prepare itself for the next unfortunate visitor to the ship's hold.

It was a very ancient creature and was used to waiting patiently in the darkness for hundreds of years for its next meal. But despite their elation at escaping the monster, the Astraxi were about to face an even greater peril.

CHAPTER 33
Shifting Sands

Outside on the upper deck it was apparent that the weather had taken a sudden turn for the worse. Dark clouds were gathering behind the dunes. Ben called Ash using his in-ear comms device.

'Hey Ash, mission accomplished buddy, get Mira to warm up some pizza to celebrate!'

'Well done team, but I think you should probably get back to the ship right away,' said Ash.

'By the way, what did you do to the sunshine?' replied Ben. The air was rapidly turning cooler, and the breeze was starting to whip up in strength. 'Now that we're done, I had hoped to get a bit of surfing in. The waves here are pretty awesome.'

'I have some concerns about those storm clouds. There's nothing on the weather satellite feed that indicates a pattern of bad weather in our vicinity. It's a total mystery. Someone or something nasty is out there in the desert and heading in our direction at speed. Make your way back to the launch now and I'll prepare to get us out of here. Ash out.'

Ash could be very abrupt without realising it, but in this instance, it was clear he was genuinely worried about the storm front that was growing behind the sand dunes and didn't want to waste time with a discussion about it. Clouds were boiling up vertically forming a large grey-black wall in the sky.

'Come on, we'd better do as he says,' said Phae as she knew that it wasn't in Ash's nature to stop them from having a little fun from time to time without good reason. He struggled to involve himself in those things that other people liked, which he felt were trivial pastimes, especially as he had so many projects that he was working on at any one time. As Nico prepared to vault the handrail, he noticed that the Blade of Astrellion was now glowing in Phae's hand, an even brighter blue than it had done in the ship's hold.

A terrible howling filled the air, like the sound of a million souls in torment all echoing on top of each other. It was accompanied by the same terrible gut-wrenching blend of fear and loathing that the team had encountered on the day Eleni was killed by the Fiend Taotie. Bitterly cold winds threw sand in their eyes and tore at their hair as the daylight was reduced rapidly to twilight levels. They struggled to keep their eyes open in the dark gritty blast, but four points of a deeper distorted darkness stretched through the space ahead of them. The shadowy shapes of all four of The Fiends were projected out from the Plane of the Undead onto the deck ahead of them blocking their exit. A simple wooden hatch cover on the deck was all that separated the Warriors from the Fiends.

Nico recognised the spirit sapping effect of the Fiends' *bane* magic from his encounter with Hundun at his mother's house but recognising it didn't reduce its potency as he felt deeply sick to his stomach.

All four of the young people felt their knees buckling in fear and their viscera felt like they were being twisted inside out and squeezed by cold grasping fingers.

'Bring them to me' hissed Hundun as he beckoned to the two weapons of power.

As Qiongqi and Taotie stepped forward on to the hatch cover, Phae found the inner strength to resist the powerful curse. She stepped forward on to the hatch to face them calling out the spell, '*Nomikí aspída*' while drawing an imaginary line across the hatch cover with her free hand.

The others began to recover their senses and their faculties as the '*shield from chaos*' spell cast by Phae partly nullified the Fiends' '*bane.*' Taotie and Qiongqi stopped short of the line drawn by Phae, while the Astraxi activated their amulets and assumed their Celestial Warrior status.

As the Four Fiends faced the four Warriors, the undead creatures changed shape. The hideous pale faces with their strange tattoos and translucent skin were replaced by more pleasant human features, yet their skin was grey, bloodless and had an uneven, lumpy texture. The Fiends' armour of dark magic faded away to be replaced by clothing of times long past, fine fabrics, leather tunics and hose. It was clothing of the quality you would expect to be worn by great kings, exquisitely embroidered, and adorned with pearls and gemstones.

Indeed, this appearance was something very close to how the Fiends would have looked before they took their evil oaths preserving their own life force in phylacteries, before stealing the souls of others. Despite the change, the four were not pleasant to look at. Thousands of years of unspeakable acts of evil had left their mark. These were the most foul and corrupt beings on earth, possibly in the entire universe.

Hundun moved closer to Phae's magical line on the hatch cover, to speak directly with her, hoping that his more normal appearance may help persuade her to his will.

'Tiger Warrior, you and your fellow Astraxi face certain destruction. The odds for your survival are practically zero. Cyax will prevail and you will die. You may as well surrender now. There is no need to suffer the same fate as your Master.'

Phae remained calm and summoned up all her courage to reply to the half-human, half-monster in front of her. She stepped forward to face Hundun gesturing the others to remain where they stood.

'I'm prepared to take my chances against Cyax or you,' she said fearlessly and with confidence that inspired her young colleagues.

A satisfied smirk curled the ends of Hundun's slit-like, lipless mouth as he tried to ingratiate himself further.

'But it need not end this way. Right now, we are at a point in time where there is a choice to be made. An alternative destiny awaits all of you. There's no need to join Xin in death. Join with us instead, and together we will rule the world.'

'Don't listen to him Phae!' cautioned Nico, who was trying to figure if he could recall any magic that would help in this situation, but in the moment of terror his mind had gone blank.

If he unleashed a fireball at Hundun as he had done at his mother's house, he would probably kill everyone else in the resulting fire. If only he had been given more time to study Dragon lore before this conflict blew up. Now the Library of the Astraxi, that place of calm and learning, seemed like a lost dream of academic treasures.

Hundun, who couldn't imagine why anyone would turn down such a lavish offer, continued his speech ignoring Nico.

'You could take the throne of the new Dark Empire and become our new Princess. With three elemental weapons, Four Fiends and Five Astraxi Warriors, together we would be invincible. We would not fear anyone, not even Cyax. You could destroy him, for ever and you could live for ever. The curse of your human mortality would be lifted. We can show you how.'

Phae gripped the Blade of Astrellion harder, its magic glowing even more intensely. 'You're no better than Cyax. You are liars and the destroyers of worlds and all that is good in them' she replied.

'If that is your answer, then we will kill you now and take the weapons anyway. But do not forget Tiger Warrior, the last time we met, how easily we destroyed your friend, the Dragon. What was her name now, I seem to have forgotten her already?'

Hundun paused for a moment taunting Phae, waiting for the impetuous anger to boil up inside of her, hoping that she would once more commit herself to some bold and ill-prepared action that would give the Fiends the advantage.

The purple stone hanging around Hundun's neck, the source of his eternal power, glowed vividly. 'Eleni, she was called, isn't that right?' he paused once more looking coldly into Phae's eyes waiting for her to make the wrong move. She gripped the sword more tightly.

'Do you even know how to use that sword?' he mocked her. Phae trembled as a tear of regret for Eleni trickled down her high cheekbone, and her bottom lip quavered, an emotion that was obvious to Hundun. The Blade trembled in her hand as she contemplated lashing out and striking Hundun down. The Blade's lawful magic could inflict great damage on the undead, even in her inexperienced hands and Hundun knew that, but he continued his mind games anyway.

Phae knew that Hundun would be superior to her in combat with a sword, but she struggled to contain her impulsive nature, as the memory of that tragic day in the ruins of the Royal palace flooded her mind. Revenge was there for the taking.

Hundun smirked, his voice adopting a tone of mock regret, 'Where is Eleni's soul now? Gone forever, what a terrible waste!' He broke into an evil sneering laughter that came from his whole body, a laughter that pounded in her ears. 'Now your pathetic mortal lives will also be ended. Such a shame!'

Phae couldn't contain herself any longer and with a massive cry of anger drove the Blade of Astrellion not into Hundun, but into the wooden hatch cover under their feet. She knew that the Blade's elemental power would split the hatch cover apart, the meta easily overcoming the wood. She also pinned her hopes on the Fiends falling into the hold giving her colleagues a chance to escape. She was prepared to take the risk to herself and make that sacrifice to save her friends.

Just like her flying kick to the door earlier, the magical sword shattered the wooden hatch cover into millions of tiny fragments.

'Head for the water' she called to the others as she tumbled into the hold. But Hundun and the other Fiends had anticipated her move and stepped back off the hold cover just as the Blade struck the wooden panel.

Hundun turned menacingly towards Ben, unsheathing his unholy sword and as he raised it over his head, a nasty looking spike on the blade detached and flew off like a dart, heading for Ben's chest. Without stopping to think, Ben's lightning-fast reflexes lifted the Shield of Fire for protection.

'That was close' whispered Ben to himself, his heart thumping. The metal spike at first appeared to stick in the highly decorated surface of the Shield, but its elemental fire energy was way too powerful for the unholy weapon and the evil spike was absorbed into the shield with a small puff of green flame.

As Hundun advanced towards him, Ben took the initiative and charged the undead king under cover of the Shield. It struck Hundun's armour of overlapping plates and scales forcing him back towards the hole in the deck that Phae had fallen through.

Ben pushed hard at Hundun with all his strength spurred on by the desire to protect his colleagues as if he had acquired the strength of a whole wolf pack working together as one, but the more he pushed, the more Hundun's enchanted armour fought back. Piece by piece the armour scales were detaching from each other and rearranging themselves, spreading out over the surface of the Shield, as if to try and absorb it.

Ben withdrew half a step pulling the Shield with him and the attached armour scales before smashing it back into Hundun with all his strength. Scorching fire erupted from the surface of the Shield in the direction of the undead king.

Hundun reeled backwards to protect himself, losing his footing on the jagged edge of the shattered deck and falling backwards into the hold. Ben was unprepared for the sudden burst of flame that came from the Shield and in his fear of being incinerated, he dropped the Shield over the edge into the hold, only just maintaining enough of his own balance to stop himself following the Fiend. Unfortunately, he was unaware that as the person wielding the Shield, he was immune to damage from its fire.

Phae had managed to soften her landing with a *'feather fall'* spell. She dropped into a pile of coiled ropes with barely a bruise and was just climbing free of them, when Hundun came crashing into the hold, followed by the Shield, which landed on top of him.

Hundun leaped to his feet and grabbed the Shield as Phae raised the Blade of Astrellion in self-defence. Still full of impetuous anger at Hundun's sneering contempt for the death of her friend Eleni, Phae charged him, pointing the glowing weapon directly at the undead creature's heart. But he didn't have a heart, at least not one with a pulse.

Hundun raised the Shield to cover himself, knowing that the Blade was potentially very deadly to undead creatures such as he, and as the Blade struck it a plume of fire was launched once more, but this time at Phae.

The Blade's elemental power provided some protection for her, as she called out *'Yoshimo!'* to invoke her own protective Shield of Harmony. The red-blue magical aura spiralled around enveloping her body in a protective cloak. Nevertheless, Phae was forced back to the wall by the heat and power of the Shield's magic, which had now set alight the tinder dry wood of the interior of the hold. Flames surged around her, ravaging the bone-dry ropes coiled up on the deck, running up the varnished timber walls and across the ceiling.

The others wasted no time in leaping over the handrail into the soft sandy slope below the ship, tumbling downwards to bottom of the dune. The three other Fiends, Qiongqi, Taowu and Taotie were slower to react, but began their pursuit.

Taotie raised his index finger at the retreating Warriors. '*Exantlisis,*' he hissed.

The three Celestial Warriors felt their legs growing heavier and their lungs gasped for enough air to keep moving as the *'exhaustion'* spell took hold. Their feet dragged through the sand as if they were weighed down by heavy burdens. Nico realised that the Fiends would soon catch and overwhelm them.

'Star shield' he called to the others and all three engaged their amulets to provide their protective energy shield. As they grouped together, the three shields merged to produce one, much stronger protective cloak. Golden lights swirled through the shield, occasionally forming the shapes of the Dragon, Monkey and Dog asterisms, before blending into other patterns. The three Fiends slowed their pursuit and eyed their prey in anticipation.

'Three Astraxi Warriors and their amulets, quite a prize!' exclaimed Taotie as he drew his unholy sword.

A communication came in from Ash. 'I'm sending another remote-control motor launch to bring you guys back.' A panel at the stern of Cygnus opened and a remotely controlled drone-speedboat shot out launching itself into the air, landing on the water with a huge splash.

Below deck in the ancient ship, Phae continued her struggle to force Hundun back as the flames around her grew higher and hotter. The magic of the Blade was in perfect balance with the magic of the Shield, and neither could force an advantage over the other.

'I gotta get out of here' thought Phae to herself, feeling the heat scorching her skin.

Hundun sensed his opportunity to overcome Phae who coughed as the heat and smoke risked overwhelming her.

'You need not die this way Tiger Warrior. It would be such a shame to see you reduced to ashes along with this old ship. Yield to me now and I will save you from the flames.'

With those words he stepped up his physical efforts, pushing the Shield hard up against the Blade and forcing Phae back towards the bulkhead, which was now fully alight and covered in raging orange flames.

But Hundun's increased assault on Phae and the proximity of the flames seemed to have exactly the opposite effect on her. Phae exploded with rage and pushed herself back at the Fiend. Hundun tried to stand his ground, but Phae let out an enormous roaring yell such that one could have imagined there was indeed a tiger in the room. Her protective magical aura seemed to intensify as she drove the creature back, summoning an internal physical strength that seemed at odds with her slender athletic body.

Hundun seemed temporarily paralysed by the deafening sound and Phae looked up at the sky through the hatch cover calling the spell '*Exo varyteis*' and imagined herself flying upwards. The inversion magic reversed the effect of gravity on her body, propelling her skywards out of the ship's burning hold. She landed in the soft sand of the dune below the ship, from where she could see the three other Fiends bearing down on her colleagues, striking heavy blows into their star shield.

Each blow from their unholy weapons drained energy from the shield, and the three, who were still weighed down by Taotie's exhaustion spell, were struggling to maintain the energy required to support their defence. The horrific wailing sound of millions of tormented souls that accompanied the Fiends grew more intense as they relished finishing off the three terrified young people behind the shield and claiming their mortal souls.

Either adrenaline or an intense need to protect her friends, or both coursed through Phae's energised Warrior mode. As she raced to the top of a nearby dune the tiger stripes in her armour flashed brilliantly in the bright blue light cast by the magic sword she was carrying. With her eyes fixed on the three Fiends attacking her friends, she raised up the Blade of Astrellion with her outstretched arm calling out '*Lux agioteis.*'

The Blade lit up like a beacon, as if a pure white light source as powerful as the daytime sun had ignited it from within. The light banished the darkness of the heavy doom-laden clouds that the Fiends had brought with them when they arrived.

Phae directed the light's intense central ray towards the three undead kings. The pure beam tore into them fiercely, ripping at their armour and pulling at their exposed flesh like a laser weapon. Plumes of black smoke rose from them, almost as if the ray of light was disintegrating their bodies into tiny fragments.

Qiongqi's cloak caught fire as he dropped his attack on the star shield and he tore it away in anger, covering his eyes in fear of the light. With the strength-sapping magic now neutralised, the Astraxi quickly regained their composure, while the three Fiends retreated to the cover of a nearby smaller sand dune out of reach of Phae's light beam using a '*blink*' spell.

Inside the ship, Hundun was far from beaten. With Phae's unexpected exit, one might have thought that he faced being incinerated alone in the ship's hold, but he had wisdom and a deep understanding of how the Shield's power really worked. Drawing the weapon of elemental power to his chest and placing both hands on its rim, he drew in a deep breath, as if to suck the fire out of his surroundings.

He was using the Shield to open a portal to the elemental Plane of Fire, which was where the weapon's power came from. It seemed as if a jet of wind was sucking the fire into the Shield.

Long tendrils of orange and yellow flames were sucked from the ship and flowed down twisted lines of flux, roaring as they converged into the gold dome that was the central boss of the Shield. Soon most of the fire had totally disappeared into the Shield, leaving the ship a smouldering charred shell.

Hundun thrust his left forearm into the Shield's enarmes and made his way through the debris to a staircase that was still strong enough to support his weight. He ran up to the deck from where he could see Phae's assault on his allies. Kicking his way through the smouldering remains of a section of balustrade, he dropped down to the sandy dune below him.

Nico knew he needed to summon some of his own lore if they were to escape the Fiends and the Shield of Fire. The DragonStone ring had been designed to draw power from the Plane of Water allowing Dragons to direct weather effects amongst other things. He recalled from a book called '*Zhao's The Five Elements and the Elemental Lore*' that if there was generative magic involved, then it may help to use an overcoming spell to counteract it. But what was that? With all that was going on he was finding it a bit difficult to remember the running order of the way the five elements interacted with each other. Maybe he should have brought a copy of Zhao's five-pointed star diagram of forces that summed it all up.

'I don't know what to do, I can't remember which order the forces work in.' said Nico, with regret written across his face.

'Why not just use the ring to blast water at them!' shouted Ciara in his ear. Nico snapped out of his mental block almost as if he had been slapped, which was what Ciara might have done next if he had remained staring blankly at his hands.

He clasped his ring finger in his other hand and summoned up a vision of a tidal wave coming in off the sea. A great dome shaped surge of water rose fifty metres high directly offshore. But Nico was worried that he and his colleagues would themselves be swamped, and he unclenched the ring collapsing the surge back into the ocean. Large waves crashed out in all directions.

'You've got to be very careful when you're throwing this kind of sorcery around, that you don't kill yourself and your friends in the process' said Nico grimly.

Ash's drone motorboat was being tossed around in all directions, swamped by the unruly sea, but it bobbed back up again like a cork, having automatically sealed itself.

Nico turned to draw a surge of water from further up the beach. The wave raised itself up high and he hurled it at the dune behind which the three Fiends had taken shelter from Phae's searing light.

As the tidal wave hit the dune, Taotie, Qiongqi and Taowu were washed away and buried in the sand. The wave continued its rush up the beach heading for Hundun who was forced to use the Shield of Fire to deflect the water that was about to engulf him.

Ash saw the chance to send the drone motorboat nearer to the shore. Phae also realised that now was the moment to escape, but Hundun was not going to let the Astraxi go. He could still take the Blade of Astrellion if he were victorious. His eyes were drawn to Phae as the burning white light faded from the magic sword and she bounded down the dune at full speed towards the water's edge. Despite the age of his undead body, Hundun was surprisingly quick on his feet and aimed to cut Phae off before she could make it to the ocean.

Her three companions were already waist deep in water climbing the ladder into the launch as Phae realised that Hundun was gaining on her and would most likely intercept her on the hardened sand nearer the water. She didn't dare hesitate, hoping that momentum would carry her where she needed to be, beyond the reach of the Fiend.

From the launch the three could see the monster closing on her as she charged down the dune with her usual surplus of raw courage over any real or even part-formed plan, roaring 'AAAHHHH!' at the top of her voice!

Hundun fired one of the deadly spikes from his jagged blade of evil narrowly missing Phae. Then he fired another which landed just in front of her, causing her to tumble to the sand as she swerved to avoid it. Leaping quickly to her feet she held forth the Blade as Hundun arrived to face her, thrusting forward the Shield and his unholy sword.

Ciara had an idea how to help Phae and uttered the spell *'Diploseis.'* In her mind she imagined a perfect duplicate of herself appearing behind the Fiend.

'You're not taking another of my friends. This time, I'll sort you out good and proper,' whispered Ciara to herself.

The replica Monkey Warrior she had created behind Hundun slapped hard him on the right shoulder, while cheekily slipping past his left shoulder as the Fiend turned to see who had shoved him. As Hundun turned back to face Phae, he was puzzled to see the Monkey Warrior standing in front of him.

'I didn't think someone as big and clever as you would fall for such a simple trick,' said the replica Monkey Warrior grinning broadly. Hundun straightened his stance and readied himself to strike the Monkey with his sword.

Phae was determined to take the fight to Hundun and rid the world of his evil presence for ever, using the power of the Blade of Astrellion. She knew that if she could strike him well enough, making enough contact with his undead flesh, there was a good chance that he would be seriously injured or even destroyed. She was more than prepared to give it a try.

Silently Ben and Nico made furious gestures to Phae, waving her on towards the boat. Hundun was still working out how to deal with two Astraxi warriors at the same time, when the illusory Monkey Warrior punched him hard in the face,

'That's for Eleni' she said, before turning to Phae and shouting, 'Run for it now, you idiot!' Phae picked up her heels quickly and sprinted straight into the water as Ash guided the drone boat to a more advantageous position for her escape.

Enraged, Hundun hacked and slashed at the duplicate Monkey Warrior which mocked him, stepping smartly aside and acrobatically dodging the blows of his sword.

Once Phae was safely aboard, the illusory Monkey Warrior thumbed her nose, blew a raspberry at Hundun, and then evaporated before his eyes. He paused to look around himself for a moment as he tried to understand what had just happened. As the motor launch raced off through the surf back towards Cygnus, he realised that he, Hundun the most feared creature of the darkness, an ancient evil warrior king of the undead had been outwitted by a young girl's clever illusion. In his anger he let loose a horrible cry of frustration that shook the ground and drove the sea into an agitated state, causing the launch to be thrown about.

Hundun was still facing the ocean as the drone motor launch approached Cygnus and safety. 'Why doesn't he follow?' asked Nico.

'It's because the Fiends fear open water,' replied Phae as the ship's robotic cargo arm hauled the launch back aboard. Once inside the ship with the hatch closed, they heard Ash's voice over the intercom.

'Strap yourselves in anywhere you can for take-off in less than one minute.' Outside the ship, the skies began to darken further as the Fiends stirred up the storm clouds, causing the sea to thrash the ship around like a cork.

Holding on to any surface they could reach, they staggered up to the central hub and scrambled into their seats as Ash guided the ship to a place well beyond the reef for take-off. Thrusters pushed the ship forward with such acceleration that they were all squashed into the back of their seats.

'I think I need to lie down, I'm exhausted,' said Ciara.

'Thanks for helping me back there Ciara. Somehow I don't think that's the last we'll see of Hundun.' said Phae.

'It was nothing,' said Ciara, 'I'm not afraid of him. But now he has the Shield and he'll probably hand it over to Cyax.'

'At least we secured the Blade' said Phae as she examined the ancient weapon. 'It's interesting when you're holding it. It feels like you were always meant to use it, like it was designed to fit your hand perfectly. Maybe I should get some fencing lessons! Mira, do you have any in the video library?' Phae was still high on the adrenaline of her narrow escape.

'Yes Phae. I have a full swordsmanship course from basic lunges, feints, and parries to the advanced use of a whole range of bladed weapons including broadswords, longswords, and specialist oriental fighting techniques,' replied Mira.

'Cool! I can't wait to give it a go,' said Phae who flexed her wrist with the sword attempting to twirl it around, but the Blade fell out of her hand dropping to the floor with a sharp clattering sound.

'Remind me to be somewhere else when you start waving that thing around again,' quipped Ben.

Mira was first to respond without a hint of irony, 'No need to worry Ben. I am fully equipped for any medical emergency with a full range of surgical options, including the precise reattachment of limbs or other body parts using a microsurgical robotic attachment. My techniques have been thoroughly tested and achieve a success rate of ninety-nine-point nine percent,' she said nonchalantly appearing on the hub's central view screens with a smile. Sadly she didn't realise just how badly this might go down with the crew.

'Er, what happened to the point one of a percent that went wrong?' asked Ben.

'Thanks Mira' said Nico, 'It's probably easier if we all just stay out of the way while she's learning to use that!'

'In that case, would anyone like some tea and sandwiches?' said Mira.

'Now you're talking my language!' said Ben jumping up to be first in the queue at the serving hatch. Mira knew that a meal would help the group relax and restore their bodies for the next challenge. Her automated galley function delivered a fabulous array of finger foods, cakes, and sandwiches via a serving hatch, which were snapped up hungrily by the young people who had lost track of when they had their last meal and were unsure when they would see the next one.

CHAPTER 34
The Eve Of War

In Thanatos, Cyax' preparations for all-out war on Astrellion were nearing completion. Despite frantic pleas for more attempts at diplomacy from all around the world, huge forces had been built up north of the border by the river which separates Golteria and Astrellion.

Legions of cyber-demons and their supporting semi-organic cyber war machines were encamped awaiting the orders that would set them loose on the northern cities of Astrellion. A smaller but much more deadly group of Morgai which Cyax had built up using the earth elemental magic of the Cup of Souls were camped far enough away from the cyber-demons to prevent them from attacking and eating their comrades.

Cyax was studying the large strategic map of Astrellion with its holographic representations of the armies gathering to fight. Tanielka and the most senior generals of her armed forces were gathered around the table waiting for Cyax' final approval. As he leaned over the table, he was still running through the battle plans in his mind, playing out various scenarios and calculating the probable outcomes and consequences of those actions and any contingency for any unexpected challenges. Cyax turned to the assembled group.

'Though the Astrellians outnumber us, they are weak and lack combat experience and will be unable to resist the ferocity of our attack. But remember that precision timing and discipline is the key to our success. My Enforcement Guards will be working at every level of command to ensure that there are no individual errors. They have been ordered to liquidate any individual or unit that deviates from the plans or shows weakness. Generals you have your orders.' With that he dismissed the group who all stepped away with a degree of urgency in their stride.

'My Lord, the stories I heard from my mother and my grandmother of your leadership and prowess in the art of war do little justice to the reality of your mastery.' Tanielka was genuinely overawed by Cyax' ability to see the outcomes of multiple battle scenarios but was even more impressed by the ruthlessness of the plan, which was to overwhelm their enemies quickly and with a ferocity that they couldn't imagine.

'Watch and learn Princess. Within seven days Astrellion will finally be mine.' Cyax turned back to the map to continue his mental calculations when the eerie howling sound of one of the Four Fiends materialising distracted him. The holographic images on the table blinked and froze temporarily as Hundun's wraith-like form warped itself into existence from a point of darkness that emanated from within the Plane of the Undead. Papers were scattered all around as a chill wind swept through the room at the same time. Hundun faced Cyax and nodded his head as an expression of respect for his long-time ally. Cyax returned the gesture while noticing that Hundun had the Shield of Fire strapped to him.

'What news my Lord Hundun?' asked Cyax.

Hundun removed the Shield from the strap holding it on his back and held it in front of himself. 'My Lord Cyax, we tracked the Astraxi to a remote beach where they had located two of the great weapons in the wreckage of a royal treasure ship.'

'And?' said Cyax, looking to see if Hundun was also carrying the Blade of Astrellion.

'We were able to secure the Shield of Fire' replied Hundun in his usual succinct manner.

'And what of the Blade of Astrellion?' continued Cyax.

'The Tiger Warrior escaped with the Blade,' responded Hundun, his rasping tone showing his distaste at not capturing either the other weapon or the young Warriors.

'We the Four Ancients, offer this weapon of power to you, to use as you wish. We trust that you will fulfil your side of our agreement.'

Hundun handed the Shield to Cyax, who held it with both hands outstretched, in admiration of the work of the ancient weapon smiths who had created it. Its polished golden rim gleamed in the light as he turned it to inspect the red and gold flames inlaid into the matt black body.

He placed the Shield on the stone flagged floor and spoke an ancient spell to summon fire demons from it.

'*Pyro daimonas!*' The inlaid red and gold patterns on the Shield came to life, flickering like real flames, as a small humanoid figure about thirty centimetres high, made entirely from living fire, emerged from the gold dome in the centre. The fire demon stood for a moment, flames running up and down its legs, arms, and torso with a flickering crown of crimson licking the air above its head. It surveyed the world into which it had been drawn, seeking something combustible to destroy. It threw itself with a sense of unbridled joy into a pile of papers, which erupted into flames as it rolled around on top of them.

Black fragments of scorched paper fringed with fire were thrown into the air as a guard intervened, trying to beat the flames with a heavy piece of curtain pulled down from the wall.

The fire demon ignited the curtain too, then climbed up the burning cloth to fight with the guard, setting his uniform on fire and burning his fingers, causing him to drop the curtain to the floor in great pain.

Fong emptied a large jug of water over the guard and the elemental creature. It writhed and hissed as the water sapped its energy, before vanishing back to the Plane of Fire through the Shield, in a puff of hot vapour.

With a look of great satisfaction at the demonstration of only a minor power of the Shield, Cyax handed it to another of the guards nearby before turning back once more to survey the table. He continued his mental calculations, this time factoring in his new weapon.

A general who was no doubt feeling the stress of the build-up to war, stepped forward nervously to address Cyax. 'My Lord would it be wise to secure the other two weapons of power before embarking on the invasion?'

'We have the Shield, the Cup, and the Wand. We also have the Snake Warrior. While they have only the DragonStone and the Blade. Where there would normally be many Astraxi Warriors, now there are only five, and they are little more than children whose Master is dead. So, we are more than ready General. Never before have we had such an advantage over our enemies. Princess, give the order.'

'With pleasure my Lord' replied Tanielka reaching for her communications pad, and with a simple touch of the screen, she set loose the most dangerous fighting force ever to be ranged against the land of Astrellion in its entire four-thousand-year history. 'General, the time has come. Prepare to move the command centre to our forward base.'

'You heard the Princess. We depart in one hour,' said the General. With that the soldiers, technicians, and battlefield commanders stepped away from their stations and filed in an orderly manner to the cyber-troop transporters waiting on the parade ground below the palace gates. The entire war machine of Golteria was primed and ready for attack. To any impartial observer, Astrellion appeared doomed, and Cyax assured of victory, even if the Astraxi made it back into the fray.

CHAPTER 35
Return To Astrellion

Cygnus was on a hypersonic trajectory to return to Astrellion as quickly as possible, reducing the flight time from Australia to around four hours compared with the usual subsonic time of sixteen hours. Cygnus was a truly remarkable vessel, being just as much at home on the edge of the vacuum of space as she was in the air, on the sea or in submarine mode beneath the surface of the oceans.

Mira effortlessly managed the navigation and other systems enabling the ship to enter a sub-orbital flight mode without Ash at the helm. The other team members were taking time out to think about their next moves after the close encounter with the Fiends on the sand dunes.

Nico, Ben, Ash, Ciara and Phae gathered in the Hub. On the screens surrounding the central console were multiple live video feeds showing the rapid advance of Cyax' forces over the Golterian border and into Astrellion's northern most regions. A war correspondent's voice broke in over the scenes of destruction.

'As Golterian troops surge through the northern regions of Astrellion, The Government and the International Organisation for Peace between Nations, have called for an immediate cease fire and the resumption of peace talks. But in response Prime Minister Fong, the official spokesman for the Golterian government of Princess Tanielka had this to say…'

The video cut to an image of Fong on a platform surrounded by microphones and reporters.

'After many thousands of years of the shameful and illegal occupation of the throne of Astrellion by usurpers, the people of Golteria have been forced to take up arms to liberate their Astrellian brothers and sisters from tyranny and return the land to the stewardship of Cyax the Magnificent, the Most-Merciful, the first-born son of Theokeis and the rightful heir to the throne of Astrellion.'

'Turn it off Mira,' muttered Nico as he swivelled in his seat with the Blade of Astrellion in his hands. He was trying to figure out what was so special about this simple short sword that the Fiends and Cyax were prepared to go to such trouble to possess it. While handling it he could sense it had special properties that couldn't be felt using just his normal five senses.

It sat well in his hand, almost as it had been designed especially for him, which Phae had said was also her first impression of the sword. The clean, bright steel of which it was made was like a mirror, apart from the small runic inscription at the top of the blade, which translated as *Morning Star*.

He carefully ran his fingers around the cutting edge of the sword, which seemed to be so fine that its edge was almost invisible when viewed from the side.

'Ouch.' Nico quickly put his fingertip in his mouth to suck up a small amount of blood from a cut. He had pushed his exploration of the sharpness of the metal just slightly too far.

'What can you tell me about the Blade of Astrellion, Mira?' he asked while wincing from what was little more than a paper cut.

Ignoring Nico's pain Mira replied, 'The Blade was forged by a master weapon smith called Astyaxes, from one of the five provinces that made up the ancient Astrellian Kingdom. As a simple sword, the Blade has special properties which enhance its accuracy and potential to do damage. But the maker also harnessed the elemental power of metal as she forged the Blade, giving it magical properties. If used in the right way, by the right person, its power is almost limitless. But it is also subject to the rules of elemental lore if other elemental forces are in play.'

Nico continued to squeeze and suck his fingertip to stop the flow, but the blood just kept oozing and forming a new red blob every time he stopped.

'So presumably, like the DragonStone, the Blade can summon elemental magic too.' His finger was now white where he had squeezed it particularly hard to try and stop the flow.

'There are some dressings and antiseptic ointment in the drawer to your left' said Mira, in her slightly nannying tone.

'You really should be more careful with that weapon Nico, it's not a toy!' Phae stepped in and took Nico's hand before cleaning off the blood and dabbing it with a ball of cotton wool soaked in antiseptic ointment. Nico just relaxed and completely submitted himself to Phae's first aid treatment.

'With the DragonStone I can summon water elementals, so does that mean there is similar magic for the Blade?' continued Nico in his enquiring tone.

Mira continued her description of the Blade, 'I can confirm that. As it is governed by the element of metal it's particularly powerful against wood elementals and can be used to enhance water elementals.'

'So, with these weapons of power, it's a bit like rock-paper-scissors, but with five objects instead of three.' Nico continued to stare at his fingertip as Phae soaked up the blood still weeping from his fingertip.

'Yes, in a manner of speaking,' said Mira. 'the Blade's main weakness lies in fire. It can be overcome by the Shield.'

'I felt that when I was attacked by Hundun,' added Phae as she unpacked the adhesive dressing. 'It seemed that despite the Blade's power, he had some sort of advantage when using the Shield against it.'

'It's also said that the weapons of power have the ability to disrupt the life energy of immortals and the undead.' continued Mira.

Nico quickly realised the implication of this fact that Mira had casually delivered. 'So could the Blade be used to kill Cyax?'

'I cannot confirm that Nico. The evidence to date appears to indicate that Cyax is indestructible,' replied Mira.

'Yes, I had noticed,' said Nico as Phae lined up an adhesive dressing against his injured finger. 'There's only one way to find out.'

'Ouch!' Nico cried out in pain as Phae squeezed the dressing into place, before patronising him with a ruffle of his floppy hair that left him looking dishevelled.

'There you are, good as new! Ready for part two of the plan then, Dragon Boy? Ash, what's our ETA?' said Phae.

'We'll be arriving in the thick of the action in just over an hour. After we come out of the hypersonic glide, I'll activate stealth mode and see how close we can get without attracting attention. Mira, I need you to start scanning the battlefield to locate Cyax' command centre and a suitable landing site nearby.'

'Scanning Confirmed Ash,' came the positive response of the ship's supercomputer.

'So, since you mentioned part two of *'The Plan'* Phae, what exactly is that plan?' asked Ciara, knowing perfectly well that Phae was unlikely to have a plan other than to dive in and try to defeat Cyax using the element of surprise.

Phae ignored her, being unconcerned by such detail, having utter faith in her own abilities and those of her colleagues.

'Mira, once you know the location of Cyax' command centre, could you bring up satellite views, maps and details of patrols and guard posts. We will need to get close to him without being detected.'

'Well, that's pretty obvious!' said Ciara with more than a hint of sarcasm. 'Even if we get into the command centre and manage to capture Cyax, which is a pretty big ask, what do we do then? I mean, he's indestructible isn't he. It's not as if we can just blast him with a fireball or get a Star Dragon to drop him into a glacier again, is it?'

Ciara had become very animated, it was clear that despite her great abilities and powers as the Monkey warrior, she was genuinely afraid of this mission.

'I wish Xin were here. He'd know what to do.' Ciara sat back in her chair and stared at the screens showing more Golterian troops overrunning towns and villages in the northern regions of Astrellion.

An awkward silence reigned in the room for a moment before Nico stood up to speak. Some internal passion inspired by Xin, had gripped him after all of the hardship he had suffered in recent times.

'Whatever happens, the one thing we need to remember is that Cyax has never ever totally defeated the Astraxi. He may have powerful weapons and magic, but there are five of us, and our lore is at least as great as his power, if not greater. As Xin always reminded us, the Astraxi are a much greater force when working together, than as individuals. The amulets chose us for this task, we all passed the test, so we should believe in ourselves. We are the Astraxi, together we can beat Cyax again. He's not going to win, not while we can still stop him. Astraxi, be strong!' Nico stood and stared at his colleagues waiting for their response.

'Whoosh!!' said Ben clapping his hands spontaneously, 'Great speech buddy, I'm with you. Let's stick it right to Cyax!' Ben leaped out of his chair to give Nico a high five and was soon followed by Ciara and Phae.

Ash as ever stood back from such obvious displays of emotion, but in his own way was very satisfied with his colleagues' reaction to Nico's rousing speech.

'Mira's tactical analysis has found us a good landing site a few kilometres from what we believe to be Cyax' command post. Let's get prepared. Your backpacks for a full combat away mission, are ready in the equipment locker. See you back here in 30 minutes, when I will have more information about our landing site.'

Ash returned to the flight deck to prepare to give his colleagues the best possible advantage, with a safe landing under the cover of Cygnus' cloaking systems, close enough to the battle front to be able to engage Cyax and his forces. The problem was that Cyax' forces were advancing so rapidly that it was impossible to decide exactly where the front line would be by the time they dropped out of their sub-orbital flight path.

'Ash, I have an incoming message from General Abara, the commander in chief of the Astrellian defence forces,' said Mira as Ash dropped into his pilot's seat.

'On screen' responded Ash as he strapped himself in.

A holographic image of the General appeared within Ash's head up display, 'Ash, I want to discuss with you any plans the Astraxi might have to get involved in this situation.'

'General, we're on our way back now and we will be turning up for the fight in less than an hour,' replied Ash as he disengaged the ship from its hypersonic flight path and began her rapid gliding descent back to earth.

The General's grim expression reflected the seriousness of the situation, 'We're taking heavy losses right now and are regrouping on the high ground of the mountain passes just north of the central plains. He'll have to come through there, so that's where we think we'll have the best chance of stopping his advance, or at least slowing him down. I'll send you the co-ordinates.'

'Astrellion can count on the Astraxi. We'll be joining you just as soon as we can General. Ash out.' The holographic image of General Abara fizzled away as Ash engaged the navigational computer on which Mira had already indicated the best landing site to get them close enough to Cyax' headquarters.

'Load in a vector to the landing site Mira and take us in automatically on this one. I'm going to make sure we're not interrupted.'

Ash spun around in his seat and with a gesture pulled up the tactical, weapons and defensive displays. A broad map covering two hundred and fifty kilometres of airspace ahead appeared on one screen where he could see the Astrellian air force taking on squadrons of Golterian fighter-bombers and troop transports. The Astrellians were managing to shoot down many of the invaders, but it was clear that they were outnumbered in the air, and it was going to be a tough battle to maintain air-superiority.

'What is your plan Ash?' asked Mira calmly as he studied the movements of groups of enemy aircraft to try and understand their strategy.

'We can't win a fight in the air on our own, so there's no point in attracting any more attention than we need. Let's just steer clear of any trouble for now, until we get ourselves established on the ground.'

'I think that's most wise Ash, that's exactly what I would have done' concurred Mira, which surprised Ash as he was more used to Mira simply reacting to his commands than offering opinions on his decisions.

'Continue on this approach vector and let me know when we are getting close, I am going to talk to the others,' and with that Ash leaped out of his seat and descended back down the stairs to the central hub.

Inside the room Mira had already transferred the tactical displays from the flight deck to the central console. Ciara, Phae, and Nico were waiting for him, but Ben had not yet appeared.

'Where's Ben?' enquired Ash.

'He's probably still carb-loading in the galley. Last time I saw him he was stuffing his backpack with snacks, while trying to eat a bowl of pasta!' said Phae. Ben walked through the door while stuffing a handful of cheesy snacks into his mouth.

'Got to get your priorities right mate! An army marches on its stomach, or so they say!' Ben was about to sit down when the ship suddenly lurched to the right causing him to spill his snacks all over the floor.

'Five-second rule applies!' he shouted as he tried to scoop up as many as he could and put them back in the bag or his mouth.

'Sorry about that Ben,' said Mira. 'I needed to take evasive manoeuvres to avoid us becoming tangled up in a dogfight, if you pardon the expression!'

'That's alright Mira,' said Ben, 'If there's a dogfight, I'm happy to get stuck in!'

'Mira, give us eyes on what's happening out there, on the ground and in the air,' commanded Ash. Immediately the view screens were ordered into a series of co-ordinated animated maps, satellite views and feeds direct from the Astrellian armed forces own military communications and some others that Mira had decrypted from the Golterian's own secure feeds. There was silence in the room for a moment until Nico spoke up.

'It looks pretty intense' said Nico in a way that suggested he wasn't really prepared for the scale and the horror of the invasion. Armoured vehicles charged through villages and towns, while squads of roving cyber-demons shot randomly at civilians who were caught in the wrong place at the wrong time.

Particularly harrowing were the images of hand-to-hand fighting between Astrellian infantry and marauding bands of Morgai demons, who behaved like packs of savage beasts ripping lumps of flesh out of anyone or any creature that got in their way. They revelled in the gore that squirted from the slashed arteries of their victims, wearing it as a terrible style of decoration. This bloody red war paint dripped from their mouths and claws and was wiped across their bodies and faces.

The Morgai were very difficult to kill, as every single fibre of their bodies was striving to cause as much terror and inflict as much pain on others as possible. They would always continue to fight on, even after taking fatal injuries themselves. While their evil hearts continued to beat, the Morgai were always the deadliest of foes.

The screens also showed live feeds from the cockpits of the brave pilots of the Astrellian air force, who were losing the fight against enemies that cared less about their own survival and were prepared to sacrifice themselves in deliberate suicidal collisions.

One terrifying feed showed a pilot's point of view, after a mid-air collision, trapped in his seat while his aircraft fell spinning to earth. Drones had also been effective for both sides, but the Golterian suicide tactics were forcing the Astrellians to withdraw to protect both their pilots and their remaining combat aircraft from this indiscriminate destruction.

'Get me General Abara again please Mira.' said Ash, having realised that the situation was deteriorating rapidly. 'General Abara, what's your status' he asked as the General appeared on a holographic screen.

'Since we last spoke Ash, we've become aware of a second Golterian force approaching from the West. Somehow it was shielded from us. Cyax has set up camp on the hills overlooking the approach to provide cover for them. We're preparing a counterattack, but we could really do with your support.'

'What do you need us to do General?' asked Phae.

'We need you to do what you're best at. Go in and disrupt his command centre. Take on Cyax directly and give us the chance to make a stand against his armies and stop their advance before it's too late. By our calculations, if we don't stop them here, they'll be in Astrapolis by tomorrow.'

For a moment the Warriors stared at each other. Normally Xin would take the lead and make the decisions, but until now they hadn't worked out who was in charge.

Phae looked around and seeing that no one else was about to speak up, she took the initiative anyway, 'General, we're on it.'

'Mira, continue on course for Cyax' command centre, get us as close as you can without them detecting us.' said Ash

'Course change for new co-ordinates confirmed Ash, estimated arrival in six minutes and thirty-four seconds.' After Mira spoke, the group continued in silence checking their equipment and preparing for the biggest challenge of their lives.

CHAPTER 36
The DragonStone

As the sun began to set on a flat piece of ground at the head of a glacial valley, small trees, rocks, and dust were being pushed around by powerful winds that appeared out of nowhere. Cygnus' retro-thrusters were positioning her vertically on to the spot identified by Mira, her landing gear creating four large rectangular compressions in the grass.

'We may be invisible, but someone's bound to have heard the huge noise that this ship makes when she lands vertically,' said Ash as he unbuckled himself from his pilot's chair. 'So Mira will get Cygnus out of here to a safe place, while we take on Cyax. But she'll be monitoring our channels and standing by to assist if we need her.'

'That is confirmed Ash, good luck on your mission. I wish I could come with you,' replied Mira.

'Maybe we'll see about that one day' replied Ash.

The five Astraxi Warriors descended the access ramp under the ship on to a patch of tufty grass beside a small lake created by a glacier, when the earth was in the grip of its last ice age.

Cygnus' noisy approach and departure had definitely been detected by a patrol of cyber-demons, whom they could see rapidly ascending from the valley below them. The five powered up their amulets and transformed into Warrior mode.

'I've got this,' said Nico firmly and he stepped forward with the Blade of Astrellion in his outstretched hand, pointing towards the approaching cyber-demons who were using their cybernetic enhancements, such as robot arms and powered body suits to scramble upwards.

Nico closed his eyes to focus his imagination more accurately. In his mind's eye he pictured a large creature rising from the earth and drawing energy from the Blade of Astrellion's connection to the Plane of Metal. As he re-opened his eyes, a huge humanoid shape was pulling itself out of the layers of flat rocks by the lake. The metal elemental quickly rose to its feet and towered over everyone, being around four metres tall.

The magical creature was made of shining bands of metal of different colours, some grey like steel, others bright and colourful like copper and brass. Instead of hands it had two massive weapons, an axe, and a mace. It's face was made from different metallic shapes, and it seemed to smile as it stared at its master waiting for a command.

Nico didn't really know what to make of this creature or how to control it, but in his mind, he directed it to attack the cyber-demons. He was just as surprised as the others when it did just that! The elemental creature slid on its heels down a short section of loose scree, bringing it directly into the path of the approaching cyber-demons who immediately attacked it with their blaster energy weapons.

Most often the energy of the weapons simply bounced off its shining metal surface, ricocheting in all directions. A ricochet unfortunately hit one of the other members of the patrol, blasting it to smithereens. Some of the energy blasts caused a small amount of superficial damage to the metallic finish of the elemental creature, but it raised its axe and hammer and tore into the hapless cyber-demons decapitating some, crushing others and slicing many more into pieces as its axe blade had almost infinite sharpness.

'I'm glad he's working for us,' said Phae her eyes transfixed by the scene below, 'Let's get out of here before they send in reinforcements.' The group moved off across the hill side followed by the metal elemental, which covered their backs from incoming blaster fire. It held its two weapons outstretched catching the energy bolts and absorbing them or deflecting them back.

As they crossed over the ridge, waiting in surprise were Cyax, Tanielka and a small force of Morgai and Golterian guardsmen. The Astraxi were quickly surrounded by the Morgai who stood snarling, waiting for their master to unleash them.

For a beat everyone present sized up each other's strengths and weaknesses, making rapid decisions about how either to attack or defend themselves. Cyax spoke first, 'Take them, alive.'

The Morgai and guardsmen hurled themselves at the Astraxi, who were equally ready to respond. Nico dived under the legs of the elemental and directed it towards Cyax, hoping that the huge creature would be as effective as he had been against the cyber-demons earlier. But Cyax was a master of elemental lore and knew exactly what to do when faced with such a creature.

While dodging a blow from the giant axe, he raised the Shield of Fire above his head and thrust it hard into the creature's other forearm. Flame flashed around the rim of the Shield as it sliced effortlessly through the metal limb. The hammer dropped to the stony ground with a resounding clang crushing the boulders beneath. As the giant metallic creature reeled from the injury, Cyax thrust the Shield firmly into its lower abdomen.

The weapon of power produced another surge of flame around its rim, and Cyax pushed it almost entirely into the creature, which buckled around its waist and crashed to its knees. Cyax withdrew the Shield and thrust it again into the metallic torso, which this time erupted in flame, causing balls of molten metal to roll down its surface.

Nico felt his mental connection with the creature suddenly stop and what was left of it collapsed around him like a broken sculpture. As it hit the ground it made a hollow ringing sound like a collection of bells that are out of tune with each other. Although he was uninjured, Nico was being pinned down by a large section of the broken elemental.

Meanwhile four snarling Morgai were edging towards Ben, their claws itching to tear him apart. The nearest of the Morgai was ready to strike, its fangs bared and drooling as it growled insanely. Ben drew the small dagger that was part of the armoured suit that protected him when the Dog amulet was activated. The advancing demonic creature looked at the blade but showed no fear as it lunged forward. Its sharp claws tore into Ben's breastplate, trying to rip away his protection, while he kept the creature's foul mouth at bay with the dagger. But the creature was very strong, driven by an unnatural hatred of humans and even with the protection the armour gave him, Ben struggled to hold it off. The three other Morgai moved in to seize their advantage.

Ben made the sharp and distinctive whistle that would magically summon canine help for him. Just as he was about to be driven to the floor, a huge Tibetan Mastiff landed on the back of the Morgai tearing at its neck while rolling it over and pinning it to the floor. Three other huge dogs followed, their orange manes giving them the appearance of lions as their muscular bodies pushed against the lightweight Morgai.

The first Tibetan Mastiff was now fully in control of its adversary and despite the demon's frantic attempts to claw lumps out of the dog, its thick coat prevented the talons from doing much in the way of harm. The dog had its jaws firmly around the demon's throat suffocating it and crushing its neck vertebrae.

Ciara took on the human guardsmen with her Monkey lore, using a variation of the illusory double she had used while evading the Fiends on the Australian beach. This time she made herself invisible at the same time, so that she could manipulate the scene from a safer position away from the action.

'*Diploseis*' she called before vanishing into thin air and being replaced by her own double, which then moved in the opposite direction to her, drawing the guardsmen away.

The duplicate Ciara then acrobatically ran up a tree to a sturdy branch high above the approaching soldiers from where she started to taunt them.

'Which of you idiots is tough enough to come up here then?' she teased. One of the less intelligent soldiers charged at the tree trunk and grabbed the lowest branch to haul himself up, but in doing so fell right into her trap. The lowest branches of the tree morphed into a group of enormous snakes, whose heads and fangs swooped down on the man, who tumbled off the tree in terror.

Ciara laughed. There had been no real need to pull this second trick, but it amused her to do so. As the other soldiers retreated dragging their terrified colleague with them, the invisible Ciara on the other side of the area summoned another spell for her mirror image, '*Extralis*.'

Confusion spread across the soldiers, who very quickly lost track of where they were, why they were there and what they were supposed to be doing. Fear and panic emptied their minds of reason, and they lost the ability to hold the even simplest conversation or respond to the commands of their leader. Those dragging their terrified friend dropped him and stared into the distance or looked at the open palms of their hands as if they had forgotten something important, while the others froze where they were standing, their faces expressionless.

Tanielka had focused her eyes on Phae. Here was the opportunity for her to prove her worth to her master Cyax, by destroying the Tiger Warrior and claiming her amulet.

'Tiger Warrior, you will yield your amulet to me now, or I will take it from your dead body,' said Tanielka as she squared up to Phae, sprouting her long, razor-sharp claws.

'I am not giving in to you, so you'll just have to take it,' said Phae as she readied herself for the Princess' imminent attack. Tanielka stared into Phae's eyes and beckoned Phae forwards, inviting her to strike first.

'Come on, have a go. You know you want to!' Tanielka was anticipating a sweet victory. She believed that her years of training as a warrior princess were about to be fulfilled and she was brimming with an electrifying self-confidence. Phae on the other hand was energised by the memories of the defeat under the old palace ruins, which were fuelling her anger and desire for retribution. She trembled as she tried to contain her feelings, think rationally, and to remember the lessons that Xin had semi-jokingly referred to as his Tiger Anger Management course. It was not a joke of course, as the old man had witnessed many times the consequences of the actions of an impetuous tiger, and it wasn't always a pretty sight. Phae clenched her fists but just couldn't resist the temptation to let rip.

'Gladly,' said Phae through gritted teeth, and she launched herself through the air feet first at Tanielka's midriff, but the Princess had anticipated this move and neatly avoided being hit while also delivering a blow to Phae on the way past, that sent her sprawling to the floor. Phae picked herself up just in time to avoid a sharp kick in the face and charged Tanielka, this time launching a blow at her head.

Once more Tanielka's combat training proved superior and she grabbed Phae's fist before it made contact and then landed a sharp punch in her ribs. The pain that rippled through Phae's torso had the effect of boosting her aggression even further and as she snapped her fist out of Tanielka's grip she swivelled and landed a kickboxing move hard in her opponent's stomach, then a karate blow at her neck as she bent forward.

Again, Tanielka was prepared and turned to deflect the blow with one arm before raking her claws across Phae's shoulder armour. The claws partially penetrated the tiger striped material and Phae winced in pain as she felt her skin being ripped open. She was now completely enraged and leapt at Tanielka wrestling her to the floor and grappling with her. As they rolled around, Tanielka laughed, enjoying the fight and the mind games she was winning against her adversary.

Ash had been standing by the edge of the field, carefully watching the outcome of the skirmishes breaking out in front of him. He was after all less of a fighter and more of a thinker, as Xin had often pointed out. After the earth elemental was broken by the Shield of Fire, Ash was helping Ciara disarm the confused guardsmen and send them back down the hillside. But Cyax spotted Ash, the descendant of the brother that he had brutally murdered in a jealous rage four thousand years ago and kicking aside the hollow remains of the elemental creature, he charged through the flames, carrying the Shield in one hand and the Wand of Xylos in the other.

'Stag Warrior you are a coward, unworthy of your ancestor. So now you will join him in death,' said Cyax raising the Wand of Xylos to strike Ash with it. Since King Theokeis had formally disowned Cyax after he was found guilty of his brother's murder, then Ash, who was also a direct descendant of Theokeis arguably had a more valid claim on the ancient throne of Astrellion. But none of that mattered to Cyax, and killing Ash was just one of the many things that he needed to do to reclaim his birth right.

Cyax was about to bring the Wand down on Ash, when Nico, who had finally freed himself from the pile of metal plates, charged at Cyax holding the Blade of Astrellion ahead of himself and roaring at the top of his voice. Cyax parried the attack away with the Wand and smashed Nico's body with the Shield in a flourish of roaring flames. Nico found himself on the floor, badly winded but not burned and had the presence of mind to roll out of the way quickly before Cyax could bring the Wand down on him.

'What sort of combat training have you had from your Master? Clearly not enough,' said Cyax as he bore down on Nico, who had now found his feet and was retreating, keeping his senses alert to the slightest possibility of another attack. Nico raised the Blade once more as Cyax thrust the Shield towards him. Flames roared out from the Shield as it clashed with the Blade, showers of sparks and jets of fire spewed out as the two magical weapons were pitted against each other in close contact.

'*Pyros exa metallo!*' Cyax quoted the rule of magical cycle of elemental lore, that Fire overcomes Metal, and as he did so the surface of the Shield raged like an inferno as if the Lord of Hell himself had taken control.

The Blade of Astrellion had been providing magical protection to Nico, by absorbing the worst of the effects of the heat and helping him physically resist the much larger figure of Cyax. Now he faced the full power of the Shield focused against the Blade, which became scalding hot in his hand, burning his palm and forcing him to drop it. Even his Dragon armour couldn't fully protect him from the intense heat. Cyax picked up the Blade where it lay, as Nico retreated and removed his gauntlet to examine the burn injury to his hand.

As Ciara and Ben dealt with the last of the confused guards, they were rushed in a surprise attack by a group of cyber-demons that had arrived to support their colleagues. With no time to think they called up a star shield to protect themselves.

Seeing an opportunity to join them, Ash burst through the cyber-demons with lightning speed, and they dived into the additional cover provided by a rocky outcrop, which protected their backs. Ash threw up his own star shield, which merged with theirs, reinforcing its energy. The cyber-demons fired their weapons at the coruscating surface of the shield, which both absorbed and deflected the energy of the blasts causing ripples of green light to spread across its surface, like the northern lights. With such a large group of cyber-demons in front of them and the stony cliff face behind, it was clear that they were trapped, without any other possibility of support or escape. It would only be a matter of time before they were broken by the prolonged effort of supporting their protective shield from attack, at which point it would collapse leaving them vulnerable.

Phae was still locked in her grappling and wrestling bout with Tanielka. Neither had gained any advantage over the other, but Phae had become aware of Nico's situation with Cyax. If he were to capture Nico, he would also take the fifth and final elemental weapon, the DragonStone. Cyax would then be unstoppable, and it would be over for the Astraxi and for Astrellion. Millions of people would be doomed to live in the dark shadow of tyranny and the rule of evil. The Four Fiends would stand to reap the rich harvest of human souls which Cyax had promised them, with all the eternal suffering that entailed. All that was good, clean, and pure would be lost, forever.

Determination gripped Phae. She was not going to let this happen, she'd had enough of losing. She opened her mouth and let out a mighty roar, the roar of an enraged Tiger Warrior.

Phae kicked Tanielka firmly in her midriff, sending her tumbling backwards to the ground where she lay motionless.

Cyax moved to attack Nico as he too lay on the ground, but Phae raced over and launched a flying kick directly into Cyax' back. Cyax retaliated with a blow from the Wand of Xylos, sucking her star energy into the wooden rod and draining her of power. Briefly she flashed out of and back into her Tiger armour. She knelt on the ground with her hands outstretched in front of her, gasping for air as if she had just run a marathon in record time. Finally, her magic faded away and she was returned to her vulnerable human state, without her Tiger armour and without enough energy to even raise her star shield. Nico looked on helplessly, he didn't know what to do to help her as Cyax seemed to be the only one with any power at that moment.

Cyax was as merciless as he was emotionless. Seeing Phae's vulnerability he raised the Wand of Xylos to strike her, but in his wickedness, he decided he would not deliver a quick blow, instead he would relish the slow suffering of both the Dragon and the Tiger in that moment.

He struck Phae's back with the weapon, but with a lot less force than he had struck Xin. She buckled slightly, then collapsed to the ground breathing heavily. Some glowing lights twinkled around her, as a small amount of her life force left her body. Nico looked on terrified as he realised what was happening. He tried to speak, but the horror was preventing him from doing so.

Cyax was enjoying the Dragon's distress as he lined up the Wand in a position to land another blow on the helpless Phae.

'So little worm, you have feelings for the Tiger. Such a pity that you will have to watch her die like you did your master.'

'Get up Phae' screamed Nico at the top of his voice, but her eyes flickered open and shut as she was losing consciousness.

'Phae, we need you!' continued Nico, 'I need you!' Nico's heart was sinking as he realised that he was once more about to lose someone that he cared for. This was just too much to bear, how could he stop Cyax from finishing her off?

Cyax raised the Wand readying himself for another blow, while watching the young man and enjoying his anguish. He hated the Astraxi deeply, especially the Dragon Warriors and in particular Dragon Magi. During his twelve-hundred-year imprisonment in the icy prison cell of the Great Glacier, many ideas for how to exact his revenge had worked their way through his mind. He hadn't expected it to be as easy as this, facing and beating five very young and inexperienced Celestial Warriors after destroying their mentor.

Nico realised that he had still one card left to play, there was one more thing that Cyax desired and killing Phae would not necessarily bring it to him.

'Stop!!' he called in desperation. 'Stop Cyax. I have something you want. If you leave her alone, I'll give you this.' He took the DragonStone off his finger and held it with his arm outstretched towards Cyax.

Cyax was intrigued and smiled malevolently, for him the day was getting better with every minute that went by.

'You would trade a weapon of such power for a mere girl? You are a fool, little worm. With that ring you could command anything you desire.'

Nico hesitated, knowing the danger in what he was offering, but in his heart, he knew he could not bear to lose Phae as he had lost so many others.

'She's not just a girl. She's my friend,' he gulped with emotion as the words slipped out of his mouth.

Cyax didn't need to think long about his answer, as he had already anticipated this trade.

'Give me your amulet and the DragonStone, then I will consider releasing your friend. But you must yield to me first.' Nico fidgeted nervously as Cyax placed the silver tip of the Wand forcefully on the back of Phae's neck. She groaned under the pressure of the magical weapon.

THE FIVE ELEMENTS

For reasons he couldn't fully explain later, Nico threw the ring about five meters to the right of where Cyax was standing. Maybe it was to buy time, because in that moment Cyax was forced to leave Phae to pick up the DragonStone. Nico seized the moment and using his amulet he summoned to earth his celestial companion, the Star Dragon Adraxa. The portal to the celestial plane roared open in a burst of starlight as Cyax bent down to pick up the magic ring.

With the Star Dragon between him and Cyax, Nico raced to Phae's side and spoke to Adraxa whose glowing body was shielding them from attack.

'Get us out of here' said Nico. Adraxa gently lifted Phae up in her claws, while Nico leaped on to the dragon's back.

The dragon jumped effortlessly into the air leaving Cyax to look on as they escaped, but he didn't care as in his hand he now held the last of the Five Weapons of Elemental Power, the DragonStone. He was very pleased with himself and let out a great roar of triumphant laughter that shook his body to the core. Absolutely nothing or no-one could stop him now.

CHAPTER 37
Desperate Times

Adraxa climbed into the sky at speed. Nico looked down to see the desperate peril which faced his three other comrades, and a pang of regret went through his stomach as he watched the volleys of blaster fire weakening their shield. He knew they couldn't hold out for much longer and Cyax would be able to add three more amulets to his list of treasures gained since he emerged from the ice.

Worse than that, Cyax would probably subject them to the same curse as he had used to turn Eduardo. The very idea that he may come up against three more of his friends, who had been turned to the darkness, made him shudder.

On the ground, the departure of their two colleagues with the Star Dragon was met with despair. Behind their weakening defence, even Ben's normally boundless optimism was fading and was being replaced by an understanding of the seriousness of their situation.

'We can't keep this up' he gasped while they directed the energy of the celestial plane through their amulets and into the shield.

'It's hopeless' said Ash, with a concise and accurate calculation of the scenario.

Tanielka had recovered from her fight with Phae and being enraged at losing to the Tiger Warrior, she turned her anger on the three others pinned down by the cyber-demons. She thrust her clawed fingers directly into the rippling energy surface of the shield, which fizzled and sparked as the celestial magic was disrupted by the dark magic of being Cyax' natural heir. A tingling sensation darted through her fingers, like a mild electric shock, which encouraged her to claw harder at the shield like someone possessed.

Whether it was Tanielka's disruptions, or whether it was simply sheer fatigue, the three Astraxi were unable to hold the shield any longer. It collapsed back to the celestial plane with a single short burst of starlight that faded slowly as it hung in the air between them. Tanielka was ecstatic, it had been many generations since any of her foremothers had captured such a group of Astraxi and their amulets. Now Cyax would see that she was indeed worthy of her position in the new empire that would be created in his name, uniting Golteria and Astrellion for the first time in history.

The young warriors cowered as the cyber-demons stepped in to restrain them, as the Princess looked on. Triumphantly she snatched their amulets as the wrist restraints were tightened behind their backs. 'Follow me' she ordered. The cyber-demons marched them in procession behind the Princess.

Cyax had moved back to his command position to review the advances being made on the battlefields below and bring his new acquisitions into the conflict. The war had reached the outskirts of Astrapolis, and the business district was in flames. Skyscrapers were burning like giant torches and citizens were fleeing in the opposite direction to the advancing army. Cyber-demons were pushing back the Astrellian armed forces in a dreadful retreat as General Abara's armies were overwhelmed. Cyax surveyed the information coming in and issued new orders to consolidate his gains, while maintaining his forces' brutal forward momentum.

Tanielka arrived in the midst of this scene with a triumphant air. 'Three more Astraxi my Lord' she said kneeling before her master with the three amulets in her outstretched hand.

'Excellent! Ready them for transport back to the Monastery,' replied Cyax as he took the three trophies before lifting Tanielka back to her feet. 'You are a Princess most worthy of the title and of being the bearer of my own blood.' He returned to his work at the Wizard's table, while the three young Warriors were put into a holding pen guarded by two particularly large and fierce cyber-demons.

On his orders, Cyax' own Wizard's Table had been set up outside his tent. He hadn't expected to be in possession of all five of the weapons so easily, but now he wanted to see what the combined power of their elemental lore could unleash. He placed the five items at their required positions on the table and summoned a powerful elemental spell, '*Tellux evano*' to connect them to the planes from which their energy is derived and to join the five of them in a power-circuit of the forces being generated.

Lines of coloured light, like laser beams linked each of the five objects, creating a five-pointed star surrounded by a pentagon. The outer concentric circles of the table rotated into positions representing the co-ordinates of places to where Cyax would now direct the most powerful magic ever wielded by a human being, or an immortal. Even Gilmane and his fraternal wizards would be awe-struck by the concentrated intensity of this power.

Cyax could now direct all five types of elemental magic to any position that he called up on the Wizard's Table. First, he directed a group of earth elementals to disrupt the roads that people were using to escape the city of Astrapolis and trap them within. He didn't want to rule over an empty capital, he wanted tribute and subservience. Indeed, what would be the point of being the King of nothing or nobody.

On his command, giant humanoid creatures burst forth from the ground next to every major highway. Their bodies were constructed from the granite and other hard minerals that existed in the ground wherever a creature emerged. Each one was slightly different in shape, but they all had a common feature, a huge boulder on the end of each arm. They attacked the roads and bridges, tearing out huge chunks of asphalt and the underlying concrete, smashing it into fragments with their rocky fists. Cars, trucks, buses, and camper vans swerved and piled into each other, blocking the roads, and creating traffic jams that went on for miles.

Huge water elementals, tens of times larger than those created by Nico during his training emerged from the sea, lakes, and rivers of Astrellion, surging over the surrounding areas like tidal waves and sweeping away people, animals, and small buildings.

Nor was the land of the Forest Folk spared from this wave of destruction. Fire demons as large as houses attacked the thick wooden walls of Dendropol taking a furious delight in igniting the ancient timbers that supported the city's greatest buildings.

The Master of Wands and the keepers of the lore of the forest were forced to withdraw from supporting the Astrellian army against Cyax to try and save their city.

Adraxa placed Phae down gently on a rocky outcrop close to where Ash had landed Cygnus. For a moment Nico thought about using the group comms system to call the ship

THE FIVE ELEMENTS

back to help but changed his mind when he realised that his friends will have had their communicators confiscated by their captors.

He climbed down from the Star Dragon's back to check on Phae, who was unconscious but still breathing and seemingly uninjured, at least from the outside.

He couldn't tell what deeper damage Cyax had inflicted on her with the Wand of Xylos. He brushed away the hair that was partly covering her face and looked at her for a moment trying to figure out what to do. He knew that some Celestial Warriors possessed powers of healing, but he had not seen these skills documented in the Dragon lore when he was in the Great Library.

He noticed that Phae was still carrying the purse on a strap over her shoulder, in which she had been keeping the Sun-Moon device. He opened it, taking the object in his hands. Maybe he could use this to help her, but he didn't really know how it worked. She had been injured by the Wand of Xylos, a weapon governed by the element of wood, so he wondered if he could somehow use the Sun-Moon to rebalance that injury. The Star Dragon was watching him and seemed to understand his thoughts,.

'Try it Dragon warrior, it might just work,' said Adraxa.

Using the very little knowledge that he had of elemental lore, he decided to set the wood governing planet of Jupiter against the moon, in the hope that the moon would degenerate the effects of the Wand's injuries. He lined up two concentric dials to set them opposite each other and placed the Sun-Moon on Phae's body just above her waistline, which he instinctively felt would be the best place to deliver its effects to her.

'I am not losing you too,' he whispered softly.

After a short period in which nothing happened, Phae stirred just a little. He held her hand gently as her eyes fluttered and opened before she gasped for air and leaned upright on one of her elbows. Fear was in her eyes, which darted around the area trying to figure out what had happened to her and where she was. Phae didn't speak, but then she looked directly into Nico's eyes as her breathing became more normal and the terrified expression faded away. She lay back down as if to rest, exhausted by the damaging effects of the Wand on her body.

Nico was massively relieved, but then he remembered the predicament of their colleagues and was ashamed that he had left them behind. He put his hands on Phae's shoulders and spoke to her.

'I'm going back for the others; you should be safe here. Wait until I get back.' Phae didn't answer as she was still too weak from her ordeal to speak. What she wanted to say was 'Take me with you' but Nico climbed on the back of Adraxa, and he directed the Star Dragon to take him back to Cyax.

The glowing figure of the Star Dragon swooped down from high above the Golterian command position with Nico gripping the spines behind her head. Adraxa let forth a great burst of dragon breath which scorched through the ranks of guards and cyber-demons. Cyax removed the Shield of Fire from its place on the wizard's table and threw it into the air with the incantation '*Horeveis.*'

The Shield now became a flying weapon, a 'dancing shield' while still being linked to the Wizard's Table by a beam of light and drawing power from its connection to the others. The Shield flew like a heat seeking missile towards Adraxa, who recognised the danger and made very tight evasive manoeuvres almost throwing Nico off her back. They soared upwards, made barrel rolls and loops, sometimes almost coming to a dead stop in the sky and then turning quickly in the opposite direction.

But the Star Dragon wasn't nearly as nimble in the air as the Shield. Many collisions with the weapon scorched Adraxa's body and wings in a way that was painful even for a Star Dragon.

Adraxa incinerated the Shield with a massive blast of dragon fire, but the weapon simply absorbed the jet, sucking it into a massive reservoir of flame on the Plane of Fire and then spat it back at her like a flame thrower. The Star Dragon dived quickly as she saw the flames shooting back from the centre of the Shield and neutralised them with blast of freezing Dragon breath. They were almost obliterated by her own fire which was being returned with malice.

Nico tried to recall some lore that might be useful to protect them from the Shield, but he was too busy trying to hang on as they were chased across the sky by the magical weapon.

If only he hadn't given the DragonStone to Cyax, he might have been able to summon something big and wet to quench the Shield's flames.

Their luck eventually ran out when Adraxa caught a blow from the Shield full square in her chest, unleashing an inferno that engulfed them both in a massive ball of flames. The Star Dragon wrapped her great wings around Nico just in time to protect him from the intense heat. They tumbled out of the sky as the intense fire scorched holes through her wings.

Cyax looked on with pleasure as he saw them plummeting to a fiery doom and summoned the Shield back to his hand. He was satisfied to have finally taken his revenge on both the new Dragon Warrior and the Star Dragon that had entombed him in the ice twelve hundred years earlier.

As the two Dragons fell closer to the earth, Adraxa unfurled her scorched and tattered wings and regained some flight control. Out of sight of Cyax, she landed heavily behind the ridge covered by tall trees, badly injured. Her magnificent scales that normally shimmered with starlight were now blackened or missing and the edges of her wings were ripped to shreds. It was clear to Adraxa that she couldn't evade the Shield of Fire and protect Nico at the same time.

'Regrettably I must withdraw Dragon Warrior. If we continue with this attack, the Shield will eventually consume us both in fire. You must continue this mission alone for now, until I return.' With that Adraxa flashed through a starlight portal back to the celestial plane to recover from her considerable injuries.

Nico was shocked to find himself alone once more. So much had happened, but there was much more to come, things he couldn't possibly have imagined.

CHAPTER 38
The Return Of The Fallen

Reasoning that a squad of guards would have been sent out by Cyax to check that he had been totally destroyed along with Adraxa, Nico summoned some of his own Dragon power and ignited a substantial fireball in the centre of a dense patch of dry woodland, causing a sizeable forest fire to break out. He hoped this would fool some lesser minded cyber-demons into believing it to be the burning remains of a fallen Star Dragon. He then climbed to the top of the high ground to get a view over Cyax' encampment and consider his now seriously limited options.

From his vantage point he could see that a small squad of six cyber-demons and a human commander had indeed set forth in the direction of the forest fire. The fire would be sufficiently intense to keep them guessing for quite a while, but he knew that eventually they would realise that the blaze was a decoy which would trigger another much larger search and probably end up with him being captured like his colleagues.

That simply couldn't happen, he desperately needed to do something. Everything now depended on him, the very situation he had been trying to avoid for most of his life and from Nico's perspective all now seemed to be truly lost. Cyax had almost limitless power and he was just one solitary Celestial Warrior. 'The Dragon Mage' potentially he may be, but that was scant consolation under the circumstances.

He recalled Xin's often repeated statement that the Astraxi had never been defeated when they worked together. Even if there were two or three of his colleagues at hand, it was hard to see how they could recover from such a catastrophic situation.

Despair took hold of his mind, causing his chest to sink inwards and his legs to fold under his body. He dropped to the ground and hunched his knees up to his chin. He felt sick and scared in equal amounts. Maybe it would be easier to simply give himself up to Cyax and get it over with.

He rolled backwards to the ground and stared upwards looking for some sort of inspiration, but all he could see were the vapour trails from combat aircraft snaking across the sky in the deepening twilight.

As he lay, he felt a pushing movement in one of his back pockets, like a small creature trying to burrow its way out through his trousers. He rolled over to reach into the pocket just as two objects came fluttering out.

He recognised the shining golden oak leaf that he had picked up after Cyax had cast Xin into the ravine. It hovered before him, just out of arm's length glowing brightly and causing him to blink. The other item floated slightly closer to him as if to invite investigation. It was another small piece of parchment, just like the one that Gilmane had sent after him the day he took the DragonStone from the shop.

Some of the despair that was swirling around his mind started to fade as he realised that here was a glimmer of hope. Gilmane must have somehow placed these two items in his pocket without him knowing. Now just when things seemed hopeless, these magical objects presented him with hope indeed, but what exactly could he do with a piece of parchment and an oak leaf made of gold?

He reached out and took the parchment, unfolding it carefully. At first the scrap appeared blank but as he stared at it, letters in an ancient script appeared, written in a dark ink by a skilled calligrapher.

'This means nothing to me' he sighed gloomily as he tried desperately to understand the mysterious magical text, rotating the sheet as if that would help. The characters, which at first appeared as a set of unintelligible lines and squiggles, were now moving before his eyes, as if some kind of a sorcerous translation algorithm was at work.

The lines soon resolved themselves into something he could read and understand. While he read the message the golden oak leaf presented itself to his other hand. Taking the leaf between his thumb and forefinger he felt compelled to read the incantation out loud. It read more like a command than something poetic, or inspiring, or magical. Perhaps the original poetry of the spell was lost in its translation to the modern language of Astrellion.

*Fallen of Astrellion, seek vengeance
against those, who wronged you.
Gather your weapons and rise once more
to defend your lands from evil.*

The golden oak leaf removed itself from his grasp then fluttered and spiralled away from his hand into an open space about twenty metres from where he stood. It floated at about head height above the ground, and a dazzling light appeared from either behind the leaf, or maybe inside it.

Nico couldn't quite tell where it was coming from, because the light came from another plane, a plane which didn't perfectly intersect with the earth, the Plane of Negative Existence. The light was golden in colour like the rays of the warmest, most powerful, and comforting sunlight, cutting shafts through the cool and nebulous atmosphere that surrounded him.

As it grew, human shaped shadows began to appear inside the light. The rays created a shimmering halo around their bodies, and the figures grew as they walked towards Nico. They looked like Celestial Warriors, but Nico couldn't identify their shadowy faces as he was having to shield his eyes against the intensity of the rays. Men and women, carrying swords, shields and other weapons emerged from the light, filling his field of view. Very quickly there were well over a hundred of them, with more following.

Down below Fong had spotted the intense light that was glowing luminously through the fog on the high ground above the command centre and felt its magical power. He called the commander of the squad of cyber-demons that had been despatched to verify the destruction of the Celestial Dragon and ordered him to investigate immediately. Fong, like other seasoned practitioners could sense when powerful magic was being deployed by other sorcerers. This was more intense than anything he had experienced in a long time, so powerful that he was almost overcome by it. But Cyax was more concerned about the destructive operations he was conducting from the Wizard's table and ignored Fong's attempts to get his attention.

As the dazzle of the light rays reduced in intensity, Nico recognised something very familiar about the people that were standing before him. They were all dressed as Warriors of the Astraxi, in armour very similar to that in which he was himself attired. There were Dragon Warriors, Winged Horse Warriors, Monkeys, Wolves, Snakes, Bulls, Stags, Tigers, and Eagles. A complete host of Celestial Warriors now stretching to five hundred or maybe more. But where did they come from and how did they get there, and what would they do next?

Nico recognised one of the Dragon Warriors near the front as the young woman whose image he had passed at the very front of the Dragon library, his predecessor Eleni. As he looked into her fiercely proud, but sad eyes she looked back at him. A feeling of mutual reassurance ran through his mind as if she were trusting him to complete some unspoken quest and that she was here to support him.

The Warriors summoned by the oak leaf started to stir, as one who was in the centre of the host made his way to the front, cutting his way through the crowd which parted respectfully to allow him to pass. After a few seconds the figure of Xin appeared at the head of the group much to Nico's total surprise.

'How did you...? I thought you were dead, and who are these people?' exclaimed Nico reaching forward to touch the old man's shoulder. Xin's body seemed slightly translucent and not of this earth. He was not dressed in his usual oriental style of clothing, rather he was in the armour of an ancient era, very ornate with bands of reinforced leather and mail. He carried his familiar short sword, small round shield and quarterstaff slung over his back.

'We haven't time to discuss the power that has brought me back here Nico. We need to act now and end this before it's too late. Many previous members of the Astraxi have followed me back from the Plane of Negative Existence, to face our deadliest foe once more. For them and for me this is a one-way journey into the void and oblivion, as there is no way back for our souls now that we have left the place which has been our home after death. Our time here is limited, but we are the Astraxi, and we took an oath to serve our land, to defeat evil, and to bring peace. Justice will prevail!'

As his inspiring words rang out, the small patrol of cyber-demons appeared firing volleys of shots from their pulsed energy weapons into the crowd. But the green flashes of energy passed through the bodies of the Fallen, scattering off the rocks behind Nico. The Fallen then turned on their attackers surging towards the hapless cyber-demons and crushing them to the ground as if they presented little or no threat to those who were already dead.

Xin climbed up on to a rock to address the host behind him which had now grown restless to complete their quest.

'My dearest and most honoured friends, for many centuries we have stood together against evil and are forever bound by ties of blood and suffering! Now I call up upon you to join me once more in this, our darkest hour. Follow me now and fight for your land, fight for your people, fight for your children, fight for their future, and save Astrellion from the eternal darkness that Cyax would bring. Astraxi, be strong!'

With a great roar the host raised their weapons in salute and followed Xin down the hill towards Cyax' command centre, with considerable speed of purpose.

'Are you joining us Nico?' asked Xin as the young man ran to catch up with him.

Nico didn't hesitate, his fighting spirit had already returned. Inspired by his old master, urgency flowed once more through his veins neutralising the hopelessness, fear, and despair, which had earlier hollowed out his courage following the downing of Adraxa by the Shield of Fire.

'Try and stop me!' said Nico with determination as the group surged downhill towards the heart of Cyax' war machine. The spirit of Xin nodded his approval with a grim smile.

As they got closer, the group, which now appeared to be almost a thousand strong, split in two to attack from opposite sides, the spirit of Xin leading one group, while Nico joined the other. Shots rang out from the Golterian guards who now found themselves unexpectedly taking defensive positions.

With quiet and ruthless efficiency, The Fallen tackled the Golterian forces with their swords and other combat weapons from across the centuries of warfare. The Golterians were unable to comprehend the fact that their modern weapons were ineffective against the spirits. The blasts of energy mostly passed through the ethereal bodies of the dead, doing little damage.

As it became apparent that the Fallen weren't easily destroyed by blaster fire, some of the Golterian defenders turned to flee, only to be cut down by their Cyax' enforcement guards, who had been ordered to make sure that every man, woman, and cyber-demon fought to the death.

The ever-watchful Fong was aware of the rapidly encroaching danger long before the commanders that were working with Cyax and Tanielka around the Wizard's table. Before this battle, known as 'The Great Liberation of Astrellion' had even begun, Fong had already pre-planned his escape, should things not go as expected. Vampires always look to the long term and grow their fortunes slowly so as not to risk being caught and destroyed by those jealous of their influence at court. Twelve hundred years ago he had been captured at the Great Gate to the citadel of Astrapolis when Cyax was defeated by Drakeidis and had himself only narrowly avoided being destroyed in the manner that most befits vampires, a stake through the heart.

A short take off cyber-copter was standing by, and Fong was already moving stealthily towards the aircraft when he was spotted by Eduardo, who had become suspicious of his movements away from the command centre.

'Hold on a second, Fong!' called Eduardo.

Fong's quick wits and deeply entrenched treacherous manner brought him to speak first, in a highly sarcastic tone designed to put Eduardo on the back foot.

'Eduardo, what important matter takes you away from your master's side at this crucial time?'

'I might ask you the same,' replied the young man, who had already transformed into his Snake Warrior guise as the host of the Fallen approached. 'Sneaking off when things get tough, eh, Fong?'

Fong didn't bother to reply and instead began an intense battle of will power against Eduardo, summoning all his hypnotic powers to bend the young man's mind to his own will.

Eduardo felt the force of the attack immediately like a hammer raining down on his consciousness, bludgeoning his self-awareness to the floor and forcing him to gather all his wits to shield himself from the unexpected psychic attack. He threw back a countercharm to Fong's overbearing force and for a short while each of them grappled with the other's minds in a kind of sub-cranial wrestling match of telepathic powers.

But despite the celestial energy flowing from his amulet, the Snake Warrior's full abilities were compromised by the spell that Cyax had used to turn him, after he had been captured in the Monastery grounds. Fong grabbed him firmly by the shoulder, pushing his clawed fingers hard into Eduardo's snakeskin armour and sending a deep physical chill through the young man's upper body, slowing his reactions even further. With his remaining physical senses numbed, and with one great mental push from Fong, Eduardo's consciousness was overturned, and he capitulated, dropping to his knees.

Two passing guards stopped at the sight but once more Fong was careful to cover up his treachery.

'I caught this one trying to escape back to the Astraxi. Take him and lock him up with the others.' Without question they picked Eduardo up, supporting him by his shoulders and carried him off. Fong needed to make sure that he wasn't seen to be running away just as things were getting dangerous, so he vanished in a cloud of grey vapour to avoid further detection.

Eduardo was delivered to the holding pen where the other three captured Astraxi were being held. As he was dumped to the floor in front of them, Ciara was shocked by the condition he was in. Since she had last seen him, he seemed haggard, as if some great torment had faded his previously handsome, youthful face. His normally stylish clothes looked shabby and unwashed.

'You look awful, what happened?' she asked. But Eduardo just shuffled over to one side of the cell and huddled up alone with his face buried in his knees, unable to speak.

'Cyax has been inside his head, and he might still be in there. We need to be careful what we say or do while Eduardo's around,' said Ash in a matter-of-fact way, not wanting to judge the Snake Warrior without the proper facts but remaining cautious. Ciara sighed and put her hand on Eduardo's head, smoothing his long fringe which was dishevelled.

'Poor Eduardo.' she whispered to him. 'What did they do to you?'

Meanwhile Xin was using his quarterstaff to clear individuals and small groups of defenders, smashing them to the ground as he whirled around as effortlessly as one would expect of a great master of martial arts.

As the Fallen approached the centre of the encampment, word of their invasion had filtered through to the group of commanders gathered by the Wizard's table.

Cyax walked over to one general who was starting to express doubts about the mission.

'My Lord, would it not be wise to safeguard your prizes and the Princess against the invaders and complete a tactical withdrawal from this location to a place from where we can secure total victory?' Sensing weakness, Cyax glowered at the man, who quickly realised the danger he had put himself in.

'My Lord, I apologise and withdraw my hasty statement. I am your most devoted servant and will obey your orders to my dying breath. Forgive me.' A thin film of sweat glowed on the man's forehead while Cyax stared at him disdainfully.

'Here it is then, your dying breath, *Aposyntethis.*' Cyax pointed his leather gloved finger at the soldier, and the man gasped for a moment before his body disintegrated into millions of tiny particles of dust that floated in the air underneath the crumbling remains of his terrified face. As his face finally vanished, the particles dropped to the ground leaving a pile of grey powder where the man had stood.

'Anyone else thinking of running away?' asked Cyax of the shocked onlookers, 'Good, now get on with your work,' he said before returning to Tanielka's side at the Wizard's table from where she was continuing to direct elemental magic against the Astrellian armies defending Astrapolis.

But despite his ruthless crushing of the dissent, the soldier's fears had made an impact on Cyax. The Fallen were now only a short distance away, cutting through the defenders with the ease of spirits that knew no fear and that their time was limited. The Golterians just needed to hold their position a little longer and the Fallen would disappear into the void, never to be seen again.

'Princess, you must hold the perimeter. Do everything in your power to stop them. Their time is running out, and they must not succeed!' Tanielka gathered a group of guards to her side and stepped forward, blaster in hand, confident in her ability to fulfil her orders.

Under Cyax' direction, energy continued to surge outwards from the table in concentric waves, powering and reinforcing the elemental magic being used to overcome the

Astrellian defenders as they fought to save their capital city. The table and its five powerful weapons needed to be disrupted, to give the Astrellians a fighting chance against their enemies. Although the Astrellians were more sophisticated in their use of technology, this didn't help when facing sorcery, or weapons that draw their power from extra-planar sources and realms of existence hostile to human beings.

Nico's group of the Fallen were now very close to the command centre. His Dragon scale armour had mostly protected him from blaster fire, but he cried out painfully after taking two direct hits, which knocked him breathless to the floor. The spirit of Eleni scooped him up and set him back on his feet before she destroyed the two cyber-demons who had foolishly stopped to celebrate their successful strike. For good measure Nico roasted them with a burst of Dragon fire.

Nico became separated from Eleni and the group of spirit Warriors and slipping past some tents found himself on the edge of Cyax' command position. The Fallen were engaged with the guards who had been ordered in to defend the area. Tanielka stepped forward to face Nico, relishing the chance to engage in physical combat with the Dragon.

Nico didn't have much time to use his Dragon lore as he was far too busy defending himself against the kick-boxing attack of Tanielka, whose martial arts skills were way too clever and dangerous for a street kid who normally hangs out with his skateboard in the park. At least he had good balance and timing which allowed him to dodge most of what Tanielka threw at him. But she was relentless, and Nico was finding it difficult to defend himself after taking a few flying kicks. To give himself a chance against the beating he was taking, he remembered a spell from the Dragon lore he had studied in the Great Library.

'*Pyros peritexeis*' he called out, drawing an imaginary circle around the Princess, and summoning a wall of flames from the Plane of Fire. Tanielka found herself surrounded by an inferno three metres high and so dense that she could barely see beyond it. The heat caused her to gasp for breath and shield her face from the intensity, giving Nico vital seconds to recover his senses. Tanielka was at first intimidated by the inferno, but she quickly recovered her courage.

'*Thias korpizo*' she called out gesturing at the walls of fire. The columns of flame wilted, being dispelled back to the Plane of Fire, and she stepped forward to find Nico sitting on the ground, his hands splayed out behind him, exhausted as if he had just completed a marathon.

With cat-like reflexes she seized her opportunity to restrain him, in a vice like arm lock, which made him wince with pain. She squeezed the arm lock a little further enjoying the gasps that came from his lips each time she twisted his arm.

'It's a shame your Tiger friend isn't here to save you this time' she said tilting her head down and staring into his eyes with a cruel smile. 'Maybe you should come back with me, and we can play a little more, Dragon boy! You're quite a catch. Maybe I will make you one of my Lords of the Chamber when we return to Golterion.' But as Tanielka was securing Nico's hands to stop him escaping, an almighty roar caused her to stop.

Xantix the Star Tiger was rampaging through the outer perimeter of the camp, reducing it to so much matchwood and torn canvas. Her giant body didn't have the warm orange tones of a Siberian tiger, rather her stripes were formed of glowing starlight in light and dark shades, which appeared to twinkle as she moved. Riding on the tiger's back was a re-invigorated Phae, resplendent in her Tiger warrior armour.

They charged through the ranks of guards and cyber-demons only stopping while Xantix picked up a particularly large and ugly cyber-demon that was keeping watch over the four Astraxi that were being held prisoner. Xantix shook it around and crushed it in her jaws tossing the broken cyber-demon to the ground. Something resembling green hydraulic fluid oozed from its broken helmet, or was it demon blood?

Phae couldn't be sure, but she didn't care, '*Lio*' she called, and the four prisoners were released from their bonds by her spell.

'Follow us and fear not!' Phae called to the four who stood looking at the sheer magnificence of her appearance on the back of the Star Tiger. She was back with her usual fully charged tigerish self-belief. They felt the blood flowing more easily through their newly released wrists, as Phae and Xantix charged through any remaining defenders that were still being hunted down by the Fallen.

'That's not an easy act to follow!' quipped Ben, who found himself inspired by Phae's actions.

They looked at each other for a moment before Ciara said, 'For once I agree with her. We need to help, but without our amulets what can we do?' They lifted Eduardo from his huddled position in the floor and followed as fast as they could, guiding the young man along. His terrified gaze exposing his inner torment.

When Xantix and Phae reached the central zone of the encampment, they ploughed forward at speed towards the Wizard's table, scattering everything and everyone in front of them. Cyax was hurled back into his command centre by a swipe from the Star Tiger's mighty paw.

With one giant bound and with Phae still on her back, Xantix leaped into the centre of the Wizard's table. Sparks radiated and fizzled as her celestial energy disrupted the elemental power radiating outwards. The five-pointed array of force lines that connected the weapons of elemental power was still glowing intensely.

'Do not touch the lines of energy flux Tiger warrior, as they are very dangerous to mortals when combined in this way,' advised Xantix.

Phae reached into her shoulder bag and pulled out the Sun-Moon. Without really having to think about what she was doing, she telepathically reset all its controls into positions that were opposite to those of the similar controls of Cyax' Wizard's table. Leaning down from the Star Tiger's back she placed the Sun-Moon into the middle, and the central red and blue conjoined jewels that were the source of its power pulsed brightly with light.

Xantix leaped down from the table, as a blinding flash of neutralising energy burst out, knocking all the surrounding people off their feet. Phae sheltered behind her Celestial companion's glowing body, as the shock wave from the blast ripped through the command centre, burying Cyax under a huge pile of debris.

As the glow faded, the Wizard's table stopped radiating energy and with their power links disrupted, the five weapons of power were ejected from their positions.

The spirit of Eleni approached Tanielka, who still had Nico in a choke hold. The Princess was dazzled by what had just happened to the Table and Nico seized this moment of uncertainty to free himself from her grip. Tanielka circled the spirit of the Eleni carefully, being unsure how to attack or defend herself against such a spectral being.

'What should I do?' called Nico to Eleni.

'Be true to yourself, Nico. Train and become the best Dragon the world has ever seen. You are the Dragon Mage, the only one who can stop Cyax.' answered Eleni as she continued her game of cat and mouse with Tanielka.

'OK then!' Nico took her literally at her word and turned towards the Wizard's Table, his eyes searching for a weapon, anything he could use against Cyax and rushed straight into the action as the various troops were recovering from the blast wave caused by Phae.

Out on the battlefields below, the reinforcing magic from the Wizard's table had stopped supporting the invaders and they were now weakened against the Astrellian defenders' counterattacks. The small bands of savage Morgai demons that had been rampaging through villages stopped suddenly as if someone had unplugged their power source. The once terrifying creatures crumbled into the ground, as without the magic of the Cup of Souls to nourish them, they turned back into the mere soil from which they had been created.

Consumed by anger and with a mighty roar, Cyax emerged from the ruins of his command centre, hurling the debris high into the air. He threw himself at the Star Tiger, behind whom Phae was still sheltering, but was rebuffed by another blow from the celestial creature's huge font paws and sent sprawling backwards. Xantix roared to warn the evil immortal from attacking her Warrior companion.

Despite everything that was going on around him, Cyax still had the determination to win at all costs. He knew that time would soon run out for the Fallen and they would fade out of existence. They would never be seen on any Plane of Reality again, their existential timelines abruptly terminated for ever. He just needed to regroup his forces once the Fallen had been taken by the void.

Nico approached Cyax with dragon flames billowing from his hands. Cyax picked up the Wand of Xylos and counteracted the jets of flame with a gush of water which immediately vapourised into a dense cloud of scalding steam. Nico winced and closed his eyes firmly as the hot water vapour scorched his face. As he fell back, Cyax kicked him firmly in the stomach, winding him, then picked the young man up by his throat, as if he were a toy.

Ash was the first of the four recently released Astraxi to reach the chaotic scene. Being an expert swordsman, he picked up the Blade of Astrellion and slowly approached Cyax, who still had the writhing Nico in his fist. Cyax threw Nico to the floor in front of Ash, which winded him once more then picked up the Shield of Fire. Ash approached Cyax quickly and nimbly with a fast series of strokes and thrusts from the Blade. Like other users of the elemental weapon, he found it beautifully balanced and fitted to his hand like a glove, as if it had been designed for him, and him alone.

In his twelve hundred years frozen in the glacier, Cyax had lost nothing of his prowess in physical combat and expertly evaded the swordsmanship of Ash. His combat experience had given him the ability to judge the next blow and push the Shield in front of it. But Ash was also a descendent of Theokeis. He held his position valiantly against Cyax, whirling the Blade deftly around himself and moving gracefully with the natural poise of a great swordsman.

'We may share the blood of our ancestor Theokeis, but yours has been diluted by centuries of breeding with lesser mortals,' Cyax mocked Ash to distract his opponent and gain an advantage.

'We have nothing in common Cyax. You should finally face the fact that your father overlooked you for a place in the Astraxi and disowned you because of your obvious character flaws.' Ash knew exactly where to place his sharp words, as much as where to thrust his sharp sword. He planted his feet firmly in expectation of a burst of explosive anger from his adversary. Cyax furiously smashed the Shield directly towards Ash, who at the last moment raised the Blade to protect himself.

The elemental weapons clashed with a resounding note and for a moment time seemed to stand still. Two magical energies surged up like a pair of tidal waves rushing towards each other. Inevitably as the rules of elemental lore predict, Fire was destined to overcome Metal, and as flame boiled out from the Shield, Ash was blasted backwards to the ground. As he lay on his back his armour was scorched and discoloured, his face singed by the flames with the Blade lying next to him.

Cyax moved in for the kill, relishing the chance to despatch yet another member of his brother's bloodline to the Plane of Negative Energy. Nico didn't have the slightest idea that Ash was such an accomplished swordsman. He appeared to be a quiet man, who spent most of his time with his head buried in engineering matters, trying to improve systems that were probably already near perfect. Ironically Ash was working on the complexities of creating a realistically humanoid artificial intelligence, while being the most reserved and least overtly 'human' member of the Astraxi.

Somehow in what little spare time he had left over, Ash had decided to honour the ancient warrior that was his ancestor, Cyrus. He had taken up training as a swordsman under the guidance of Xin, without ever anticipating that this skill would ever be needed and under such duress.

After the flash caused by Phae's disruption of the Wizard's table, the spirit of Xin realised that events were moving at pace in the centre of the camp. As he arrived, he drew his staff to defend Ash against Cyax, who relished the opportunity to destroy his old servant once more.

'I killed you once, and now it seems I will kill you again, old man.' Cyax, who had fought against The Fallen last time they had been summoned, raised his hands, and fired lightning bolts at the spirit of the ancient warrior.

Xin knew that the energy aimed at him would disrupt and possibly destroy his spectral body, so he darted out of the way before launching his own attack on Cyax with two swift blows from his staff. The two old adversaries became engaged in a desperate battle for superiority, but each was the match of the other and so extraordinary was their struggle that even Cyax' guards disengaged from their fight with the Fallen to watch.

Phae came across Tanielka and the spirit of Eleni still trying to outmatch each other in combat. A wave of anger burst through Phae's heart as she saw the figure of her lost colleague again, still feeling the guilt of having been responsible for what happened to Eleni underneath the ruins of the Royal Palace.

In her impetuous manner, she broke into the fight without considering the risks, throwing herself at the Princess. Tanielka had seen Phae coming and dropped her hands to her sides as if to invite the blow. As Phae threw a punch Tanielka ducked the blow and in the blink of an eye disappeared, rematerialising right behind Phae, kicking her in the back and sending her tumbling to the ground. Eleni stepped into the space between them, and the Princess hesitated, being unsure of how to fight a member of the Fallen.

Cyax continued his fight with Xin, while Nico was tending to the injured Ash. Nico remembered his parting exchange with Gilmane, where he had declared that he was going 'nowhere' but he also knew that going nowhere was not truly in his character. All his outbursts of temperament and denial of responsibility were a defensive shield, which allowed him to run away from life and the struggles of growing into an adult and making an effort to achieve the things that people expected of him. 'The Greatest Dragon Mage, really?' That was just too much responsibility to bear, but now as he sat next to his injured friend, he realised that this was the moment where he should stand up and be recognised.

'Step up to the plate, Nico' as Xin often said.

'Which plate would that be?' he used to think to himself jokingly imagining Xin presenting him with a plate of freshly cooked noodles or some chilli prawn dim sum!

Nico saw the Blade lying in front of him, glinting in the light of the many fires that had broken out, caused by of the incendiary outbursts of the Shield.

'Time to do something and make a difference,' he thought as he picked up the magic sword. He walked slowly towards Cyax and the spirit of Xin, who were still trying to outmanoeuvre each other. He waved the Blade around trying to get a feel for how to swing it and not be humiliated, as he had been when he last tried to use it on Cyax.

Nico closed in on Cyax from behind. Timing would be everything, because if he got it wrong Cyax would certainly finish him off. Xin launched another attack, this time with his short sword and Cyax raised the Shield to parry the blow. Seizing the moment, Nico thrust the Blade towards Cyax. It was a poor piece of swordsmanship, by anyone's standards, but the sword's inherent magical power guided the tip to make a small cut in Cyax' arm, which was buckled into the Shield.

Cyax paused to contemplate the injury to his arm. But then like an angry bull, he charged around the scene smashing the Shield into anything that got in his way. Normally a minor flesh wound to Cyax would heal instantly, but as this one bled he felt the pain intensely.

Tanielka also stopped and gripped her arm, gasping in pain even though she hadn't been hurt. A telepathic bond had always existed between the Princesses and their ancestor, brought about by the original sorcery which had made him immortal.

Tanielka raced to her master's side and feeling his pain she reached for her communicator.

'Fong, get us out of here now!'

Tanielka knew that Fong would have an escape strategy and wasn't fooled by his cool, apparent compliance with orders to stay and fight to the last. Cyax' explosion of pain and anger had created a large space in which people were too afraid to step, for fear of getting in his way.

Cyax was unsure how to react to this injury. He was not one to run in the face of an enemy. Although his armies had suffered defeats in the past, he had always left the field in an honourable way as a soldier. As a tactician though, he sensed that now was not the time to continue the fight, as the small wound to his arm was affecting him in a way that he had not felt during his entire immortal time on the earth.

'You haven't got much time left old man. Have no doubt I will come back and finish this.' Cyax taunted Xin who was standing around the perimeter with other members of The Fallen that had gathered.

Cyax unbuckled the Shield of Fire from his wounded arm and thrust it hard into the earth. The ground shook, as if an earthquake had struck. It heaved, surging up and down causing people to lose their balance and structures to collapse. A rift appeared where the Shield had been planted, and as Cyax pulled it from the earth, the crevice widened splitting the ground apart.

The fissure opened at an astonishing rate and soon became a deep chasm between the opposing sides, over a hundred metres long and ten metres wide. It seemed as if the land had been injured, like a deep flesh wound in the earth's own skin, bleeding red-hot magma, which as it cooled, scabbed over the injury leaving a rough black scar.

Flames roared out of the gorge and more crimson red-hot lava was spitting over the edges as a huge fire demon climbed out from its home, a magma chamber below the surface. The soldiers nearby ran to save their lives, some of them in flames as the evil creature belched its infernal breath over them.

The fire demon stood over ten metres tall, from its clawed toes to its head that was crowned with fire, its powerful body formed of the glowing magma from which it had emerged. It fixed its white-hot gaze on the Astraxi and strode towards them, hurling handfuls of molten lava, sending them diving for cover.

'Use the banishing spell to send it back Nico!' called the spirit of Xin to the young man. 'I am unable to use such sorcery in my current condition.'

'I don't know the word for fire demon in ancient Astrellian' replied Nico, with anxiety rising in his voice as the creature got closer.

'*Pyriam*' was Xin's sharp response, 'The word for fire demon is *pyriam*.'

'*Pyriam: Yoshara kalente*' called Nico, and celestial energy surged in narrow lines of starlight from his amulet through his outstretched palm, wrapping around the demon as if weaving a net around it. The glowing net tightened around the flailing demon until it shrunk the creature into a small but intensely hot point of flame that glowed brightly before disappearing from sight.

Across the chasm a cyber-copter pilot swooped her part machine, part demonic creature into the space behind Cyax in the near vertical style of landing for which the vehicles were famous. Fong beckoned the Princess and Cyax aboard and the strange flying vehicle launched itself almost vertically into the air at great speed.

The Astraxi and the Fallen gathered by the wreckage of Cyax' wizard's table, where they recovered not just the Sun-Moon device, the DragonStone and the Cup of Souls, but also their captured amulets.

On the nearby battlefields, Astrellian soldiers now found themselves facing a Golterian army, which was disintegrating without the magical power flowing from the Table. Inspired by their sudden change of fortune, the defenders became attackers and in a great rout, they drove the Golterians back to their own borders, crushing many of them into the ground.

CHAPTER 39
A Farewell To Comrades

The six Astraxi Warriors Nico, Phae, Ben, Ciara, Ash, and Eduardo gathered around the spirits of Xin and Eleni.

'Xin, we thought you were gone forever,' said Ben with a look of sheer elation at being reunited his mentor.

'How on earth did you manage to lose this Nico?' asked Ciara as she handed the DragonStone ring to him.

'Sometimes you have to make a personal sacrifice to help others,' said Nico, slightly embarrassed by Ciara's question.

'Wise words indeed young Dragon. You've really stepped up…'

'…to the plate, by any chance?' Nico finished Xin's sentence. They laughed as a group for the first time since the attack on the forward base that marked the start of hostilities.

'This has been a day of triumph and tragedy for Astrellion, but you, young Dragon, you have showed your true worth. Well done. In fact, you should all be proud of yourselves,' Xin looked at his team of warriors with immense pride.

'I have recalled Cygnus. We should get out of here,' said Ash with a tone of genuine concern in his voice.

'It's not that simple,' said Xin with a deep sigh, 'My return is only temporary. Soon the Fallen and I will be gone forever.' The group's elation quickly turned to sadness, realising that time was running out for their Master.

'I'm really sorry Eleni,' said Phae quietly with her head bowed to the spirit of the Dragon warrior. 'If I had known what was going to happen, I wouldn't have dived in like that to get the Cup of Souls. I was sure I could get it, but I was wrong.' Phae was still feeling deep regret for what had happened to her friend.

'Don't be sad Phae' replied Eleni, 'It was my destiny, but I was fortunate to be given one more chance to fight for the Astraxi and now it is time for me to leave. Farewell to you all and good luck, especially to you Dragon Warrior.' As Eleni finished speaking, she bowed, and her translucent figure disappeared before their eyes as if a breeze had blown in and swept her away like a cloud of twinkling golden lights. Other members of The Fallen were also saying their last goodbyes to each other and disappearing into the night.

Xin sighed deeply, trying to delay for as long as possible his departure from this plane and into the eternal void. The others could see that his figure was already starting to fade around the edges and a collective sense of tragic loss filled their hearts.

'Wait Xin. Don't leave us!' called Ben.

'You can't go, we need you,' pleaded Ciara.

Xin was about to speak to reassure them, when a strange visual disturbance appeared behind him, as if the surrounding space were blurring, wavering, and shimmering like a mirage. A human shaped figure merged out of the disturbance and stepped forward towards Ciara with great purpose. He was very old and wore the robes of an ancient Astrellian court official, including a pork pie hat perched on his head. The old man took the Cup of Souls from Ciara's hands and spoke in his familiar deep tones.

'The Cup of Souls will save you, Xin. But we must move fast.'

'Gilmane?' gasped Xin in surprise. Gilmane lifted the Cup and exhaled a long, forceful breath across the top of the artefact. A silver liquid condensed out of Gilmane's breath into the bottom of the Cup, swirling around as if it had a life force of its own. Its mercurial surface rippled and swelled, almost as if it were breathing.

'Drink it quickly' Gilmane's order was direct, and Xin took the Cup by both of its dragon shaped handles, pouring the elixir into his mouth. As the fluid progressed through Xin's body, parts of him lost their eerie translucency becoming more solid. First around his stomach and spreading up through his lungs and his neck into his head, and at the same time spreading down through his midriff and down through his legs until he was once more entirely opaque and solid.

'Gilmane, can you bring back Eleni too?' said Phae.

'I'm sorry Phae, but it's too late for her,' said Gilmane regretfully. Phae hung her head once more in remorse.

Xin looked at himself to check for any problems caused by the transition back to fully fleshed human being.

'You never fail to surprise me Gilmane, thank you. This lore hasn't been seen for over four thousand years. I didn't expect it, and I am eternally grateful.'

'Well, as an immortal you certainly have the opportunity to be *eternally* grateful, I suppose!' said Gilmane with a twinkle in his eye. 'I made a promise never to use this magic again, but promises are made to be broken, as humans often say!' Gilmane tried to appear cheerful as he patted Xin on the shoulder, but the vow he had just broken would almost certainly carry a serious penalty.

'That's the gift of wizards!' he continued, 'But as usual, I've got far too involved again and no doubt this time it will get me into even more trouble with the others.'

Xin was uncertain as to whether he was still fit to be the leader and spiritual guide of the Astraxi.

'Am I fully restored, Gilmane? Just as I was before Cyax sent me into the abyss?'

Gilmane stroked his whiskers pondering the question and the answer.

'Hmm. Too early to tell. The Potion of Eternity can have a few nasty side effects, so you had better be careful. Take some time off. Maybe a century or two!' Gilmane winked as he stepped back and bowed before dematerialising in the opposite way to which he had first appeared.

'Xin, who were all those people that came with you and Eleni?' asked Ciara.

'They were the spirits of your predecessors, Astraxi Warriors from the past. Many, many dear friends of mine, who were lost in previous battles. Sometimes I used to see them in my dreams, and for a while I was walking amongst them again. So much tragedy, that time does not heal.' Xin was briefly silent again, as if in prayer or mourning.

'But Ash is right, we need to get out of here. Cyax will come back stronger next time. We must be ready.'

Inside Fong's cyber-copter, Cyax was examining the small flesh wound that Nico had left on his arm. The skin looked old and wrinkled in a way that Cyax had never experienced as an immortal. Prior to this, even when he had been seriously wounded, his body had always regenerated.

This wound ached and showed no signs of healing, which disturbed him. The Blade of Astrellion had injured him in a way that no other normal weapon had ever done in the past.

He became wary of its power, but eager to reclaim possession of it.

'Does it pain you, my Lord?' said Fong drily, suspicious of his master's injury, but also hinting at the loss they had just suffered.

'What do you mean by that Fong?' Cyax was angry, and in the confined space of a cyber-copter it wasn't wise of Fong to provoke him further. Cyax might just throw him out of the door.

'I mean nothing my Lord. Simply that the battle is lost,' said Fong calmy and concealing any insinuating tone.

'Nothing is lost. There is another way to win this war. All men fear me, and I fear nothing. I am fear,' replied Cyax staring into Fong's watery red eyes that were deeply set into their dark grey eye sockets behind his tinted circular glasses.

'We will find the missing Astraxi Warriors and turn them against the others, neutralising their power,' he snapped.

'I shall begin the search immediately my Lord,' replied Tanielka. Since his re-appearance, Cyax had not disappointed her. He was a truly fearsome being, equipped with amazing strength, courage, and powerful sorcery, but something about him disturbed her.

Although she was totally committed to the cause of regaining the throne of Astrellion, she was privately worried about such an enterprise. It seemed to her that Cyax considered no cost too high to achieve his ends. The taking of Astrellion could just as easily end in cataclysmic destruction for everyone, with Cyax left governing what was little more than a massive smoking graveyard from the charred ruins of the old Royal Palace. Victory at any cost? She didn't find that particular destiny appealing in the slightest.

Chapter 40
Picking Up The Pieces

Ash flew the team back to Astrapolis, where he moored Cygnus at her usual berth in the badly damaged but still functioning commercial harbour. A small welcoming committee sent by the President of Astrellion had been hastily assembled to greet them and offer thanks for their service to the country and its people.

In a short speech Xin thanked the armed forces of Astrellion and that the saving of the land was for the citizens to celebrate, as the Astraxi would take satisfaction in knowing that they had once more been able to fulfil the vows of their ancestors.

Xin was then surrounded by news cameras, who had heard the stories of his fate on the mountain and wanting to know how he had managed to return from death. As ever he was reticent to discuss the fine details of any part of the operation, preferring to keep the practices of the Astraxi a closely guarded secret.

Fame and the search for individual glory had almost destroyed the Astraxi on previous occasions, by causing rivalry and factionalism in the ranks, as some Warriors of a more arrogant temperament had looked down on others whom they felt made less of a contribution to the group. Public adulation and hero worship always made this worse. The Astraxi would only function at their best when they were a team of equals committed to working with each other. Xin made maintaining that team bond his primary task above others.

So, he shielded his young group from the noisy throng of reporters as they made their way down to the shuttle, which would return them to their base underneath the Perpetual Motion Café.

As they sped silently under the streets of the city, they were spared the sights and scenes of destruction that the Golterian forces had unleashed on its peaceable inhabitants. The damage was indiscriminate with debris scattered over large areas, here a school or a hospital, there a parade of shops or an apartment block.

Many people had fled the city before Cyax had closed the main highways in and out. Some of the refugees had already started to return, especially since Fong had been quoted on the main news channels as saying that his government would be prepared to negotiate a final settlement to his master's ancient claim to the throne of Astrellion.

'I don't trust him. I never did. He's just buying time to regroup and come back harder than ever' said Xin as he watched in the operations room. 'It's interesting that Cyax didn't make an appearance. He'll already be planning his next attack for sure, and we will need to be ready as ever. Training will resume in the morning!' and before Xin finished speaking the others groaned their disappointment, hoping for at least a short break of a few days from the action.

The operations room had survived the war intact. Even though Fong's scouting party had made it to the front door of the Perpetual Motion Café, its magical entrance through the store cupboard and its secret password were still holding up, even though anyone who knew chef Xin well enough would probably be able to guess it.

They headed through the store cupboard and into the café's main serving area. The plate glass window had been blown in by Fong's cyber-demons. Tables and chairs had been randomly thrown across the room, some were broken or ripped apart, and everything was covered in dust. Nico noticed that the perpetual motion machine was moving again, in its apparent defiance of the laws of physics.

'What a mess!' Xin let out a sigh when he saw the damage, but nothing was too far beyond repair. He picked up a chair and moved it back into place while sweeping away some broken glass with his shoe. The others joined in to help and within a short time a semblance of order was re-established, but without a front window the café still had the feeling of a bomb site.

'I imagine that carpenters and window fitters are going to be hard to come by for a while,' said Xin with an air of resignation.

Phae had an idea and powered up her magic without transforming into the Tiger warrior.

'*Olokliros*' she said quietly as in her mind she remembered how the windows had looked when they were intact. It was as if time was running backwards. Shards of broken glass and splintered wood rose from the floor and carefully re-assembled themselves, each piece merging with the next one smoothly as if nothing had ever been broken. Before long the window was fully restored.

'That's a very useful piece of magic!' said Xin gratefully. Let's get to work straightening this place out. '*Masfina mataris!*' said Xin, summoning his invisible assistants, which picked up brushes to sweep the floors and rearrange the kitchen like a small team of invisible cleaners.

'Good, now I'll make some tea for everyone,' he said with a look of satisfaction.

Phae brought two cups of the green tea that Xin had managed to rustle up and joined Nico at a table. He had been cleaning up the serving area, deep in thought about everything that had happened to him since the day he first entered Gilmane's shop and stole the DragonStone ring.

Phae's expression showed that she had something on her mind, but for once was she finding it difficult to express herself and was reeling out trivialities such as 'I wonder what happened to the old ship in the dunes?' or asking Nico about his favourite music, while she built up to saying what she really wanted to say.

Nico didn't really realise what was really going on inside Phae's head, as like many teenage boys he found the internal workings of girls' minds something of a mystery. At times she seemed more complex than he could personally imagine. He listened to her random chit chat and nodded and smiled as she rambled on about perhaps taking up her wildlife studies again or wondering when the university would re-open. She asked Nico about his plans for the future, which he hadn't really thought much about, since most of his past had recently been taken away from him one way or another by people who didn't even stop to ask his opinion.

Eventually she decided to get to the point and as she spoke the pitch of her voice went up slightly, 'Er, I never thanked you for what you did for me Nico.'

'Thank me? What for?' Nico was a little surprised as he hadn't considered anything that he had done for Phae was worthy of or required some expression of gratitude.

'Well, for saving my life, I suppose.' Phae stopped and stared straight into his eyes looking for something that would indicate that he recognised her feelings about this. The tragic memory of Eleni and her brief return with the Fallen, had affected Phae deeply, bringing up to the surface how much she cared for those people who were her closest friends. She had been feeling particularly protective about the young man with the floppy hair and long spindly limbs since he rescued her from Cyax.

'But you saved me too when I fell off the back of Adraxa. Does that make us even now?' was Nico's slightly awkward response, being unsure about where this conversation was leading.

'I guess so' she replied, slightly disappointed that Nico was not reading her signals. But then she remembered that she was a little older than him after all, and maybe he wasn't mature enough to realise what she meant. Maybe her feelings were misplaced, and perhaps she was having an emotional over-reaction to the moment when he had sacrificed the DragonStone to save her from Cyax. Nico on the other hand was starting to understand what she may have been implying.

'Well, maybe we should…' The moment was suddenly broken by Ben. 'Is it noodle o'clock yet? I could eat a horse!' he said, barging in between them with his usual brand of good humour and laying down some serviettes, bowls, and chopsticks in anticipation of a lunch service.

Phae looked away and as the moment had evaporated, decided to let the conversation drop, while Nico resumed his teenage introspection.

As if on cue Xin said, 'I am not sure I have a horse, but I am sure I'll find something in the storeroom that I can warm up in the wok!'

Ciara pulled Ben to one side to berate him about his total lack of sensitivity. 'That was just getting interesting. Why do you always have to mess things up?' she whispered, trying to be discreet, but not quite managing it.

'What do you mean, mess things up?' he said surprised. Ben really didn't understand.

'Look at them. There's something going on between them. Isn't it obvious?' Ciara said with a little conspiratorial smile.

Phae realised that her feelings had been exposed and was a little embarrassed that the young Irish girl had read her like a book.

'Oh shut up Ciara,' she said indignantly. Nico didn't really know what to say, but he quickly worked out that he was caught in the middle of something, which could be emotionally dangerous!

Ciara smiled mischievously. She had achieved her aim of provoking a little bit of embarrassment, because she too was quite fond of the young man.

'Ever seen a Tiger eat a Monkey?' Phae chased Ciara around the café and trapped her in a booth, flicking her with the cloth she was using to dust the benches, in revenge for the young girl's impertinence.

'Ow, ow, Xin, she's hurting me, make her stop!' Ciara pleaded, trying to get sympathy from the old man.

'Make sure she suffers good and proper Phae!' quipped Xin, encouraging Phae's chastisement of the younger girl.

Suddenly the newly restored front door swung open and a woman with long, flowing, hair strode in. She was physically imposing, carrying with her an air of authority that couldn't be ignored. Her energetic, youthful face was fringed by pure white hair, in complete contrast to the black mane that covered the rest of her head. She was dressed in an armoured suit, edged with some sort of protective technology, like a deflector shield.

In a holster she carried a modern blaster weapon and strapped to her back was a samurai sword. She had a foxy smile, the sort you reserve for close friends, people that you can be rude to, knowing that they would understand you were just having a bit of fun.

'Look what happens when I leave you alone for a little while old man!' said the woman, who surveyed the chaotic scene in front of her.

'Now now, less of the old man routine, you're not much younger than me, remember!' Xin's face lit up as his companion walked across the room towards him.

'Yes, that is a fact, you're not much younger than Xin. The difference in your ages amounts to only a very small percentage. Less than one percent in fact,' said Ash as if to confirm Xin's statement.

'Thank you, Ash,' said Xin in a slightly sarcastic way that was lost on Ash but brought a smile to the faces of the others.

'I heard a nasty rumour that you were dead,' the woman continued.

'You don't get rid of me that easily!' replied Xin walking over to embrace the woman with great warmth.

'Admit it, I am the one that keeps you young around here!' the woman teased him, stepping back to look him up and down. 'You don't look too shabby, considering where you've been and that you've had to fend for yourself for a while!'

'You're insufferable, but it's great to have you back!' said Xin, clearly delighted to see his dear friend after many years of being apart.

'These young people look pretty hungry to me; I think you should get back to the wok while I introduce myself' she said looking at the six young people working out which Warrior was which.

Phae spoke first, 'Are you...?'

'Cally' warmly shaking both of Phae's hands. 'Yes. You must be Phae.'

'This is Nico, and Ciara, Ben, and Eduardo...' continued Phae.

'...and I already know Ash!' said Cally. Ash nodded in acknowledgement. She looked at Nico and was about to say something about Eleni and the prophecy about the Dragon Mage but decided that discretion would be better for the time being.

'Where have you been these last few years, Cally? You've missed all the fun!' said Xin ironically as he stirred the contents of his wok, carefully adding in some extra mushrooms, lemongrass, and fish sauce.

'I've been everywhere including some places that were un-earthly to say the least. Sorry I wasn't around to help,' replied Cally. 'And how was Cyax? Twelve hundred years in deep freeze doesn't seem to have cooled his temperament?'

'Oh, you know him, just as difficult as ever, but we managed just fine without you, while you were off on your holidays. No need to worry, nothing to see here!' Xin continued his teasing of the woman who had been his closest companion for over four thousand years.

"Hah, I don't think so. Look at this mess!' she retorted.

'And were you successful in finding the others. I must admit they have been on my mind. We will have to bring them in before Cyax gets to them,' he responded.

'Well, I had some success, but it wasn't easy after all this time and I am not sure all of them will be persuaded to come back,' added Cally, dipping a fork into the wok, lifting out a mushroom and putting it in her mouth. 'Mmm, that's just as good as I remember. At least you've still got it where cooking is concerned!' she said struggling to speak as the delicious but slightly too hot food burned her palate and tongue.

"When can we start? asked Nico, excited at the prospect of seeing the real potential of a larger group of Astraxi warriors.

"There's no time like the present,' said Cally.

'But aren't we going to eat first?' said Ben in a slight panic at losing his eagerly awaited meal.

'Engage brain before opening mouth Ben!' said Ciara.

'Chilli prawn dim sum, anybody?' said Xin triggering laughter amongst the group at the sound of his favourite magic words.

To be continued!

ABOUT THE AUTHOR

Stephen Salam read physics at Durham University before joining a film production company working on advertising, broadcast, and industrial film in the '80s.

In 1992 he founded his own production company, writing and directing films and TV programmes for clients all over the world, and winning many national and international awards.

Over the last twelve years, Stephen has been developing and writing a range of fantasy content and screenplays aimed at young adults.

The Five Elements is the first of a series of books and screen content set in the mythical land of Astrellion.

For more information visit:
www.stephensalam.com

Contact: astraxiwarriors@gmail.com

Social media:
TikTok: stephensalamauthor
Facebook: Stephen Salam Author
Instagram: stephensalamauthor

Printed in Great Britain
by Amazon